SUFFER THE CHILDREN

Thomas Potts Mysteries by Sara Fraser from Severn House

THE RELUCTANT CONSTABLE
THE RESURRECTION MEN
THE DROWNED ONES

SUFFER THE CHILDREN

A Thomas Potts Mystery

Sara Fraser

This first world edition published 2011
in Great Britain and in the USA by
SEVERN HOUSE PUBLISHERS LTD of
9–15 High Street, Sutton, Surrey, England, SM1 1DF.

British Library Cataloguing in Publication Data

Fraser, Sara.
  Suffer the children. – (A Thomas Potts mystery)
  1. Potts, Thomas (Fictitious character) – Fiction.
  2. Police – England – Redditch – Fiction. 3. Poor
  children – Crimes against – Fiction. 4. England – Social
  conditions – 19th century – Fiction. 5. Detective and
  mystery stories.
  I. Title II. Series
  823.9'14–dc22

ISBN-13: 978-0-7278-8035-2 (cased)

All Severn House titles are printed on acid-free paper.

Severn House Publishers support The Forest Stewardship Council [FSC],
the leading international forest certification organisation. All our titles that
are printed on Greenpeace-approved FSC-certified paper carry the FSC logo.

Typeset by Palimpsest Book Production Ltd.,
Falkirk, Stirlingshire, Scotland.
Printed and bound in Great Britain by
MPG Books Ltd., Bodmin, Cornwall.

ONE

Foxlydiate Hamlet, Parish of Tardebigge, Worcestershire
Thursday 4th October, 1827

D ragged by three sweating, labouring horses the long wagon lurched up the sloping roadway. Through the dark hours of the drizzly night, while its cargo of fitfully sleeping young children huddled close beneath the barrelled canvas roof, two children had sat apart from the rest exchanging urgent whispers.

'Come on, Sukey, we can jump out now while he's snoring.'

'No we can't!'

The boy gripped her hand. 'Yes we can. We can be miles away afore he wakes up. Come on!'

Joey Dowler, the man lying crossways on the boards at the rear tailgate, snorted loudly and jerked his head, making the girl gasp in fright.

She shook her head. 'No, Jack!'

Desperation throbbed in the boy's voice. 'Well I'm going. I'll leave you if you don't come this minute!'

'No!' She shook her head in equal desperation. 'He'll grab you and then you'll catch it!'

The boy shook his head too. 'He's too drunk. Now come on!'

She snatched her hand free of his grip. 'I aren't coming.'

'I'm leaving you then!' he hissed in angry frustration and rose to move stealthily towards the tailgate. He reached the snoring man and began to step over his prone body, seeking a foothold on the top of the tailgate. Then he shouted in shock and pain as a hand suddenly shot upwards and grabbed his thin thigh.

'You little bastard! I'll learn you your lesson!' Dowler threatened drunkenly as he scrambled up into a kneeling position and, using both hands, lifted the shrieking boy and slammed his skinny under-sized body against the tailgate.

Bones cracked audibly; the boy's shrieks instantly stilled.

Dowler lifted the inanimate body clear of the tailgate, and as he did so blood dripped from the boy's ears and mouth.

Sukey vented long drawn-out shrieks of horror, rousing the other children who added their own frightened wails to create an uproar. The driver cursed, brought the horses to a juddering halt and bellowed at the children. 'Shurrup! Shurrup!'

He slashed the long carriage whip through the air, cracking it again and again until the children subsided into choked sobs and whimpers.

'Enoch, you'd best take a look at this!' Dowler called nervously.

Enoch Griffiths climbed down from his seat and went to the rear of the wagon grunting irritably.

'What the fuck has you done? Hand him down here so I can take a look at him.'

He took the boy in his arms, moved some distance away and, laying the limp form on the ground, knelt to examine it closely.

Joey Dowler climbed over the tailgate and followed.

'He's as dead as a door nail,' Griffiths hissed furiously. 'You could hang for this, you stupid bastard!'

'Oh my God!' Dowler groaned in fearful dismay. 'I ne'er meant to kill him!' He started to beg frantically. 'Help me, Enoch! Help me! I ne'er meant to kill him!'

'Shurrup and let me think,' Griffiths snarled.

'Let's just chuck him in the ditch and get away from here,' Dowler pleaded.

'If you don't shurrup and let me think I'll chuck you both in the fuckin' ditch,' Griffiths growled savagely.

Both men fell silent as Griffiths, head bent, thought hard. Dowler, hands kneading together, had fearful eyes locked on the other's face.

After long seconds Griffiths said, 'Was it just this 'un who was trying to scarper?'

'He was talking to the wench, Sukey Crawford. He wanted her to go with him, but she was too feared and she said she 'udden't.'

'Bring her to me.'

Dowler went back to the wagon tailgate and ordered gruffly, 'Sukey, get down here.'

There was no movement within the almost impenetrable gloom

of the interior, and the only sounds were the stifled sobs and whimpers of the huddled children.

'Don't you make me come in there after you, you little bitch,' Dowler shouted. 'Or I'll tear your bloody head off!'

He shook the tailgate as if he were going to climb up over it, and one child squealed frantically.

'Her aren't here. Her's gone!'

Other children added their frightened assurances. 'Her's jumped out o' the front! Her's gone! Her's gone!'

Griffiths came at a run and levered himself over the tailgate and into the wagon. One after another he dragged children from the writhing huddle and put them aside, mouthing the tally as he did so.

'One, two, three, four, five.' Then he roared in rage. 'Her's done a runner! The little bitch has done a runner!'

He clambered across the driving seat, jumped down and ran along the roadway for some yards shaking his clenched fists in raging frustration at the night-shrouded scrub and woodland of the surrounding countryside.

'Any sight of her?' Dowler came hurrying to join him.

Griffiths turned on him savagely. 'There's more chance o' sighting a needle in a bloody haystack. We'll need to tread on her afore we can see her. This is all your fault, you stupid bastard.'

His fist crunched against flesh and bone, bringing blood spurting from the other man's lips.

Dowler staggered backwards and fell to his knees on the muddy track.

Griffiths stepped towards him, fists poised to strike again, but Dowler made no attempt to raise his hands in defence, only cowered submissively like a terrified dog cowering before its brutal master.

'Now listen well,' Griffiths growled. 'I need to get this lot settled in well afore crack o' light so I'm going on ahead. You get rid of that little fucker, and make sure you hides him deep.'

'But I aren't got a shovel to dig with!' Dowler protested plaintively.

'Use your fuckin' hands! And when that's done you search high and low until you finds that little bitch,' Griffiths snarled. 'And you'd better bring her back in one piece or I'll slit your fuckin' gizzard.'

He turned and went back to the wagon.

Dowler stared miserably after the vehicle as it lurched away and disappeared into the darkness. Then he picked up the boy's limp body, slung it over his shoulder and went into the nearby woodland.

Crouched up to her neck in the fetid muddy water of the roadside ditch, the small girl heard the horses' snorts, the great iron-shod wheels crunching only a yard distant from her head, and crammed her fingers into her mouth to stifle her terrified moans.

TWO

Redditch Town, Parish of Tardebigge.
Sunday 7th October

I n the high pulpit of St Stephen's chapel, John Clayton, the tall, muscular curate, sighed inwardly. 'It's going to be slim pickings this collection,' he muttered to himself.

The blustering rain and winds had deterred a great many of the congregation from attending the morning service. The segregated cushioned pews of the rich in the front of the chapel and the plain wooden benches of the poor at the rear were half empty.

He began the 'Order of Morning Prayer', declaiming in his pleasantly sonorous voice three different verses from the Scriptures, then the Exhortation.

The congregation knelt and intoned the General Confession, the Absolution and the Lord's Prayer.

'Oh Lord, open Thou our lips,' Clayton requested.

The congregation chimed in. 'And our mouth shall shew forth Thy praise.'

'Oh God, make speed to save us,' Clayton beseeched.

'Oh Lord, make haste to help us,' echoed the congregation.

All rose to their feet.

'Thank Christ for that, me bloody knees am killing me!' Fat, red-faced innkeeper Thomas Fowkes' grunted sigh of relief was overlaid by John Clayton's stentorian cry.

'Glory be to the Father, and to the Son, and to the Holy Ghost!'

'Hallelujah, Brother! Hallelujah! Glory be to God! Hallelujah!' Fat, red-faced Gertrude Fowkes shouted exultantly. All eyes turned in unison towards the tiny side pew in which she and her husband were crammed together.

Seated above the heads of the congregation, in the front row of the narrow, newly erected North Gallery, two pretty, blonde-haired girls erupted with delighted giggles, but their companion, the fat, red-faced Lily Fowkes, exclaimed in utter mortification, 'That's me Mam showing me up again! The silly daft cow!'

Joseph Davis, Chapel Clerk, rose majestically from his seat at the base of the pulpit and, pointing his hand at the offender, thundered furiously, 'Be silent, woman! This is the ordained House of God, not a cesspit of viperous, ranting Dissenters!'

John Clayton, struggling to hide his own amusement, was quick to intervene.

'Let us praise Our God with Psalm ninety-five. *Venite Exultemos Domino*.

The organ sounded.

'*Oh come let us sing unto the Lord; let us heartily rejoice . . .*' Clayton's rich baritone filled the air.

His flock dutifully joined in. '*. . . in the strength of our salvation.*'

The more buxom of the two blonde girls in the gallery craned her neck to stare at the people beneath.

'Tom Potts aren't here, Amy. We'd be sure to see him if he was. Why aren't he come, I wonder?'

'Because he's had second thoughts, that's why,' Lily Fowkes spat out spitefully. 'He knows that now he's got a bit o' money he can do better for himself than to wed a common barmaid.'

The buxom blonde turned angrily on her. 'You nasty cow! For two pins I'd knock your block off!'

Lily scowled defiantly. 'You just try it, Maisie Lock, and see what you gets!'

Sitting between them, Amy Danks scolded, 'Stop showing us up! Everybody's looking at you.'

The pair became conscious of the disapproving frowns and verbal tuttings of their immediate neighbours and subsided into sullen silence.

After a second Psalm, Clayton read the First Lesson taken from the Old Testament.

Her pretty face frowning anxiously, Amy Danks continually glanced surreptitiously at the rows of faces along the gallery and in the seats below, praying silently. 'Oh let him come. Please God, let him come.'

The Lesson ended. All rose, the organ and massed voices sent the '*Te Deum Laudamus*' heavenwards.

'We praise thee, oh God; we acknowledge thee to be the Lord . . .'

'He aren't coming, is he?' Lily Fowkes hissed triumphantly into Amy's ear. 'I knew this 'ud happen. There'll be no Banns called for you this morning, my wench. He's cancelled 'um, and that's why he aren't here.'

Amy blinked down at the hymn page, its printed words blurred by the tears welling in her blue eyes.

'Oh Lord in Thee have I trusted; let me never be confounded.' The final chords died away and with much coughing and shuffling of feet the congregation reseated itself to listen to John Clayton read the Second Lesson, this time taken from the New Testament.

Maisie Lock took Amy's hand in commiseration, whispering, 'Ne'er you mind, my duck. You can do better than bloody Tom Potts, lanky streak o' piss that he is. Just wait 'til I gets hold of him. He'll wish he'd never been born!'

'. . . And I will execute vengeance in anger and fury upon the heathen, such as they have not heard. Here endeth the Lesson.' Clayton closed the vast bible and stared up at the gallery. His eyes sought and found Amy and his tough ugly features were softened by the warmth of his smile as he announced, 'I publish the Banns of Marriage between Master Thomas Potts, Constable of this Parish, and Miss Amy Danks, Spinster of this Parish. If any of you know cause, or just impediment, why these two persons should not be joined together in Holy Matrimony, ye are to declare it. This is the first time of asking.'

'That's shot you up your fat arse, aren't it, Lily Fowkes!' Maisie Lock crowed exultantly. 'Tom Potts and Amy am certain sure to be wed now their first Banns has been called.'

Lily Fowkes huffed petulantly.

Amy Danks emitted a heartfelt sigh of relief.

John Clayton waited for a few seconds for any objection to be stated, but no voice was raised. Then he flicked a wink to Amy before calling to the congregation.

'Let us now join together in Hymn five hundred and forty-seven, "The ransomed of the Lord shall return and come to Zion with songs".'

Amy rose to her feet and joined with gusto in the opening chorus.

'Children of the heavenly King, As ye journey sweetly sing . . .'

In her mind Amy was savouring the prospect of having children of her own to surround her with their own sweet singing through the years to come. But at the same time she was also thinking resentfully, 'You should have been here with me to hear our Banns called, like you promised to be, Tom Potts! When we're done here I'm going straight to give you a piece of my mind.'

THREE

I t was near to noon and raining heavily when top-hatted, cape-clad Constable Thomas Potts and his companion in the pony trap reached the isolated storage shed and the elderly smocked-rustic standing outside its closed and barred door.

'Oh, there you be at long last, Master Pettifer! You've took a deal o' time getting here. I could have had me throat cut by now,' the rustic accused angrily.

'It's above six miles to Redditch and back, Joe Eden, and you should be grateful that I did you the favour of fetching Master Potts. He was supposed to be listening to his first Banns being called this morning.' Farmer Will Pettifer reined in the pony.

'You look so warlike, Master Eden, I doubt that anyone would dare to try and cut your throat.' Tom Potts smiled wryly at the pitchfork wielded by the man. 'Master Pettifer says that you have a witch trapped inside your shed. Now who exactly are you talking about?'

'How should I know? But it's got to be the same bloody witch who's been casting evil spells on me all this bloody year. It started when me ewes dropped their lambs and two on 'um died on me. After that I've lost a dozen or more hens. Last week me best dog was run over by the bloody stagecoach. Me missus has been lay abed sicking her bloody guts up for three days and nights past and aren't able to do a stroke o' toil, and me bloody mare went lame on me yesterday forenoon.'

'And you believe that it's a witch's spells that have caused these things to happen?' Tom frowned incredulously.

'O' course I does. There's naught else it can be!' The old man scowled. 'And now I'se got me new crop o' carrots and wurzels stored she's come to put a curse on 'um, so she has.'

Tom stepped down from the trap and the old man gaped in astonishment.

'Bugger me, Master Potts, I been told you was a lanky, narrow bugger but you'm a sight more lanky and narrow than any bloke ever I saw afore.' His toothless mouth emitted a raucous cackle of laughter. 'I'll bet when the clouds am low you thinks that you'm in a fog.'

'Yes, Master Eden, that's exactly what I think.' Tom nodded wearily. 'Now can we get on with the business at hand?'

'I'll leave you and this loony old bugger to it, Master Potts. I've got some very pressing business of my own to attend to.' Pettifer grinned. 'And I'm sure that you're well able to deal with any number of witches.'

The trap rattled away.

'This female, Master Eden, how old might she be, and how active in body? And does she have any companions?' Whenever he was faced with the likelihood of violent physical confrontation, Tom was all too painfully aware of his own deficiency in muscular strength and athleticism.

Joe Eden gurned in contempt. 'Don't you know any bloody thing? How can I know what her looks like now? Witches can change everything about 'um, at any time they wants, so her could be any shape of a thing. What you got to do is the minute you spots summat moving inside there, shoot it dead.'

As on so many other occasions Tom didn't know whether to laugh or weep at the degree of superstition still flourishing in this modern age of scientific progress. He drew a long breath and asked again.

'When you saw the female enter the shed, what shape was she then, Master Eden? And was there anyone else with her?'

'Her was all bent and scrunched up and walking funny-like, but I knew her was the witch because I saw a toad following after her and everybody knows that witches has cats and toads as their familiars. And there must have been another of her evil spirits waiting for her in the shed because I heard her crying out to 'um after I'd crept up and barred the door shut. So you'd best charge your pistols afore you goes in there.'

'I've brought no pistols. But I'm sure this will suffice well enough as a weapon.' Tom hefted his yard-long, crown-topped, red, gold and blue staff of office.

'No pistols?' the old man exclaimed. 'Am you bloody sarft-yedded? No pistols?' He turned and hurried away, shouting back over his shoulder, 'You can open the bloody door by yourself, you gert lanky fool.'

'Dear God, give me strength!' Tom muttered in exasperation and, lifting the bar from the door, pulled it slightly ajar. Peering into the gloomy interior he called, 'I'm Thomas Potts, Constable of Tardebigge Parish. Come to the door and identify yourself.'

There was no answering word or movement.

'Could there be a gang laying in wait for me?' Tom wondered. His deeply ingrained timidity made him reluctant to enter the darkness inside.

From a distance Eden shouted angrily, 'What's you hanging about for? Am you feared or what? Do your duty. Get in there and fetch 'um out.'

Tom waited. Called. Waited. Called and waited yet again.

'Why don't you get in there? Am you too windy-gutted, or what?' Eden taunted.

Heart pounding, throat tightening, breath shortening, Tom dragged the door wide and, holding his staff raised to strike, stepped across the threshold.

His eyes slowly adjusted to the gloom as he scanned the roof-high layers of mangold-wurzels and the stacked barrels of carrots. He crept cautiously along the narrow walkway and drew a sharp intake of breath as he detected a dark shape on the ground at the far end of the shed.

'You there, come towards me. I swear that I'll not harm you,' he called, and receiving no answer went warily to the crumpled heap.

He frowned in concern. It was a small girl, her mass of tangled hair and the rags on her frail body sodden with rain and thick with mud and slime. She was unconscious, her breaths a strangulated wheezing. Crouching low he laid his hand gently on her forehead and felt the burning heat from her skin.

'The poor little mite's consumed with fever.'

He gathered her up in his arms and hurried from the shed.

'Killed her, has you? I never thought that you'd got the stomach for it. Bloody good on you!' Eden crowed delightedly.

Tom momentarily lost his temper. 'Hold your noise, you old fool! Of course I've not killed her. She's a mere child and very sick. Lead on to your house, we must get her clean and put to bed, before anything else can be done.'

'What?' The old man scowled and raved furiously. 'Let a bloody witch across my doorstep? Put her to bed in my house? Not bloody likely you won't. If you aren't going to kill the evil bitch then just get her off my land as quick as your bloody legs can carry you. Because the only way you'll bring her under my roof is over my dead body!'

Realizing the futility of further argument Tom crouched and balanced the girl's limp body across his knees while he shrugged out of his greatcoat and wrapped her in its capacious folds. Then cradling her close he hurried onwards through the pouring rain.

At William Pettifer's house it was the farmer's wife who opened the door in reply to Tom's knocks.

'What on earth have you got there, Master Potts?' She peered short-sightedly at the limp bundle in his arms, then exclaimed, 'Bless me! It's a kiddy, aren't it?'

'It is indeed, Mrs Pettifer, and I fear she's ill. Can I bring her inside?'

The woman frowned doubtfully. 'What's amiss with her? I got my own kids to think about. I don't want them catching the smallpox, or the cholera.'

Tom could understand and sympathize with her concern, and answered honestly. 'In truth, ma'am, I don't know what's wrong with her. She's burning with fever. But as you can see the poor little soul is so filthy wet and dirty that until she's been washed and cleaned there's no way of telling what is ailing her.'

'Well, who is she?' the woman questioned.

Tom could only shrug. 'I don't know her name, ma'am. Or anything about her.'

'Hold on a minute.' Mrs Pettifer's tone sharpened. 'Is this one of them who was thieving from Old Joe's shed?'

'There were no others, ma'am; she was alone in the shed. And I don't know that she was thieving anything,' Tom protested. 'I've found nothing that would indicate that she was committing any crime whatsoever.'

'Then what was she doing in Old Joe's shed where she had no rights to be? And Old Joe said she cried out to others when he barred the door. So where are they?'

Tom's anxiety for the child drove him to snap impatiently. 'For God's sake, ma'am, there were no others and this poor child needs help. So will you kindly let me bring her inside?'

The woman bridled instantly. 'Don't you take that tone with me, Master High and Mighty Constable! You're not talking to one of your Redditch slum rats now. Me and my husband pays the Parish rates that you lives off. So take that thieving little tramp and put her in the bloody jail with all the other bloody thieves that we has to pay to keep with our hard-earned money.'

She slammed the door in his face.

Tom could only chide himself wryly. 'That went rather well, didn't it, Potts! Now what will you do?'

He briefly considered his other options then whispered gently to the unconscious child, 'I'm sorry, my dear, but I've no other feasible choice than to take you to the Poorhouse.'

Rainwater dripping from his top hat and clothes, boots squelching in the mud, he trudged away from the farm.

It took him more than an hour to reach the large semi-derelict old house and outbuildings which constituted the Tardebigge Parish Poorhouse. As always this visit to the Poorhouse lowered Tom's spirits. He knew only too well the sad histories of many of its fifty or more current inhabitants. Parentless children and infants, aged enfeebled men and women, pregnant girls abandoned by lovers, wives abandoned by husbands, the destitute sick, the mentally infirm, the cruel roll call of life's casualties.

The elderly stooped male porter opened the front door to Tom's knock. Like all the others who dwelt here he wore on his shabby coat the grey cloth badge bearing the painted red letters TP, the emblem widely regarded as a badge of shame, the emblem of the Tardebigge Parish pauper.

He recognized Tom and wordlessly beckoned him to enter, then shuffled away down the corridor shouting in a wavering voice, 'Master? Mistress? The constable's brung you summat.'

Tom crouched to balance the child on his knees and draw back the folds of the wrapped greatcoat so that he could check her condition.

He sucked in a sharp breath of concern. Her eyes were open but deep sunken, blankly staring as if she saw nothing, and although her skin was radiating heat her body was shivering violently.

Footsteps sounded on the bare planked floor.

'What's this you've brought us, Master Potts?' Edwin Lewis, the middle-aged, broad-shouldered Poorhouse master with the stiff-backed bearing of the veteran soldier, bent to examine Tom's burden. Then he straightened and bellowed.

'You'd best come here directly, Mrs Lewis. This falls within your line o' duty.'

A short, sturdy woman dressed in severe black and wearing a man's broad-brimmed slouch hat came hurrying down the corridor with a loud clumping of hobnailed boots.

'Be good enough to let the dog see the rabbit will you, Master Lewis?' She pushed her husband to one side and went down on to her knees, feeling gently over the child's head, face and body with both hands.

'There don't appear to be any bones broke. Give her here, Master Potts.' She took the child in her arms, rose and hurried back down the corridor shouting, 'Becky, Abigail, get the kettle on the fire and sort me out some clean towelling. I'll be in the washhouse.'

'You looks like you been dragged backwards through a river, Master Potts. There's a good fire in my parlour so come in and dry yourself by it while you're telling me all about this kiddie,' Edwin Lewis invited.

When they were seated in the neat parlour before a blazing fire Tom quickly related what had happened.

The Poorhouse master frowned doubtfully. 'Has there been any missing kids reported lately?'

Tom shook his head. 'I'm wondering if she's been deliberately abandoned. Or if she was with a tramper who's lying dead somewhere.'

'Well, the Vestry aren't going to be best pleased wi' me for taking her in here without their permission . . . And what if she dies on us? You know well that they won't pay to bury her until they've searched high and low for her rightful parish. The poor little soul could be laying in my salting trough for months.' Lewis paused momentarily, then burst out angrily, 'This bloody country has got some bloody rotten laws, aren't it!'

'Indeed it has.' Tom's agreement was heartfelt.

He hated the draconian Laws of Settlement which ruled that no man, woman or child was entitled to receive help from any Parish Relief Funds unless they had been born in that particular parish. An individual could come to work and live in a parish, pay local taxes, serve that community. But should that individual become destitute for any reason, they were not entitled to be relieved by the Parish, and could be returned forcibly to their parish of birth. This included the sick and the dead. All too often pauper corpses remained unburied for long periods while the ruling 'Select Vestries' of parishes disputed as to which of them should pay the burial fees of an infant, child or adult.

'But don't worry, Master Lewis. I'll take full responsibility for whatever she might cost the Parish. No blame for this will fall on your shoulders because I'll explain everything to the Vestry.'

It was an hour later and Tom's clothing was still damp in parts when Hilda Lewis came into the parlour.

'How is the child, ma'am?' He rose from the wooden armchair.

'Burning with fever, Master Potts.' She frowned accusingly. 'And the pitiful little soul has been sore-treated without a doubt. She's carrying bruises and weals on her poor little body that was made by a whip if I'm any judge; and I've seen enough whiplashes to be a very good judge of whiplashes.'

'Well she's suffered no ill treatment from me, and neither from Joe Eden, I'm positive,' Tom hastened to assure this formidable woman. 'But is she able to speak, ma'am, because I need to ask her some questions?'

'Speak! You ask me if she can speak!' The woman glared at Tom as if he were an idiot. 'She might be on this world, Master Potts, but she aren't aware of being on it, I can tell you. She might be breathing and her eyes might be open, but her spirit's wandering only God knows where. You may ask your questions until you're blue in the face, Master Potts, but the poor little soul will not be able to give you any answers.'

'Well please may I at least sit with her for a while, ma'am?' Tom supplicated humbly. 'She was so covered in muck and slime that I'm not able to describe what she really looks like, and if I can't do so then I've little chance of discovering her identity. Also she might regain some awareness in a couple of hours or so.'

'You may sit with her, Master Potts, but don't try to rouse her, will you?'

'I wouldn't dream of doing so, ma'am,' Tom truthfully affirmed.

'I don't doubt you, Master Potts. Come with me.'

Like a monarch, Hilda Lewis regally led the way and Tom followed, a submissive courtier.

FOUR

Afternoon, Sunday 7th October

The rain had ceased but the skies were still blanketed with cloud, the air dank and chill. Wet, weary, footsore, Joey Dowler bewailed his ill fortune as he stumbled up the steeply rising trackway.

'What am I going to do? Enoch's going to smash me face in.'

The wind gusted suddenly, carrying a spattering of fresh raindrops and Dowler cursed in self-pitying anger. 'Fuck this for a game o' soldiers. I could catch me death o' cold out here! Her's more than likely laying dead in a ditch by now, and that's why I aren't spotted her.'

He reached the top of the climb where the trackway debouched on to the newly constructed gravelled turnpike road which ran north to south along the top of the long spine of high ground known as the Ridgeway. A half mile to the north the road passed through the village of Astwood Bank and on for a further four miles through its almost contiguous villages of Crabbs Cross and Headless Cross. Then down the long incline known as Mount Pleasant and into the hilly town of Redditch, which was centred on a plateau at the extreme northern end of the Ridgeway overlooking the broad valley of the Arrow River. The town and its satellite settlements, although surrounded by vast swathes of woods and agricultural land, were industrialized. Specializing in the manufacture of needles and fish hooks, they were collectively termed the 'Needle District' and were fast achieving worldwide supremacy in that particular trade.

Joey Dowler turned and hurried northwards until he reached a wayside alehouse. He pushed open the door and stepped thankfully into the dry warmth within.

The small, low-beamed room was furnished with high-backed wooden settles around the walls. In its centre men seated on stools surrounded a solitary table bestrewn with playing cards and coins. The air was thick with the fumes of smoking tallow candles in wall-fixed sconces, burning peat, strong harsh tobacco, cider and the mingled stenches of farmyard muck and unwashed flesh emanating from the dozen or so smock-frocked farm labourers staring curiously at this newcomer.

'How do,' Dowler greeted.

'How do,' one solitary voice replied.

'Is the landlord around?' Dowler asked.

'I keep this house.' The owner of the solitary voice rose from the settle next to the peat fire and questioned suspiciously, 'Who might you be?'

Dowler was not perturbed by the landlord's unwelcoming attitude. In isolated rural alehouses strangers were invariably regarded with suspicion.

'I'm just passing through, Master, and wants a drink.'

'Where are you passing to?' The landlord stepped forwards and another man moved to block the doorway.

Apprehension struck through Dowler, and he asserted nervously, 'To Redditch. Me name's Joey Dowler. I lives in Hill Street on Unicorn Hill down in Redditch there.'

His questioner came to stand directly in front of him. 'Who can vouch for that?'

'Well, there's a good many in Redditch who knows me! I'm speaking truthful! Honest I am!'

The questioner ostentatiously sniffed the air and turned to ask the eager listeners, 'Has one o' you farted, or is Joey Dowler shitting himself?'

There came a roar of laughter, and the landlord chortled with satisfaction. 'We'em just having a bit o' fun wi' you, Joey Dowler. What's your pleasure?'

'Bloody Hell!' Dowler exclaimed in relief. 'You was putting the fear o' Christ up me. I'll need a flagon o' gin to settle me nerves after this.'

'And you shall have it.' The landlord grinned. 'Find a seat for yourself by the fire; you looks half perished wi' cold.'

'Half perished wi' bloody fright, more like,' Dowler blurted, and more laughter rang out.

Dowler took a seat on a high-backed wooden settle, the gamblers returned to their game, and interrupted conversations were resumed as the landlord delivered the flagon of gin.

Joey Dowler took a deep swig of the raw spirit and gasped with pleasure as it burned down his gullet to begin spreading warmth through his chilled body.

Another be-smocked labourer came through the outer door and was greeted by his friends.

'You'm late on parade, Ezra. Where you bin?'

The newcomer was animated with excitement. 'I been over at Bank Green. There aren't 'alf been a game at Joe Eden's this day. The loony old bugger reckons that that witch he's been shouting on about for ages was in his shed this morning. He got Will Pettifer to fetch the constable and they caught her in the shed. Old Joe said that her was in the shape of a little wench but her was all black and slimy. Her stunk like summat out of a bloody cesspit, Old Joe said, and her was pretending that her was senseless.'

Joey Dowler caught his breath and listened intently.

'What's they done with her, Ezra?' the landlord asked.

'Well, the constable reckoned that Old Joe was off his yed for believing in witches. He wanted Joe to give her shelter. But Joe 'uddn't have her under his roof, so the constable took her to

Pettifer's place. But Pettifer's missus told him to bugger off and take her to the Poorhouse, so that's what he must ha' done.'

Once again apprehension struck through Joey Dowler.

'If her's a blacky her might be a gyppo,' a man offered. 'I saw a tribe of the buggers passing yesterday.'

Ezra stroked his stubbled chin reflectively. 'Her could be, I suppose. Anyway, from what they'm saying her looked to be in a real bad way and she'll more than likely die.'

'Well, be her gyppo or tramper it's good riddance to bad rubbish because they'm a plague on the land, all of 'um,' another man put in.

'Ahrr, you'm right there. They'm all lazy thieving bastards.'

'They ought to be hung, every last one of 'um.'

There was a fervent chorus of agreement, then the talk turned to other matters.

Joey Dowler sat silent, taking swigs of his gin, trying desperately to decide on a course of action.

'What if it is her? What if her don't die? What if her lives and tells tales? But what if it aren't her?'

His flagon of gin was almost empty before he came to a reluctant decision.

'I'm going to have to tell Enoch.'

He drained the last dregs of the raw spirit and stumbled drunkenly out into the night.

FIVE

Night, Sunday 7th October

The centre of Redditch Town was an open long-sided triangular green with its points at due North, East and South. Radiating outwards from the Green were a network of streets and alleys and courts, close-packed houses and tenements, shops, taverns, workshops, factories and mills. At the eastern point of the Green where its bordering roadways met and forked was the two-storied, stone-fronted, castellated 'lock-up', standing detached from its neighbours. It was the only public building in the Parish, and the lodging of Tom Potts and his mother, the Widow Gertrude Potts.

It was close to midnight and the town was quiet and in pitch darkness when Tom returned from the Poorhouse to the Lock-up. There was no lamplight glowing from the upper storey windows where he and his mother had their living quarters, and none from the arrow slits that flanked the large gothic-arched entrance door.

'Dammit, she's not lit the passage lantern yet again.' He groaned inwardly. 'And no doubt she's left something inside for me to trip over.'

He mounted the three steps on to the front platform of the building, unlocked and pushed on the heavy iron-studded door to discover it was barred on the inside.

'Here we go!' He sighed resignedly. 'She's having another of her martyrdom moments. Wicked me, rudely waking her from her well-deserved slumbers. Oh well, so be it.'

He grasped the iron bell rod on the door post and tugged repeatedly.

Bells jangled on both lower and upper floors sounding preter-naturally loud in the stillness of the night.

Almost immediately the casement of the window above the door opened and a strident female voice shrieked threateningly. 'Be off with you, you drunken villain, or I'll empty the pisspot over your head!'

Tom instantly jumped sideways as a liquid stream cascaded down from above, missing him by inches.

'Goddamn it! You surely knew it was me!' He shouted furiously as rancid smelling urine splashed upon his boots and stockings.

'How could I know it was you?' Widow Potts' almost conver-sational tone held a note of satisfaction. 'What sort of son would come in the dead of night and frighten his poor pitiful invalid mother half to death?'

She instantly shrieked the answer to her own question. 'A wicked fiend of a son who delights in making his mother's life a constant torment! A veritable purgatory!'

Knowing only too well the futility of responding aggressively Tom sighed and requested quietly, 'Will you please come down and unbar the door, Mother?'

'Only when you have apologized for terrifying me so,' she stated flatly.

For a brief moment Tom was sorely tempted to hurl his staff at the opened casement, but he controlled himself and said through clenched teeth, 'I apologize for disturbing you, Mother.'

'Disturbing me, he says! Disturbing me!' She vented high-pitched wails. 'Oh my dear God, what have I done that I should have given birth to such a cruel, vile creature as he who stands below? What have I done, my dearest Lord?'

The bedroom window of the nearest house opened and a man bellowed irately.

'You've woke me up, that's what you lot's done! And I got to be at my work by five o' the clock. So stop your bloody skreeking will you and let decent hard-working folk get their rest!'

The Widow Potts' casement slammed shut and Tom silently blessed the irate neighbour. But many more minutes elapsed before the glow of lamplight shone through the arrow slits and he heard the wheezing, grunting grumblings of his mother as she unbarred the door.

He stepped inside and for several moments they stood silently facing each other. As always the physical contrast between them evoked in Tom's mind the nursery rhyme of 'Jack Sprat and his Wife'. Tom exceptionally tall and narrow built, with a lean aquiline face. The Widow Potts exceptionally squat and fat, her ballooned features and hanging jowls framed by the voluminous mobcap bearing a strong resemblance to a scowling toad.

'That saucy slum-slut that you're stupid enough to want to marry has been pestering me and making my life a misery since this morning.' There was a gleam of cruel enjoyment lurking in the widow's slit puffy eyes and spittle flecked from her toothless mouth. 'She's very angry because you've made a fool of her before the entire congregation by not being in the chapel to hear your own Banns called.'

Dread shivered through Tom. 'Did you not give her my message? Did you not tell her that I'd been called out on urgent official duties, and that I was sorely distressed not to be able to be there with her?'

Even as he voiced the questions he knew with dismayed certainty that her answer would be in the negative. Disgust burgeoned so strongly that he could only shake his head and snap angrily.

'Don't even bother to make any excuses, Mother. I really don't want to remain in your company a moment longer this night.'

He locked and barred the door and walked past her down the stone-flagged, cell-lined passage, at the far end of which was a rear door and to its side the steep narrow stairway to the upper floor.

From a wall cupboard flanking the door he took a strip of towelling and a cake of soap. Then he stripped to the waist and went through the rear door into the square yard which was enclosed by high, spike-crowned walls. The water pump stood in a corner facing the privy in the opposite corner. Tom removed his boots and stockings before vigorously working the pump's long handle to fill the wooden bucket beneath the spout, lathered, sluiced and dried his head, upper body, feet and legs. Then he washed his stockings, and the urine off his boots.

By now feeling virtually spent, he decided, 'I'll light a fire first thing in the morning to dry these out.'

Upstairs, lying in his narrow cot, his mother's snorting snores sounding loudly from the adjoining room, Tom tried to sleep. But troubled thoughts and vivid images plagued him.

'That poor child, what dreadful things may have happened to her? Will she live? And Amy is right to be angry with me. She'll be thinking that I broke my promise to be with her to hear our banns called. Dear God, why did you give me such a spiteful, nasty shrew as a mother?'

Even when sleep finally overcame him, disturbing dreams caused him to restlessly toss and turn and wake at intervals all through the night.

Up in the Poorhouse little Sukey was also restlessly tossing and turning in a feverish coma, at times screaming in terror and choking out snatches of words. Sitting on a stool next to the narrow cot, Hilda Lewis stroked the girl's forehead, murmuring soothingly. 'Lie still now, little one. Lie still and be easy. You'm safe here wi' me.' She sighed sadly. 'What is it you're trying to tell me, I wonder.'

From the adjoining cot an old crone was listening intently, and after yet another outcry from the sick child, she croaked, 'Them's nursery rhymes her's a shouting out, Missus.'

'Don't talk so sarft, Abigail,' Hilda Lewis reproved sharply. 'How can you tell what she's saying when you're nigh on as deaf as a post?'

'I'm only deaf when I wants to be, Missus.' The crone cackled with sly laughter. 'I can hear a needle drop when I needs to.'

'As I've suspected many a time, you crafty old baggage,' her mistress snapped, just as the sick child again writhed violently and spilled out mangled words.

'Alright then, Abigail!' Hilda Lewis challenged. 'What did the poor little mite just say?'

'Her said that Jack's got his crown broke,' the crone asserted triumphantly. 'That's what her said. I heard it as plain as plain. And that's that 'un that goes, "Jack and Jill went up the hill . . ."'

'To fetch a pail o' water.' Her mistress chimed in. 'And Jack fell down, and broke his crown, and Jill came tumbling after.'

'That's it, Missus!' The crone cackled with satisfied glee. 'That's it! That's it!'

'Alright, Abigail. Now just go to sleep, will you. You'll have me as daft as you are if I has to listen to any more of your nonsense this night,' Hilda Lewis ordered sharply, and turned her back on the other woman.

Abigail laid her mobcapped head on the pillow and contentedly sucked her toothless gums until she drifted into sleep.

SIX

Early morning, Monday 8th October

In the darkness lights were beginning to glimmer from the rows of buildings surrounding the Green. Soon the bells of the needle mills and factories would commence their clangour and from the hovels and tenements men, women and children would come flocking in answer to this summons to yet another long grinding day of hard toil.

Tom Potts rose from his cot and used tinder and steel to light the bedside candle, and kindle a flame of sticks and coal in the small iron fire range. Then still in his nightshirt and long-tasselled nightcap he fetched his damp clothes from the yard and arranged them in front of the fire to dry out.

'Thomasss! Thomasss! Where's my breakfast? Do you mean to starve me to death?' Widow Potts shrilled querulously from her bed. 'You get lazier by the day, I swear. The morning's nigh on gone and you're still laying abed, you idle devil! Thank God your poor sainted father is in his grave, because it would break his heart to see what you have become.'

'I may well become a matricide if I have to live with you for much longer,' Tom thought with grim humour, and called back. 'Don't distress yourself, Mother, I'm going to make breakfast directly.'

He dressed in shirt, stockings and breeches, pulled on boots, took up the lighted candle and went back downstairs to the cupboard and shelf-lined alcove which served as the larder. Widow Potts' breakfast took only seconds to prepare. A bowl of milk with a raw egg beaten into it and topped with a layer of cone sugar, plus two slices of bread which she would dip into the liquid and noisily suck and champ on.

When he carried the bowl into her room she sat up in bed and berated furiously.

'Why didn't you knock and warn me you were coming in? Have you no manners at all, you brute beast? And what about my candle and my fire? Do you intend me to freeze to death in the dark? You'd like that, wouldn't you?'

An angry retort rose to Tom's lips, but he bit it back as the image of his beloved father's face came into his mind, and the memory of his father's dying pleas that he, Tom, would care for and be kind to this woman until the end of her days.

He placed the bowl and bread on the bedside chair, lit her candle from his own then laid and lighted a fire in the grate.

'Is there anything else you need, Mother, because I have to go out very shortly?'

Noisily slurping, sucking and champing, she totally ignored him, and with an overwhelming sense of relief he closed her door behind him.

Downstairs again he lit a bull's-eye lantern and shone the ray of light inside the open door of the lower cupboard, sighed ruefully and went out into the yard. He stripped to the waist, sluiced his head and upper body with pump water, brushed his teeth and towelled himself dry. His mood was sombrely regretful.

'There's naught else for it. It has to be done now.'

He filled a bucket with water and set it to one side, took up the lantern and returned to the lower cupboard.

Bathed in the pool of light a litter of newly born kittens writhed blindly, mewing piteously for warmth and food.

'Goddamn you, Bathsheba! This is the third litter you've abandoned,' Tom muttered in disgust. 'I swear you're just such a mother as the one I've got upstairs!'

He gently gathered the tiny bodies into his hands, took them out to the pump and slipped them into the water-filled bucket, covering it over with a square of wood board.

A small black cat came out from the shadows and, purring loudly, rubbed its head against Tom's legs. He smiled ruefully and bent to stroke its soft fur.

'This is you all over, isn't it, Bathsheba? Hiding away for days on end until I've done the deed and then coming crying for your breakfast. I don't enjoy drowning the abandoned offspring that you leave to starve to death, you shameless hussy.'

He lifted her into his arms and she rubbed her head against his chin as he carried her back indoors.

After he had made a hasty breakfast of bread and cheese Tom came out from the Lock-up and stood for some moments wracked by indecision.

'Go and see Amy? Check on the poor child at the Poorhouse? Which one first?'

Fronting the Green midway along its southern border, the lights of the Fox and Goose Inn were shining through its latticed windows.

'Amy will be busy with the early trade. She'll not be best pleased if I go bothering her now, and neither will Tommy Fowkes. It might be better if I go to see the child first, then report to Blackwell, and see Amy afterwards,' Tom decided, but in the next second berated himself angrily. 'Don't be such a damned coward! Go and face Amy and take your punishment like a man! And be damned to Fatty Fowkes!'

The long Tap Room of the Fox and Goose was packed with the lower social ranks of the town's workers. Odorous unshaven men clad in grimy work clothes were clamouring for service, exchanging stories, oaths and raucous laughter.

In the smaller Snug Room were congregated the respectable middle ranks of the labour force. The overseers, the clerks and timekeepers, neatly clothed, faces freshly washed. Their behaviour sedate, voices muted and conversations mainly centred on their pursuits of self improvement and social advancement.

The large, well-furnished Select Front Parlour was the undisputed domain of the accepted aristocracy of the town. Needle Masters, Factory Owners, Doctors, Lawyers, and those thrusting 'Up and Comers' who aspired to join these exalted ranks.

Thomas Fowkes gloried in his role as Innkeeper of the Fox and Goose, and now that he had achieved a considerable degree of prosperity thought himself to be the equal of any, and far superior to most of his fellow men. He spent the vast majority of his time lording it in the Select Parlour, chatting with his select clientele and even deigning on occasion to serve them with his own hands. With a shrewd eye for business he usually had his two pretty barmaids, Amy Danks and Maisie Lock, working in here. His wife oversaw the Tap Room with the help of a pot man. His daughter Lily was normally relegated to the duller, less profitable Snug Room – much to her chagrin, for she fiercely envied the opportunities enjoyed by Amy and Maisie to flirt with the rich young bloods of the town.

As Tom Potts walked up to the door of the Fox and Goose the summoning work bells began tolling from near and far and he halted to allow a clear exit to the inn's customers. The first to emerge were the frequenters of the Snug Room, and many of them civilly greeted Tom as they passed.

The next group to stream through the doorway were the Tap Room habitués.

'Look who's here, lads, fuckin' Lanky Balls himself wi' his bloody truncheon at the ready!'

'He makes a beanpole look like the fattest oak tree in England, don't he?'

'Does your Mammy know you'm here? She'll tan your arse for you if she finds out!'

'Why don't you come wi' us and do a proper day's work for a change!'

'No, you'd sooner crawl to the Masters to get your bread, uddn't you!'

Tom stoically ignored the gibes and insults mouthed at him as they dispersed to go to their different places of work. He had long sadly accepted that large numbers of the local population saw him as the willing tool of that rapacious governing class which ruthlessly exploited the poor and landless masses.

No mass exodus followed from the Select Parlour. There was no necessity for it because as one Needle Master often proclaimed: 'I don't answer to the bells until I choose to, because I'm the man who owns those bells!'

Tom stepped into the broad entrance passageway just as the door of the Select Parlour opened and Amy Danks came through it. He called to her.

'Amy, can you spare me a moment? I need to explain about yesterday.'

She came to front him, her cheeks flushed, her eyes hard with anger.

'Look, I'm really sorry that I couldn't be with you to hear our Banns but I was called out. My mother should have explained where I'd gone,' he told her hastily.

'Don't you dare blame your mother for what you didn't do, Tom Potts. And that was to come and tell me yourself! You know very well that the rotten old cow hates me and that she'd never explain anything to me.'

'Amy, I'm not trying to blame her—'

His nervous denial was cut short.

'Just you listen to me, Tom Potts,' Amy snapped furiously. 'I was really worried when you didn't come to chapel, and I went running to the Lock-up to find you. And that old bitch of a Mam of yours insulted me, so she did. Spoke to me as if I was a piece of dirt!'

'I'm very sorry!' he blurted desperately. 'I know that she can be very rude at times. I'll take her to task about it.'

'I'll take her to task about it!' She mimicked him angrily, then stormed on. 'No you won't! She treats you like a dog and you haven't got the courage to put her in her place.'

He lifted his hands in protest and tried to speak, but she waved him to silence.

'No, don't even try to say anything. I'm telling you now that as long as that evil old bitch is beneath your roof then I'll not marry you. I'd sooner be in my grave than under the same roof with her. So it's her or me, and you must make your choice. And don't dare to come near me until you've got shot of your Mam, and you'd best do it quick because there's plenty of other chaps who're eager to wed me.'

She swung about in a flurry of petticoats, ran down the passage and disappeared into the rear rooms.

'Oh my God, what a start to the day.' Tom sighed glumly and left the inn.

At the central crossroads a middle-aged man came running and shouting from a shop doorway to intercept him.

'Hold hard, Tom Potts! I wants words with you!' Timothy Munslow, portly stomached Pie Man and General Confectioner, angrily brandished a small, dead, soaking-wet dog beneath Tom's nose. 'I've just fished this up out of my well. That bloody King William is trying to poison me water!'

King William was a harmless, deranged, harelipped man in his early thirties who until her recent death had been cared for by his widowed mother. Now he was homeless and without family the Select Vestry had ordered him to be kept in the Poorhouse, but he continually ran away from there to roam around the parish. Many of the local people treated him kindly, giving him food and often temporary shelter. But there were some who used him as the butt of their cruel jokes, getting him drunk and egging him on to create mischief.

'How can you know that it was King William who threw this dog into your well?' Tom sought clarification.

'O' course it was him, I knows that for a fact.'

'Did anybody witness him throwing the dog into your well?'

'How could they? He did it in the dead o' last night when everybody was sleeping, didn't he.' Munslow puffed in exasperation. 'He aren't bloody sarft enough to do it in broad daylight when he can be seen, is he?'

'Then you've no proof of his guilt, Master Munslow. It might have been anyone who has a grudge against you that put this poor beast in your well.'

Munslow's face reddened and he shouted angrily. 'Ohhh no!

It's him alright! And I knows that for a fact, because this bloody cur was with him at the Big Pool yesterday, and when I walked past him it tried to bite me. Naturally I stamped the bugger flat and kicked it into the pool.

'It's certain sure the Loony come back later and fished it out and chucked it down my well to poison my water. That's certain sure that is; and I'm telling you now that if you don't find the bugger and lock him up this very day I'm going direct to the Vestry to lay complaint that you'm neglecting your lawful duty.'

Munslow hurled the dead dog to the ground and stamped away, muttering aggrievedly to himself.

Tom sighed down at the bedraggled dog. 'I'd best put you into the ground, you poor beast.'

He carried the dog back to the Lock-up, put it in a sack together with the drowned kittens, took a shovel and went to a stretch of waste ground beyond the Big Pool, where he buried the animals.

'I'll have to postpone seeing the little girl and find King William before he gets himself into any further troubles,' Tom reluctantly decided. 'But it's going to be a very long day, I fear.'

SEVEN

Birmingham.
Midday, Monday 8th October

The clock of St Martin's church displayed the noon hour as Enoch Griffiths, the very epitome of the prosperous countryman with beefy red face beneath wide-brimmed hat, powerful physique clothed in brass-buttoned coat, breeches and leather gaiters, walked through the bustling market stalls of the Bull Ring.

On the other side of the market place Griffiths went into an alehouse which was thronged with feather-bonneted, garishly rouged prostitutes and their potential customers.

'Hello, Master Enoch, is it me you're wanting again this fine morning?' A strapping young woman pulled down the top of her tawdry low-cut gown to flaunt her full breasts before his eyes. 'Here they be all ready and waiting, fresh and sweet-tasting just like you likes 'um.'

He grinned regretfully. 'Not right now, Elsie, I've got very pressing business to attend to. I'm looking for the Duchess.'

'That stinking hag?' Elsie's eyes widened in exaggerated shock. 'I can't believe what I'm hearing, Master Enoch! Would you really rather shag that poxed-up old bitch than me?'

He chuckled amusedly. 'Well you know the saying that there's many a fine tune gets played on an old fiddle.'

'Not when all its bloody strings be broke.' Elsie's fine teeth shone in laughter.

'Do you know where she is?' Griffiths' tone abruptly hardened. 'I've no more time to waste gaming about with a slut like you.'

'I saw her going into Chinky Chong's house not long since,' the young woman told him hastily. 'And listen, I was only having a bit o' fun wi' you.'

He nodded and smiled once more. 'I know that, my lovely girl, and after I've done my business I'll be coming back for you. We'll make a night of it.'

'I'll be here waiting for you, Master Enoch. Honest I will,' she assured him volubly.

Griffiths left, and another woman said to Elsie, 'You've got another all-nighter with your regular then, you lucky cow. I've heard he pays well.'

Elsie nodded thoughtfully. 'Oh yes, he pays well, but there's been a couple o' times when he's made me skin crawl.' She hesitated, searching for words. 'It was like I saw summat in his eyes which made me feel I was looking into me own grave!'

Her companion laughed hoarsely. 'Well if it happens again just close your eyes and try to think of England.'

The door at the end of the narrow blank-walled passageway was iron barred. Griffiths hammered on its thick planking with his meaty fist, and a small eyehole trap momentarily opened and closed. Chains rattled, bolts clunked and the door swung inwards.

'Welcome, Master Griffiths, you couldn't have picked a better day to honour me with your presence.' The shaven-headed, fashionably dressed Chinaman greeted his visitor with outstretched hand and smiling face. 'I've just taken delivery of the very finest Afghan, and your favourite divan is waiting for you.'

'And I'm in sore need of a puff of the best, Chong, but it'll have to wait.' Griffiths shook the proffered hand.

'Take a sniff of this, and you'll know that I'm not exaggerating, Master Griffiths.' The Chinaman held a small ball of raw opium to Griffiths' nose.

Griffiths sniffed loudly and nodded appreciatively. 'That'll do me fine. Save a room for me and me whore tonight. But now I needs to have words wi' the Duchess. Is her head straight today?'

The Chinaman chuckled. 'As straight as it'll ever be, I suppose. She's in the kitchen. You can be quite private there. In the meantime I'll get your pipes and room prepared.'

'And can you arrange a decent-looking carriage and pair for early tomorrow. I need the Duchess to go on an errand for me.'

'To hear is to obey, Honoured Mandarin.' The Chinaman caricatured a Kow-Tow.

Griffiths went into the smoke-filled, rank-smelling kitchen at the rear of the house. The woman he sought was sitting crouched on a stool before the range fire with a mangy-furred cat on her lap.

She didn't turn to look at him as he entered, but said loudly to the cat, 'Look who's here to see us, Sweetie-pie. It's my own dearest friend come again to beg my forgiveness for his ill-usage of me.' Her accents were those of a Gentlewoman.

The cat lifted its head to stare at the newcomer, then suddenly arched its back high, sprang from the woman's lap and disappeared beneath the dresser where it stayed hissing and growling.

'You're a much cleverer girl than I've ever been, Sweetie-pie.' The woman applauded mockingly. 'You recognize the devil when you see him, don't you? How I wish I'd done so.'

Enoch Griffiths didn't move from the doorway. He pitched coins tinkling and rolling across the stone-flagged floor, and ordered grimly, 'Listen to me well. I've arranged for a carriage for you first thing tomorrow morning. You'll go to the Tardebigge Poorhouse. There's a little wench just been took in there, age about eight years, name o' Sukey Crawford. You'm to claim her and fetch her out of it. Now word has it that she's out of her head, so make up a story to cover that.'

Still keeping her face turned to the fire, the Duchess asked, 'Where am I to deliver her?'

'Take her to Marlfield. Tell Doll, the wench must be kept separate.'

He turned and left, closing the door quietly behind him.

The Duchess remained motionless, listening to the impacts of his iron-studded boots on the flagstones. Then when all fell silent she went on to her hands and knees to gather the coins strewn on the floor, whimpering aloud as she did so.

'God forgive me! What choice do I have? There's naught else I can do! May God forgive me!'

EIGHT

Night, Monday 8th October

I t was almost midnight; the skies were virtually cloud-free but the sliver of the new moon shed little light upon the dark earth. Hungry, tired and dispirited from the fruitless search for the elusive King William, Tom Potts came slowly trudging up the long sloping road which led on to the eastern side of the town's central plateau.

When he reached the plateau he came to a standstill where the roadway divided to skirt around the deep waterhole known as the 'Big Pool'. It was virtually surrounded by rows of jerry-built tumbledown tenements inhabited by some of the needle district's poorest, most wretched inhabitants. Without access to spring-fed wells or deep-piped pumps, the Big Pool was their water source, and in their squalid ignorance they both used and abused it and were sickened and killed by it.

Tom had seen dead dogs, cats, rats floating in its murky depths. Human and animal faeces, rotting food waste and household rubbish. Even on occasion the corpse of a man or woman driven to suicide by the hopeless desperation of their existence. In hot summer weather it emitted a foul miasma that carried far on the air, and even now in the cool of autumn its stench percolated its immediate environs.

As always the sight of the Big Pool's thick-scummed surface provoked an angry disgust in Tom.

'We are living in the richest, most powerful, most advanced scientific and modern nation in the world, and here it's still the Dark Ages.'

A soughing breeze came from the west as he walked slowly on towards the Green, reached the Lock-up and thankfully inserted his key in the door. A sudden sound of human voices was carried to his ears by the wind. He turned his head, listening intently, and again heard voices and a burst of laughter. For a brief moment his longing for food and rest battled with his sense of duty, then reluctantly he accepted.

'I'll have to check that there's no mischief afoot.'

Shouldering his staff he headed towards the southern side of the Green where he judged the sounds had originated.

He reached the wall of the chapel yard and halted, listening intently, peering hard, but could not distinguish any movement in the darkness. Keeping close to the wall he moved cautiously onwards towards the central crossroads, passing the front of the Fox and Goose and its immediate neighbours.

Another brief snatch of muffled voices and laughter sounded from his front, and Tom crouched low, breath catching in his throat as against the skyline he spotted a solid black silhouette moving from the chapel wall into the middle of the roadway facing Timothy Munslow's shop on the crossroads corner.

In the next instant glass shattered, raucous laughter erupted, and a voice shrieked unintelligibly mangled words.

'Stand where you are!' Tom went forwards at a run, shouting at the top of his voice. 'In the King's name! Stand where you are!'

Above the shop front a casement was flung open and Timothy Munslow's voice roared. 'You loony bastard. I'll fuckin' well swing for you, you loony bastard!'

Tom was only yards from the black silhouette in the middle of the roadway when a heavy weight cannoned into his side sending him toppling helplessly, left foot twisting beneath him. For brief instants he lay sprawled face downwards, then tried to scramble back to his feet but as he attempted to stand his left ankle gave way and sickening agony shafted through his leg as he collapsed to the ground again.

He bit hard on his lips to hold back a shout of pain as he pushed himself into a sitting position and bent forwards, feeling with tentative fingers in an attempt to ascertain whether his ankle was broken.

'Get after him! Damn you, Potts! Get after the loony bugger!' Timothy Munslow came bellowing from the shop.

Other neighbours came hurrying, shouting.

'What's up!'

'What's all this racket?'

'Bloody King William smashed my bloody windows again!' Munslow bawled furiously. 'And bloody useless Jack Sprat here has let the loony bugger get away wi' it again!'

Tom was too engrossed with his own troubles to argue the point. His ankle was swelling rapidly, throbbing painfully, and he struggled to unlace his high boot.

Another neighbour brought a lighted lantern into the gathering group and knelt to gently remove Tom's boot and knee sock.

Clenching his teeth, Tom kneaded the swollen flesh, checking that the skin was unbroken, wriggling the toes of the bootless foot, feeling relieved that the injured ankle must only be sprained, not broken.

'Am you going to get after him, or what?' Munslow bent to shout aggressively into Tom's face. 'Or am you just going to stay here sitting on your arse all night?'

'I'm not able to get after anyone at this instant, Master Munslow,' Tom told him. 'My ankle appears to be badly sprained.'

'Sprained? Sprained?' The other man scoffed derisively. 'How can a short-arsed little weakling like King William sprain a girt lanky lump like you?'

'I don't know who knocked me over.' Tom's own temper was becoming strained. 'And I don't know whether or not it was King William who smashed your window. There could have been two or three people here.'

'O' course it was King William; I could hear him shouting and so could you. Wi' that bloody harelip of his he can't sound any word proper, can he? There's no mistaking him when he tries to spake, is there?'

'That's true enough,' Tom was forced to admit.

'Come on, Master Potts, I'll get you back home.' The man with the lantern intervened. 'Help me carry him, you lot.'

Half a dozen men lifted and bore Tom back towards the Lock-up, but Timothy Munslow petulantly refused to help, and shouted after Tom.

'I'm going to report you to the Vestry, Tom Potts, for failing to do your duty; and I'm going to lay complaint afore Lord Aston as well if they don't gi' me satisfaction. You just wait and see if I don't.'

NINE

Morning, Tuesday 9th October

A t 11.30 in the rainy morning the Reverend John Clayton came into the yard of St Stephen's chapel to join the men waiting at the locked side door of the vestry.

'Good morning, Gentlemen,' he greeted them. 'This is an uncommon hour for the start of a Vestry meeting, is it not?'

'You can blame me for that, Parson.' Timothy Munslow scowled. 'Or better still blame our bloody useless Constable!'

'Why so? What has my friend Tom Potts done to deserve blame?' Clayton asked.

'Dammit, Parson, can you not save your questions until we're inside out of this poxy weather!' Samuel Smallwood, Needle Master and Select Vestryman, interjected irritably.

'I most heartily second my colleague's proposal, Parson Clayton.' William Hemming, Needle Master and Select Vestryman smiled pleasantly. 'I fear that if we remain standing here any longer we are all in danger of catching our deaths from damp.'

'Pray forgive my lack of consideration, Gentlemen.' Clayton apologized and quickly unlocked the door and bowed in invitation. 'Please go before.'

The two vestrymen seated themselves across from each other at the long table which dominated the vestry room. Clayton, who supplemented his paltry income by acting as Clerk to the Vestry, occupied a stool behind the small writing desk in the corner and hurriedly readied an inkstand, quill pens and ledgers. As befitted his lowly standing in the presence of this ruling body of the Parish, Timothy Munslow remained standing.

'Dammit all, where is himself?' Smallwood grimaced sourly at the empty throne-like chair heading the table. 'We're not his servants that he should keep us hanging about like this.'

As Smallwood spoke a man came through the door behind him. William Hemming and John Clayton rose and bowed.

'Please be seated, Gentlemen, and pray accept my humblest apologies for being tardy in attending. Believe me I do not make a practice of keeping even my lowliest servant waiting, and most certainly never Gentlemen of such importance as your good selves.' The latecomer was small, thin and stoop-shouldered. His pallid features were hollow cheeked and deeply lined.

Smallwood flushed with chagrin and blustered. 'I meant no offence to yourself, Master Blackwell, but I've many pressing affairs of business to see to this morning, and need to deal with them as soon as possible.'

'I appreciate that fact, Master Smallwood, and do assure you that I take no offence.' The thin lips of Joseph Blackwell, Attorney at Law, Chairman of the Select Vestry, Clerk to the Magistrates, Acting Coroner, and de facto controller of the Parish Constabulary, twisted in a mirthless smile.

He hung his top hat and cloak on the row of wall pegs and took his seat on the throne-like chair.

'Very well, Gentlemen, since we constitute a quorum, I declare this meeting open and empowered to deal with any lawful Parish matter brought before it.' He nodded to Timothy Munslow. 'State your case, Munslow.'

The pie-man immediately launched into a furious tirade. 'That bloody useless Tom Potts aren't doing his duty! That loony bugger, King William, poisoned me well on Sunday night and then last night he come and smashed me shop windows. What I wants to know is why our bloody useless Constable . . .'

Joseph Blackwell closed his eyes, steepled his fingers and bent his head to rest his chin on their tips.

TEN

'Well now, Master Potts, I concur fully with your own diagnosis. It's a simple sprain, and using the cold compresses and strapping to reduce the swelling is of course the best form of treatment.'

Doctor Hugh Laylor, considered by many female admirers to be the most handsome, elegant and eligible bachelor in the Parish, if not the entire county, straightened up from his examination.

'When Blackwell told me to come and examine you, I did point out to him that it was a waste of Parish funds, since your knowledge of human anatomy is without doubt equal to my own. Why did you not finish your studies?'

Sitting up on the narrow cot, Tom shrugged philosophically. 'Call it fate. My father was a military surgeon and I was his apprentice. Then later I walked the wards and studied in London, and was very close to receiving my doctorate when his death left my mother and me totally bereft of finance, and in debt. I had to abandon my studies and find whatever work I could to keep us fed.' He paused, then asked somewhat hesitantly, 'I suppose that I'm the laughing stock of the parish yet again?'

Laylor answered hesitantly in his turn. 'There are those who are mocking you for being rendered *hors de combat* by the village idiot. But I believe most sensible people accept your account of others being present at the scene who intervened to enable King William to get away.'

'There was at least one other, for certain fact,' Tom asserted, and sighed resignedly. 'But I've come to terms with the fact that I'm a target for mockery.'

The Lock-up bells jangled loudly and Widow Potts' strident complaining erupted from the adjoining room.

'Ohhhh God! Did ever another pitiful tragic soul suffer as I am suffering? How can I drag my poor agonized body down the stairs yet again? Why must I be tormented so?'

Laylor's white teeth glistened in amusement, and he called out, 'Stay where you are, Madam, I beg of you. I shall go immediately and answer the door.'

'Ohhh, God bless you, Doctor. How I wish that I had had a son like you, instead of the cruel beast that I've been cursed to slave for through all these benighted years.'

Laylor winked at Tom like a mischievous urchin. 'I'm convinced, Madam, that God is testing you so grievously in this life, so that he may justly reward you all the more bounteously when you are called to Heaven.'

'How very wise you are, Doctor Laylor. You have undoubtedly spoken truly.' Widow Potts sounded extremely gratified. 'And just as undoubtedly my unnatural son will roast in Hell's fires.'

Tom grinned wryly, shook his fist in mock threat, and whispered, 'Get out, Doctor Laylor, before I do you a mortal injury.'

The other man bowed with a flourish and departed. A few seconds later he shouted from below. 'There's a gentleman wants to speak with you, Master Potts. Shall I send him up?'

'If you please,' Tom called back to the accompaniment of his mother's strident wail.

'Am I not to be allowed a single moment of peace and quiet? How I long to die and have an end to my torments.'

'May I enter, Constable Potts?' The caped man framed in the doorway holding a black billycock hat in his hands was of middle height, his sun-bronzed features framed by longish black hair. 'I'm sorry to trouble you, but I'll be as brief as I can.'

'Please come in,' Tom invited and, stifling a grunt of pain, stood to his feet. 'How can I help you?'

The man stepped into the room. 'I'm not sure if you can. You see I'm trying to trace a wagon load of children.'

Tom was forced to sink down upon his cot to ease the pain of standing, and indicated the stool by the window. 'Please, sit down there and tell me the full story.'

The man sat upon the stool hesitated, as if to marshal his thoughts, and then spoke hurriedly.

'My name's Matthew Spicer, and I'm a seafarer. An old friend of mine, Ruth Telton, had settlement through marriage in the Brimfield Parish in Shropshire. She was a widow-woman and she fell ill, and died some months past. Her child, Jack, he's ten years old, was taken into the Brimfield Poorhouse. I knew nothing of this until I visited Brimfield a few days since. When I found out what had happened I went to take the boy out of the Poorhouse and bring him back to Bristol with me. But he and another child, a girl named Sukey Crawford, had been sent off as Parish Apprentices the day before I came back. So naturally I went after him in order to free him, but I've not yet found him.'

'I see.' Tom nodded thoughtfully. 'I take it the Brimfield Vestry had advertised the children were available for apprenticeship?'

It was common practice for poorer rural and urban vestries to rid themselves of the expense of the pauper children who were Poorhouse inmates by apprenticing them to industrialists, tradesmen, or anyone else who applied to take the children away from their Parish Settlement. Tom was very much opposed to this practice, which in all too many cases committed the children to a life of virtual slavery and abuse, because the unpaid Parish Poor Overseers delegated to make enquiries as to the applicants' bona fides rarely did so, and even more rarely enquired after the children once they had been moved into another parish.

'Just the usual.' Spicer frowned. 'They stuck a poster on the Poorhouse wall offering a premium of four guineas to anybody who'd take the boy and the girl both. I went straight to see the Overseer who'd given them over. I found that all he had in the ledger was the man's mark for the four guineas of premium, and the parish he was taking the children to. The man claimed to be a nail maker, James Barry of Catshill village in Worcestershire. He said that he needed a boy to train to the nail making, but he'd take the girl as well and his wife would teach her to keep house. There's a nail-making village of that same name next to Bromsgrove.'

'And this is all the information you have?' Tom queried.

'The Overseer said that Barry was just an ordinary sort of labouring man and thickheaded with it, who he judged was about thirtyish or so. But he got a good look at the wagon that Barry took the children away on. It's a barrel-topped, roller-wheel wagon with a three-horse team harnessed in unicorn fashion. The wagon body was in bad condition and the canvas was torn and flapping. The Overseer could hear other children in it as well. That's how I've managed to trace the likely route it took from Brimfield. A wagon and team of that description paid tolls at Tenbury, Ombersley and Bromsgrove; and the timing of its passage fits very well. I went to Catshill but there's no nail maker named James Barry there. So I hunted around, and yesterday in Finstall hamlet I found a man who told me that he'd seen a wagon of that description in early morn last Thursday passing through the hamlet on the road towards Redditch.'

'So early morn last Thursday it was seen on the Bromsgrove road about four miles distant from here, and heading this way.' Tom mused aloud. 'Have you checked with our southern tollgate at Headless Cross?'

'Yes, but man and wife both say that no traffic had passed through their gate during those hours. But we both know that no gatekeeper is ever going to own up to leaving the gate open for a while at that time o' the morning so that they can get a nap. So I think there's a chance that the wagon might be from hereabouts, and what I'd ask you to do is tell me if anybody local owns such a wagon.'

'Well there's considerable cargo trade through the needle district, and as well as the regular carriers a few of the Needle Masters have their own roller-wheel wagons for sake of the cheaper tolls. I can give you a list of the owners I know of hereabouts,' Tom offered readily. 'And if I can be of further service then please call on me.'

'I'm grateful to you, Constable Potts. God bless you for being so kind.'

From the adjoining room the intently eavesdropping Widow Potts emitted a loud snort of derisive disagreement.

When his visitor had left Tom pondered unhappily on what he'd been told. The unexplained disappearance of friendless, unprotected pauper children was not a rare occurrence. What was somewhat unusual was that in this case someone cared deeply enough to go in search of them.

'I hope to God that you find your old friend's boy, Matthew Spicer.' He wished this with all his heart.

ELEVEN

Tardebigge Poorhouse
Afternoon, Tuesday 9th October

'What are you pestering me about now, Abigail? Can't you see I'm busy?' Hilda Lewis frowned as she stirred the bubbling mess of gruel in the great iron pot on the kitchen range fire.

'There's a woman at the door who wants to spake to the Master. Her spakes like Gentry, and her's come in a carriage as well,' the old crone told her.

'Then go tell the Master that there's a Gentlewoman come to see him,' Hilda Lewis snapped.

'I 'ud, but I can't.' The crone sibilantly sucked her toothless gums. 'He aren't here, is he? He's gone out, he has.'

'Dear Christ above!' her mistress hissed angrily. 'If he's gone to the bloody pub again, I'll have his guts for garters when he comes back.'

'That's it, Missus!' Abigail cackled, nodding gleefully. 'That's it! Have his guts for garters! I shall like to see you do that, I shall.'

'Here. Get stirring.' Hilda Lewis handed the long wooden ladle to the crone. 'And if you lets the porridge catch and burn, I'll have your guts for garters as well, you idle old besom.'

'That's it, Missus!' Abigail cackled, nodding gleefully. 'That's it! Have me guts for garters! I shall like to see you do that, I shall.'

When Hilda Lewis opened the front door she found herself facing a woman dressed in full mourning weeds, a thick black veil concealing her features. Hilda Lewis instantly evaluated the quality of the caller's clothing, and the single-horsed carriage with its dark-clad driver, hat pulled low over his eyes, lower face muffled in a scarf.

The woman proffered an ornately embossed calling card.

'My name is Mrs Adelaide Carnegie. Wife to the Reverend Alistair Carnegie, of Henley-in-Arden in the County of Warwickshire.'

Hilda Lewis took the card and bobbed a curtsey. 'Will you be
so good as to step inside, Ma'am? I'm Mrs Lewis, wife to the
Poorhouse Master.'

The woman entered.

'How can I be of service to you, Ma'am?' Hilda Lewis asked.

'My husband is the Guardian-Director of the Saint Christopher's
Child Refuge of Henley-in-Arden. We take in orphaned pauper
children from the Poorhouses and train them for domestic service.
Then find them positions with reputable families. You will of
course know of our charity.'

Hilda Lewis didn't, but anxious not to offend this gentlewoman
immediately professed, 'Indeed I do, Ma'am. It's very well known
for its good works and charity.'

'Just so, and from the depths of our hearts my husband and I
give thanks to our Blessed Saviour for having showered his sweet
mercies upon us with such abundance,' Mrs Carnegie acknowledged fervently.

'Amen to that,' Hilda Lewis intoned solemnly.

'I'll come immediately to the reason for my calling upon you,
Mrs Lewis. A little time ago we received into our care a girl-child
who had been sorely ill-treated and misused. We believe the poor
little mite to be about eight years of age. She is an orphan of
sickly mind and body. A tragic condition inherited from her mother.
A young tramper woman, who most wickedly transgressed our
Sweet Lord's commandments, and died of a foul venereal distemper.
Namely the Syphilis.

'Some nights past the child went missing from our care. I confess
we are at a complete loss as to how this was possible. Since that
unhappy night we have had wide-ranging enquiries made for any
sighting of her. Yesterday we were informed that a small girl had
been found wandering in this parish and had been brought here
to the Poorhouse. Naturally I've come post-haste to discover if it
could be our tragic child.'

As she listened the pieces of a mental jigsaw were rapidly slotting together to form a composite, wholly recognizable picture in
Hilda Lewis' mind.

'Runaway tramper child! About eight years old! Bearing marks
of ill usage. Feverish! Wandering in her mind!'

Aloud she invited, 'You'd best come straight upstairs and take a look at her, Ma'am. From what you'm telling me, it sounds like it could well be the one you'm seeking.'

'I pray with all my heart that it is her.'

Upstairs as Hilda Lewis opened the door of the bedroom she told her companion, 'I must spake truthfully, Ma'am, and confess that I've been forced to heavy dose the poor little mite with laudanum. The shame is on me for giving her such heavy doses, but hers been so distressed and fevered, shouting out gibberish and tossing and turning all the time, that if I hadn't dosed her I do believe she'd have become so worn out she'd have give up the ghost and died. But thanks be to God, her fever's eased.'

'Dear Mrs Lewis, I beg of you not to feel any sense of shame,' the other woman gushed fulsomely. 'Our Sweet Lord sees all, and understands all, and He knows that you have acted in the best interests of this poor child.'

'Thank you, Ma'am, you've given me great comfort by saying this.' Hilda Lewis led the way into the room.

Mrs Carnegie moved to bend over the pale, drawn face of the child lying motionless in the cot, and suddenly went down on to her knees, clasped hands held high above her head.

'Thank you, Lord! Thank you from the very bottom of my heart for this mercy you have bestowed upon me, this miserable sinner before you.'

'Is it her, Ma'am? Is it the child you'm looking for?' Hilda Lewis questioned eagerly.

Mrs Carnegie stood up and grabbed Hilda Lewis' hand between her own, pumping it up and down as she poured out her gratitude.

'Yes, this is little Sukey Crawford! God bless you, Mrs Lewis! God bless you! My dear husband will be so joyfully relieved that we have her back into our safekeeping. You will be forever remembered in our prayers, and this poor afflicted child will know of you and how you have saved her life! God bless you, Ma'am!'

TWELVE

I n the churchyard of St Martin's, shielded from the noise and bustle of the Bull Ring market, Enoch Griffiths stepped out from a recess in the church wall to confront the undersized, weakly built man dressed in the cheap top hat and poor quality dark clothing of an ill-paid counting house clerk.

Ishmael Benton's thin white face twisted in surprise and he exclaimed in a reedy, high-pitched voice, ''Pon my soul, Master Griffiths, it's been some considerable time since we last met.'

He looked the burly man up and down, evaluating the expensive clothes, fine beaver top hat and general appearance of an affluent countryman.

'You look to be enjoying health and prosperity?'

'Oh yes, Master Benton, these days I'm my own man with plenty of irons in the fire. But I'm told that you've fallen on hard times through the gambling, and you'm presently back living with your brother Judas in Redditch.' Griffiths leered knowingly. 'But maybe fortune is smiling on you once more, or at least that's the hope that's brought you here at this particular hour, is it not?'

Benton's eyes narrowed as realization came to him. 'It was you who sent the message.'

'Aghhh, still as bright as a new needle, aren't you, Master Benton?' It was a sneer rather than a compliment. 'But do you still have your contacts among the Chavy-Shaggers?'

'I do.'

'Well I've some brand-new specimens of those particular commodities for sale, that those gentlemen are keen to buy.'

With an effort Benton controlled his excitement, and asked quietly, 'And you can guarantee that the commodities are in prime condition?'

'O' course they am.'

Benton smiled sneeringly. 'And of course you're bound to say that, and of course I believe you, Master Griffiths. Nevertheless I shall have to view them myself before I notify my gentlemen that a sale is imminent. Also I require a commission of thirty per cent of sale total, and an advance on that commission of ten guineas to be paid today. I'm sure you'll understand that if we are to enjoy an amicable business relationship then you must gain my trust by agreeing to my terms without further discussion.'

'You'll get no advance from me, and not more than seven per cent commission on sales. Good day to you, Master Benton.'

Griffiths turned away and the smaller man hastily reached out to stop him leaving.

'Now don't be so hasty, Sir. If the goods are of high quality then I'm sure we shall be able to negotiate a mutually satisfactory agreement as to the commission.'

'The commission is what I say it shall be. I'm not some thick-yedded, easy-gulled yokel; and any fuckin' cheapjack like you that tries it on with me is always soon taught that they've made a very bad mistake.' The big man's features were still impassive, his tone flat and unemotional, but his eyes glinted with menace.

Benton forced an obsequious smile. 'I beg you not to take offence, Master Griffiths. I was only testing your business acumen, as I would with any new supplier. Of course I'm happy to accept your terms.' He paused, then asked tentatively, 'And the merchandise? When may I view it?'

'Come to Marlfield Farm at midnight on Saturday. And in future, little Ishmael, just remember who's the master when you're having dealings with me.' Griffiths contemptuously brushed away his companion's restraining hand and walked off towards the noise and bustle of the market.

Ishmael Benton's small eyes reddened with anger. His tongue snaked wetly across his thin lips as he mentally vowed, 'It's you who's just made the very bad mistake of insulting me, you stupid, ignorant yokel; and you'll find that out to your cost some day.' He went out of the gate in the opposite direction, where a shabby dog cart was waiting for him.

'Well?' rat-featured, fang-toothed Judas Benton, pawnbroker of Redditch Town, demanded eagerly.

'Well what?' Ishmael Benton was poker-faced.

'Oh, don't come the cunt, our Ishmael! You knows what!' His elder brother whined irritably.

'Oohhh, you means that, what! Well why didn't you say it was that, what, in the first place, Brother Judas?' Ishmael Benton baited, and then grinned and nodded.

'We're in business.'

THIRTEEN

Morning. Saturday 13th October

Two miles east of Redditch the ancient Roman road of Icknield Street ran north to south through sparsely inhabited, rolling scrubland. Marlfield Farm stood secluded at the end of a narrow track leading off Icknield Street.

Enoch Griffiths reined in his fine hunter stallion to a walk as he turned into the narrow track which led to Marlfield Farm. The day was fine and clear with a soft southerly breeze and as always Griffiths took pleasure from the sight of the house, its extensive outbuildings, and the neat hedgerows of the surrounding pastures where horses, sheep and cattle were grazing.

'Not bad going for a one-time poorhouse brat, is it? Tenant of the best farm on the Icknield Street.' He smiled with self-satisfaction.

He rode round the house to the cobbled stable yard at the rear and two burly figures, smocked, knee-breeched, hobnail booted, came from a doorway to hail him gruffly.

'Mornin' Brother Enoch.'

'Mornin' Brother Enoch.'

'Sister Deborah, Sister Delilah.' He acknowledged them smilingly. 'You'm both looking particular fresh and beautiful this morning.'

His twin sisters, though some years younger, closely resembled him in their facial features and physical build, but while his eyes were bright with sharp intelligence, their eyes were dulled with their shared mental retardation.

'Where's Doll?' he asked.

'Her's wi' them kids.'

'See to this 'un, will you?' He left the horse with them and went into the house.

The attic room was large, clean and airy, furnished with several wooden cot beds, a long washstand with plentiful bowls and water jugs, and against one wall a row of covered chamber pots.

Doll Griffiths heard the clumping of her brother's boots upon the stairs and ordered sharply, 'Get into line! Not there, you fool! Come here so the Master can get a clear look at you.'

The group of small naked children rushed pushing and jostling to obey.

Enoch Griffiths entered and his sister's lipless mouth opened in a snarl, disclosing one single blackened tusk in the front of her lower gum.

'You've took your time getting here. I was expecting you yesterday morning.'

He grinned genially at her. 'Don't pull your face about like that, my love, it makes you look particular old and ugly, and you birthed two years after me, and me still looking so young and handsome. It aren't no wonder that no man ever wanted to wed you, is it?'

Short and stockily built, Doll Griffiths wore a black dress and bonnet. Her lank greasy hair hung in tendrils around a grey-complexioned, deep-lined face that was a mask of bitter resentment.

'Where's the little wench the Duchess brought you?' he questioned.

'In the end gable room,' Doll Griffiths confirmed. 'I've kept her separate like you wanted. I'm buggered if I know why you had her brought here. You must have known that her bloody mind's gone, and if her aren't kept well dosed her keeps on shouting bloody gibberish. If you ask me, I don't reckon anybody 'ull ever buy her!'

Enoch Griffiths' expression hardened and he hissed, 'But nobody is asking you. So don't poke your nose into where it's not wanted, or I'll break it for you and make you even uglier than you am, if that's possible.'

As he turned from her and went to the row of small boys her eyes glared hatred at the back of his head.

Enoch Griffiths bent to each child in turn. Examining their puny bodies closely, he asked them, 'Have you been good, boy? Have you been eating all the nice things we're giving you? Are you looking forward to going to your nice new home?'

He smiled and patted their heads as they timidly returned affirmations.

The inspection completed, the two adults left the room, which Doll Griffiths secured with a huge padlock, and went to a room beneath the end gable.

In the room's single cot the small girl was lying comatose on her back. Enoch Griffiths pulled the covering blanket back and closely examined her naked body, turning her carefully, and when finished covered her again with the blankets.

'You've done a good job with these kids, Doll,' he praised. 'They're starting to look fresher by far. I reckon they're near ready for market.'

'All but this 'un,' she asserted aggressively. 'Every time the dose wears off she shouts bloody gibberish and acts up like a bloody mad thing. There's nobody 'ull ever want her!'

This time he did not react aggressively, but smiled smugly. 'I've got one o' the sharpest, slyest little rats in the kingdom sniffing out the market for my merchandise. I guarantee that he'll know a buyer who'll be panting and slavering to pay the top price for her. If I'm wrong then I'll let you kick my arse from one end of Icknield Street to the other. That's a solemn promise, that is.'

She made no reply, but in her mind silently promised him: 'Some day it'll be your head I'll be crushing, not your arse that I'll be kicking, you evil bastard!'

FOURTEEN

Midday, Saturday 13th October

'Well met, Constable Potts. Come through to the kitchen, will you, it's nice and warm there,' Hilda Lewis smilingly invited at the door of the Poorhouse, and as she led the way through the building told him, 'I'm glad you've come, because I've got some good news to tell you.'

'And I shall be glad to hear some, Ma'am,' Tom answered.

In the kitchen two old crones were sitting on small stools in front of the range fire and Hilda Lewis ordered, 'Becky, Abigail, move over a bit will you and let this gentleman in to warm his bones.'

She brought another taller stool to the range. 'Set you down on this, Constable. Will you take summat to ate or drink?'

'Nothing, I thank you, Ma'am, but I'm very grateful for the stool.' Tom exhaled with relief as he seated himself and the painful throbbing in his injured ankle began to lessen. 'And what is this good news you have for me?'

'It's about the girl child you brought to us. Here's the calling card that the lady brought with her . . .' Hilda Lewis handed Tom the ornate card and went on to relate in detail the visit of Mrs Carnegie. 'So all's ended for the best for that poor little soul, has it not, Constable Potts? It was plain to see that that good woman who came for the little mite has a heart of pure gold. I do believe it must have been God himself who guided Mrs Carnegie here.'

'And a bloody good job He did as well! I never got a wink o' sleep wi' that little wench a-shriekin' and a-blartin' bloody nursery rhymes all bloody night and day! "Jack and Jill went up the bloody hill, Jack fell down and broke his crown", night and bloody day I had that dinning in me earholes. "Jack fell down and broke his bloody crown!" Night and bloody day I had it, so I did.' Old Abigail cackled with laughter. 'God did me a favour when He had her took away, else I'd have died o' weariness, so I should.'

'Hold your tongue, Abi!' Hilda Lewis scolded. 'This gentleman don't want to be hearing your silly nonsense! Just ignore her, Constable.'

Tom's interest had been sparked, however. 'I'm curious about this, Ma'am. Did the child manage to say anything to you about what had happened to her?'

'Nooo!' Hilda Lewis shook her head, and smiled regretfully. 'The poor little mite did shout out at times, but it was just gibberish that couldn't be understood. Truth to tell, in the end I had to keep dosing her heavy to make sure she had some rest.'

'It warn't gibberish!' Abigail spluttered furiously, spraying flecks of saliva from her toothless mouth. 'I heard as plain as plain what her was saying. Jack an' Jill went up the hill to get a pail o' water, didn't they? And Jack fell down and broke his bloody crown, didn't he? And Jill come bloody well tumblin' down after him, didn't her?'

Hilda Lewis chuckled, winked meaningfully at Tom and stroked the old crone's forehead with her fingers. 'Yes, Abi, they did. You've got the right of it, my dear. Now you be a good girl and quiet yourself, and I'll let you and Becky have a pipe of the Master's bacca each.'

'A pipe o' the Master's bacca!' Abigail clapped her withered hands with delight. 'Did you hear that, Becky? We'em having a pipe o' the Master's bacca.'

Hilda Lewis led the two old women from the room.

Tom once more scanned the calling card and accepted that the mystery of the girl child was now explained. He felt genuine relief that the child had found safe refuge. 'I hope fate serves you better from now on, child.'

When Hilda Lewis came back she accompanied him to the door, and as they parted Tom asked, 'I forgot to ask you, did the lady give a name to the child?'

Hilda Lewis frowned with the effort of recall, and then shook her head in frustration. 'Do you know I can't remember, Master Potts. What with being so excited and all that when she come, and having so many other things on me mind that I'd got to see to, I can't remember if she did or not.'

'Oh, it makes no matter, Ma'am. All that's important is that the child has now found a safe refuge.' Tom dismissed the matter from his mind.

It was early evening when he painfully completed the two-mile journey from the Poorhouse and limped back into the noisy thronged market place lining the southern side of the Green. His most pressing task now was to check the licences of the market's assorted stallholders, peddlers, dealers, cheapjacks. All shouting their wares, cajoling, wheedling, begging for a share of the payday coins in the purses and pockets of the toil-grimed men, women, youths, girls and children released from their grinding drudgery until the work bells rang out early Monday morning.

Before he could begin the checking, however, Tom had to go to the Lock-up to fetch his Constable's staff, which denoted to the world at large that he was an Officer of the Law on duty, and empowered to act in the King's name.

He limped through the market and halted outside the Fox and Goose.

'I must speak to Amy before I do anything else; she's surely had time enough to calm her temper by now.'

Since she had stormed away from him Tom had been miserably wrestling with the problem besetting his relationship with Amy Danks. That problem was his mother.

Tom had sworn his solemn oath to the dying father whom he had loved, admired and respected above all other men, that he would support and care for the Widow Potts until the end of her days.

Now he mentally assured his dead father, 'I'll continue to support and care for my mother, come what may. But also come what may, I love Amy and intend to marry her.'

'Why are you skulking about outside here, Tom Potts? Are you too feared to come in and face me?' Amy Danks, pert and pretty, arms akimbo, hands on hips, suddenly confronted him.

Startled from his reverie Tom could only stammer. 'Oh, Amy, I was coming to see you this very moment.'

'Why? Whatever could you say that holds any interest for me?' she demanded frostily, but the spark of mischievous amusement in her eyes belied her tone of voice.

He drew a long breath and, struggling to keep his voice firm and measured, told her, 'Amy, I love you more than anybody or anything in this world. My one desire in this life is to wed you, and to spend the rest of my days striving for your happiness. When we're married I'm sure that I can persuade my mother to let me find a nice little cottage for her to live in, so that you and I will be by ourselves in the Lock-up. Of course I shall have to continue to support her financially, but I'll not ask you ever to have any personal dealings with her of any kind.'

A satisfied smile hovered on Amy's full red lips. 'Our Banns are to get their second calling tomorrow, Tom Potts. Do you solemnly swear that you'll be at my side in chapel to hear them called?'

'Of course I do,' he assented eagerly.

'And you must also solemnly swear that after the service you and I will speak to Parson Clayton, and you will tell him that you'll be moving your Mam out of the Lock-up before our third Banns are called.'

'But that's within a week!' he protested. 'I'll need more time than a week to find a suitable home for her.'

'I'm not arguing about this, Tom Potts.' She dismissed his protest with an imperious wave of her hand. 'If she's not gone from the Lock-up by this time next week, then there won't be any calling of our third Banns. I'll see you tomorrow in chapel.'

Before he could say anything she ran back into the inn, leaving him unhappily contemplating troubles to come.

FIFTEEN

Evening, Saturday 13th October

The two young men with dogs at their heels left Redditch after sunset and walked westwards from the town towards their goal: an alehouse in the tiny woodland-shrouded hamlet of Foxlydiate some two miles distant.

'Well now, you pair o' rogues, what can I do you for?' From behind his serving board, Pat Bull, the grizzled proprietor of the alehouse called out in warm welcome.

The reaction of the few drinkers in the dim-lit shabby room was less welcoming as they saw that the newcomers were dressed alike in red shirts, leather waistcoats, knee breeches, thick woollen stockings, heavy boots, brightly coloured neckerchiefs around their throats and squared brown paper hats on their unkempt heads. This style of clothing was the identity badge of the notorious Redditch Needle Pointers, men whose work – the dry-grinding of needle points during which they constantly breathed the fine dust of stone and steel into their lungs – was a virtual guarantee of premature death. Choosing exceptionally high pay and short life over low pay and longer life, their wild debauchery, contempt for death and propensity for savage violence had made them feared throughout the Midlands.

Surreptitious grimaces were exchanged, and the atmosphere became charged with tension. One man hastily drained his quart pot of cider and made a hurried exit.

'I'm glad you'm glad to see us, Pat. But perhaps there might be some here who aren't so pleased.' The sandy-haired, scar-faced, powerfully built Ritchie Bint stared challengingly around the room. 'And if anybody present holds any grudge and wants to go a few rounds wi' me, then I'm more than willing to oblige 'um.'

'And if you don't fancy your chances wi' my mate, then you'm more than welcome to try me out.' John Hancox, younger, shorter, more broad-shouldered than Bint, issued his own challenge.

Heads were shaken, disclaimers muttered, and Ritchie Bint grinned contemptuously, but then told the landlord, 'Quarts of your best Scrumpy for me and me mate, if you please, Pat, and give all these gentlemen a drink of whatever they fancy on my slate. And when they've drunk that drink, then give 'um another on me mate's slate. And after that 'un, they can have another on me. Never let it be said that us Pointer Lads am tight wi' our money.'

The tension in the room immediately disappeared as the topers applauded their benefactor.

'God bless you, Master.'

'One o' the best, you am!'

'That's right, that is! One o' the very best!'

One man lifted his pot of cider high above his head and shouted, 'Let's have a toast, lads. Here's to the good health o' the Redditch Pointer Lads. May they have merry lives, keep on earning lots o' the gold 'uns, and keep on winning every fight they ever gets into!'

His audience cheered enthusiastically, and drank deep.

Pat Bull leaned over the serving board to look closely at the Pointers' dogs. Terriers with hard, wiry, black and tan coloured coats, flat skulls and wide-set eyes, standing fifteen inches in height and weighing around twenty pounds.

'These are them Welsh 'uns if I'm not mistaken, Ritchie. They looks to be prime,' Bull praised.

'They am,' Ritchie Bint affirmed. 'They're red hot on foxes, badgers and otters.'

Bull beckoned Bint to come closer and whispered in his ear.

'It's all set for tonight, and our customer's got the rhino waiting for us. We'll be able to have a clear run at that sett down in the Lydd Wood that I told you about. I knows for a fact that Danks and all his blokes am going to be in the Grange Wood 'til dawn tomorrow.'

'How so?' Bint asked.

'Because I've seen to it that Danks has got the true word that Sonny Jakes is going up there for pheasants tonight.'

'I thought that you and Sonny was good mates?' Bint frowned in surprise.

'Not any more. The fly bastard has tried one time too many to gammon me over a bit o' business. I'll see him bloody hung afore I'm done wi' him.'

Bint grinned appreciatively. 'Remind me to always be straight wi' you, my mate.'

'Oh I will. Don't you fret about that, my mate.' Bull grinned back.

It was past midnight, the sky was virtually cloudless and the waxing half moon helped to illumine the tracks and glades of the ancient woodland.

Two of the four men moving in single file along a track carried spades, short wooden stakes and stout canvas drawstring sacks. The other pair each led two dogs on ropes. They were deep in the wood when the leader, Pat Bull, called a halt.

'This 'ull do, lads. The sett's about half a mile dead ahead. We'll do the drive from here.'

A soft wind moaned in from the south and Ritchie Bint hissed with satisfaction.

'This 'ull carry any noise we makes away from those bastards down in the Grange. We couldn't have asked for a better night, could we?'

Pat Bull issued instructions. 'Right then, me and Ritchie 'ull stop the earths; and I wants you two to get at least ten score yards distant from each other. Then wait until you hears me blow me horn twice afore you looses the dogs an drives 'um straight towards the sett.'

Pat Bull and Ritchie Bint continued onwards with their loads. When they reached their target, a long high bank which had a series of large burrow holes along its base, Ritchie Bint moved close to study these entrances and exclaimed in pleased surprise.

'Bloody Hell, Pat, it looks promising.'

'I reckon there's near half a dozen good-sized sows and boars.' His companion came to join him. 'You get stopping, mate. I'll sack this 'un, an that 'un further along there, and them three at the end. That should give us a good haul.'

They set to work with a will. Ritchie Bint shovelled earth into his sacks and blocked the burrow entrances with them. Pat Bull pushed the bottom of his empty sacks down the chosen tunnels, and arranged the open drawstring tops of the sacks around the circumference of the burrow entrance, with the ends of the drawstrings firmly staked. The badger bolting panic-stricken into its lair would be completely enveloped by the tough canvas and as it struggled to push on, the drawstring would be pulled tight, closing the sack neck and trapping the beast.

This age-old method of hunting was effective because badgers are nocturnal, normally only leaving the sett at night to forage for food. Notoriously shy and timid, badgers bolt in panic to seek refuge in their burrows at sound or sight of predators such as humans or dogs.

As Ritchie Bint knelt to push earth-filled sacks into the tunnel entrances the musky smell of badgers filled his nostrils, but then at an entrance isolated from the others another stench overlaid it. A cloying, sickly stench that Ritchie Bint instantly recognized.

'We've got a dead 'un in here, Pat. Maybe somebody's been here afore us and poisoned the buggers.'

'Fetch it out and let's have a look at it.' Bull came to join him.

Bint cautiously inserted his hand and felt a small hard object. He explored and gripped it with his fingers, tugged hard, pulled it out and exclaimed in surprise.

'It's a kid's clog!'

He inserted his hand into the hole again and felt carefully around. Then suddenly he jumped to his feet, snatched up his shovel and started to dig out the top of the tunnel.

'What the hell are you doing that for?' Bull demanded. 'The bloody keepers 'ull know we've been here when they sees that's been dug out.'

Bint ignored him and kept on digging furiously. Within scant time he broke through the top of the tunnel, then used his hands to remove the last of the loose soil.

He straightened, shaking his head and muttering in shock. 'It's a kid! It's a dead kid!'

'It can't be a kid.' Bull pushed him aside and gaped down in disbelief at what he saw. Doubled up and jammed hard between the sides of the tunnel was a small figure, reeking of rotting flesh. 'It must be a fox or summat.'

'Foxes don't wear clothes nor fuckin' clogs, does they?' Ritchie Bint was fast recovering from his initial shock. 'It's a kid alright, but I can't make out if it's a boy or girl.'

Bull snatched up the spade and started to shovel loose soil back on to the figure. 'Don't say nothing about this to the others. We'll cover it up, then do what we come for and get well away from here.'

'It aren't Christian to leave the poor little cratur here like this,' Bint protested

'Bugger being Christian!' There was desperation in Bull's voice. 'Look, Ritchie, I've got to get these badgers tonight. I owes a lot of rhino to the Worcester Yids and they'm threatening to have me arrested and committed for debt if I don't start paying 'um back a bit rapid.'

'You hold hard now.' Ritchie Bint gripped Bull's arm and pulled him back from the burrow. 'How does you think that kid come to be in there?'

'It don't matter, do it? It's just a piece o' rotten meat now. It's more likely that the brocks dragged it in.'

'Oh no.' Bint shook his head in firm rebuttal. 'The brocks 'ud ate it where it lay, and it couldn't have crawled in by itself and got stuck like that. It's been shoved hard into there, that's why it's so tight stuck.'

'Well whatever it is, it's got naught to do wi' us. Listen, Ritchie, you knows very well that the fuckin' Earl 'ull have us transported if we're known to have been on his land with dogs. Bugger me, you got six months' hard labour for trespass for just larking in his fuckin' woods wi' your wench, didn't you? What we've got to do is to cover this kid up, and keep this just between our two selves. We can't risk breathing a word of it to anybody else, not to Danny nor John neither.'

Accepting that his friend only stated the plain truth, Ritchie Bint fell silent, thinking hard for some moments before deciding 'Alright then. We'll cover the kid up.'

He took the shovel from his friend and after a brief spurt of hard effort the dead child was completely buried from view.

'Right then,' he growled. 'Give your horn a toot, and let's get these fuckin' brocks sacked up.'

SIXTEEN

Sunday 14th October

When he rose from his cot as dawn was breaking Tom felt both happiness and uneasiness.

'I have to tell her today. Give her due warning that her life is going to change.'

The image of his father's face rose in his mind, and guilt flooded through him. 'I'm not breaking my word to you, Father. I shall still be supporting her, and ensuring that she has a comfortable life. I'm not doing this on a selfish whim, but because Amy and she hate each other, and it's not possible even to hope that they could ever live in harmony beneath the same roof.'

He smiled ruefully. 'As you well know, Father, if my mother goes into an empty room, she rushes to pick a quarrel with the nearest wall.'

The clanking of the bells broke into his train of thought, and he hurriedly pulled on breeches and went downstairs to the front door.

A woman was outside, shawl pulled around her head to hide her features.

'Please excuse my state of undress, Ma'am. What brings you here so early?' Tom asked politely.

'You'm to go straight away up to the top o' the clay pit in Muskats Way. Somebody's waiting there for you. And they says it's real urgent that you goes up there as quick as quick. They says it's a matter o' murder.' She gabbled hurriedly and ran swiftly away.

'Murder? A matter of murder?' But by the time Tom had fully absorbed the import of what she had said she had already disappeared from sight.

'Is she gammoning me? Is this a hoax of some sort?' he wondered, and for a brief instant was inclined to accept that it was. But staring around and listening hard he couldn't detect any signs or sounds of onlookers in the misty murk of this early dawn.

The clay pit was about a mile distant, situated on the Muskats Way, the public track which bisected the hilly Pitcher Oak Wood a mile to the west of the Lock-up.

Reluctantly he accepted that he must do his duty and investigate further, consoling himself that he could limp to the clay pit and return in ample time to prepare his mother's breakfast, then wash, shave and don his Sunday best clothes to accompany Amy to the chapel for the calling of their second Banns.

The clay pit was deep and wide, surrounded by trees and undergrowth. When Tom reached it his ankle was already throbbing painfully. The thought struck him that the narrow pathway circumventing the steep sides of the pit was an ideal spot for an ambush, closely hemmed in by trees, bushes and thick undergrowth.

'Somebody could be hidden only a yard from me and I wouldn't be able to see them until it was too late. A simple push would send me down into the pit.' His heartbeat quickened nervously.

'You damned coward!' Deep in his mind a voice jeered at him. 'You've a stout walking stick in your left hand, and a constable's staff in your right hand. Surely even a weak-bodied poltroon such as you is well armed enough. Your staff's crown is lead weighted, isn't it? One blow with that can crush a man's skull!'

The image of his father's face rose in his mind.

'No, I'll not disgrace your memory. You were always brave.' Tom gripped his staff hard and limped on.

He had only covered a few yards when a man stepped out from the bushes ahead. Tom gasped in fright and lifted his staff in readiness to strike.

'I'm glad you've come, Master Potts. I was feared you might think it to be a gammon.' Ritchie Bint was grimly serious. 'It's a bad business this.'

Tom was struggling to control his jangling nerves, and managed to ask, 'And what is this bad business, Master Dint?'

'It's a dead kid, and I reckon it's murder!'

'Dead kid? Murder?'

'I reckon so.' Bint shook his head sadly. 'I'm a rough sort o' bloke, Master Potts, but I don't like to see little kids being cruelly used. I suffered too much of it meself when I was a nipper.'

'Explain fully what this is all about, if you please, Master Bint,' Tom invited.

'Can I trust you to act fairly by me?' the other man asked.

'We've always been straight with each other. You can trust me to act fairly.'

'I do,' Bint accepted. 'But this is going to have to be a case of "no names, no pack drill". What I tell you is for your ears only. I want no mention made of me.'

'Very well, I agree.' It was Tom's turn to accept.

'I found a dead kid stuffed up one o' the tunnels in a badger sett in the Lydd Wood last night. I'm bloody sure that the poor little sod couldn't ha' got stuck in there by itself.'

Tom reacted instantly to this information. 'Take me there.'

'No.' Bint refused flatly. 'We nigh on cleared every prime brock from there last night, so I can't risk being spotted in the Lydd by any of the Earl's keepers. They keeps count of the brocks in that sett, and when they finds it's been raided and they've spotted me in the wood, they'll swear it's me that's took 'um.'

'But you'll be with me and I'm on the King's business,' Tom argued.

'No, I'll not come with you.' Bint was adamant. 'We agreed, "no names, no pack drill", didn't we? Go and find Josiah Danks, and get him to take you to the sett. You'll think of summat to tell him how you heard there was a dead kid to be found there.'

'Alright, Master Bint, I'll do that.' Tom accepted defeat, and on impulse added, 'I'll not forget how honourably you've behaved in informing me of this. You may rest assured that your name will never be mentioned by me in connection with this matter.'

He held out his hand and Ritchie Bint shook it, and grinned. 'I hopes I can also rest assured that none o' my mates 'ull ever come to know that I'se shook the hand of a bloody constable neither. Me name 'ull be mud if they ever finds out.'

SEVENTEEN

Sunday 14th October

The bell was tolling and the worshippers were filing into the chapel. At the chapel yard gate Amy Danks stood peering anxiously towards the Lock-up.

'He should have been here waiting for you, Amy. But it don't look as though he's coming, does it?' Lily Fowkes baited. 'What a rotten thing to do, to promise you faithfully that he'd be here and then not bother to turn up again. He's having you on for a fool.'

'Hold your tongue!' Maisie Lock rounded on her angrily. 'Don't you pay no attention to this spiteful cow, Amy. Tom 'ull have good reason not to be here, I'm sure.'

'That's just what I said, didn't I?' Lily Fowkes riposted. 'The reason is that he's having her on for a fool, and believes he can treat her like dirt.'

The bell ceased tolling, and Maisie Lock took Amy's arm. 'We needs to get inside quick, my duck, or Old Davis 'ull be making a show of us for coming in late.'

'You go on in.' Amy pulled her arm free, her pretty face flushed with chagrin. 'I'm going to the Lock-up to see where he is.'

'Me Dad 'ull be spitting feathers if we aren't all at the service when it starts,' Lily Fowkes warned.

'He can be spitting the whole bloody bird for all I care,' Amy retorted and left at a run, skirt and petticoats flying up around her shapely legs.

It took several repetitions of frantic tugging on the Lock-up's iron bell pull before the casement window above Amy's head opened and Widow Potts' glowering face poked out to shriek stridently.

'Have you come to murder me, you wicked girl? Well the door's bolted and barred and you'll not be able to break it down, no matter how hard you try. So be off with you!'

'I'll not leave until I speak with Tom,' Amy retorted.

'He's not here.'

'Then where is he? Why aren't he in chapel to hear our Banns called?'

It took a couple of seconds for Widow Potts to grasp the connotations of that question, then her pig-like eyes half buried in balls of fat sparked with malicious delight.

'Well now, I would have thought that even you, Amy Danks, would have understood why a man born and raised as a Gentleman's son isn't in the chapel to hear his Banns called. It's because he's realized his mistake.'

'What mistake might that be?' Amy challenged.

'The mistake of ever thinking that he wanted to marry such an ignorant, caterwauling slum rat like you. Now be off with you, and don't ever come back here!' the old woman rejoined triumphantly, and slammed the casement shut.

'You're a bloody liar, you rotten old bitch!' Amy shouted furiously up at the closed casement, and the next instant realization assailed her. 'Oh my God! That's what I'm doing! I'm sounding just like a caterwauling slum rat!'

A sense of utter mortification flooded her mind, and she anxiously looked about, fearing that there might be onlookers. She breathed a sigh of relief when she saw none, but that relief was quickly superseded by a nagging sense of dread.

'She must be lying. Surely she's lying. Tom can't be wanting to break our engagement? Can he? I can't face going to the chapel now, and him not being there again to hear our Banns called.'

Tormented by doubts Amy slowly walked back to the Fox and Goose and went upstairs to the room she shared with Maisie Lock. Once there her doubts suddenly solidified to absolute conviction.

'You've deliberately broke your solemn oath that you'd be at the chapel this morning, Tom Potts. You've betrayed me again! What a fool I've been to trust you.'

She slumped on to the bed, head in hands, and wept angry tears.

EIGHTEEN

Sunday 14th October

It was turned midday when in the Lydd Wood, Tom Potts gently scooped away enough of the loose earth to disclose the maggot-infested body of the small child. Next he carefully dug the side of the tunnel out and the two men lifted the body and laid it face upwards on the flat ground.

'The poor little soul's been here more than a few days judging by the stink and the maggots,' observed Josiah Danks, Head Gamekeeper of the Earl of Plymouth's Hewell Estate, and Tom's prospective Father-in-Law.

Tom crouched close to study the corpse. 'It looks as if the badgers left it alone. I thought that they feed on carrion as well as live grubs and worms.'

'They do, but it might be that the scent of human kept them away.' Danks frowned thoughtfully. 'Look, Tom, you know that I've got to report what we've got here to the Estate Factor, and when the Earl comes back from London he'll have to be told as well.'

'Of course.' Tom nodded.

'The Earl also has to be told that this sett's been nigh on robbed out, and he'll go bloody mad, because he was going to use these brocks for baiting. He'll not rest until he finds out who took 'um.' Danks frowned uneasily. 'It's certain sure that the bloke who told you this kid was here is one o' them who poached the brocks. You're going to have to tell us his name.'

'I gave that man my word, Josiah, and I'll not break it. You'll never hear his name from me,' Tom replied firmly.

'The Earl won't take no for an answer, Tom. He hates poachers worse than death. He'll very likely have you jailed if you don't turn informer.'

Tom inwardly quailed at the prospect, but stubbornly asserted, 'If he does, then I'll just have to grin and bear it.'

'You might be able to grin and bear it, but what about my Amy? She won't want her husband in jail, will she?'

Tom shook his head ruefully. 'At this moment she might be thinking it's just what I deserve. She'll be really angry with me because I promised that I'd be with her to hear our Banns called.' He rose to his feet. 'Look, Josiah, at this moment this poor child has to take precedence over all else. I have to take him back to the Lock-up and make my report to Blackwell.'

'So be it. I've said my piece and you know now what might happen. I'll go and fetch a cart and driver from the Grange, and something to wrap the kid in.' Josiah Danks walked away.

Tom carefully selected a large number of wriggling maggots from the corpse and wrapped them in his handkerchief, then began digging and searching through the soil in front of the burrow.

It was nearing dusk when Josiah Danks returned. 'Sorry for being so long, Tom. One of my keepers was fighting with a footman at the Grange and there's ructions with the butler. The cart's waiting for you on the road. I'll help you carry the kid to it and then I'll have to get back to the Grange.'

It was full dusk as the cart creaked slowly past the Fox and Goose and Tom stared wistfully at the lighted windows of the inn. He longed to go inside and seek out Amy, but knew that that must wait until his tasks were done.

'I'm telling you again, I'll not share my house with stinking carrion! How dare you bring it here? Take it away this instant, you vile beast!' Widow Potts shrieked furiously.

'The child's body will be out in the yard, Mother. It will not discommode you in any way.' Tom spoke through clenched teeth.

The argument in the open doorway of the Lock-up had raged for the twenty minutes since his return.

'Not discommode me? Are you mad? It would discommode any decent civilized person to forever be forced to share their house with stinking carrion! I'll not do so! I'm sick and tired of my home being treated like a charnel house. Take it away! Take it away this instant!'

'Be you a-going to unload this little cratur, Master?' the cart driver shouted. 'I'se got to get back to the Grange.'

'No, he's not going to unload it! Take it away from here, you oaf! And take this vile beast of an unnatural son with you as well!' Widow Potts tried to slam the door in Tom's face.

His sorely strained patience finally snapped, and he forced the door back against her weight, moved inside and gripped her arms.

'It's you who are leaving here this very moment,' he gritted out. 'I'm taking a room for you at the Unicorn Inn and you'll stay there until I can find a cottage for you to live in.'

'You can't do this!' She gasped in shock. 'You can't treat your poor suffering invalid mother with such cruelty! You vile beast, you!'

'Oh, but I can, and I'm doing so immediately. You needn't worry, because I shall make sure that you do not lack for anything pertaining to your bodily comfort and welfare,' he grimly assured her, and called to the cart driver. 'Please bring the child inside, and then I want you to give this lady a lift to the Unicorn Inn just beyond the crossroads there. I'll accompany you and pay you well for your trouble.'

Late night had come before Tom had successfully installed his bitterly complaining mother in a comfortable room at the Unicorn Inn, and completed the various tasks at the Lock-up. There still remained the overriding necessity to go and make his report to Joseph Blackwell. He limped past the now solitary lighted window of the Fox and Goose and mentally promised, 'I'll be as quick as I can reporting to Blackwell, Amy, and then come directly to you.'

In the imposing Red House at the northern point of the Green, overlooking the steep Fish Hill and the broad Arrow valley beneath, Joseph Blackwell sat behind the desk in his lamp-lit study, resting his chin on steepled fingers, listening intently.

When Tom finished speaking he snapped brusquely. 'And who is this informant, Master Potts? No doubt he is a poacher!'

Tom experienced a tremor of dread, but steeled himself to state firmly, 'I can't give you the person's name, Sir. I gave my word that I wouldn't identify them.' He waited nervously for a furious reaction.

But the other man only smiled bleakly. 'As you well know, Master Potts, over these past many years I have cultivated a very wide variety of useful acquaintances. People who find it advantageous to

their well-being to endeavour to satisfy my appetite for knowledge.
Need I remind you that your own future well-being is greatly
dependent on your own efforts in that direction?'

He paused to let the veiled threat take effect.

Tom swallowed hard, but refused to surrender. 'With all respect,
Sir, I won't break my given word to that person, no matter what
unfortunate consequences that might hold for me.'

He waited with bated breath for the verbal axe to fall on him.

All that came was a reedy chuckling plaudit. 'Good! You've
proven yet again that you are a truly honourable man, Constable
Potts.' Smiling bleakly, Blackwell waggled his forefinger in a mock
gesture of reproof. 'But I'm a little hurt that at this advanced stage
in our relationship, you still do not appear to trust me as implicitly
as I trust you.'

'I do have implicit trust in you, Sir!' Tom protested. 'But you
know how virulently the Earl hates poachers. My informant was
risking transportation, perhaps his neck even when he told me of
this. I can't break my word to him, no matter what trouble it brings
down on my head.'

Blackwell became very serious. 'Listen well to me now, Thomas
Potts. I already knew that that badger sett was to be poached. I
knew because Patrick Bull has been one of my informers for more
years than I care to remember.'

Tom gasped in utter dismay at the realization that, if arrested,
Ritchie Bint would undoubtedly believe that he had betrayed
him.

Blackwell's pale eyes glinted with satisfaction at Tom's reaction.
'I shall now entrust you with yet another of my secrets, Constable
Potts. I don't really give a damn about poaching. The poor deserve
to taste a little fine game meat now and again. But I do not permit
it to get out of hand in this Parish. So, every now and then I expect
Bull to give me some poachers – Sonny Jakes and his gang for
example. In return I allow Bull a little sport on occasion, but he
must always tell me in advance the what, where and with whom.
Such as the badger sett, in the Lydd Wood, in company with
Richard Bint, John Hancox and Daniel Boyd. Bull will most surely
bring me his account of the discovery of the body. However, you
need have no fears for your informant. I also consider that the
man has behaved with decency on this occasion.'

'Indeed he has, Sir,' Tom agreed with heartfelt relief.

Blackwell frowned. 'Such a callous method of disposal of the body persuades me that this child met his end by foul play, and above all other crimes I abhor child murder. I want you to give this matter absolute priority, and bring the perpetrator to book.'

'I shall do my utmost to do so, Sir,' Tom promised fervently.

Blackwell assembled a quill pen, inkwell, sheet of notepaper and wrote a brief note, which he waved in the air to dry.

'Unfortunately my old friend Doctor Price is ill at this time, so Doctor Laylor will have to perform the post-mortem. Since you've previously demonstrated that you possess an abundance of medical knowledge and experience, you will assist Laylor in the task.'

Tom's immediate reaction was gratification. 'I thank you for your confidence in my abilities, Sir.'

Blackwell's tone was cold but warmth lurked in his eyes. 'I trust, Constable Potts, that my confidence in your abilities is not found to be misplaced.'

He folded the note and handed it to Tom. 'This is the post-mortem authorization. I want the work completed without delay, so deliver this to Laylor immediately. God only knows where he might be at this hour. Mayhap entertaining one of his fancy women. Nevertheless you must seek him out this very night. It is an absolute priority.'

Outside the house Tom was racked by indecision. 'Shall I go and see Amy first, or search out Hugh Laylor? If I don't go to see her straight away the pub will be locked down for the night and she'll be in her bed.'

'Absolute priority! Absolute priority!' Blackwell's words echoed in his mind, coupled with the visual memory of the pathetic little corpse, and he made his decision.

'It has to be Laylor. Amy will understand when I tell her why.'

NINETEEN

Tom rose long before dawn and spent time poring over some of his father's casebooks. As soon as there was sufficient daylight to see clearly he painstakingly examined the maggots he had selected the previous day. He then dissected some of them and studied the parts under a microscope.

Hugh Laylor came to the Lock-up a couple of hours after sunrise and Tom led him into the walled rear yard where the child's blanket-covered body lay on a trestle table within a temporary canvas shelter.

Laylor nodded appreciatively when he saw the row of glass jars and buckets of fresh water which Tom had made ready. 'You've prepared well, Master Potts.'

Tom removed the blanket. 'To save time I've cut his clothes off and washed him clean. There are abrasions on his skin, but nothing to indicate that he was stabbed.'

'Well done.' Again Laylor was appreciative. 'Have you an opinion on time of death, and the evidence for it?'

'Judging from the various conditions of the maggots, and allowing for the average air temperatures, I think that it's between nine to twelve days.'

'Judging from the maggots' conditions?' Laylor's eyebrows rose in surprise. 'I've not heard of this before.'

'My father had great interest in entomology and made a study of blowfly larvae and their stages of development. He taught me about their life cycle.'

'Tell me about it.' Laylor's curiosity was fully roused.

'Both blue and green-bottle blowflies for preference lay their eggs on fresh rather than putrefied flesh. The eggs hatch into first-stage instars, maggots, between eight to fourteen hours later depending on temperature. The colder the weather the longer delay of the hatching. Then after two or three days the first skin is shed and a larger larval instar emerges, this is the second-stage maggot. Within seven to eight days this skin is shed and the third-stage maggot emerges. This stays feeding on the body for a further five or six days. Then, when it's a fully grown maggot it leaves the body and travels a little distance, buries itself in the soil and pupates. That pupal stage lasts approximately twelve days.

'I found no pupae in the ground around the burrow, and none of the maggots were as large as I would expect them to be if they were close to their time of leaving the body. Hence my estimate of the time of death.'

'My God, but you're an ingenious fellow, Master Potts,' Laylor exclaimed admiringly. 'And I'm perfectly content to accept your estimate of the time of death. Now tell me, do you have any opinion as to the *cause* of death?'

'There is crepitation in the first and second cervical vertebrae and the mastoid process of the skull. But of course that might have been inflicted after death.'

'Fractured neck and skull, you say. Well let us begin there.' Laylor opened his surgical chest and took from it a long-bladed dissecting knife, scissors, a mallet, chisel and handsaw.

'Here.' Laylor smilingly proffered the knife. 'Let me find out what else you can teach me today.'

'I doubt that I can teach you anything you don't already know about dissection, Doctor Laylor.' Tom removed his coat, rolled up his sleeves and took the knife. 'I shall try to impress you with my dexterity, however.'

Tom had assisted his father at many post-mortems, and from harsh experience over long years he had trained himself to regard a dead body purely as an anatomical specimen. Yet now he still mentally begged the child, 'Please forgive me for what I must do to you.'

They turned the body on to its front. It took only brief minutes for Tom to slice and carefully peel away the flesh from the entire rear half of the skull and the uppermost vertebrae of the spinal column to reveal the crushed bones.

'Neat work, Master Potts,' his companion acknowledged. 'It looks to have been a savage impact to have caused this measurement of actual crushing. And see how the fractures radiate right up into the cranium. I do believe that we have the likely cause of death here. Would you agree?'

'Fractures radiate right up into the cranium. Into the crown!' Words jumped unbidden into Tom's mind, and he muttered, 'Jack fell down and broke his crown.'

'What's that you say?' Laylor asked. 'I didn't quite catch it.'

Tom was struggling to marshal a swirling confusion of memories and thoughts from among which the old crone Abigail's cracked voice suddenly rose to dominance.

'I never got a wink o' sleep wi' that little wench a-shriekin' and a-blartin' bloody nursery rhymes all bloody night and day! Jack and Jill went up the bloody hill! Jack fell down and broke his bloody crown! Night and bloody day I had that dinning in me ear'oles, so I did. Jack fell down and broke his bloody crown!'

'Is anything the matter, Master Potts?' Laylor stared curiously at Tom's strained expression.

Tom didn't hear him. Instead the voice of the seafarer Matthew Spicer was now reverberating through his head. *'Jack, who's ten, was took into the Brimfield Poorhouse . . . the kids had been sent off as Parish Apprentices the day before I came back . . . In Finstall hamlet I found a man who told me that he had seen a wagon of that description in very early morn last Thursday passing through the hamlet on the road towards Redditch . . . Jack, who's ten . . . Jack, who's ten.'*

'Master Potts? Are you alright? Did you not hear me?' Laylor reached across the trestle and gripped Tom's shoulder, startling him back into awareness and he flustered.

'My apologies, Doctor Laylor, I was lost in thought. What was it you were saying?'

'I was wondering if you agreed that the likely cause of death would be these injuries to the mastoid process and upper vertebrae?'

'Certainly they could be,' Tom concurred.

'However we'd best open him up and check the internal organs just to be sure.' Laylor smiled wryly. 'Blackwell is a stickler for following correct procedures, is he not? You carry on excising and I'll examine and test.'

The afternoon was well advanced when the final tests were completed and both men were satisfied that the crushed mastoid process and vertebrae were indeed the cause of the boy's death.

They moved the dissected organs and tissues from the bowls and jars back into the corpse and sewed it up. Then took turn about to work the handle of the pump and lave their hands, arms and heads.

When they were drying themselves using strips of rough towelling, Laylor asked curiously.

'Why do you remain in this thankless post, Master Potts? It's widely known that you have an income from the fund the Mackinnon family established for you when you rescued their relative from her maniac of a husband. You can surely well afford to resign from the constableship and resume your medical studies. You'd very quickly obtain your doctorate with the knowledge and experience you already possess.'

Tom grimaced ruefully. 'I owe a debt to the Parish Chest which Lord Aston insists that I pay back in the sum of only one shilling weekly. Until the debt is cleared, which will take almost eight years, I'm obligated to remain in this post.'

'But you can clear the debt at one swoop with a lump sum from your trust fund,' Laylor objected.

Tom shook his head. 'I found out after a little time that Lord Aston had prevailed upon the Mackinnon family to include a clause in the trust contract which prevents me from doing so. Also if I simply resign from this post against Lord Aston's wishes, then the Trust Fund is dissolved and I am again rendered penniless. Lord Aston guarantees that he will then have me committed to the Debtors Prison – and you well know that he wields the power and influence to do it.'

'This is absolute tyranny!' Laylor protested.

Tom shrugged. 'Mayhap so, and there are times when I am a most reluctant Parish Constable. But there are other times when I actually relish being lawfully empowered to try and hunt down evil wretches, such as whoever killed this poor child.' He grimaced wryly. 'And on occasion it also gives me opportunity to practise my medical skills, does it not?'

'Indeed so,' Laylor agreed. 'I'll go and see Blackwell and recommend that the body be buried post-haste. It's decomposing so fast that it'll have to be poured into a jug and splashed into a grave else.'

*   *   *

After Hugh Laylor had left the Lock-up Tom sat pondering possibilities.

'Jack fell down and broke his crown.' The sentence nagged like a toothache, giving Tom no respite. 'Broke his crown . . . Broke his crown.'

According to what Matthew Spicer had told him the wagon carrying the abducted children could have passed through Foxlydiate hamlet and the Lydd Wood on the 4th of October. Tom's estimated time of death spanned that date, so could the boy have been on that wagon? Could he be the Jack Telton that Spicer had spoken of?

And the little tramper girl Tom had taken to the Poorhouse – could she have also been on that wagon? Old Abigail claimed that the child had continually recited the nursery rhyme of 'Jack and Jill'. Was it possible that the child had merely been saying that Jack's crown was broken, and could it be that same Jack was this dead boy?

The mental condition of the girl could possibly have been brought on by the trauma of witnessing Jack's death. Her physical condition could certainly have resulted from wandering abroad through the wet, chill-winded days and nights between the 4th of October and Sunday the 7th of October when Tom had found her.

'Might her mind be clearer now?' he asked himself, and was gripped by an overwhelming compulsion. 'There's only one way to find that out. I have to go to the Children's Refuge this very day. But first I'll go and see Amy . . .'

Lily Fowkes was standing in the doorway of the Fox and Goose when she saw Tom coming across the Green, and on impulse went to meet him.

'Hello, Lily.' He smiled. 'I'm come to see Amy.'

'Ohhh, she's not here, Tom. My Pa's sent her on an errand,' she told him truthfully.

'That's a great shame.' Tom's disappointment was palpable. 'I have to go to Henley now, and I need to see her and explain what I've been doing these last days. When will she be back, do you think?'

'Ohhh, that's hard to say. Maybe . . .' Lily was about to say 'in an hour or so', but her jealous spite of Amy abruptly became dominant, and instead she lied. 'Maybe late on Wednesday, or perhaps even the day after that. She's got a powerful lot of errands to do in Bromsgrove, and in Droitwich as well.'

'Oh well, it can't be helped, can it?' Tom accepted his disappointment philosophically. 'If by any chance Amy should return early, would you please tell her that I'm dreadfully sorry to have missed the calling of our Banns, and that I will explain everything just as soon as I see her.' On impulse he couldn't resist adding with an embarrassed flush, 'And please would you tell her that I'm sorely missing her.'

'Of course I will, Tom,' Lily assured him with a smile.

TWENTY

Evening, Monday 15th October

The village of Henley-in-Arden was in Warwickshire, some eight miles east from Redditch. Hampered by his injury the walk took Tom more than three hours and it was dusk when he reached its nearest straggled buildings. He stopped a passer-by and asked for directions to the Refuge.

'The place you wants is down the far end o' that lane there. You can't miss it because there's a big high fence all round it, but it aren't there any more,' the man told him. 'I mean to say the house is still there, and still called the Refuge, but it aren't took in kids for years as far as I knows. I think it's a loony bin now. But you'd best go and take a look for yourself.'

An increasing sense of foreboding filled Tom as he limped up to the house, which had no lights showing from its barred windows.

After repeated knocking a small spyhole opened in the door and a male voice questioned. 'What do you want?'

'Am I addressing the Reverend Alistair Carnegie, Sir?' Tom enquired.

'You are not, Sir. My name is Charles Hewitt,' the voice snapped curtly. 'What's your business here?'

Tom quickly explained why he had come.

'I know nothing of any children or Carnegies. This is a private lunatic asylum. Now go away, or I'll send for the constables to take you up for trespass,' the man threatened.

'But, Sir, please may I just ask you one more—'

'Go away this instant, damn you, or be arrested! I'll not warn you again!'

Tom reluctantly accepted that to continue trying to question the man was fruitless. His position of authority carried no weight here. His legal powers as a Constable only extended to the boundaries of his own Parish of Tardebigge, just as magistrates' legal powers only extended to the boundaries of their individual counties. He also knew that the local constables were exceptionally quick to deal with any report of trespass. The reason being that Henley-in-Arden bore the unusual distinction of having several private madhouses located within its boundaries, and any trespassing stranger could well be an escaped inmate from one of those establishments.

Feeling bone weary and dispirited Tom set out to limp his way back to Redditch.

Charles Hewitt continued watching through the spyhole until Tom had gone from his view. Then he went back down a flight of stone steps into a warren of adjoining windowless cellars.

The most spacious of these was well lit, its atmosphere hot and muggy from the heat and fumes of the many burning oil lamps ranged around its bare lime-washed walls. In the centre of the slate slab floor was the largest article of furniture the room contained: a big heavy hospital operating table, fitted with thick leather restraining straps and shallow channels and vent-holes to drain off blood and fluids.

Set against one wall was another table fitted with castors so that it could be wheeled about. On its top, arranged in a hollow square, were four identical wooden troughs, each forty inches long, nine inches broad, seven inches high, and pitch-lined to make them watertight. A young man was carefully slotting flat metal plates into vertical grooves cut into the longest interior sides, thus forming a series of equally measured cross divisions along the entire length of the troughs.

'Who was that at the door?' he asked when Hewitt returned.

'He said his name was Potts, and that he was the Constable of

Tardebigge Parish. I sent him away very sharply.' Hewitt's manner was supercilious. 'The fellow proved to be as spindly in spirit as he is spindly in body. He scuttled away like a whipped cur.'

'What did he want?'

'He wanted to know if I was the Reverend Carnegie.' Hewitt's smile was a sneer. 'I very firmly disabused him of any such nonsensical notion.'

He moved to examine the troughs, running his forefinger over the tops of the plates. 'I need to be sure that you've made no error this time, Henry . . . Zinc, cloth, silver, cloth, zinc, cloth, silver, cloth, zinc, cloth, silver . . .'

Henry Atkins reacted with good humour. 'Unless I change my mind, and then it will be copper, cloth, zinc, copper, cloth, zinc! And today the liquid is the dilution of muriatic acid, to be one to five parts water. Unless of course I should change my mind yet again, and then it will be the dilution of one part sulphuric acid to fifty parts water.'

Within seconds he slotted the final metal plate into position, and began to stuff the spaces between the plates with folded cloths, saying as he did so, 'This will take but a minute or two, and I've already prepared the dilution. I hope you've taken equal care when preparing the patient, Charles. We don't want another failure resulting because of your carelessness, do we?'

Hewitt tossed his head and clucked his tongue indignantly. He then flounced to the doorway and shouted, 'Mackay, bring the patient.'

Within seconds a powerfully built man came through the doorway leading like a dog with neck collar and leash a small, naked, shaven-headed, shrivelled, doddery shuffling man, his torso grotesquely twisted by spinal deformity.

'Where in God's name did that cheating bastard Benton dig this one up from? He must be ten years older than bloody Methuselah. He'll probably shiver to bits at the first induction of the fluid.' Atkins spat out disgustedly.

He turned on Hewitt in sudden temper. 'Why must you always give me material like this to work with? I've told you a hundred times that we need young specimens with healthy organs and elasticity in their bones if we are to achieve success.'

The older man flinched before the onslaught, and gabbled, 'Such specimens are very hard to come by, my dear, as you well know. But Benton has sent word to me that he has at last managed to find a prime one for us, and he'll call on us tomorrow to finalize price and delivery.'

'You've told me this before, and he's failed you before.' The younger man glowered sulkily.

With a tentative smile Hewitt whispered pleadingly, 'Come now, let us be friends again. I'm very eager to see the results of the new variations you propose to use today. Please, my love, let us be friends.'

Atkins shrugged, and conceded. 'Oh, very well then. I suppose that I must forgive you . . . yet again!'

Hewitt clapped his hands in joy, and ordered Mackay: 'Make all ready.'

The big man led his captive to the side of the operating table. He unbuckled the leather collar and bodily lifted the old man in his arms to gently lay him upon the table, then stood crooning soothingly to him, stroking his wrinkled face and head. The old man's sunken eyes stared blankly up at his captor, and saliva dribbled from the corners of his toothless mouth.

Mackay then swiftly and dexterously fixed the table straps to the old man's arms, feet, legs, passing others across his hips, waist, chest and shoulders, yet the old man appeared unaware that he was being securely trussed.

Atkins interconnected the interiors of the boxes with copper strips and from two adjoining boxes trailed out from each a single long copper wire with wooden sheathing insulators near their ball-topped ends. He filled the boxes with watered acid from a large demijohn, took a sheathed wire in each hand, struck a dramatic pose and announced theatrically, 'Behold, Gentlemen, I present to you the miracle of the Etheric Fluid!'

He tapped the brass balls together. There was a blinding flash of light, a loud cracking report, and a fleeting pungent whiff of metallic acidity.

Hewitt clapped and cheered, Mackay remained expressionless, while the third member of the audience stayed staring blankly upwards, saliva trickling from the corners of his mouth.

Atkins' voice throbbed with fanatical conviction as he pointed the balls at the old man's face and told him, 'I see, Sir, that you're unimpressed by this demonstration of the Etheric Fluid. However, after I have passed this fluid through your head, you will come to appreciate how truly miraculous it is. Within mere days you will have attained sufficient powers of reason and speech to express your grateful thanks to myself, and my esteemed associates.'

He wheeled the box table to stand directly behind the head of the old man, and nodded to his companions. 'Come then, Gentlemen, let us commence the treatment.'

He distanced the brass balls an inch away from each side of the old man's skull and announced, 'I shall firstly direct the fluid through the temporal bones.'

He pushed the brass balls against the skull. There was a crack, a hissing of burning flesh, a momentary high-pitched squeal from the old man as his eyes bulged, his features twisted, his jaw chattered and his entire body violently convulsed.

Trudging towards Redditch, Tom was repeatedly asking himself if he was going in the wrong direction. Four miles from Henley he came to a halt.

'No matter how tenuous it might be, the only immediate lead I have at this moment is the Carnegies. And I'm unlikely to find out anything about them in Redditch.'

He turned and stubbornly limped back towards Henley.

TWENTY-ONE

Monday, 15th October

During the hours that Tom Potts was limping painfully to, from and back to Henley-in-Arden, several closed carriages, dog carts and gigs had individually arrived at Marlfield Farm, and their male drivers and passengers were met and led into the main house by Enoch Griffiths. In the spacious, well-furnished drawing room plentiful food and drinks had been laid out and were eagerly consumed by the visitors. A convivial festive atmosphere soon permeated the gathering.

'Gentlemen, your attention, if you please. It's time for business,' Enoch Griffiths shouted with a jovial grin. 'Time for what you've all been waiting for.'

'And about time it is too!' a half-drunken gentleman in clerical tie wig and clothing snapped pettishly. 'My lady wife will be wondering where I'm got to.'

'You can tell her that you've been taking Master Griffiths' advice on which boy's arse will prove the salutary cure for your syphilis. I'm sure she'll be greatly relieved to hear that,' a wag quipped and was loudly applauded.

'Order, Gentlemen, if you please!' Griffiths moved to the side of the ornate marble fireplace and tugged on its flanking silken bell pull.

Almost immediately a side door opened and Doll Griffiths entered holding the hand of a small, naked, frightened-looking boy. She pulled him with her across the room, displaying him to the audience.

Feet shuffled for vantage, heads craned forwards, pince-nez were raised and focussed, sharply indrawn breaths hissed audibly.

Enoch Griffiths' gaze flitted from face to face and his voice became low pitched and husky.

'There now, Gentlemen, he really is particular fresh and beautiful, aren't he just; and guaranteed never to ha' been touched. He's as pure, sweet and toothsome a virgin cherry as ever I've had the pleasure of beholding. But I warn you fairly that the Gentleman who's lucky enough to take his cherry is going to have to pay very highly for that privilege. He's worth a small fortune is this sweet morsel. What am I bid, Gentlemen?'

'One guinea!' the clerical gentleman hiccuped.

'What a teasing wag you are, Reverend.' Enoch Griffiths chortled jovially. 'You know well that the only thing you might get for a guinea is a bit of the grass he wipes his arse with.'

Other bids began to flow.

'Two guineas!'

'Three!'

'Four!'

'Gentlemen! Gentlemen!' Griffiths raised both arms. 'Surely I don't have to remind you that it's "Woman for Pleasure", but "Boy for Paradise"!'

He flicked his fingers at Doll Griffiths and she pulled the boy into the midst of the men as her brother went on. 'Feel his flesh, Gentlemen, feel how soft and warm it is. Smell his body, Gentlemen, as sweet to the nose as any perfume. Look how he trembles and shrinks when he feels your hands on him. Is that not exciting, Gentlemen? What a timid, helpless little virgin he is! Just imagine what you can do to him when he's yours. When you own him body and soul, to do whatever you like with him, whenever you choose.'

'Eight guineas!'

'Nine!'

'Ten!'

'Eleven!'

The bids came hot and fast and Griffiths grinned with satisfaction.

Standing unobtrusively in a corner of the room Ishmael Benton nursed his bitter resentment of Griffiths' contemptuous treatment. He stared at the other man's red beefy face and promised himself: 'I'll wipe that grin off your face someday, Griffiths, and if I have to wait a long time for that day to come, then so be it. As the Spaniards say, "Revenge is always a dish best eaten cold".'

TWENTY-TWO

Early morning, Tuesday 16th October

In the kitchen of the Fox and Goose, Thomas Fowkes, his family and staff were breakfasting on fat bacon and fresh eggs. The main topic of conversation was the discovery of the dead child in the Lydd Wood, the news of which had spread throughout the parish during the course of Monday.

When Amy Danks had heard that news on Monday it invoked an initial reaction of joyful relief. 'That's why Tom couldn't come to the chapel. What a bitch I am for doubting him.'

She had wanted to rush immediately to the Lock-up to see him, but had been firmly dissuaded by her employer.

'Neither you nor nobody else can go there today, my wench. From what I've been told Blackwell and Lord Aston has strictly forbid anybody going there. Doctor Laylor and Tom Potts will be doing a post-mortem and it'll be Heaven help anybody who goes disturbing them.'

'Tom 'ull come and tell you all about it when he's finished, Amy,' Maisie Lock had assured her, and Amy had reluctantly accepted.

Later that day Maisie had excitedly imparted to Amy another titbit of welcome information. 'You'll never guess what's happened, my duck! You'll never guess!'

'Well tell me then!'

'It's Widow Potts! Her's living in the Unicorn. Tom's chucked her out!'

'When?' Amy gasped with surprise.

'Last night, when he brought the dead kid back to the Lock-up. Him and the old bitch had a terrible fight, and he chucked her out of the Lock-up. Jimmy Smith, the potman at the Unicorn, just told me about it. He said that the first thing this morning her was creating merry hell with John Mence over something or other, and Mence was shouting that for two pins he'd chuck her out on to the street like her son had.'

Pure exultation pulsed through Amy, which as the afternoon lengthened was punctuated by disturbingly repetitive shafts of guilty unease. These she tried to assuage by telling herself: 'When Tom comes to see me, I'll tell him that I'll help his mother when she's moved into a cottage.'

Afternoon became evening, became night, and as the hour for closing the inn drew inexorably nearer Amy's mood became ever more tense and anxious. 'Why hasn't he come to see me? When that old bitch said he was not wanting to marry me any more, was she speaking truly after all?' The questions were a self-torturing inquisition.

Lily Fowkes had earlier sensed how troubled Amy was becoming, and periodically popped into the Select Parlour to spitefully torment her.

'Terry Prescott's just been in the Snug, and he said that he saw Tom going into the Crown an hour ago. He's sure to pop in and see you later though, my duck.'

'I think I've just seen Tom passing outside. I can't be sure, but it must have been him because there's nobody else so tall in the parish, is there?'

'Amy, there's lights on in the Lock-up, Tom must be back there. Why aren't he come to see you, I wonder? He knows that you'll be worrying to death about where he is.'

When the inn was closed and locked up for the night, Amy waited until everyone was sleeping then snuck out and ran to the darkened Lock-up. For long minutes she rang the bell but the door remained shut and no light appeared in the upstairs windows.

Now sitting silent and subdued at the Tuesday breakfast table, Amy came to a fear-invoking decision which she had been struggling with all through a virtually sleepless night.

'I'll do it! I'll ask the Witch Man to tell me what's going to happen to me, be it good or bad!'

TWENTY-THREE

The White Swan Coaching Inn, Henley-in-Arden
Early morning, Tuesday 16th October

Tom Potts was woken by his bed-fellow's crushing weight suddenly rolling upon him, and he shouted and struggled violently in shocked fright, rousing the snoring fat man into fuddled awareness.

'Dammee! Dammee! But you ain't my missus! I beg pardon, Sir. Humblest apologies, Sir! Humblest apologies!'

The crushing weight lifted and Tom hurriedly vacated the bed. The fat man rolled back over on to his side of the bed, released a resounding, stinking fart and recommenced snoring.

Tom smiled wryly. 'It's a good job I wasn't undressed else God only knows what I might have woken to find up my backside.'

He hurriedly re-strapped his ankle, laced on his boots, donned his waistcoat, coat, and top hat, took his walking stick and exited the foul-smelling room, which was little larger than a cubicle.

Outside on the extended sleeping-quarters balcony, which over-looked the elongated inner courtyard of the large inn, he gratefully breathed in the fresh chill air of early morning, counted the money in his pockets and formulated his plans.

'Breakfast here in the Swan. Then get shaved, washed and brushed in the village barber shop.'

Tom had learned from past experience that barbers were fruitful sources for local gossip and information.

'Oh yes, Sir, I get a good class of passing trade. Commercial and professional gentlemen who, like yourself, Sir, are stopping at the Swan.'

The barber was keen to chat. 'I'm Henley born and bred, Sir, like my father and his father afore him. Of course in their day there wasn't the same amount of traffic on this road, was there, Sir? Not like today with all these coaches passing through here going up to Birmingham and down to London. These new macadam roads am remarkable, aren't they, Sir? Who'd have thought that a Scotchman would have the brains to think of that way of road-making? People travel with the speed of the wind these days because of him, don't they, Sir?'

Tom asked about the Children's Refuge. 'St Christopher's, Sir? Oh yes, I remember it well. From all accounts there were some very funny goings on there, Sir.'

Tom raised an eyebrow. 'Oh no, Sir. I don't mean funny haha. I mean strange and mysterious like.

'Well, Sir, the Reverend Mitchell and the Reverend Carnegie and his wife opened it about twenty years past, very charitable people they were as well. They had local folk working there, and they'd bring the orphans and foundlings to church and out for walks and suchlike. Then Reverend Mitchell died sudden like, and it all started to change.'

'How did it change?' asked Tom.

'Well there seemed to be a lot fewer kids took in, and all the local folk was given their sacks, Sir, and nobody was let through the gate any more. The kids stopped coming to church and stopped going out for walks. In fact nobody hardly ever sighted anything of them at all. Then some years past the place was closed up and left empty, until last year.'

'Who lives in the Refuge house now?' Tom queried.

The barber was quick to share his knowledge. 'Well, it's been turned into one of those private madhouses we've got several of hereabouts. I've been told that the proprietor is one of those scientific gentlemen. Hewitt's his name, I think. But he keeps himself to himself, and don't welcome visitors. I've never set eyes on him close up myself, Sir.'

'Where did the Carnegies move to?' Tom asked, but without much hope that the barber would know.

'They went to Birmingham, Sir, and it was my next-door neighbour, Edgar Williams, who took their chattels up there on his cart. The poor chap's housebound these days, but his mind's still sharp and he'll no doubt be able to recall what street they moved to. Especially if he gets a little refreshment for his memory, if you get my meaning, Sir.'

The barber had finished his work. 'There now, Sir, all done. And if I may say so, you look every inch the fine Gentleman you are, Sir . . . Why thank you, Sir, this is more than generous. I do hope that I shall be honoured with your patronage when you're next in Henley.'

The barber's confidence in his neighbour's memory was justified: half an hour later Tom had a Birmingham street name, and also some extra information. The Reverend Mitchell had once mentioned to Edgar Williams that the Carnegies had a son of their own, but Williams had never seen the child and knew nothing more of him.

Like a hunting hound which had found the scent of a quarry, all Tom's instincts were now centred on giving chase: to go immediately to Birmingham some twelve miles distant. He counted his few remaining coins.

'It's likely most of this will be needed to buy information, so I'll have to go by Shanks' Pony. But I've had a good breakfast, and if I step carefully my ankle should last it out. I can be there by nightfall.'

He set out eagerly, his thoughts so focussed on what he might discover in Birmingham that he was unaware of the dog cart coming down the long straight main street towards him, and suddenly pulling to a halt.

'Christ Almighty! It's Potts, right enough! What the fuck is he

doing here?' Judas Benton demanded in shocked alarm. He stared
around, desperately seeking a hiding place. 'Let's get out of his
way afore he sees us.'

Ishmael Benton was equally perturbed, but kept his head. 'No!
It's best that we find out why he's here. Stop pissing your britches,
and play the man for once. Now try to look calm, will
you . . . . Giddup.' He whipped the horse into a trot.

When the vehicle neared Tom, Ishmael Benton shouted in mock
surprise.

'Well this is an unexpected pleasure, Master Potts. Good
morning to you.'

'Good morning to you, Master Benton, and to you also, Master
Benton.' Tom bowed to each man in turn. He knew Judas Benton
well, having frequently pawned articles with him during his years
of penury. Ishmael Benton he had only recently and briefly met
when the man had returned to live in Redditch.

'Can I give you a lift, Master Potts?' Ishmael Benton offered.

'Only if you are going in the direction of Birmingham, and I
see that you are not.' Tom smiled.

Benton reacted instantly. 'Well, contrary to appearances, that is
exactly where we are going, just as soon as I've watered my horse
at that trough down by the Swan there. We have to meet a business acquaintance of my brother in the Jewellery Quarter, isn't
that so, Judas?'

Judas Benton nodded dumbly.

'Come up, Master Potts,' Ishmael Benton insisted warmly. 'I'll
not accept refusal and we shall be most glad of your company.'

Tom happily accepted the offer. 'This is turning out to be a
lucky morning for me, Gentlemen.'

Sitting in his study back in Redditch, Joseph Blackwell Esq. was
thinking precisely the opposite about the progress of his own
morning. He had slept badly, his manservant had nicked his chin
twice while shaving him, his cook had burned his breakfast
kedgeree, his scullery maid had broken his finest porcelain tureen,
and for the past three quarters of an hour he had been enduring
the complaints of the Widow Potts. At last he could bear no more,
and held up both hands in surrender.

'Enough, Ma'am! I have heard enough. Kindly return to the

Unicorn and I will send my manservant to you within the hour.
Good day to you, Ma'am!'

TWENTY-FOUR

The horse was strong and fast and the travellers made good
time to Birmingham. Tom found himself enjoying Ishmael
Benton's company. The man proved to be well-read and
widely travelled and they initially talked about books and their
own personal travels, while Judas Benton remained silent. It was
not until they had entered the outskirts of the city that Ishmael
Benton referred to the dead child.

'I heard that Master Blackwell has arranged for the child to be
buried today in the paupers' plot. The Vestry is paying the costs
and John Clayton performing the last rites.' Ishmael Benton
scowled and observed heatedly, 'It's a terrible thing to have
happened to a child. Whoever is culpable should be hung, drawn
and quartered, but firstly put in the public stocks for a few weeks
so that people can demonstrate their abhorrence for what he did.'
He paused and sighed regretfully. 'That is assuming it's a man
who did it. In this day and age of blatant female license and
immorality it might even have been a woman.'

'Well yes, it's possible,' Tom agreed. 'I've encountered certain
of the female sex who are capable of committing any crime.'

'Forgive my curiosity, Master Potts, but I can't help wondering
if your reason for coming to Birmingham is to do with the poor
child's death.'

Tom hesitated momentarily, but then could see no harm in
admitting, 'Yes, Master Benton, it is. I'm trying to trace the
Carnegie family, who once superintended a children's refuge in
Henley-in-Arden.'

'Oh, that's something of a coincidence,' Benton exclaimed. 'I
once encountered a Reverend gentleman who said that he was
superintending such a refuge in the vicinity of Henley.'

'He could be the very gentleman I'm going in search of. What
can you tell me of him?' Tom questioned eagerly.

'I can't even recall his name, I'm afraid.' Benton regretfully shook his head. 'I only met him the once, and we were in a numerous company among general conversation. He seemed to be a very polite gentleman.' He winked roguishly. 'Unlike a certain senior one of our own parish clerics whom I will not name.'

'I think I may be able to guess that cleric's identity.' Tom chuckled.

As they penetrated deeper into the city the dog cart's pace was forced to slow by the teeming traffic in the narrow, dirty, smoke-aired streets, where from all sides there came the clanging clattering of the myriad industrial processes which had earned Birmingham the sobriquet of the 'City of a Thousand Trades'.

Tom looked about him. 'I think we've arrived in Deritend?'

'We have indeed, Master Potts,' Ishmael Benton confirmed. 'Is this your destination?'

'Yes, the address I seek is somewhere about here. So I'll part from you now, with many thanks for your kind assistance.'

'It's been our pleasure, Master Potts. Unfortunately I don't know how long our business here will take us, or in fact where it will entail us going on to. So I'm not able to offer to carry you back to Redditch with any certainty as to a time and place we could meet up with you.'

'No matter, Master Benton, I'm well able to use Shanks' pony.' Tom got down from the dog cart and waved them goodbye as they drove off. 'Many thanks to you both.'

The dog cart turned a corner and halted.

'Take them.' Ishmael Benton pushed the reins into his brother's hand.

'Wait for me at the Anchorage,' he instructed, then dismounted and moved to look cautiously around the corner. He instantly sighted Tom's tall hat bobbing clearly above the intervening heads of the passing bustle and smiled grimly. 'You make a very fine signpost, Potts; this is going to be easy.'

The three-storied terrace-end house was as smoke-grimed and shabby looking as its neighbours, but unlike them it was double instead of single-fronted, and had a prominent sign in one of its ground-floor windows: 'Rooms to Let. No Irish need apply.'

The black-clad, severe-looking woman who answered the door silently examined Tom from head to toe before announcing in a broad Irish brogue, 'I'm Mrs Bridget O'Toole, the mistress of this establishment. You look to be respectable, but I shall still require references, and a deposit of three months' rent in advance.'

Tom bowed politely. 'I regret, Ma'am, that I'm not seeking accommodation. I'm come here to enquire for a gentleman whom I've been informed resides here. The Reverend Alistair Carnegie, Ma'am.'

She stared at him in stony silence, until he felt driven to introduce himself.

'My name is Thomas Potts, Ma'am. I'm the Constable of the Parish of Tardebigge, and I have urgent need to speak with the Reverend Carnegie. Would you please be kind enough to inform him that I'm here.'

She made no response, but only continued to stare stonily at him until in desperation he offered, 'I will pay you for performing that service for me, Ma'am.'

She proffered a cupped palm.

Tom hastily felt in his pocket, took out some coins, selected a sixpenny piece and put it on to her palm. She frowned in negation, and sighing in defeat he gave her the solitary silver shilling, leaving himself with pitifully few copper pennies and half-pennies.

The cupped palm became a tight-closed fist, and she nodded acceptance.

'Should I wait here for him to come to me, Ma'am?' Tom asked.

She shook her head. 'That'll serve no purpose, Master Potts. The old man's been dead and buried this last month.'

It was now Tom who stood silent as he digested this unwelcome news, while she became increasingly voluble.

'This was his room, the one with the sign in the window. Lived there solitary ever since he came here nigh on five years past. Kept himself to himself as well. Never spoke to any of my other lodgers, and only spoke with me when he paid his rent, candles and coals, and even then it was only strictly business, not a morsel of gossip or a single pleasantry. No trouble at all though, not a bit!'

'Did he have visitors, Ma'am?' Tom momentarily interrupted the flow.

Her manner changed; her face became animated, she glanced from side to side as if checking for an eavesdropper, then inclined her head closer to Tom and in a conspiratorial tone told him, 'That was the strange thing about him, Master Potts, nobody ever came knocking the door for him. But he used to go out sometimes and come back in the dead of night, and then I used to think that I could hear him talking to somebody in his rooms. But my rooms are across the hallway, you see, and the walls are thick, so I could never make out what they were saying.'

'Man or woman?' Tom queried.

'Both,' she replied. 'At times it could have been a woman's voice, and other times a man's. But I never ever saw them coming into the house, nor leaving it neither.'

She paused, inclined her head even more closely towards Tom and whispered breathily, 'Another thing about him was that one of my lodgers saw him more than a few times down at the Bull Ring market talking to the gay girls that plies their trade there, and going off with them all arm in arm, close pressed together like they was panting to do it there on that very spot. And him wearing his priest's clothes as well! Wouldn't you think he was behaving something shameful to do such? To go gadding about with the gay girls when he was dressed as a Man o' God!'

An irresistible mischievous urge impelled Tom to question. 'Do it on that very spot? Do what, Ma'am?'

'Get away with you!' She smiled archly. 'I'm too old a bird to be caught like that.'

'Indeed I recognize that you are a very shrewd and wise lady.' Tom flattered her. 'Could you tell me how did he die, was he long ill?'

'Ill? Good God no! He was as hale and hearty as a brewer's dray horse.' She paused for effect then announced dramatically, 'He cut his own throat! I'd heard nor seen nothing of him that day and naturally, being concerned for his welfare, I took the liberty of unlocking his door and peeping inside. Just to make sure he wasn't laying there ill, you understand.'

'Of course I do, Ma'am,' Tom could only mutter, startled by this information.

'He was sitting in the chair in front of the fireplace with his throat cut from ear to ear, and the razor on the floor beside him, and a bit of a note. There was blood all over the floor. It took my charwoman a whole day to scrub the boards clean. Thanks be to

God that the chair hadn't got any coverings and cushions else they would have been ruined entirely.

'Anyway, because he'd committed the mortal sin of killing himself, he couldn't be buried in holy ground, could he? Even though he was a Man o' God. There was some talk of putting him under a crossroads with a stake through his heart. But in the end they shoved him down with all the unshriven babies and whatnots at the far end of the Potters Field.'

'Has no one come forward to enquire about him? Because surely he must have left various possessions?'

'Well, that's another mystery. There was no watch, nor money nor anything worth a penny piece like rings or keepsakes in his room, and no relative has yet come forwards to lay claim to anything. And the note on the floor just had the same words, "Nothing left", written again and again all over it. "Nothing left", that's all he'd writ. The only thing that I can think is that he was indeed penniless, and that drove him to kill himself. Mind you, if he'd had anything to leave it would have been forfeit to the Crown anyway, wouldn't it? The constables tried it on with me, so they did. They tried to say that all the furniture in his rooms was his property and forfeited to the Crown because he'd committed self-murder. But I'd got all my bills of sale so that shot them up their backsides.'

'Did he ever owe you rent, Ma'am?' Tom couldn't resist enquiring.

'Oh no!' the woman stated emphatically. 'My lodgers pay in advance, and should they be an hour tardy in meeting their obligations, then out they go! I may be a poor, forlorn, frail-bodied widow woman, Master Potts, but I've the heart of a lion.'

For a fleeting instant a mental image of his mother assailed Tom, and with heartfelt sincerity he assured his companion, 'I do not doubt that fact, Ma'am.'

'Good day to you, Sir.' The woman closed the door and Tom slowly walked away, thinking hard about what he had learned.

From his concealed vantage point in an alleyway Ishmael Benton had seen the money change hands, and surmised from the length of time the pair had talked together that considerable information had been exchanged. He waited until Tom had gone out of sight before hurrying to the house and hammering on the door.

When the same woman opened it, he held a gold sovereign before her eyes.

'Good morning to you, Ma'am. I do truly believe that a brief conversation between us will be to our mutual advantage.'

Tom knew that until he had more money in his pockets to pay for information it would be fruitless for him to go to the Bull Ring market and attempt to find the prostitutes that Carnegie had met with. He was also beginning to question whether or not this particular trail was worth pursuing any further, and the germ of self-doubt was beginning to wriggle in his mind.

'I could well be embarked on a wild goose chase in the case of the Carnegie family so perhaps it might be best to concentrate first on finding Matthew Spicer and seeing if he's traced that wagon . . . But I can't make progress either way until I get back home and replenish my pockets.' He pulled out his fob watch, saw the hour and grimaced unhappily. 'It's going to be a long, hard night, I feel.'

TWENTY-FIVE

Early evening, Tuesday 16th October

Jack Smith, the 'Witch Man' of Redditch, walked ponderously into the large Tap Room of the Fox and Goose and stood balefully regarding the drinkers. Some were playing dominoes and cards on the rough hewn tables, others clustered talking and laughing at the bar counter, another group was pitching quoits in the far corner.

Jack Smith's strange dark hazel eyes were unusually penetrating, but only one of the attributes which combined to make his physical appearance a singular sight. He stood barely five feet in height, with a massive upper body, no visible neck, and extremely short legs. He wore a shabby black tailcoat, the tails of which dragged on the ground behind him, and a tall black hat pulled low over his misshapen ears. Coupled with a hairless head and eyebro-

he presented an altogether eccentric appearance, in keeping with his habits and manners.

'What's your pleasure, Master Smith?' Lily Fowkes asked from her post behind the counter.

'My pleasures are none o' your business,' he growled. 'My needs are a pot of ale and a pipe, which you can bring to that table over there.' He went to sit by himself at an empty table.

Lily served him and then hurried into the Select Parlour to tell Amy Danks.

'Jack Smith's in the Tap, Amy. Miserable as sin, like he always is.'

Amy followed her friend back to the Tap Room and went to speak to the Witch Man.

'Now then, my maid, what does you want with me?' Jack Smith glowered.

'If you please, Master Smith, I need my fortune telling.' Amy Danks' usual pert confidence was not in evidence as she faced the Witch Man across the table.

'And I need rest and relaxation, my maid, which is the express reason why I'm choosing to sit by myself at this table trying to enjoy my pipe and ale in peace and quiet.'

'I wouldn't come bothering you if it wasn't really important, Master Smith, and it's only you that can help me.' Amy produced some coins and showed them to him. 'Look, I've got money to pay you with, and if this aren't enough I can get some more. Please help me. I'm in sore need of your magic.'

Smith sensed that she was truly under stress, and although he continued to glower, his heart softened at the sight of troubled youthful beauty.

'What is it that's upsetting you, my maid?'

She glanced around at the other drinkers in the room, some of whom were taking an interest in her and the Witch Man's interchange. 'I can't tell you here, Master Smith, there's too many big ears listening. Can you come into the back parlour? I'll carry your pot and pipe for you.'

'Bloody hells bells! Can't a man ever get to enjoy a drink in peace wi'out having daft women pestering him?' he grumbled etchily, but rose to his feet. 'And I can carry me own pot and pe. I aren't lost the use of me hands yet.'

In the parlour they sat to face each other across the table.

'Now before we starts you've got to cross me palm with silver.' Smith held out his hand.

Amy sorted through her meagre store of coins and put the solitary silver sixpence into his palm.

He expelled a noisy snort of indignation. 'All this tanner 'ull buy you is a bit of scrying!'

Her pretty face radiated dismay. 'But I thought that you'd read my stars, Master Smith. That's the only piece of silver I've got. But I've got another four pence in coppers you can have.'

'I can't read your stars, my maid, because me astrology books are in pawn to the Unicorn and it's going to cost me a half-sovereign to fetch 'um out again.' He saw her escalating distress and again softened towards her. 'Now don't moither yourself because I'll do a proper scrying for the tanner, and you can keep them coppers. Get me a small bowl.'

When she brought the bowl to him he poured some of his ale into it, and instructed, 'Take this tanner back off me, kiss it three times and put it in the bowl.'

She did as he asked.

'Now don't you be feared of what's going to happen next, my maid. I'm going to put meself into a trance, and when you sees me head drop forward then you must ask me your question, and that must be the only question you ask.'

He closed his eyes and began to draw long rasping shuddering breaths. Amy stared at him with wide-eyed apprehension, her own breathing shallow and quickening.

His head fell forward and she started in shock. His eyes opened and stared glassily at the dark liquid in the bowl.

Amy's hands clenched tightly and she gasped. 'Will I wed the man I'm betrothed to?'

Fear flooded through her as she saw Smith's eyes dilate and roll up until only the whites showed, and his breathing metamorphosed into a series of strangled groans. All her instincts were impelling her to flee from the room, but she forced herself to stay seated.

She emitted a faint scream as Smith abruptly straightened his glistening white eyeballs met her frightened gaze.

Then his pendulous lower lip quivered violently, an

high-pitched voice he told her, 'You shall wed the man you chooses to wed.'

His head slumped forwards, his eyes closed, and his breathing slowly eased.

As the seconds ticked by Amy's jangled nerves calmed and she was able to dwell on what she had been told.

'I shall wed the man I chooses to wed.'

A feeling of relief stole into her, which strengthened and took firm hold. Her mood soared happily.

'Then I shall wed Tom.' Her imp of mischief roused itself and she giggled. 'That's unless I changes my mind and chooses not to.'

Smith's head lifted and his penetrating gaze fixed upon her. 'Did the spirits bring you any answer to your question?'

'You know that already, Master Smith.' She was puzzled by his words. 'It was you who told it me.'

'Oh no, my maid.' He shook his head. 'I don't know what comes out of my mouth when I'm scrying. The spirits uses my eyes to read the pictures in the magic bowl and then it's them who speaks, not me. I don't ever remember anything that comes through my mouth. I'm only the channel for them to pass their message through.'

He fished the sixpence out of the bowl and pressed it into her hand. 'Be a good maid and fetch me a drop o' brandy, this scrying takes a lot out o' me these days.'

Amy went to the Select Parlour and Tommy Fowkes scolded her.

'I don't pay you good money to go having your fortune told on my time. Bloody lot o' nonsense it is as well. It's only silly sarft wenches like you that keeps that lazy old shyster in drink and tobacco, when he ought to be doing a proper job o' work to earn his keep.'

Amy's eyes glinted mischievously as she answered in a subdued tone. 'I'm glad that you thinks fortune telling is all nonsense, Master Fowkes.' She deliberately kept a sombre expression on her face. 'Because although at times you can be such a miserable mean man work for, I really wouldn't like anything bad to happen to you.'

She handed him the sixpence, poured out a large measure of and went to leave the Tap Room. 'I'll only be two ticks.'

'Hold on a minute.' The landlord's fat sweaty face betrayed a trace of anxiety. 'What do you mean, something bad happen to me?'

Amy's sombre expression betrayed nothing of her inner mischievous glee. 'I mean it's like you say, it's most probably all nonsense anyway. You're right to pay no heed to it. I know I'm a fool to believe in it, but isn't it just amazing how he told me of my best-kept secrets!'

Again she went to leave, and again he stopped her. 'Wait a tick, will you! Tell me what he said about me?'

She shook her head. 'Oh, I can't tell you that. Master Smith talks to the spirits, you see, and they gets real angry if their private predictions are told to others. One of the things that's most important when you have a fortune told is that you must never tell what was told to you, even if you want with all your heart to warn somebody who's in danger. Otherwise bad things will happen to you.'

She sighed regretfully and shook her head, exclaiming emphatically, 'A pack of wild horses couldn't drag it from me, Master Fowkes! As much as I'd like to tell you what the spirits warned of, it's more than my own life is worth.'

Shaking her head as if truly regretful she left him staring worriedly after her.

A few moments after her return, Fowkes told her, 'I've got business to attend to, my dear. It's quiet tonight so you'll be alright by yourself, won't you? Maisie 'ull be back from her errand any minute now.'

'Of course I shall. You take as long as you wants,' she assured him dutifully.

He drew a large tumbler of brandy from the keg and carried it with him as he left.

Amy quickly slipped after him, and watched as he went into the back parlour, hearing him say, 'Just come to see how you're a-doing, Master Smith. I've brought you a measure of my finest brandy, and it's on the house. You see, I've been wanting to have a little chat with you for ages now . . .'

Tears of hilarious amusement sparkled in Amy's blue eyes and she crammed both hands against her mouth to smother her delighted laughter.

When Maisie Lock returned Amy excitedly related what Jack Smith had said, and how Thomas Fowkes was even now having his own fortune told.

Maisie laughed uproariously, then told her, 'I saw a light upstairs in the Lock-up, so your Tom must be back there now. If you'm quick about it you can run down and see him while old Fatty's wi' the Witch Man.'

Amy snatched up her shawl and ran from the inn. As she sped across the dark Green she was happily picturing how he would greet her, and how she would treat him.

'He'll be desperate to tell me how sorry he is to have missed our Banns, and I'll be very haughty with him at first. Until he's begged me to forgive him and been humbled enough. Then I'll give him a kiss, and tell him that I forgive him. A bit later on I'll tell him that I'll help him care for his Ma when she's living in her cottage. But that can wait until after we're wed.'

She bounded up the steps, grabbed the bell pull and tugged hard, giggling mischievously. 'When he calls down to see who's here, I won't answer, but keep on ringing until he comes and opens the door. Then I'll jump out at him and scare him half to death.'

'Is that you, Thomas?'

The strident shout struck Amy like a physical blow.

'Will you stop ringing these bells, and give me answer, you great stupid oaf!'

Amy shook her head in disbelief. 'It can't be! It can't be! I'm imagining this!'

'Answer me, damn you!' The mobcapped head of Widow Potts thrust out from the casement.

A rushing onset of fury vanquished Amy's wishful disbelief. 'It's her! He's took the evil old bitch back! Well bugger him then! I'm done with him forever!'

She pulled her shawl over her head and ran back across the Green, with the shrieking of Widow Potts ringing in her ears.

'You saucy strumpet! Don't you dare come pestering my son ever again! He's done with you, d'you hear! He's done with you!'

TWENTY-SIX

Tom had grossly overestimated the extent of his injured ankle's recovery, and after covering five miles was being forced to halt and rest it every two or three hundred yards. It was nearing midnight when he finally reached the Redditch Green. Experiencing a disturbing mingling of both joyful anticipation and nervous apprehension, he made his painful way to the Fox and Goose.

'As I crossed over Salisbury Plain, A dainty fine sight I did behold, As lasses were crying and tearing their hair, Oh the route is just come for the Blues.'

The tuneful tenor singing sounded clearly as Tom neared the inn. He smiled in recognition. 'It's the Apollo Glee Club meeting, isn't it? John's in fine voice this evening.'

'Then each one home to their mothers did run, My heart is undone it is true. I'll pack up my clothes without more delay, And boldly I'll march with the Blues.'

A small crowd of listeners had clustered outside the Select Parlour's windows and on impulse Tom halted by them.

'Our ship had been rigged and we all set sail. How sweetly the French Horn played too. Then everyone gave a loud Huzza! Success to King George and his Blues.'

The song ended, from within the room came loud applause and stamping of feet, and the listeners outside added their own plaudits.

Tom limped into the inn and, racked by a sudden disturbing doubt, hesitated outside the closed door of the Select Parlour.

'Will it be a scowl she'll greet me with?' He drew a deep breath. 'Be kind to me, Lady Luck.'

The room was crowded with members of the Apollo Glee Club, the self-considered cultural elite of the Parish, the air clouded with the smoke from their tobacco pipes and cheroots, and loud with the hubbub of talk and laughter. Tom eagerly looked for but could not see Amy.

Sitting at one of the tables, John Clayton waved and called, 'Tom, come and join us.'

The curate was in company with Hugh Laylor and Richard Hemming, the son of the Needle Master William Hemming.

Behind the serving counter Lily Fowkes smiled slyly and poked Maisie Lock in the ribs.

'Maisie, look what the cat's just dragged in. I don't know how he's got the gall to show his face in here after what he's done to poor Amy. Now's your chance to give him a piece of your mind, like you've been saying you will.'

Maisie Lock's eyes fired with anger. 'I'll give the rotten bugger more than a piece o' my mind. Just you see if I don't.'

Socializing with a group of club members on the public side of the counter, Tommy Fowkes as always was maintaining an eagle-eyed watch on all that passed in the room. He leaned across the counter and hissed warningly at Maisie.

'Just you behave yourself, my girl.'

'The rotten bugger's got to be shown up!' she hissed back defiantly. 'He's broke poor Amy's heart!'

'What will you have to drink, my friend?' Clayton invited as Tom sat down, and like the others removed his top hat and placed it brim uppermost on the floor beside his chair.

'I strongly recommend that you take a glass of brandy, Master Potts,' Hugh Laylor advised smilingly. 'Because tonight we are truly witnessing a miracle akin to Jesus changing water into wine, are we not, Gentlemen? For once in his sinfully greedy life, Fatty Fowkes has miraculously neglected to change spirituous liquors into virtual water.'

'I'll just have a glass of ale, thank you.' Tom could not stop himself from glancing about in search of Amy.

Clayton lifted his hand high above his head, and Maisie Lock immediately came to the table.

'A glass of ale, and three brandies, if you please, my dear,' Clayton ordered.

Maisie bobbed a curtsey and hurried back to the counter.

When she returned with the tray of drinks, Tom asked, 'Where's Amy tonight, Maisie? Nothing's amiss with her, I hope?'

The young woman made a deliberate show of ignoring him and,

smiling radiantly at his companions, set their individual drinks on the table before them.

'There you are, Sirs. One for you, one for you, and one for you.'

'Maisie?' Tom could not understand why she was behaving like this. 'Is anything the matter?' Anxiety struck through him. 'Amy is alright, isn't she?'

'No, her's not alright!' She rounded on him furiously, shouting at the top of her voice. 'Her's real upset because you'm forever letting her down, you rotten bastard!' She lifted the glass of ale, hurled its contents into his face, dashed glass and tray on to the floor, and ran from the room.

Ale dripping down from his face and hair, Tom sat rigid with shock.

The room erupted in a thunderous uproar of mocking jeers, cheers, laughter, hands clapping, feet stamping.

John Clayton reacted instantly. By sheer strength he dragged Tom up from the chair and propelled him from the room, out of the inn and across the darkness of the Green.

They had reached the Lock-up steps before Tom could gather his senses and struggle in vain to break free from Clayton's iron-like grip.

'What possessed Maisie to do that, John?' he questioned in utter bewilderment. 'I must go back there and see Amy immediately!'

'You're going back nowhere, my friend. There's been more than sufficient mockery already inflicted on you for this night.' Clayton relentlessly propelled Tom up the steps to the door.

'I must go back there,' Tom protested.

'Not tonight, you won't.' Clayton was obdurate. 'Try to see sense, Tom. Whatever is amiss between you and Amy will not be put right by you going back there this night. All that will do is to give the fellows there further opportunity to jeer and mock you; and they'll most certainly include Amy in their sport. How will that make her feel? Consider that, my friend, and see sense for her sake.'

Tom could not bear the prospect of Amy being mocked and humiliated, but at the same time he could not bear not knowing how he had so grievously hurt her, and argued.

'But John, I can't leave it like this. I must know what I've done to hurt her!'

'The same as you've done to me, you hound of Hell!' The strident shriek shrilled from the upper casement. 'You've made my life an endless torment!'

Tom looked upwards in horrified shock.

'Ohhh yes! I'm back in my rightful place, you evil fiend!' Widow Potts was gloating. 'And here I must remain. By the express command of Joseph Blackwell, Esquire.'

Tom took two sideways steps and sank down on to the top bar of the stocks. He buried his face in his hands, and groaned in despair.

TWENTY-SEVEN

Wednesday 17th October.

After he had spent a virtually sleepless night, breakfast for Tom Potts was a lavish portion of overheated recriminatory tongue pie from his mother. This, coupled with his worries about his relationship with Amy Danks, served to destroy any appetite he might have had for actual food.

Unable to bring himself even to reply to Widow Potts' verbal assaults, he silently washed, shaved, cleaned his teeth and left the Lock-up as the first mill and factory bells were ringing the initial warning summons to their work forces.

Opposite the Fox and Goose he came to a halt, racked with uncertainty.

'Shall I go in and see Amy? It'll be full of people now though. What if they mock us both? Perhaps it's best if I go to see her when everyone's gone to work? And Blackwell will be waiting for me to report, won't he? Perhaps it's best all round if I come back later and talk with Amy.'

He walked on, castigating himself for his own cowardice, yet at the same time unable to deny his feeling of relief in postponing what might prove to be a very painful confrontation with the girl he loved.

*   *   *

In the impressive Red House at the top of the Fish Hill, Joseph Blackwell was already at work in his study. As always he listened intently to Tom's lengthy report, making no comments until it was finished. Then he asked, 'This Reverend Carnegie business, what do you make of it, Master Potts?'

Tom answered thoughtfully. 'Well his suicide leaves many questions that need answers, Sir. Such as what has happened to Carnegie's wife? Why didn't she come with him to the Deritend lodging? The identities of his mysterious visitors? His openly consorting with prostitutes?'

Blackwell next asked, 'This seafarer fellow, what of him?'

'I need to find out if he has succeeded in tracing the wagon which collected the children from Brimfield.'

'You will have to do a deal of travelling about so you may have the loan of my younger saddle mare; and since Hollis is still deranged and Bromley is of little use, I shall direct the Vestry this very day to appoint another deputy constable to cover for you during your absences.' He smiled thinly. 'Since hearing Patrick Bull's account of what happened in the Lydd Wood, I've had in mind a most suitable man for the post. All costs of your investigations will be met by the Vestry, my mare including. I bid you good day and good hunting, Constable Potts.'

'Thank you and good day, Sir.'

As Tom turned to leave, Blackwell gestured for him to halt. 'Oh, I was forgetting that I owe you an explanation concerning your lady mother's return to the Lock-up. Unfortunately there was no other choice but to have my man reinstall her in there. Master Mence was expelling her from his premises, and no other lodgings could be found for her at such short notice.

'I trust that as soon as this present investigation is done with, you will make arrangement for a suitable dwelling place for her, should you not be able to reconcile your differences.' Again the thin smile touched his lips. 'Take comfort from the old adage, Constable Potts, that one can choose one's friends, but not one's relatives.'

Outside the house Tom was yet again beset by the quandary of whether he should go to the inn to see Amy, and yet again his courage failed.

'Perhaps it's wisest to leave it a while longer and allow the situation to cool somewhat . . . And anyway it's of the utmost urgency that I try to trace Spicer . . . I'll make the rounds of the wagon owners as quick as I possibly can, and then go to see Amy before I go to Birmingham.'

Drawing what scant comfort he could from that decision, he went to the stables at the rear of the Red House to collect Blackwell's horse.

TWENTY-EIGHT

Wednesday 17th October

B reakfast for the Benton brothers in the kitchen of Judas Benton's pawnbrokers shop on Unicorn Hill was fraught with tension.

'I should never ha' let you talk me into this. I should ha' known that it would end bad. Everything you've ever touched has ended bad. I wish you'd never come back here,' Judas Benton declared glumly for the eighth time in succession.

'For fuck's sakes give it a rest, will you?' Ishmael Benton snapped irritably for the eighth time in answer. 'How many times must I tell you that we've got nothing to worry about?'

'But bloody Potts is sniffin' around, aren't he? And he might look to be a sarft-yedded bastard, but he aren't! Look how quick he was to track Carnegie down.'

'And look what good it's done him!' Ishmael jeered. 'He's found a dead man, and dead men can't tell tales, can they?'

He rose from the table. 'Right, I'm off to Henley first, to finalize the price for the girl. Then I'll collect her from Marlfield and deliver her. Come nightfall we'll have a nice few more of the gold 'uns to play with. It's money for jam.' He ran his tongue over his lips as if savouring a pleasurable taste, and repeated with salacious satisfaction, 'It's money for jam, our kid.'

At the Refuge in the village of Henley-in-Arden, breakfast was interrupted by Mackay coming to inform Charles Hewitt and Henry

Atkins that the subject of the previous day's experimentations had died during the night.

'Goddamn and blast! What rotten luck! We were getting some very promising results with him,' Atkins grumbled more in resignation than anger.

Charles Hewitt was quick to offer comfort. 'Never mind, my love. I'm positive that Benton will bring us good tidings today.'

'Shall I box him up and take him to Samuelson?' asked the dour-featured Mackay.

Hewitt smiled archly at Atkins. 'Shall he, my love?'

The young man shook his head. 'Not yet. I'm going to open him up and pass the fluid directly through the main organs to see what effects it will have on them.'

'But you know how much Samuelson hates them being opened,' Hewitt objected.

Atkins shrugged dismissively. 'Damn Samuelson! We must all make sacrifices in the cause of scientific discovery.' His tone hardened. 'You're displaying an ever-increasing tendency to question my every decision.'

Hewitt made no answer, and Atkins' eyebrows lifted in interrogative challenge.

After brief seconds it was Hewitt who blinked in surrender and muttered, 'I don't mean to do so, my love.'

The younger man smiled benevolently. 'You're a sweetheart, Charlie.' He turned to snap curtly at Mackay. 'Get the box prepared, and make a decent job of it this time, not the usual rubbish you produce!'

Mackay left the room, and Hewitt sighed reproachfully. 'I do declare, my love, that you always speak to poor Mackay as if he were a dog.'

Atkins chuckled amusedly. 'But of course I do, Charles. I can't help but feel that while our own relationship is akin to Romeo and Juliet, our relationship with Mackay is akin to the relationship of Prospero and Miranda with Caliban.'

TWENTY-NINE

I t was afternoon when Tom rode into the yard of Abel Morrall's Needle Works, which stood on the outskirts of the sprawling village of Studley, some three miles southwards from Redditch. In coming here he had crossed the Tardebigge Parish and the county boundary, so could only act as a private citizen. However, Tom had met the Needle Master before, and was confident that he would be willing to answer any queries.

There was a two-horsed, roller-wheeled wagon parked in the yard with two men examining its wheels. Tom recognized Abel Morrall. He was something of an eccentric figure, a man in his sixties who still dressed his hair in the old-fashioned pigtail, and wore the tricorn hat, extra-long waistcoat and full-skirted topcoat of another era.

As Tom came up to them both men turned to look at him.

'Long time no see, Constable Potts. What brings you here? Not brought any sad tidings for me, I hope?' Morrall greeted in a friendly manner.

'No indeed, Master Morrall.' Tom dismounted and the two men shook hands.

Morrall introduced his middle-aged, ruddy-complexioned companion. 'I don't reckon you two knows each other, do you? Well, this is Billy Nokes here, Constable Potts. He's got the wainwright's yard down at Alcester.'

Tom bowed politely. 'I'm honoured to make your acquaintance, Master Nokes.'

'Likewise, Constable Potts.' Billy Nokes grinned. 'I likes to be on friendly terms wi' the constables. You never knows but when you might need their help, does you, them being legal people so to speak.'

'I'm afraid I've no legal powers beyond Tardebigge Parish, Master Nokes.' Tom grinned wryly.

'That's a pity, because you seems to be one o' the good sorts.'
Nokes grinned back. 'I'd best be away then, Abel, if I'm going to
get these wheels proper fettled for you.' He mounted the wagon
seat and drove away.

'What can I do for you, Constable Potts? Have you come to
dun me for me debts?' Morrall smiled jokingly.

'I merely wanted to enquire if you have had a man named
Matthew Spicer call on you recently to enquire about your wagon?
I'm trying to get in touch with him,' Tom explained.

'Aye, there was as a matter o' fact; he called on me the day
afore yesterday. He wanted to know if my wagon had been out
journeying in foreign parts around about the start o' this month.'
Morrall grimaced sourly. 'Chance 'ud be a fine thing.'

'Did he tell you why he was enquiring about this?' Tom asked.

Morrall appeared a little shamefaced. 'Yes, he said he was trying
to trace some pauper kids the wagon was carrying. But to be honest
I was a bit short with him, because that old wagon o' mine was a
pain in the arse to me! There was a bloody jinx on it, so there was!'

'How so?' Tom asked.

'Well I bought it dirt cheap, and it's proved the truth of the old
saying, "You gets what you pays for in this life; and if you buys
dirt cheap, then in the long run you pays filthy dear for it!" There
was trouble with the boards, axles, spokes, felloes, naves, bloody
everywhere. Billy Nokes was forever having to fix it up for me.'

'So was your wagon journeying away around the start of the
month, Master Morrall?' Tom asked.

'No, worse luck for me business!' Morrall spat out disgustedly.
'I'd got rid of it by then. Sold it to Billy for any bits and pieces
he could salvage from it. And trust my rotten luck! Last week I
bought that one that Billy's just took away now, because a couple
o' the wheels has gone a bit wobbly already. I reckon I'd be better
off paying the carriers to do me fetching and sending all the time.'

'Did Spicer mention where he might be heading to next, or
where he was lodging?' Tom asked.

'No, but him and the horse looked very fresh and clean, so I
reckon he was lodging at the Barley Mow, or maybe the Marlboro.'

'My thanks, Master Morrall, I'm much obliged for your help.'
Tom bowed, and after exchanging mutual goodbyes, he remounted
and left.

This had been the final wagon owner on his list, and he was now accepting that it wasn't a locally owned vehicle that had carried the children from Brimfield. He called at the two inns that Morrall had suggested, and at the Barley Mow was told that Spicer had indeed lodged there on the night of Sunday, but had left the following morning.

'There's no point in me continuing to look for him hereabouts. He'll be much further afield by now,' Tom decided. 'I'll head directly to Birmingham and seek out the prostitutes the Reverend had connection with. It's not much of a connection, but it's the only one I have.'

He thought of Amy, and was torn between the desperately poignant longing to see her, and his obsessive compulsion to hunt down the killer (or killers) of the boy, and to find the little girl.

'Every hour that passes gives whoever killed the boy and took the girl more time to cover their tracks. More time to kill again! Amy will understand that I've no other choice.'

With grim determination he turned his mount's head northwards in the direction of the turnpike road to Birmingham.

It took Billy Nokes, with the fresh team and empty wagon, less than an hour to travel the four miles south along the turnpike from Studley to his large wainwright yard in the ancient market town of Alcester, Warwickshire. As he reined in the team and clambered down from the wagon his workman came to talk to him.

'That bloke there wants a word wi' you, Billy.'

The horseman was standing by his mount's head in front of the forge, and smiled pleasantly as Billy Nokes introduced himself.

'I hear that you sometimes deal in and hire out carts and wagons, Master Nokes.'

'Yes, you heard rightly, Master, I do a little bit o' dealing in second-hand carts and wagons sometimes, and sometimes I'll rent one out.' Billy Nokes pointed to an old cart in the corner of his work yard. 'That 'un's available if you'm interested in buying, and I'll do you a fair bargain for it. But now don't you take offence, will you, but the truth is I don't rent out to anybody who I don't know.'

'And very wise too. If the renter made off with the team you'd very quickly be a bankrupt.' Matthew Spicer smiled understandingly and, glancing around the outbuildings, remarked casually, 'I would imagine that the expense of keeping sufficient horses to rent out with the wagons must cost you a pretty penny anyway?'

'Ohhh, I only keeps me own pair.' Nokes grinned. 'Anybody who wants to rent has to supply their own team.'

'Really? You surprise me, Master Nokes!' Spicer exclaimed. 'I would have thought if they could afford to own a large enough team to draw a full loaded roller-wheel, then they would own that same vehicle.'

'That's the usual way of it.' Nokes nodded his head in wry acknowledgement. 'But this business still surprises me on occasion – and I've been in it all me life, and me old faither afore me. Why only last month a bloke from Redditch who scratches about for odd jobs to earn his bread, come in here wi' a triple team of as fine cattle as I've seen for years, and rented a bloody wreck of an old roller-wheeler that I'd just bought for spares. Paid me ten days' rent for it wi'out haggling either, so he did, and a bit extra because I had to rig up a unicorn harness for them, you know, a leader and two wheelers.

'I says to him, "Where in Hell's name did you get these fine cattle, Joey Dowler, and money to burn as well by the looks of it?" And he says to me, "I've found meself a rich widow-woman to work for, Master Nokes, and she wants to wed me."' Nokes gurgled with laughter. 'And I says to him, "Ask her if she's got a rich widow sister who might want to wed me!"'

Spicer joined in the laughter. 'I could do with marrying a rich woman myself, Master Nokes. I shall give some thought to buying your cart and let you know what I decide. Now I have some other business which I must attend to, so I'll bid you good day.'

'You'll find me here, Sir. Unless I find that rich widow in the meantimes.' Still gurgling with laughter, Billy Nokes went back to his workshop.

THIRTY

'Where's Doll?' Enoch Griffiths came bellowing into the kitchen, eyes bloodshot, breath stinking pungently of gin and tobacco.

Sitting opposite each other at the large table, his booted, breeched and smocked younger sisters instantly stopped eating the bowls of stew before them and exchanged nervous looks.

'Well, Sister Deborah? Where is her?' Griffiths scowled.

The women stayed motionless, staring fearfully at each other.

Griffiths stepped behind Deborah, lifted the wide-brimmed slouch hat from her head and dropped it on to the bowl of stew. She flinched and emitted a squeak of fear.

His thick fingers closed around her throat as he bent to whisper hoarsely in her ear. 'Where's Doll, Sister Deborah?'

'Her's with Joey!' It was Delilah who cried out. 'Her's in the hay shed with Joey. But her said we warn't to tell you.'

Her brother's wide-gapped, brown-yellow teeth bared in a snarling grin. 'Now I'm particular gratified that you've give me that information, Sister Delilah. So particular gratified in fact that I'm going to let this one finish her grub . . . After I've pushed a bit o' sense into her thick yed.'

He lifted the hat from the bowl and, using both hands, crammed it hard down on Deborah's head, brutally pressing on it, savagely twisting it from side to side while she whimpered with pain.

'Ohhh! Don't stop! Don't stop!' Doll Griffiths squealed with pleasure, raking her fingernails across Joey Dowler's naked back as he thrust deeper, faster, harder into her sweating body. In the next instant he emitted a shuddering groan, and collapsed upon her gasping for breath.

'God strewth! You'se come already! You'm fuckin' useless, you am!' she shouted angrily.

'Now don't be hard on him, Doll. Not when he's the only man in the kingdom who's able to get a hard-on over you. How much are you paying him this time?' Enoch Griffiths jeered from the doorway at the couple lying in the hay.

The woman was unabashed by his entrance, and spat defiantly, 'Not half as much as you has to pay any woman to even come within ten yards of you.'

'Get off her, Joey,' Griffiths ordered. 'And you bugger off out of here, you ugly cow, afore I kicks your arse.'

Nervously eyeing the other man Joey Dowler obeyed and started to get dressed.

Glaring hatred at her brother, Doll Griffiths gathered her clothing and, still naked, scurried from the shed.

'Her makes me shag her, Enoch! Honest!' Dowler blurted fearfully. 'Her says that she'll tell you a pack o' lies about me pinching stuff from here unless I shags her. Honest her does!'

'Shurrup and listen well,' Enoch Griffiths growled. 'I was down in Studley last night and had a drink in the Barley Mow wi' Abel Morrall. It seems that a bloke named Spicer called on him a few days past making enquiries about if his roller-wheel wagon might have come back from a longish journey round about the beginning o' this month. And if it might have been carrying some Poorhouse kids. Then yesterday afternoon, bloody Tom Potts called on Abel as well and asked him the very same questions as Spicer did.'

'Bloody hell!' Dowler grimaced unhappily. 'What if Potts finds out that we rented a wagon from Billy Nokes? He'll come asking us questions as well, mightn't he?'

'Us?' Griffiths reacted with an exaggerated air of puzzlement. 'What d'you mean, us? It was you who rented it from Nokes, not me. I never went near to Alcester that day, did I? My name was never mentioned, was it?'

'Only because you told me that it hadn't got to be. But we went together to collect the kids, didn't we!' Dowler wailed in protest.

'Well I've got no recollections of going anywhere near to Brimfield, or anywhere else collecting kids.' Griffiths shook his head as if bewildered.

Dowler's bovine features were contorted with strain as his

limited intelligence struggled to comprehend the implications of what was now happening.

Griffiths sighed heavily and shook his head. 'This is a sad mess you're in, my buck. This Spicer bloke's on your tail now, aren't he, and Potts is as well. If you'm arrested by Potts and took back to Brimfield, the Overseer 'ull recognize you, won't he? Because if you remember, it was you he handed the kids over to, warn't it?'

'But you was there as well,' Dowler protested plaintively.

'I was outside the gate sitting on the front of the wagon with me back to him, Joey. I never come near him, did I, and because of me toothache I had me scarf wrapped round me face, didn't I? So nobody who passed could know my face again.' Again Griffiths sighed regretfully and shook his head. 'It sore grieves me to say this, my buck, but this is all your own fault. You didn't bury that kid like I told you to, but shoved him up a hole instead. Now this bloke Spicer and Tom Potts as well am hot on your tail, and you're deep in the shit.'

Dowler appeared near to tears as he pleaded desperately. 'Help me, Enoch. Tell me what to do! You've got to help me!'

'Shurrup and let me think!' Griffiths commanded. He began to pace up and down, head bent, brows furrowed in ostentatious cogitation, lips moving soundlessly.

Dowler's head turned from side to side, keeping his gaze fixed on the other man's face like a dog anxiously waiting for its master's word of command.

After long minutes Griffiths halted and grinned reassuringly. 'Don't worry, Joey, I won't let the hangman put his rope around your neck.'

Dowler's face crumpled and he sobbed with gratitude. 'I know you'll save me, Enoch. I know it.'

'Now shurrup and listen well!' Griffiths snarled, and with a lowered voice issued a series of instructions. While he listened, Dowler's agitation visibly increased.

'Now do exactly as I've told you, Joey, and all will be well. I fuckin' guarantee it! But don't mess up again, or I'll have your fuckin' guts for garters,' Griffiths finished with a threatening scowl.

'I'll do it, Enoch. Honest to God, I'll do it just like you tells me to,' Dowler gabbled and ran from the shed and down the lane towards the Icknield Street.

With a contemptuous snarl Griffiths watched him go. 'By Christ, Joey, you'm becoming a liability now! I'll be well rid of you, and sooner rather than later!'

Ishmael Benton was driving the dog cart into the lane entrance when Dowler burst from it and ran headlong past him. Benton continued up the lane into the farmyard. As he reined in his horse he saw Enoch Griffiths standing frowning in the doorway of the hayshed and called out.

'What's got into Dowler? He's just come haring past me as if all the hounds of Hell was chasing after him!'

'Never mind him! What news have you got for me?' Griffiths demanded sullenly.

'It's very good news, Master Griffiths. I'm come to fetch the girl.'

'How much?'

'Twenty-five!'

'Twenty-five?' Griffiths was visibly surprised.

'Twenty-five it is, and guineas, not sovereigns,' Ishmael Benton announced with preening self-satisfaction. 'Now perhaps you'll appreciate what a very valuable asset I am to you?'

Griffiths' sullenness metamorphosed into welcoming good fellowship and he smilingly confirmed, 'Indeed I'm beginning to, Benton. And to prove my words I'm going to pay you a full ten per cent commission on completion of this particular transaction.'

'That's most generous of you, Master Griffiths. Most generous indeed. I am most grateful to you.' Benton's fulsome words were in sharp contrast to his innermost thoughts.

'Step into the house and take a drink while the girl is made ready for the journey,' Griffiths invited, and then as if in afterthought added casually, 'Who's the buyer, by the way?'

'I'm sorry, Master Griffiths, but the paramount condition of this sale is that he insists on remaining anonymous. I tell you truthfully that I myself don't know his real identity.'

'How can I be sure of that, Benton?' Griffiths was instantly suspicious.

Benton only smiled and calmly pointed out, 'Because if I was trying to gammon you, Master Griffiths, surely I would have told you that the offered price was, say, twelve sovereigns, and that his name was John Smith. I could then very easily have produced a Master John Smith who would have confirmed that identity and paid the money over to the pair of us in company.' He paused momentarily to evaluate the effects of his words, and then gently chided, 'Come, come, Master Griffiths. You must learn to trust me as completely as I trust you if our joint venture is to continue to flourish; and to prove that you can trust me, I've got some information you might be interested in. I gave Thomas Potts a lift into Birmingham yesterday, and guess where he was going to?'

A wary gleam came into the big man's eyes, but he only gestured dismissively.

'Why should I want to know where that bloody beanpole went?'

Ishmael Benton's decayed teeth momentarily bared in a wolfish grin. 'Oh, I'm sure you'll want to know this, Master Griffiths. He went to the old parson's lodgings in Deritend and had a long talk with the landlady, Mrs Bridget O'Toole.'

'That's of no interest to me.' Griffiths shrugged.

'Oh, I wouldn't say that.' Benton winked knowingly. 'I had a long talk with the lady myself, and I found what she had to tell me was of great interest. But it didn't come cheap, if you get my meaning, Master Griffiths. Information always carries a price, don't it?'

The big man came to the side of the gig, smiled and beckoned Benton to lean closer. 'I don't want the girls to hear what we're talking of, Master Benton.'

Benton's decayed teeth showed again, this time in a grin of triumph. He bent closer. 'That's very wise, Master Griffiths; and you may trust me not to overcharge you for the information.'

Griffiths moved with lightning speed, and Benton's eyes bulged as his windpipe was agonizingly clamped by massively strong hands, which dragged him off the gig and smashed him on to the ground.

Griffiths released his grip and straightened to stand hands on hips, waiting for his choking, gasping victim to recover his senses.

When Benton had done so, and was lying nursing his throat and dragging wheezing breaths into his lungs, Griffiths growled menacingly, 'Learn your lesson this time, you little rat, and don't ever try again to keep things from me. Because the next time you upsets me, it will be the last!' He hawked and spat in Benton's face. 'Now spit out that information about Tom Potts that you've got for me; and give me the name and whereabouts of the girl's fuckin' buyer!'

THIRTY-ONE

Birmingham
Saturday 20th October

It was three o'clock in the murky drizzling morning and the vast majority of the great city's industrious and respectable inhabitants were in their beds. The streets were dark and virtually deserted except for the few patrolling watchmen, the occasional shelterless wanderer, furtively scurrying thief, ragged scavenger, and drunken homeward-bound roisterer.

Yet here and there in the fetid narrow alleyways surrounding the Bull Ring market place, talk, laughter and singing still sounded, lights still shone through the cracked, gapped shutters of low-life taverns and brothels.

For several hours Tom Potts had been cautiously exploring this seedy, perilous underworld where disputes and brawls could erupt without warning, and dangers always lurked. He was tense and nervous, but well prepared to deal with any threat to his bodily safety.

On arrival in the city on Wednesday night he had stabled his horse and taken a room at the Albion Coaching Inn on the High Street. Then he had gone out and bought the workman's peaked cap and jacket he was now wearing, and the pair of small pocket pistols now concealed in the inside pockets of the jacket. The next day, Thursday, he had commenced his search.

Tom was following the same pattern of behaviour in each tavern he went into. He bought a pot of ale, and waited to be approached by the prostitutes touting their wares. To his grimly ironic amusement every such encounter so far had followed a similar pattern, despite the differences in the women and girls, and he had so far not found what he was seeking.

In this particular noisy, smoke-filled tavern he bought a drink, moved to stand away from the serving counter and the pattern began repeating yet again.

'Hello, my sweetheart. Are you looking for a bit 'o fun wi' a nice girl like me?' She was an attractive, strapping young woman wearing a tawdry low-cut gown.

'I might be if the price suits.' Tom grinned.

'Well, if you're as long in the prick as in the body, I might do it a bit cheaper for you. Every girl likes to feel a good long 'un inside her. So let's say a shilling for a short timer. Or, just because I likes the look of you, I might consider giving you an all-nighter for five bob. I swear you'll not get a better offer than that anywhere in Brummagem. Just you take a peep at these, and think of how sweet they'll taste when you're sucking them.'

Displaying her unusually fine white teeth in an enticing smile she fleetingly pulled down the top of her gown for him to glimpse her jutting breasts.

Tom had been celibate for a long time, and an involuntary surge of lust now disconcerted his thoughts.

Her experienced eyes noted his reaction and she invited, 'Come on, dearie, let's go to my room and have a nice time.'

By sheer willpower he brought his rampaging imaginings back under control, and managed to reply quietly, 'I'd love to spend the night with you, my pretty, but it will have to be some other time.' He saw the instant anger rise in her at this rejection, and hastened to add, 'But I can offer you the same money you'd earn for an all-nighter, for just a bit of information you might be able to give me.'

'Oh yes, and what might that be?' she questioned suspiciously. 'Because my name's Elsie Page, not fuckin' Polly Peachum! I don't never peach on my mates.'

'I'm not asking you to peach on your mates, Elsie.' Tom was now back in full control of himself. 'I'm only looking for my old master; he's a clerical gentleman, name of Carnegie. The Reverend Alistair Carnegie. I've got some good news for him.'

'Oh yes, and what might that be?' she asked with an equal degree of suspicion.

'I can't tell you that, Elsie, it's private between him and my present master, Reverend the Lord Aston. They're very old friends.'

She stared at him speculatively, and for the first time in this search Tom experienced an unbidden intuitive flash of certainty. *She knows something!*

He forced himself to stay silent, and to display nothing of what he was feeling. He lifted the pot of ale to his lips and drank a couple of mouthfuls, then turned away from her and went to the counter to ask the bartender, 'Give me a pipe, will you?'

'That's tuppence.'

Tom gave him the two copper coins and in return received a short clay pipe already filled with tobacco. The barman lit the pipe with a flaming taper and, puffing clouds of acrid-tasting smoke, Tom returned to stand facing the young woman.

'You knows my name, dearie, now tell me yours,' she asked.

'I'm Tom.'

'Tom what?'

'Tom Potts.'

'Well then, Tom Potts, what's what I might know worth to you?'

'If you can tell me where he is, and I find he's really there, I'll give you the five bob.'

'Well, I know the bloke you're looking for.'

'How do you know he's the man I'm after?'

'We gets parsons coming here regular looking for women, but not one particular woman, like he did.' She grinned contemptuously. 'And the fuckin' parsons who come here looking for a shag don't never wear their churchgoing clothes neither, like he did. So just for curiosity I followed him one night all the way back to Deritend, and saw him go into a house there. So I asked around the neighbours and found out his name was Carnegie, and that he was a proper parson.'

Tom only shrugged carelessly. 'I expect you thought that you might get a few sovs out of him if you told him that you knew where he lived, and was thinking of telling his neighbours what he was getting up to at nights.'

She took no offence at his suggestion and merely shook her head dismissively. 'No, the blackmail has never been one o' my games. But I talked very civil with him a few times after I knew his name, and he was always good enough to slip me a couple o' bob if I was in need. But the last time I met him he told me that he was leaving Brummagem for good, and I aren't seen him since.'

'That's a shame for you,' Tom commiserated. 'And it's a shame for me, because I would have gladly paid you the five bob if you'd known where he is now.'

'Well I can tell you where to find the woman who he used to come to see. We calls her the Duchess,' she offered. 'That's worth summat, surely?'

'I'll tell you what I'll do, Elsie,' Tom counter-offered. 'You take me to her, and I'll give you a couple of bob. Do we have a bargain?'

'Alright.' Elsie nodded agreement, and her fine teeth gleamed as she laughed. 'You might find that you knows her already. I've often wondered if she's his missus!'

Excitement coursed through Tom, but he only said casually, 'It's been a good few years since I last saw Mrs Carnegie. I expect she's changed a great deal in her looks. People do, don't they?'

'Well women can hide their faces, can't they? Like the Duchess wearing a black veil every time her went out. That's what I'll do if I ever gets old and ugly like her.' Elsie laughed.

Tom's excitement intensified. The woman who took the girl from the Tardebigge Poorhouse had worn a thick black veil, and had the manners of a Gentlewoman. Had he succeeded in running Mrs Adelaide Carnegie to earth?

'Let's go then, Elsie, and see the Duchess.'

'Oh, we can't see her now. You meet me here Sunday night and I'll take you there then.'

'But I need to see her urgently,' he protested.

'Well you'll have to wait 'til tomorrow,' she reiterated. 'One o' my regulars has just come in, and I've got me living to earn.'

'I'll pay you double,' he pressed her. 'A full four shillings.'

'Be told, will you! Meet me here Sunday night,' she snapped irritably, and flounced away to begin talking animatedly with a man who had just entered the room. Within scant minutes she and the man had left together, and Tom was forced to accept that he would have to wait until Sunday night to meet the Duchess. That acceptance brought with it the realization of his own need for sleep and he laid the half full pot of ale and unfinished pipe on the counter.

'Be yow leaving 'um, Cully? Can we have 'um?' asked one of a group of noisy youths, all dressed in the garishly styled coats and the 'Look Lively' stiff-peaked caps of the latest flash fashion.

Tom nodded and went out into the darkness of the alley, walked a few yards in the direction of the Bull Ring, heard the brief outburst of noise from the tavern as its door opened and closed and the multi-footsteps coming after him. Pulling the pistols from his pockets he stopped and, heart pounding, turned to face them shouting, 'Get back or I'll shoot!'

'Get stuck into the cunt, he's got fuck all!' one of the pursuers jeered.

The blast of the pistol resounded off the grimy walls as the lead ball smashed against the brickwork.

'Fuckin' 'ell! He's got barkers!' the same voice screamed out.

The multi footsteps abruptly retreated, and Tom turned and ran headlong towards the Bull Ring.

When finally he slowed and halted outside the Albion Inn on the corner of the High Street he was panting heavily, sweat streaming down his face and body. He slumped with his back against the wall, and waited for his thudding heartbeat to slow and his juddering nerves to steady.

As they did so another completely different emotion overlaid all others he had experienced that night: a sensation of totally exhilarating elation.

'Bloody Hell!' He could only shake his head and marvel at it. 'Why do I feel so wonderfully joyful? So abso-bloody-lutely, wonderfully joyful!'

THIRTY-TWO

Redditch
Mid-morning, Saturday 20th October

Outside the door of the Lock-up Charles Bromley, the middle-aged, pot-bellied, Tardebigge Parish Deputy Constable and sole proprietor of Bromley's Stationery Emporium for All Articles of Stationery, Rare and Antique Books and New Literature, took off his crumpled top hat and mopped his pink bald pate with a grubby handkerchief.

'A moment, Master Bint, I beg of you. Allow me to catch my breath,' he beseeched mellifluously, his eyes alarmingly magnified by his bulbous-lensed spectacles, his ill-fitting bone false teeth slipping up and down as he spoke.

He carefully stretched and plastered long strands of greasy grey hair across his pate, replaced his hat, and brushed the dust from his threadbare clothing with his pudgy hands, before going on.

'Your appointment has come as a great shock to me.'

'It come as a bloody-sight greater shock to me, Charley Bromley!' Ritchie Bint declared disgustedly. 'My old dad must be turning in his grave this very minute.'

'Your father has doubtless been turning in his grave ever since your wickedness drove him to it!' Widow Potts shouted down from her window. 'It's a disgrace that such a rogue as you should have been appointed as a constable. The Vestry have all gone mad! That's the only explanation I can think of!'

'Oh, my dearest one, pray don't upset yourself so,' Bromley anxiously beseeched his wife-to-be. 'I'm sure that Master Bint will prove to be a most diligent and worthy holder of his office.'

'Indeed so, Master Bromley.' A smiling John Clayton came walking towards them. 'Is it not a proven fact that reformed poachers make the best gamekeepers?'

'I've heard such, Parson Clayton. I trust I find you well?' Bromley bowed to this welcome ally.

'I am very well, I thank you.' Clayton returned the bow and then called up to the widow. 'Have you received any word from Tom, Ma'am?'

'Received word from Thomas Potts?' She angrily spat the question and its answer back at him. 'Of course not! He's the worst son in Christendom and his cruel, vicious neglect of me is driving me to an early grave, and that grave will be a merciful refuge for me, I do assure you. I feel eager to go to it this very moment!'

She slammed the window shut, and Ritchie Bint anxiously urged Charles Bromley, 'You'd best run up quick to her, Charley boy, cos she could be doing herself an injury this very second.'

'Oh my God!' Bromley gasped in horror and scurried into the Lock-up, shouting, 'Calm yourself, dearest one, I'm coming! I'm coming!'

'That was very wicked of you, Master Bint.' John Clayton chuckled.

Despite the Needle Pointers' notoriety as hard-drinking, brawling, poaching reprobates, Clayton admired their physical courage and their demonstrable contempt for death, and knowing that despite his fearsome reputation, Bint was at base a good-hearted, straight-dealing man, he had both respect and liking for him. Clayton was also prepared to hazard a shrewd guess that it was Bint who had informed Tom Potts about the dead child in the Lydd Wood. Now he couldn't resist teasing the pointer.

'It seems a long time since we enjoyed a decent badger-baiting in the town, Master Bint.'

Bint roared with laughter. 'I blames that noble Gentleman who lives up in Hewell Grange for that, Parson. He likes to keep all creatures great and small for the pleasures of just himself and his lordly friends. Even though God put fishes, birds and beasts on the earth for everybody to share in. You ought to preach a sermon against such greed and selfishness.'

'If I ever inherit a fortune, then I will most certainly do that. But until such a miracle occurs, I am regretfully in no financial condition to challenge those whom the Good Lord has set to rule over me,' Clayton admitted wryly, then requested, 'If you should meet with Tom Potts before I do, would you please tell him that I urgently need to speak with him? Impress upon him that I want him to come directly to seek me out the very moment he returns.'

'I'll do that, Parson, there's my word on it,' Bint promised, and in his turn said wryly, 'And now I've got to collect my constable's staff from inside, and make my first patrol of the market. Thank God most of my mates 'ull be at their work, so my shame won't be seen by them 'til later.'

John Clayton laughed, but as he walked away his amusement was overlaid by his concern for Tom Potts.

'Poor Tom, how are you going to receive the news that Amy Danks has this very morning cancelled my third calling of your Banns?'

THIRTY-THREE

Tardebigge Vicarage
Saturday evening, 20th October

The Right Honourable and Reverend Walter Hutchinson, Lord Aston, Vicar of Tardebigge Parish, Justice of the Peace for the County of Worcestershire, exuded the pomposity of self-importance to match his immense girth.

Now as flames leapt in the ornate marble fireplace, and in each of the twin candelabras on the table six tall wax candles burned, adding even more heat to the already excessively heated room, Aston sat at the head of the long dining table noisily chewing his supper of broiled pigeons and capons washed down with copious draughts of claret. His fat purple face glistened with sweat as at frequent intervals he laid down his knife and fork and mopped his face and bulging jowls with the voluminous napkin that was covering the vast expanse of his chest and belly.

Seated facing him at the bottom end of the table, Joseph Blackwell Esq. was speaking in measured, concise sentences. '. . . And so, my Lord, despite his injury our constable is now fully engaged upon the investigation into this unfortunate child's death, and I have given him full leave to go wherever he needs to pursue his enquiries. I've also appointed a new deputy constable, Richard Bint. He's a noted pugilist and well able to give a hiding to any troublemaker.' Blackwell waited for his de facto employer's reaction.

Aston lifted the decanter and emptied the last few drops of wine into his glass, glared drunkenly at the empty container, then bellowed furiously, 'Damn you, Webster, where the devil are you skulking, you idle hound? I need another bottle.'

His bent-bodied, smock-clad old manservant limped into the room carrying a full decanter of wine, which he plonked heavily down before Aston.

'By God, I could have died of thirst waiting for you to move yourself. You useless creaky old bag of bones.' Aston scowled.

'Humph!' the old man snorted indignantly. 'There's no fear o' that happening, is there, Vicar? You'se already took aboard enough grog to sink a three-decker.'

'Don't you use that tone towards me, you insolent villain. Or by God I'll make you sting for it,' Aston bellowed, and snatching the short-queued clerical tie-wig from his shaven head he hurled it at the old man's face. Webster instantly ducked, and the tie-wig sailed across the room to land directly upon the fire, where it puffed and flared into flames.

'Har har har!' the old man cackled derisively. 'That's another 'un you've chucked on the bloody fire aren't it! What a waste o' money!'

'Blast you, Webster! I'll break your damned head for you, blast you!' Aston tried fruitlessly to lever his huge bulk from the wooden armed chair it was crammed in.

Still cackling with derisive laughter the manservant scuttled from the room.

'Damn and blast that insolent old bastard's eyes!' Aston ranted furiously. 'I'll have him thrashed and sent to the damned Poorhouse, I'm damned and thrice damned if I don't!'

Eventually Aston abandoned his struggle to get to his feet and subsided into the chair, causing it to creak as it took his weight once more. He gulped down two more glasses of wine in quick succession, emitted a long loud belch and shouted, 'Damn you, Webster! Where's my pipe, you idle old dog?'

Within seconds the manservant entered with a large silver tray on which were laid long-stemmed clay pipes, small silver bowls of tobacco and a sheaf of spill-tapers.

'Here you be, Vicar. That be Virginia, that be Eye-giptian, that 'uns Turkeyland, and I'm bollixed if I can bring to mind what that other 'un is. But you'se drunk too much grog to know any different anyway. Now does you want me to prepare a couple o' pipes for you, or not? Make your mind up quick because I'se got me chores to do and can't be wasting time buggering about wi' you.'

'Get out of my sight, you stink-skinned old wretch!' Aston snatched up a tobacco bowl and hurled it.

Webster skipped spryly aside, the bowl smashed into the wall scattering the expensive tobacco and with another derisive cackle Webster scuttled from the room.

'He'll be laughing on the other side of his ugly face when I kick him into the Poorhouse tomorrow,' Aston threatened, and with podgy fumbling hands filled a pipe and lit it.

A smile hovered on Joseph Blackwell's thin lips as he waited for the other man's drunken tantrum to pass. He always drew much ironic amusement from this bizarre relationship between master and manservant.

The physical act of puffing out clouds of savoury-scented smoke appeared to soothe Aston's choleric drunken temper but when he spoke his slurred tone still held a spiteful edge.

'I've had other visitors before you, Master Blackwell. So I know that that lanky gangly clown whom you're so fond of received his injury when he was put on his arse by a damned lunatic, and is the laughing stock of the parish yet again.'

'That may well be so, my Lord,' Blackwell replied evenly. 'But the fact should not be overlooked that many of those who now rush to mock Thomas Potts were rushing to cheer him on occasions in the past. You yourself have also publicly praised him highly if my memory serves me.'

Aston grunted sourly and after a somewhat strained silence between them proffered a verbal olive branch.

'I am prepared to concede that there has been the odd occasion when he has not made a complete fool of himself.'

'Just so, my Lord,' Blackwell accepted the peace offer.

Aston's expression became one of glowering resentment. 'Now, Master Blackwell, let me come to the reason why I've sent for you to come here at such short notice. The Earl returned from London yesterday, and this afternoon he sent a footman to summon me to the Grange. To summon me to come post-haste! Summoning me as if I were his lackey. Me! The Lord Aston! Whose ancestors were Armigers when his family were muck-stinking cowherds!'

With an effort Aston controlled his anger, and continued acidly, 'Apparently the noble Earl has questioned all his servants and is convinced that Potts' informant was one of the scum who poached his badgers. He insists that this poacher and his accomplices must be brought to book.'

'I fully understand the Earl's justified anger in regard to the poaching of his badgers, my Lord, but unless we continue to grant anonymity to informants, such as the man in question, then I fear we shall forfeit a great amount of useful information.'

'I know full well, Master Blackwell, that guarding the anonymity of our informers is of paramount importance in the enforcement of law and order. But the Earl is adamant that he will not be gainsaid on this occasion.'

Aston assumed that that was the end of the matter, but Blackwell did not accept it and persisted.

'In this particular case, my Lord, Potts seems fully persuaded that this informant behaved as a Good Samaritan by bringing the dreadful fate of this poor child to our attention. In fact I fear he will simply refuse to name the fellow.'

'Refuse? Potts will refuse?' Aston's eyes bulged in total astonishment, then he roared in anger. 'He can't refuse me! I'll have the lanky bastard's guts for garters if he dares to refuse. I'll have him rotting in Worcester Jail for the rest of his days if he dares say nay to me!'

Blackwell's pale, deep-lined features remained impassive, betraying none of the deep concern he was feeling at this turn of events. He knew that Aston – whose power and influence throughout the county was second only to its greatest landowner, the Earl of Plymouth – was perfectly capable of acting mercilessly when crossed, and could make this threat a reality.

Blackwell exercised a degree of mental dominance over Aston, and now he prepared to exert it in order to protect Tom Potts. When Aston's roaring subsided into aggrieved mutterings, he ventured, 'My Lord, with your permission may I respectfully make a suggestion?'

'You may,' Aston grunted.

'Thank you, my Lord.' Blackwell inclined his head submissively. 'The salient fact is that the vast majority of the law-abiding inhabitants of this Parish are horrified by the discovery of this child. They applaud the action of this informant in coming forward as he did. What I want to say now may rouse your anger, my Lord, yet I must somehow find the courage to speak out.'

Blackwell made a mock show of nervous indecision, staying silent until Aston urged impatiently, 'Speak out, man! I'll not bite you!'

With the facial expression of a condemned man on a gallows,

Blackwell hesitantly obeyed. 'The truth of the matter is, my Lord, that in this Parish the people hold you in much higher esteem than they do the Earl. They know well that you are of infinitely superior intellect to the Earl. In their eyes you are the rightful ruler here, and not the Earl. It is you that they trust to uphold the law and dispense true justice.'

As Aston visibly preened, Blackwell inwardly smiled with contempt. *I have you now, you conceited drunken ninny.*

Aloud he continued, 'As you rightly say, my Lord, Thomas Potts is undoubtedly a lanky, gangly clown, but nevertheless have there not been occasions when he has proven to be a most diligent and effective investigator of crimes?'

The other man nodded a grudging acceptance.

Blackwell also nodded. 'I am grateful that you should give me such a timely reminder of those occasions, my Lord.'

Aston gulped his glass empty, belched and reached for the bottle, but clumsily knocked it over so that its contents spilled across the table. He stared owlishly at the spreading puddle of wine and bawled, 'Bring me a drink, you stink-skinned old wretch!'

Webster was there almost immediately, slamming two uncorked bottles on to the table, chortling derisively. 'Let's see if you can manage to pour these all over the table. This is how a glass gets filled, Vicar, and even a scabby babby could manage to do it.'

As he poured wine into Aston's glass Webster stared questioningly at Blackwell, who answered with a barely perceptible nod. Webster moved to stand behind his employer's chair and silently mouthed an emphatic assent to Blackwell.

Blackwell waited until Aston had drained this new-filled glass and Webster had refilled it yet again, then enthusiastically praised, 'This is an excellent plan, my Lord! I will make bold enough to congratulate you on your remarkable percipience. Unlike myself you have recognized that here we are presented with a golden opportunity to rid your Parish of miscreants, and most impressively of all, to be able to do so with the applause of even their fellow slum rats.'

'Plan? Miscreants? Fellow slum rats?' Aston blinked in befuddlement.

'It's a master stroke to allow Potts to concentrate firstly on solving the matter of the dead child, and lull his informant and the rest of the scum who poached the Earl's badgers into believing they have got away scot-free.'

'Master stroke?' Aston hiccupped.

'A master stroke indeed, my Lord.' Blackwell's voice throbbed with admiration. 'May I congratulate you on it!'

Still not comprehending what was happening here, Aston demurred modestly. 'I would not wish to claim any unearned plaudits, Master Blackwell.'

Blackwell got to his feet and declared warmly, 'These plaudits are well deserved, my Lord. When the killer of that poor child is apprehended the entire county will ring with your praises for having the moral courage to stand against the Earl and set the value of an innocent child's life above that of mere badgers. So, as you advise, I shall instruct Potts that he is not to identify his informant at this time. Instead he is to concentrate on investigating the death of the child.

'It's a superb plan, my Lord! It will demonstrate to the world that you are not the man to let any over-proud Johnny-come-lately ride roughshod over the heartfelt wishes of God-fearing, hard working, law-abiding people.'

Aston slammed his fist down upon the table and slurred drunkenly, 'By God, you're right! The over-proud puppy dog will find that I'm not a man to be trifled with. He'll sorely rue the day that he dared to treat my lineage with such contempt.'

Blackwell clapped his hands in applause. 'Indeed he will, my Lord! As have so many other upstart puppy dogs during your years of ruling this parish. And now, if you will excuse me, I must bid you a good night, my Lord.'

Aston waved to him in gracious farewell, then bawled at the top of his voice, 'Damn your stinking hide, Webster! Pour me a drink, you idle old dog.'

With a satisfied smile curving his thin lips, Joseph Blackwell left the house. Outside the door he took a gold sovereign from his purse and placed it under the shrub from where Webster would retrieve it later.

In the house Aston blinked owlishly. 'I'm damned if I can entirely recall that conversation. What did I just agree to with Blackwell?'

'Don't you moither about that now, Vicar.' Webster grinned. 'You just swig your wine, and I'll tell you all about it tomorrow.'

THIRTY-FOUR

Late night, Sunday 21st October

Before leaving his room at the inn Tom Potts carefully primed and loaded his pistols, at the same time fervently hoping that there would be no necessity to fire them. He had no wish to kill or maim, but grimly accepted that if the first shot against the wall had not stopped his assailants, then he would have been forced to shoot to kill with his second pistol.

Although it was close to midnight and the Sabbath worshippers and strollers had long since gone to their rest, the streets were thronged with incoming carts and wagons bringing the multi-commodities which fed the insatiable varied appetites of the city. Long before tomorrow's dawn tens of thousands of men, women and children would come swarming out from their homes, furnaces would be roaring, tall chimneys belching smoke, hammers and anvils ringing, machinery stamping and grinding to produce the wealth that fuelled the nation.

When he reached the entrance to the narrow alley that led off from the Bull Ring, Tom's footsteps slowed and halted. He was dreading the prospect of another confrontation with the gang who had chased him the previous night. Once, twice, three times he took a couple of steps into the alley, and each time backed out again as his nerve failed him.

'God damn me for being such a coward!' His stomach felt as if it were tight-knotted, and a chill of sweat oozed from his pores.

He forced himself to visualize the ravaged body of the dead child.

'If I don't get justice for him, then who will?'

His father's face rose vividly into his mind, and he whispered aloud, 'I'll not dishonour your name by running away from this.'

He felt the outlines of the pistols in his inner coat pockets and resolved grimly, 'If that gang comes at me again, then so be it.'

He stepped into the alleyway and this time kept walking steadily forwards until he reached the tavern door. There he paused, sucked in a long deep breath and, summoning all his determination, pushed the door wide and entered the noise, smoke and smells. There was a momentary lessening of the noise as curious eyes examined the newcomer. Tom's own eyes were darting around the crowded room as he moved to the serving counter. As he reached it Elsie appeared at his side and, smiling tipsily, linked her arm with his. 'I've heard that you're a flummot cove, who's a dab hand with the barkers.'

He grimaced in puzzlement. 'What do you mean?'

'Oh, come on now, Tom, you don't need to act the green yokel any more,' she mock-chided. 'You really put the shits up them flash ramps men. They wasn't planning on bludging a flummot cove wi' a brace o' barkers up his sleeve.' She beckoned to the bartender. 'I'll have a gin, and my Gentleman here will have whatever he fancies having.'

'A pot of ale, if you please,' Tom ordered.

'I do please; and it's my pleasure to serve you, Cully.' The bartender grinned admiringly. 'Those young bastards needed having the shits put up 'um. They was getting too cocky by far, they was.'

As the drinks were served Elsie declared, 'Do you know summat, I've always reckoned that I can read a man's character in the first minute that I meets him. But you really had me fooled, you did. I never took you for a flummot cove.'

'What does that mean? "Flummot cove" and those other terms you use?' Tom questioned once more.

'It's our cant, Tom. Bludging is battering and robbing somebody, and rampsmen are the coves who does it. A flummot cove is a dangerous man; and you must know what a "brace o' barkers" is, surely?'

Tom nodded. 'A pair of pistols.'

'Hurrah for you.' She laughed. 'Well that lot last night are rampsmen, and it's always four or five of them bludging some poor soul who can't fight back. I've known the gutless bastards even strip women of everything they've got, and then kick the poor cows half to death just out o' badness.'

She lifted her glass of gin and toasted Tom. 'So here's good health and long life to you, my flummot friend.'

Tom waited until she had emptied the glass before urging, 'I need to get on with this business, Elsie. Will you please take me to see the Duchess now?'

She lifted her hand in front of his eyes and rubbed her fingers and thumb together.

'Don't worry, you'll get your money as soon as I meet the Duchess,' Tom assured her.

She grinned cheekily. 'I'd sooner have it now, because if you won't pay me when you sees her, then how can I ever get it off a flummot cove like you?'

'Here.' He gave her a silver shilling. 'You'll get the other half when I've seen her.'

'But that 'ull still be only two bob. You promised to give me four bob last night.' She pushed the shilling back into his hand. 'I don't trust you now.'

Tom came to an instant decision to call her bluff. 'Alright then, Elsie. There's no more to be said.'

He put his pot on the counter and walked out of the tavern. He had taken only a few steps when the tavern door slammed and Elsie came running after him, shouting, 'I was only having a bit o' sport wi' you. There's no need for you to get so arsey wi' me. I'll take you to her now.'

He kept his expression grim. 'Lead on then, and let's have no more of your nonsense. You'll get your money.'

She guided him through a maze of blackly shadowed, stench-filled passages and alleyways thickly strewn with faecal waste and rotting rubbish. Tom surreptitiously transferred his pistols to the outer pockets of his coat and kept his hands on their butts.

'This is it.' She halted by a narrow black-shadowed passage entrance. 'Stay here, I'll not be two ticks.'

She disappeared into the black passage and Tom heard her knocking on a door and calling her name. A speck of light glowed briefly, bolts clunked, and a door opened to illume the short passageway with lamplight.

Elsie spoke rapidly to the man silhouetted in the doorway, then called softly, 'Come on, Flummot. Be quick now!'

'It'll cost you a tanner to see her, Master.' The man held his hand out as Tom joined them.

'Pay him quick and let's get inside,' Elsie hissed. 'We can't be caught hanging about in this fuckin' doorway at this hour.'

The man bit the coin and pocketed it, jerked his head for them to go past him, and as they did so quickly shut and bolted the door.

Tom stood stock-still with shock, his nostrils, mouth and throat filled with the mingled stenches of rotting flesh and vinegar: the sick, cloying, acrid reeks of a charnel house, where on one side of the long room a row of shrouded corpses rested on raised stone slabs, each corpse's feet protruding from the shroud with an identifying label tied to dangle from their big toes.

'Why didn't you tell me she was dead?' He rounded angrily on Elsie, who was standing pressing a handkerchief to her nose and mouth.

'I thought you knew she was!' Her words were muffled by the cloth.

'D'you want to look at her, or not?' the mortuary porter grunted impatiently. 'I aren't got all fuckin' night to waste.'

Tom took a grip on his temper and nodded.

The porter led him to the far end of the row and roughly stripped the shroud from a woman's shaven-headed, naked, emaciated body, with a stitched-up dissection wound running the length of its torso. 'This is her. Brought in Thursday, her was.'

Elsie came to Tom's side and exclaimed, 'See, that's why she always wore a veil. The pox has ate her nose away.'

Tom stared down at the raw stump of flesh in the centre of the dead woman's face and grimaced sympathetically. 'Yes, it looks to be the syphilis right enough.' He studied the gaping longitudinal slash in her throat. 'I can't believe that's her own handiwork.'

'No, that's what the sawbones did,' the porter informed. 'They wanted to see how the opium ball was stuck.'

'Ball of opium?' Tom queried.

'Look, you can see it! The ball's still in there,' Elsie put in excitedly and pointed into the slash. 'She swallowed it right down into her gullet and choked herself to death. Chinky Chong, who keeps the opium den, found her laying dead in the alleyway close to his house.'

'Look, you got to go now!' the porter chivvied them.

'Wait a moment.' Tom acted on impulse. 'What about her clothes or any other of her belongings? Do you have them here?'

'What's that to you?' The porter scowled.

'I'll pay a tanner for a quick look through them,' Tom offered.

The porter bit and pocketed the coin. Left the room through an inner door to return within seconds carrying a bundle of women's clothing.

Tom quickly sorted through the costly but now odorously soiled articles, some of which bore the inside name tag of Adelaide Carnegie. There was one badly stained silken handkerchief which bore the clumsily stitched, embroidered inscription: 'To my Mamma. From Martin.'

'So there was a child, a boy. Where might he be now?' Tom wondered, and asked aloud, 'Have there been any gentlefolk come here to see her?'

The porter's broken, blackened teeth bared in a snarling grin. 'There's always gentlefolk coming here to view the dead 'uns. Treats it like a regular peep show, they does. That's why my boss took the stitches back out of her neck, so he could show the gentry folks the ball of opium in it. They pays my boss to let 'um in, and he gets a bit more rhino from 'um if he's got summat a bit out o' the ordinary to show off, like this 'un. The tight bastard ne'er gives me a brass farthing of it. He got a good price for this 'un's hair as well, but it's me who always has to shave 'um off. Anyway come on, you've got to go in case he comes. He's always sneaking in here to try and catch me making a bit o' rhino for meself.'

Out in the alleyways once more, Tom and Elsie walked side by side, each engrossed in their own thoughts until Tom broke the silence.

'Where can I find this Chinky Chong you talked of?'

'You aren't paid me for the Duchess yet,' she rejoined. 'And Chinky Chong 'ull cost you extra.'

Tom pulled the few remaining coins from his pocket. He'd paid in advance for his room and stabling at the Albion Inn, and now had just six shillings and five pence halfpenny. He showed her the coins.

'Listen, Elsie, this is all the money I've got left.'

'Well it aren't nearly enough for the Duchess and Chinky Chong both. So pay me what you owes me, and we'll part company.'

Tom tried to bluff once more. 'What's to stop me walking away now, and not giving you a single penny?' he challenged.

She smiled knowingly and slowly shook her head. 'You won't do that, Tom Potts. If there's one thing that I've learned all about, then it's men who likes knocking women about. You might be a flummot cove when somebody has a go at you, but I'll stake my life that you've never served any woman badly.'

Tom sighed in resignation and handed her all the remaining coins. 'Here, I'm giving you all I've got as a token of goodwill.'

'I told you I know all about men, didn't I? I knew from the first time I talked to you that you're a good soul.' She crowed triumphantly. 'And because you've treated me kindly I'm going to do you a favour in return. I'll take you to see Chinky Chong and it won't cost you a penny more. Wait here for me while I go and ask him if it's alright to bring you there. I'll not be long.'

When Elsie ushered Tom into the luxuriously furnished, incense-scented room, the shaven-headed, fashionably dressed Chinaman smiled and bowed in greeting.

'I am Chong, Sir. I am honoured to receive you to my humble house.'

Tom returned the bow. 'I thank you, Sir.'

'Miss Elsie has told me that you were desirous of asking me about the Duchess, who Miss Elsie says was well known by you?' Chong sought confirmation.

Tom made another instant decision to use bluff. 'That is so. But whether the lady would have recognized me on sight, I can't say. It's been many years since we last met.'

The Chinaman's gaze pointedly travelled from Tom's face to feet and back up to his face. 'With all respect, Sir, I have to venture the opinion that anyone who has met a gentleman of your quite exceptional height would not quickly forget him.'

'Can you tell me what you knew of the lady?' Tom asked.

'Very little that will be of help to you, I fear.' Chong's tone was apologetic. 'You see I cater to a very select clientele, and because they are people of wealth and power I have to respect their desire for anonymity. I knew her solely as the Duchess.' He paused and then again sought for confirmation. 'But Miss Elsie tells me that you knew her as a Mrs Adelaide Carnegie and you were once in service with her husband, the Reverend Alistair Carnegie?'

'That is so,' Tom confirmed.

'And you are seeking for the Reverend Carnegie because you have good tidings for him? That is most interesting.' Chong's head bobbed several times in rapid succession. 'I only wish I could assist you in your quest for him, Sir. All I can tell you however is that when the lady I knew as the Duchess became ill and fell on hard times I took pity on her, and occasionally gave her food and shelter in my kitchen.'

'I beg you not to take offence, Sir, at my asking if you also gave her the ball of opium she choked on?' Tom tentatively requested.

'I take no offence, Sir,' Chong replied equably. 'The answer is, I did not give it to her, she stole it from me. Supplying opium is my livelihood, not my charity. But I did not know that she had choked on a ball of opium. As I told you, she had been in ill health for some considerable time, and when I found her dead I naturally assumed that she had been struck down by apoplexy or whatever. I immediately sent for the Night Watch to come, and they removed her to the mortuary.'

He smilingly bobbed his head. 'That is the sum total of my knowledge of the Duchess, Sir. And now I have other matters to attend to, so if you'll excuse me . . .'

'Of course, Sir. Thank you very much for your courteous reception of my enquiries,' Tom told him sincerely, and took his leave accompanied by Elsie.

Frowning in thought, Chong went upstairs and entered a small room where the fumes of burned opium thickened the air and a snoring, comatose man lay face upwards on a divan couch, his glazed eyes staring blankly at the ceiling.

The Chinaman scowled and hissed sibilantly. 'When you have recovered your senses, Master Griffiths, you and I will be having a discussion about a gentleman named Thomas Potts.'

Outside in the alley Elsie invited Tom, 'Come and stay the night with me, Flummot. I've taken a fancy to you, so it won't cost you a penny.'

He was genuinely touched by her offer, but could only refuse gently. 'I can't stay with you, Elsie. I like you very much and truly think you to be beautiful; but I'm in love with a girl, and we are to be wed. Our third Banns were called this very Sunday, in fact, so hopefully we will marry before this month ends.'

Elsie's immediate reaction was a snort of disbelief. 'You're turning down a freebie wi' me?' Followed by a furious accusation. 'You must be a fuckin' dollymop who only shags wi' men!' Then she stormed away, screeching, 'I only offered because I felt sorry for you. You fuckin' ugly lanky freak!'

Tom could only sigh regretfully at the manner of their parting as he watched her disappear into the night.

THIRTY-FIVE

Afternoon, Monday 22nd October

With his mount at a walk Tom made slow progress back to Redditch, mentally grappling with the problem of how he could make any further progress in the search for the missing girl, and for the killer of the dead boy, now that his only leads had been blocked.

A sense of frustration was tormenting Tom. He had known many other instances of husband and wife both dying within days or weeks of each other – and there were blatantly obvious reasons for the Carnegies' deaths: the woman's sufferings with the syphilis, her husband's suicide because of his heartbreak at seeing his wife in such a miserably degraded condition.

'And yet? And yet? It's just a little too much of a coincidence for me to accept entirely. There are too many questions left unanswered.'

When he reached the padlocked northern tollgate of Redditch and rang its bell an old crone came hobbling from the tollgate cottage.

'Hello, Granny Lock, I've no money with me but I'll come back directly and pay you.'

As she removed the padlock and opened the gate she peered at him with sympathy in her rheumy eyes. 'The Trust won't miss four pence, Master Potts, so you can pass through for nothing today. I was real sorry to hear your bad news. That girl must be mad to cast off a nice man like you be.'

'What?' He stared at her in puzzlement.

'Me granddaughter, Maisie, told me yesterday. I said to her, that girl must be mad to cast off a nice man like you, so I did.'

'What did Maisie tell you, Granny Lock?' Tom's mouth was drying with apprehension.

'Her told me about Amy Danks stopping your Banns being called. I said to her, that girl must be mad, so I did.'

She was speaking to his receding back as he kicked his horse to a gallop. He dismounted at the Fox and Goose, tied the reins to one of the hitching rings in its wall, and rushed inside calling for Amy.

Gertrude Fowkes came frowning out from the rear parlour closely followed by her daughter and Maisie Lock.

'It's no use you shouting and bawling for Amy, Master Potts. Her don't want to see you,' Gertrude Fowkes informed him frostily.

'Well where is she?' he demanded anxiously.

'Her's in my parlour, and she's told me to send you packing, and to bar you from this house. And for the little amount of money you passes across our counters, you'll be no great loss to our trade. So be off with you!'

'I'm not going anywhere until I've spoken with Amy,' he replied, and stepped to go round her towards the parlour.

'You shan't pass. Help me stop him, girls!' Gertrude Fowkes shouted and the three women formed a human barrier.

Tom could not bring himself to force his way through them but stubbornly stood his ground. 'I'm not leaving until I've spoken with Amy.'

The door of the parlour opened and Amy appeared. Her expression was grimly determined. 'You're wasting your time, Tom Potts. I told you that you must choose between me or your rotten bitch of a Mam, and you chose her. I'm never going to wed you now, so you can go away and stop pestering me.'

'You can't mean that, Amy?' Tom could hardly believe he had heard her correctly. 'I promised you that I'd find a separate place for my mother to live in, and you know that I mean to do that.'

She shook her head and spat out angrily, 'You've had me for a fool, and I'll not stand for it. I don't want to speak to or see you ever again. So just bugger off, will you.'

She stepped back into the parlour and the door slammed shut. Its sound impacted upon Tom like a physical blow.

Gertrude Fowkes saw his stricken expression and felt pity for him. 'You'd best go, for all our sakes, Master Potts,' she told him quietly. 'When Amy's in this mood there's no telling what she might end up doing. Go away now, there's a good man.'

'Yes, you get going, or I'll chuck another pot of ale over you,' Maisie Lock threatened.

'That's enough of that sort o' talk, Maisie,' Gertrude Fowkes warned her sharply, and told Tom, 'Just go away please, Master Potts; you'll change nothing by staying here.'

For a few moments Tom battled with himself, and then grudgingly accepted that at this time there was nothing he could hope to gain by stubbornly standing his ground.

'Amy,' he called. 'I can only hope and pray that you'll talk to me when you're calmer. Because believe me there is nothing I want more than to be your husband, and to spend the rest of my days cherishing and caring for you.'

He walked sadly out of the tavern, and unhitched the horse. He patted its neck and told it, 'Let's get you home to your stable first, and then I'll tell your master about my failure.'

In the study of the Red House, Joseph Blackwell listened in silence to Tom's account and when it had ended commented thoughtfully, 'I've known cases where someone has choked to death on various objects, but never before have I heard of someone choking to death on a ball of opium. Do you think it was an accident?'

'It could well have been an accident, Sir. Perhaps she was sucking on the ball and involuntarily swallowed it?'

'Yes, she could have,' Blackwell agreed, and then told Tom, 'You're still free to continue your investigation, Master Potts. I've appointed Richard Bint to act as a deputy constable, and he has proven to be most satisfactory in that post.' A brief smile quirked the thin lips. 'In the early hours of Sunday morning he arrested our very own King William in the act of assaulting Timothy Munslow's windows.'

Tom was simultaneously shocked and concerned by this information. The concern was for the plight of King William, whom he had often befriended. The shock was the appointment of Richard Bint as Deputy Constable.

Noting Tom's expression, Blackwell chuckled dryly. 'You need have no concern for King William, Master Potts. He is safely lodged back in the Poorhouse, and the admirable Mrs Lewis is caring for him. There will be no further proceedings taken against the poor fellow.'

'I'm relieved to hear that, Sir.' Tom grimaced wryly. 'But I fear it will not be welcome news for Master Munslow.'

'Our new Deputy Constable has already smoothed Master Munslow's ruffled feathers. He persuaded two pointer lads, Thomas Chance and Simon Cook, out of the goodness of their hearts, to pay a handsome sum in compensation to Munslow in return for that gentleman not pressing charges against King William.'

Tom couldn't help but appreciate this example of rough justice. Tommy Chance and Simmy Cook were two of King William's principal tormentors. He could well accept that Bint had known it was them who had been egging the simpleton on to smash Munslow's windows, and one or the other had been the assailant who was responsible for his own injured ankle.

'It appears that Master Bint has already proven to be a great asset to our constabulary, Sir.'

'Indeed so,' Blackwell heartily agreed, and then became serious. 'Have you any idea as to how you will further your current investigation?'

'At this moment, Sir, I've not,' Tom admitted. 'But I'm totally confident that I shall succeed in solving this matter.'

'And I share that confidence.' Blackwell picked up his quill pen and bent over the open ledger on his desk. 'I bid you good day, Constable.'

Outside the front door Tom asked himself grimly, 'But now just what can I do to achieve my boast of success? I'm damned if I've got the faintest idea!'

He walked reluctantly towards the Lock-up, inwardly dreading the prospect of his mother's triumphal glorying over his split with Amy. Yet at the same time feeling an inexorable hardening of his resolve to move his mother into a dwelling place of her own.

'I've had all that I can bear of her vicious temper, Father, and

I'll not tolerate living with it any longer,' he told the mental image of his beloved dead parent.

The Lock-up door was bolted and barred on the inside and Tom tugged the iron bell-pull, calling, 'It's Tom, Mother, will you please open the door?' He stepped hastily back, warily watching for the upper casement to open and discharge the contents of his mother's chamber pot.

However, the casement stayed closed so he repeated the process three more times.

After a few seconds he heard the bars and bolts being drawn and saw the door open wide, but no one appeared in the doorway.

Tom's immediate reaction was to suspect that she had prepared some type of booby trap to welcome his return.

'Are you there, Mother?' he called.

'No, Sir. It's me, Sir.' The voice was a tremulous, childish treble.

'What the . . . ?' Tom was momentarily taken aback. 'Who's me?'

'I'm me, Sir.' A diminutive, barefoot young girl wearing a huge floppy mobcap, ragged dirty dress, voluminous apron and a nervous expression stepped out from behind the door.

Tom immediately saw how pale and drawn with weariness her face was, and spoke very gently. 'Don't be feared, child, I'll not harm you. What's your name?'

'I'm called George Hanover, Sir.' The girl bobbed a curtsey.

'George Hanover? But surely that's the King's name?' Tom spoke without thinking.

'I know, Sir. But me Dad said that them Germans are all bastards, and because I'm a bastard as well, he called me George Hanover. That was afore he went off to be a soldier, Sir.'

'And how old are you, George Hanover?'

She bobbed another curtsey. 'I think I'm eight years old, Sir, but I can't be certain because me Dad never told me. He said it was for him to know, and for me to find out, Sir.'

Tom hid an amused smile at the gravity of her manner. 'Didn't your mother, or your brothers and sisters ever tell you?'

'I've never had a Mam, nor any brothers nor sisters neither, Sir. There was only me and me Dad, and now he's gone for a soldier, there's only me meself, Sir.'

Pity roused in Tom. 'What brings you here in the Lock-up, my dear?'

'Master Bromley give me this cap and apron and brung me here yesterday morning to skivvy for Mistress Potts, Sir. Like I skivvied for me Dad, Sir. Only the Mistress aren't here now, Sir. She said I'm to tell anybody who comes asking for her that she's gone to have her tea at Master Bromley's, Sir.'

'Well, my name is Thomas Potts. I'm Mistress Potts' son, and I live here as well. So if you'll let me come in, you and I will have our tea together. While we do so you can tell me all about yourself, and in return I shall tell you all about myself. Do we have a bargain?'

'Very well, Sir.' She bobbed a curtsey and stood aside, head bowed submissively.

Looking down at her solemn little face and submissive posture Tom suddenly experienced an emotion so poignant that it brought a lump to his throat. It took him several moments to recognize that what he was feeling was a rush of protective paternalism.

He bent towards her and said huskily, 'Your name is now Georgina, but I shall call you Georgy; and you don't need to call me Sir, or to curtsey to me. You shall call me Tom. Come now, we'll go look in the cupboards and decide what we'll have for our tea.'

'Very well, Sir.' She bobbed a curtsey.

He chuckled and told her, 'Now say after me, "Very well, Tom." Come now, let me hear you say it, and say it without curtseying. "Very well, Tom", and no curtsey.'

She appeared undecided, but he pressed her.

'Very well, Tom,' she whispered.

He laughed. 'I can't hear you, Georgy. Say it again, only louder this time.'

'Very well, Tom,' she blurted.

'Good!' He applauded. 'That's very good! Now let's get something to eat. I'm positively starving.'

'Very well, Tom.' Her smile beamed as he took her hand and led her towards the larder at the far end of the corridor.

In Tom's room, while they ate bread and butter and drank small beer, he drew Georgy's story from her.

She had been raised in a hovel in the nearby village of Feckenham by her father, a feckless drunkard. A relative of Charles Bromley had lived nearby who was a Poor Law Overseer. When her father deserted her this relative had agreed that Bromley could take her as a Parish Apprentice to be trained in domestic duties. Bromley in his turn had given the child over to Gertrude Potts.

'Have you had any schooling at all, Georgy?'

'No. Me dad always said that schooling wasn't for the likes of me. He said I was put on this earth to skivvy for him.'

'Would you like to have some schooling?' Tom asked.

'I sometimes think that I should like to be able to read and write, and do sums. But it's not for the likes of me to do such, is it, Sir?'

'Ahem! Not Sir!' He held up a warning finger. 'My name is Tom.'

She blushed and whispered, 'Sorry, Sir . . . I mean Tom.'

'That's better.' He smiled.

'Please can I get on with me work now, Tom?' she requested timidly. 'Only the mistress said she wants all the downstairs washed and scrubbed like a new pin afore she comes back.'

'Where did you sleep last night, child?' Tom had a disquieting thought.

'Downstairs in one o' them rooms.'

'Show me.'

She led the way downstairs and indicated a cell.

Tom frowned when he saw there was no bedding on the narrow stone-flagged sleeping platform.

'Where's your bedding, Georgy?'

'I haven't got any. But the mistress said that if I was a good girl and worked very hard she'd give me some later on.'

Tom displayed none of the rising anger he was feeling. He saw with pity how utterly drawn and weary she looked, and told her gently, 'You are not going to do any more work this day, Georgy. Instead you're going up to my room, and you are going to sleep in the cot there.'

'But the mistress will be angry with me if I don't do me work!' the girl protested nervously.

'No, she won't!' Tom said firmly, and ushered her back upstairs.

He selected one of his books and smiled. 'I'm going to go next door and read, and you are to go to bed and rest. I'll wake you tomorrow morning.'

'But where will you sleep if I have your cot?' she asked.

'I shall sleep in one of the rooms downstairs. You rest now, Georgy, and don't fret about anything at all. I'm sure that all will go well with you from now on.'

THIRTY-SIX

Evening, Monday 22nd October

Tom answered the summons of the clanking bells to find his mother facing him at the door.

'So you're back, are you?' She noisily sucked her toothless gums as she scowled at her only living child. 'Of course, I should have remembered that it's the bad penny that always turns up again.'

Grunting and wheezing she shuffled across the threshold, demanding, 'Where's my skivvy? It's her duty to be here to meet me.'

'She's asleep in my room.' Tom braced himself for the inevitable outburst.

'My skivvy is sleeping in your room? What wickedness is this? Have you gone mad?' The Widow Potts violently shook her head, her hanging jowls swinging from side to side, shrieking incredulously. 'Are you mad? I can only believe that you are, and that the Lord inflicted you upon me as a punishment for my youthful, innocent vanity. That's the only explanation I can find to explain my birthing of you. You were sent as my cross to bear.'

'Don't shout so loud, Mother; you'll wake the poor child up, and God only knows she needs some rest after the way you've been slave-driving her.'

The Widow Potts again noisily sucked her toothless gums as she glared at her son, but before she could return to the attack, Tom's patience gave way and he took the offensive, telling her ~~ated~~ly, 'Listen well, Mother. I'll not tolerate any more ill-~~~~ment of this poor child, and she'll not be used as your personal ~~~~ She'll not sleep down here in the cells either, but will have my cot until the gable room has been made suitable for her to sleep in. Furthermore, I intend to have her Guardianship signed over to me. I also intend that she is to have schooling. You will treat her with kindness and care for her well-being, or you will leave here.'

'Who are you to give orders to me?' Widow Potts spluttered indignantly.

'I'm the man who pays the household bills. I'm the man who will be providing your bed, board and upkeep until you wed your betrothed husband-to-be, Master Charles Bromley. Should that blessed day ever come, which at times I doubt!'

'I'll not stand here a moment longer to be so grievously bullied and insulted by such a vicious, evil cur of a son!' Widow Potts hissed, and with a nimble alacrity belying her bulk she pushed past him and disappeared upstairs.

Immersed in his own anger, Tom didn't detect the arrival of fresh callers until the clanging of the bell startled him into awareness. He saw a ragged, barefoot boy standing in the doorway in front of a huddle of other small figures.

'Can you come, Sir? Can you come quick to our house?' the boy pleaded in a quavering voice.

Tom's immediate involuntary reaction was a surge of resentment at this unwanted intrusion into his own problems.

'Why must you come pestering me now, boy? What do you want?' he challenged curtly.

'Me Dad's bashing me Mam up, and her face is all blood! Come quick, Sir! Please!' The boy's voice wailed into loud, terrified sobbing.

Realization of the child's distress brought instant shame shuddering through Tom.

'I'm behaving like a brute bully!' he castigated himself in disgust, and aloud questioned, 'What's your name, boy, and where are your parents now?'

'I'm Jimmy,' the child choked out. 'They'm in our house!'

Tom's thoughts raced. His constable's staff was upstairs but he feared to lose valuable time in limping to fetch it. He reached down and gripped the child's hand.

'Take me to your house, Jimmy.'

With the other children tailing behind, the boy led Tom down the left forked road leading eastwards from the Lock-up towards the Big Pool. After only a few steps a sudden intuitive foreboding impelled Tom to seek for an unwelcome confirmation.

'Are you one of Paddy O'Leary's children, Jimmy? Is your house in the Salters Yard?'

'Yeah it is, and Paddy's our Dad, and our Mam's called Mary. Does you know 'um, Sir?'

'Oh yes, I know them, Jimmy.' Tom gulped hard.

The Salters Yard was a row of ancient half-timbered tenements standing midway between the Lock-up and the Big Pool, and hod-carrier Paddy O'Leary was its most notorious inhabitant. A big, raw-boned Irishman, who when sober was invariably pleasant and inoffensive, but when drunk metamorphosed into an aggressive brawler.

'I can bate any man in this bloody town, so I can! Come out and fight, you yellow-bellied bastards. Come out and I'll take any six o' youse wi' one hand tied behind me back, so I will. Come out and fight!'

The sudden onset of the bellowing voice caused Tom to halt the small procession still some yards distance from the Salters Yard.

'That's me Dad,' Jimmy whimpered.

'I thought it might be,' Tom acknowledged ruefully. 'Now you stay here with your brothers and sisters.'

Mouth dry, heartbeat pounding, Tom went on alone to the entrance in the waist-high brick wall which fronted the cobbled forecourt of the tenements, inwardly praying fervently. 'Dear God, give me courage. I beg you, please give me courage.'

The moonlight shone on the big man staggering about the forecourt, stripped to the waist, shaking his fists at the dark closed windows of the houses.

'Come out, youse cowards! I know youse are hiding in there! Shitting yourselves like the yellow-bellied rats youse are.'

Tom crouched down and cautiously peered over the top of the wall at the house he knew to be O'Leary's. Like the rest, no glow of candle or rush-light showed through the windows, but he could see that the door was wide open.

'My first concern has to be the woman. She could be lying sorely injured, or even dying in there. But how do I get to her?'

His body was trembling with fear, his breathing rapid shallow gasps.

'How do I get to her? How?'

'By going in there, you damned coward! By acting like a man, not a quivering jelly! Now stand up and go in there!' The voice coming from deep within his mind was scathingly contemptuous, and impelled by shame, Tom obeyed its command.

He rose and walked through the entrance towards the open door. He covered half the distance and the bellowing roar filled his ears.

'Ahharr! Trying to creep up on me from behind, was yez? Too fuckin' yellow-bellied to come at me from the front, are yez? I'm going to break the back o' yez now.'

Tom turned to see the Irishman lurching towards him from the far end of the forecourt. Adrenaline pumped through his body, rousing the conflicting atavistic reactions of fight or flee.

'Fight or flee? Do I stand or run?'

The image of his father's face rose in Tom's mind, and he vowed grimly to that image, 'I'll not shame you by running, I swear.'

He went to meet O'Leary, then as if from nowhere a man came leaping over the brick wall and hurled himself at the Irishman.

Before O'Leary could react the newcomer punched his head with lightning speed once, twice, three, four times, sending the Irishman sprawling, senseless and bleeding.

The newcomer stepped back from his handiwork. All along the tenements darkened windows opened and cheers and plaudits rang out.

Tom could only stand and stare in bewilderment as Ritchie Bint turned to face him, and grinned.

'Us constables has got to stick together if we'em to uphold the law, Constable Potts.'

Mary O'Leary, big and blowsy, came charging from her house screaming furiously. 'Leave my man alone, you bastards.'

She went down on her knees by her prone husband. 'I'm here, me darlint! I'm here! They'll not touch you again, me darlint, I'll kill the bastards first.'

'Come out of the way, Mary, and let me and my mate get him back to his bed.' Ritchie Bint laid his hand on the woman's shoulder. 'You get them kids o' yours seen to.'

She rose to her feet and Tom saw the bloody swollen lump that was her eye. Noting the expression on his face, she grinned.

'The bastard caught me wi' a Judas when I was having a sup o' gin, or it would ha' been a different story else.'

Ritchie Bint laughed. 'That's true enough, Constable Potts. Paddy comes off worse nine times out of ten when he toes the line wi' Mary.'

O'Leary stirred and groaned and Ritchie Bint and Tom lifted him to his feet and half-carried, half-dragged him back into his fetid tenement and laid him on the foul-smelling bed.

Mary O'Leary brought her children into the tenement and told Ritchie Bint, 'You can fuck off back to your shite hole in bloody Silver Street now, Ritchie Bint, and leave us be.'

'Alright Mary, we'em going. But I'm telling you now that the next time I have to come and keep the peace in your shite hole, then your man is going to find himself in the stocks.'

'Oh, just fuck off, Ritchie!' She waved him away in disgust. 'I never thought I'd see the day when you'd turn traitor and take the side o' the Masters against us.'

'The only side I'm on is the side that's carrying this hat on his head.' He tapped his square brown paper hat with his forefinger and, beckoning Tom to follow him, went out on to the yard.

As they walked away from the yard Bint grinned. 'Right, Constable Potts, we'd best be getting on with our patrol. I've heard a whisper that there's a couple o' likely lads been eyeing up Bartleet's warehouse lately. We might find 'um lurking about there.'

Tom was ironically amused at this illustration of the truth of the adage about the reformed poacher making the keenest gamekeeper.

They both halted in the street and Bint asked, 'Is there another place we should check on first, Constable Potts?'

Tom shook his head. 'No, there's not. Firstly I want to thank you most sincerely for coming to my aid tonight. Also, what we need to do now if we are to be colleagues – and I trust friends also – is to use familiar terms with each other. I am to be simply Tom to you, and you must be Ritchie to me.'

He offered his hand, and Bint shook it heartily. 'I likes that, Tom.'

'Now the other thing is that normally as Constables we wait to be sent for by those in need of our assistance. We only patrol nightly when there are ongoing cases of theft or repeated blackguardism by a particular group or individual. As a Deputy Constable you are virtually unpaid except for certain expenses that you're entitled to, as I am myself. I also get monetary fees for certain of the duties I'm called upon to do, but no money for my duty of keeping the King's peace. As the full-time Headborough Constable of the Parish I live rent-free at the Lock-up, but I still have to pay my own money for candles, coals and whatever other essentials I need.

'So don't forget, Ritchie, that you still have to earn all your bread and board at the pointing trade. I would advise you as a friend to only patrol the Parish or do other peacekeeping duties when you are sent for to do so. Many people hate the constable's staff of office, and you don't want them to begin hating you personally for being over eager to wield it, do you?'

'I take your advice as being very kindly meant, Tom.' Ritchie Bint grinned, and for a moment resembled a cheeky, mischievous urchin. 'And I shall remember it. But you have to remember in your turn, that all me life I've been on the other side of the fence. Being on this side of it is a novel thing for me, and I'm loving it. There's a great many people who hate us needle pointers anyway for being the roughs what we are, so a few more nor less hating me gives me no cause for any concern.

'As for anything else, them who knows me will tell you that I'm not a man to bully and lord it over them who're weaker than me. So you've no cause to worry about how I shall do me duty as a constable. I'm well able to run with the hares and hunt with the hounds.'

'With all my heart I do believe you, Ritchie. So let me bid you a warm welcome to the Parish Constabulary. Now I'm going to my bed. Whether you choose to do the same or to make a patrol is entirely up to you, my friend. I'll bid you a very good night.' Tom smiled, and with a final warm handshake they parted company.

THIRTY-SEVEN

Enoch Griffiths was still drowsy and fuddle-minded from the after-effects of his opium debauch when Chong brought a bottle of wine and a glass to the small lamp-lit room.

'Here, Master Griffiths, I'm sure you will be very glad to wet your whistle.'

Griffiths groaned as he sat upright and put his feet on the floor. 'That Afghan was real strong, Chinky. I feel like me head is still floating on the ceiling.'

Chong filled the glass with wine and handed it to the other man, who greedily slurped it down, and held the glass out.

'Fill her up, Chinky.'

Chong poured more wine and, as Griffiths lifted it to his lips, told him, 'Elsie brought a gentleman to see me last night.'

Griffiths slurped the glass empty and again held it out, grumbling, 'This is cat's piss, but I'll lay odds you'll be charging me a fortune for it, you robbing heathen!'

The Chinaman only smiled as he refilled the glass, and asked, 'What do you know of an exceptionally tall man, who has the speech of a gentleman, and says his name is Tom Potts?'

A wary gleam came into Griffiths' eyes. 'Why do you ask me that?'

'Because that was the man who Elsie brought here last night. He claimed to be an old servant of the Carnegies. But I'm sure that he lied.'

'What did he want to know?'

'Anything I could tell him about the Duchess.'

'And what did you tell him?'

'Nothing that he didn't know. Elsie had already taken him to the mortuary to see the Duchess. Now you tell me who he is.'

'He's the constable of the fuckin' Tardebigge Parish, and he's poking his fuckin' nose into my affairs. I'll break fuckin' Elsie's fuckin' neck, so I will!' Griffiths raged furiously. He jumped to his feet, hurled the full glass of wine against the wall, and stormed out of the room.

THIRTY-EIGHT

Morning, Tuesday 23rd October

It was well before dawn when Griffiths galloped his sweat-frothed, labouring horse into the yard of Marlfield Farm. He reined in by the kitchen door and bellowed up at the window above it.

'Get down here, you lot! Get down here!' He hurled his riding crop at the window. 'Get down here!'

He continued bawling until the casement opened and Delilah Griffiths peered down at him through sleep-blurred eyes.

'Get here double quick, you cow!' He shook his fist at her. 'Or you'll be having a taste o' this.'

Her face disappeared and within seconds the bolts rattled and she ran out of the front door.

Griffiths dismounted. 'See to the beast.'

She took the reins and led the horse away.

Griffiths went into the house, bellowing, 'Get down here, you lazy cows! Get down here now!'

'I'm in the kitchen, Brother Enoch!' Deborah shouted fearfully. 'I'm just lighting the fire to cook your breakfast.'

'Where's fuckin' Doll?' The kitchen door smashed back on its hinges as he crashed into the candlelit kitchen.

'Her's still abed.' His sister's normally ruddy face was blanched with fear.

'No her's not! How can a body sleep wi' all this bloody racket going on?' Doll Griffiths spat out as she came into the room behind her brother and angrily challenged him. 'What's all this shouting and blarting for?'

He swung to face her with his fist raised threateningly.

Doll Griffiths flinched, but stood her ground. 'Punching my lights out aren't going to serve any useful purpose, Brother Enoch. So why don't you just sit yourself down, and tell me what you wants me to do?'

For some moments he remained motionless, fist still raised, face purple with rage, dragging air into his lungs and expelling it with loud snorts.

'Come now,' she coaxed and moved cautiously to ready a chair at the large board table. 'Set yourself on this and have some vittles. Deborah 'ull cook you a nice bit o' bacon and egg in a couple o' shakes, won't you, Deborah?'

'I'm doing it for you now, Brother Enoch,' the younger woman blurted anxiously as the range fire kindled and she rushed to place a heavy iron skillet on the flames.

The man's heavy breathing began to ease, and he let his fist fall then seated himself on the readied chair, and growled, 'Get me some ale, Doll, and you look sharp wi' my grub, Deborah.'

The women's relief was patent as they bustled to obey him.

Doll drew a pot of ale from the large barrel in the rear scullery and hastened to place it in front of her brother. 'Does you want a pipe, Enoch?'

He nodded and again she hurried to fill a short clay pipe with tobacco, hand it to him and proffer a flaming spill for him to light the pipe.

He puffed rapidly, drawing the smoke into his body and expelling it in dense clouds until it wreathed around his head.

Judging that the immediate danger of assault had passed, Doll asked, 'What's happened to upset you so, Brother Enoch?'

'Naught that I can't deal with.' He grunted. 'Has Joey been here while I've been away?'

'No, we aren't seen hide nor hair of him since last Thursday, when you sent him off.' Her eyes glinted resentfully.

'Well go up to Redditch right away, and tell him to get here as fast as his legs 'ull carry him.' Enoch Griffiths grinned savagely and jeered. 'Have you got enough money saved up to pay him for a shag? Maybe he'll give you one on credit.'

Furious hatred reddened her eyes as she snatched her shawl and bonnet from the wall hook and hurried out of the room.

When she reached the Icknield Street she turned and shook her fist at the farmhouse, mouthing, 'You'll get what's coming to you, Brother. Just you wait and see if you don't!'

The darkness of pre-dawn still blanketed the town but lights shone from the mills and workshops where the workers had been toiling for hours, and the sounds of hammers tapping steel came from a myriad tenements and sheds where the 'soft workers' of the needle industry earned their bread in their homes. In virtually every tenement and court of Hill Street, candle- and lamp-lit windows denoted the labour of these women, small children and aged 'soft workers'.

Joey Dowler lived with his old father in one of the courts, a small cramped square of tiny one-up, one-down terraced hovels facing into a yard entered by a narrow covered passage, and dominated by the stinking midden pit in its centre.

The feeble glow of a solitary rush light came from the single downstairs window, and when Doll Griffiths knocked on the ramshackle door a quavering voice answered from inside.

'It aren't bolted, Hetty.'

She lifted the catch and pushed the door ajar. 'It's not Hetty, Master Dowler. I'm looking for Joey.'

The old man was sitting on a broken-backed wooden chair in front of a minute, rust-covered empty fireplace. He turned his head to look at her, and whined peevishly, 'I thought you was me neighbour, Hetty, bringing me a bit o' breakfast. She's bloody tardy coming with it this morning.'

'I'm looking for Joey,' she repeated. 'Where is he?'

'How the bloody hell should I know? The bugger comes and goes and comes and goes, and never so much as gives me the time o' day. Never mind telling me where he's going or been gone to.'

A woman carrying a small bowl of gruel came out from the adjoining hovel, and asked, 'Can I help you, Missus?'

'I'm looking for Joey. I'm a friend of his.'

'Does he owe you money as well, Missus?' As she spoke the woman pushed past Doll Griffiths and went in to the old man. 'Here's your breakfast, you miserable old bugger. I could hear you moaning about me.'

She grinned at Doll Griffiths. 'He forgets that these walls am as thin as paper, and you can hear a pin drop through 'um.'

'No, Joey don't owe me anything.' Doll forced a smile.

'Leastways not this week. But I've got a job for him, and it needs doing a bit quick.'

'Well I heard him going out last thing last night. It's more than likely he went to the marsh aback of the old windmill down Bridley Moor. He told me yesterday that he'd been laying eel traps there, and he might have an eel for me today. But watch your step on the marsh. There's some queer goings on there at times. They do say as how it's haunted and there's evil spirits roaming around it.'

'I'm well used to them. I lives wi' one o' the buggers.' Doll sighed self-pityingly. 'Anyway, thanks for your help, Missus. If Joey should come back meanwhiles, could you tell him that Doll Griffiths needs to see him urgent about that job we was speaking of.'

'I will, my duck,' Hetty Drake assured her.

Bridley Moor was an undulating stretch of gorse-strewn barrens and marsh a half-mile to the west of the town. The skies were paling with the oncoming of dawn as Doll Griffiths tramped up a hillock of gorse topped by the ruinous tower of a derelict windmill. A strong wind was gusting as she reached the tower and stood screwing her eyes against the buffeting wind, peering down at the several small ponds dotted about the marshland to the west.

Scattered sheep were grazing, birds were flighting, but there was no immediate sign of any humans.

'Where the bloody Hell has you got to, Joey? Where am you hiding?' Doll muttered aggrievedly, then was assailed by the sharp need to urinate. 'Well you'll have to wait while I takes a piss!'

She sought for shelter from the wind on the lee side of the tower, but the gusts still swirled about her. She picked her way cautiously through the dark gap of the doorway and all was still. She pulled her skirt up around her waist and squatted, sighing in relief as the urine spurted from her over-strained bladder.

She lifted her head to look into the shadows about her, and thought she detected a slight movement. The flow of urine eased, trickled and ceased. She straightened, stepped carefully around the steaming pool, let her skirt fall, squinted her eyes to peer and detected more movement.

'I know somebody's there! Is it you, Joey? Am you trying to frit me, you bastard?' She took quick steps forwards, halted abruptly, her eyes widening as she stood face to face with the man, then she shrieked in horror and staggered back and out of the doorway.

In the shadows within the tower the hanging corpse of Joey Dowler continued to sway and turn in the penetrating draughts of the wind.

'Where the bloody Hell have you been, and where's bloody Joey?' Enoch Griffiths demanded angrily as his sister burst through the kitchen door.

'He's dead. He's hanging in the windmill on Bridley Moor,' Doll Griffiths panted.

'Dead? Hanging in the bloody windmill? Joey's hanging in the bloody windmill?' Enoch Griffiths bellowed, jumped from his chair and grabbed his sister's throat, dragging her to him so that he could sniff her breath. 'How much bloody gin have you had to make you rave so, you drunken cow?'

'Let me go, you bastard!' She struggled free and shrieked. 'Joey's topped himself in the windmill on Bridley Moor. I went in to have a piss, and there he was. Fritted me half to death, it did. I've run all the bloody way back here. And I aren't had a drink neither. But I needs a drink now. By God I does!'

Enoch Griffiths took a grip on himself and told her, 'Sit down and catch your breath, Sister Doll.'

He took a bottle of gin from a cupboard and placed it in front of her as she slumped down at the table, her shoulders heaving, her hands visibly trembling.

'Take a couple o' swigs, and calm yourself down,' he instructed. 'And then you can tell me all about this.'

He waited while she drank, and when her shoulders stopped heaving and her gasping eased, he asked her quietly, 'How come you was looking for him on Bridley Moor?'

She related her visit to Joey Dowler's hovel, and the exchanges with his father and neighbour.

'I'll have to go now and tell his dad what's happened to hi
she finished, and went to stand up.

'Hold hard!' Griffiths gestured for her to stay seated. 'L

to think about this for a bit. You have another drink.' After pondering for some time he asked, 'What exactly did you say to his dad and the neighbour?'

'I just said that if Joey come back meanwhiles could they tell him that Doll Griffiths wanted to see him about a little job I got for him.'

'Alright.' He nodded.

'I'll go up now and tell his dad that's he's dead.' Once more she made as if to stand, and again he gestured for her to remain.

'No, you stay here. Leave it for some other bugger to find him, and they can go and tell his dad. Get it into your head that you never found Joey. You didn't see him on the marsh, and you never went into the windmill. You came back here and told me that you hadn't been able to find him. Have you got that? You never found him! You don't know that he's dead! And say naught to the girls about this!'

'Why should I do that?' she questioned, and he glowered menacingly.

'Because I say that you're to do it,' he growled. 'Now I'm only going to tell you this once, so listen very carefully. There's something strange going on here which I need to get to the bottom of. Something that might well have you and me both in our graves if I don't get to the bottom of it a bit bloody sharpish. So you just do what I tell you. Keep your mouth shut about finding Joey!'

Knowing her brother as she did, Doll Griffiths recognized that he was deadly serious, and his warning about their graves was not empty blustering. A frisson of fear shivered through her, and she nodded obediently.

'I don't know that Joey's dead. I never seen him on the marsh, and I never went near the windmill, Brother Enoch. And I'll say naught to nobody.'

THIRTY-NINE

Mid-morning, Tuesday 23rd October

Maisie Lock finished polishing the top of the table in the window nook of the Select Parlour and straightened her body, rubbing the small of her back and looking idly out through the latticed window. 'Bugger me!' She blinked hard and pressed her nose against the glass pane. 'Bugger me! It is him!'

She turned her head and shouted excitedly, 'Amy! Come here quick! Look at this! Quick! Quick!'

Amy Danks hurried to her friend's side and pressed her own nose against a glass pane. She gasped in shock. 'Who's that scruffy kid he's got with him? And where's he taking her? Just look at them! They're hand in hand like a bloody dad and child!'

'You'd best follow and find out what he's up to,' Maisie Lock urged.

'Phooo! Why should I care! Let him do what he will; I couldn't care less.'

Amy's feigned indifference did not fool her friend, who took pity on her.

'Well I'll go. If Fatty Fowkes asks where I am, tell him I'm chasing that bloke who did a runner last night without paying his score.'

Before Amy could make any reply Maisie Lock was gone from the room and outside hurrying past the window.

Hand in hand Tom Potts and Georgy Hanover turned left at the central crossroads and went north along the High Street until they reached and halted before a double bay-windowed shop with ornate gilt lettering on the sign above its door, proclaiming:

Mesdames Elizabeth & Sarah Henbath
Mantua Makers & Milliners
To
The Nobility

'What does that sign say, Tom?' Georgy asked timidly.

'It says that this is a very grand dress and hat and ribbon maker's shop that caters exclusively for the nobility.' Tom winked broadly. 'So I shall have to introduce you to the Mesdames Henbath as Lady Georgina Hanover, who has taken residence at Lock-up Castle, with Lord Thomas Potts and his mother, the very grand Dowager Lady Gertrude Potts.'

Georgy's smile beamed, and Tom made a mental note that today he must remember to buy her a toothbrush, tooth powder and various other toiletries, and to order a hip-bath from the ironmonger. He also intended to introduce Georgy to her primary education in the shape of the elderly Henry and Agatha James, the proprietors of a small private school for young children, after she had become accustomed to maintaining a high standard of personal hygiene. An attribute which Tom felt was grievously lacking in the vast majority of his fellow citizens.

Now he hid a wry smile as he realized: 'My God! I'm already beginning to regard her as my adopted daughter, am I not?'

Inside the shop he was greeted with welcoming smiles and curious eyes by the Henbath sisters – fashionably dressed, attractive spinsters in their mid-twenties, who both considered Tom to be a very eligible bachelor, and believed he was lowering himself by his courtship of Amy Danks.

'And who is this interesting-looking child, Master Potts?' Elizabeth, the dominant sister, wanted to know.

'This is Miss Georgina Hanover, who has come to live with my mother and myself.'

Georgy bobbed a curtsey, and Tom went on to explain.

'She needs a complete outfitting of new clothing. Workaday and Sunday best gowns, bonnets, and all the other articles of clothing, including slippers and shoes, which young ladies require. I would also much appreciate your kind help in purchasing any other articles of toilette which you consider to be necessary for a young lady who is to embark upon a course of education and etiquette which will enable her to take her place in polite society.' Suddenly becoming aware of how pompous he was sounding, he bowed and flustered. 'Pray forgive my excessive verbosity, ladies. But this is the first time I've ever had to deal with this sort of transaction.'

Sarah Henbath lifted her gloved hand to her mouth to stifle a snort of laughter.

Elizabeth Henbath bobbed a curtsey, and told him gravely, 'You are forgiven, Sir.' Then she turned to Georgy. 'Take off that awful mobcap, child. Stand straight and hold your chin up. Sarah, follow me.'

The two sisters walked very slowly round and round the blushing girl subjecting her to an intense critical scrutiny which lasted so long that Tom was becoming uneasy.

The inspection finally ended and Elizabeth Henbath told him, 'Please excuse us for a moment, Master Potts. My sister and I need to have a brief discussion.'

They withdrew to the far corner of the room and spoke in animated whispers for some time. Tom was now invaded by a sense of tense apprehension. They came back to him, and Elizabeth acted as spokeswoman.

'My sister and I have a proposal to put to you, Master Potts, and that is that you should allow the child to come to us each weekday and we will instruct her in all aspects of dress, etiquette and manners of polite society. Reasonable fees to be negotiated, and mutually agreed between us prior to her first period of instruction. What say you to this proposal?'

Tom sighed with relief. 'I'm more than happy to accept, ladies, and very grateful as well. I don't foresee any difficulty whatsoever in the matter of our coming to an agreement regarding the fees. So when can she begin receiving this instruction?'

'This very minute, Master Potts.' Elizabeth Henbath smiled. 'This first period of instruction will be concerning aspects of personal hygiene. The measuring for her new clothing will then commence. After that we shall outfit her in some suitable workaday clothing for immediate wear. Then a visit to the shoemaker, followed by the purchasing of her articles of toilette. We'll bring her back to the Lock-up this evening after she's dined with us. So you may go about your duties with full peace of mind that Miss Georgina Hanover is being very well cared for. I bid you good day, Sir.'

'Good day, ladies, and many thanks.' He smiled at Georgy. 'I'll see you later, my dear.'

'Alright, Tom.' Her smile beamed, and he left the shop feeling utterly content with what had been arranged. He walked back towards the crossroads humming happily, immersed in this strange new pleasure of being in the position of a de facto father.

'Who's that little scruff you was with?' Maisie Lock ambushed him.

'Oh my God! Where did you spring from?' He was taken completely off guard.

'In the entry here. You'd have seen me if you hadn't got your yed in the clouds, like always. Now, Amy wants to know who the wench is?'

He felt a spurt of annoyance. 'If Amy is so curious about the child, why doesn't she come and ask me herself?'

'That's a daft question aren't it, Tom Potts?' Maisie scoffed. 'It just goes to show how little you knows about how women think. It should be you telling her without her needing to ask you.'

'I accept the fact that I don't know how women think, Maisie. But have you forgotten what happened the last time I tried to speak to Amy?'

'O' course not! And you deserved it!' Maisie retorted scathingly. 'You lets her down time after time, and then bowls up as if butter wouldn't melt in your mouth. No wonder she gets mad at you. If you was my betrothed I'd bloody well swing for you!'

Hope sprang up in Tom. 'Do you think she might speak to me now, and allow me to explain about the child?'

Maisie shook her head. 'No! She's still very angry with you for breaking your promises. But you can tell me about the kid, and I'll tell Amy.'

Tom felt despondency replace hope, but went on to explain about Georgy, and how he intended to act as her surrogate father.

The young woman's eyes momentarily softened, but then she frowned and asked, 'How are you going to protect the poor little mite from your bloody mother's nasty temper? That's the first thing that Amy will want to know.'

'You may tell Amy that she need have no worries on that score. I've made it very clear to my mother that she is to treat Georgy with kindness.'

'And pigs might fly!' Maisie's temper flared. 'I could kill you for the way you've let your bloody mother treat poor Amy, and tread all over you. Don't you dare try to talk to Amy until you've got rid of the evil old bitch, or I'll be chucking more than a pot of ale at your yed.'

She turned and ran, leaving him staring unhappily after her.

FORTY

Evening, Tuesday 23rd October

For Tom it had been a long and frustrating afternoon. One of his responsibilities as Constable was the administration and guardianship of the Pound Meadow, the field at the bottom of the Unicorn Hill where lost, stray or suspected stolen farm and domestic animals were impounded until their rightful ownership could be established. Just before midday two men had come to the Lock-up each claiming that a stray ram being kept in the Pound was their property. Tom had gone with them to the Pound, where each disputed the other's claim to ownership. Eventually the argument became so heated that fisticuffs had erupted, and in endeavouring to separate them Tom had caught a heavy blow on his nose, which had bled copiously for several minutes. The two men had then gone their separate ways vowing to appeal to the magistrates for settlement of the dispute.

Tom had returned to the Lock-up to clean the blood from his face and clothing, and had been subjected to a diatribe of abuse, punctuated by paroxysms of wailing self-pity, from his mother.

The woman who came once a week to thoroughly clean the Lock-up had then arrived, only to tell Tom that she would never ever clean the Lock-up again because of his mother's continuous complaints about the standard of her work.

Desperate for respite, Tom had escaped and gone to try and find other accommodation for his mother. There were three empty properties which would have made ideal homes for her, but unfortunately for Tom the landlords of each property refused point blank to have his mother for a tenant.

'If it was for you alone, Master Potts, I'd gladly rent it to you. But with all respect your Ma has the name of being a terrible harridan. Only last week she rowed with my missus about something which was none of your Ma's business anyway. Sorry.'

'Is the cottage for yourself, Master Potts? Ohhhh, it's for your mother. I'm sorry, Master Potts, but I don't want her for me next-door neighbour. I'd never get a moment's peace and quiet, would I?'

'No bloody chance!'

This final and briefest refusal sent Tom back to the Lock-up feeling increasingly despondent, only to be greeted by more querulous, whining complaints from his mother.

'How am I going to be able to care for myself in my parlous condition? I'm a sick woman and I need a skivvy! Bromley brought that girl here to serve me. You've got no right to take her from me. She's here to be my skivvy!'

'No she's not!' He was adamant. 'She's here to be educated and brought up decently, and to be treated with loving kindness. So let's hear no more from you about this matter.'

His mother waddled into her room and furiously slammed the door behind her.

He went back downstairs and stood outside by the side of the stocks, drawing in long breaths of the chill damp air. He felt momentarily cheered by the expectation that little Georgy would be returning shortly from her day with the Mesdames Henbath. But then his mood clouded once more.

'Am I doing the best thing for Georgy to have her living here with me and my mother? How can I ensure that during my absences my mother will treat the child kindly? Is there anyone I can employ to stay here in the Lock-up to care for Georgy and to shield her from my mother's spitefulness when I'm absent?'

His thoughts went to that other small girl who had been spirited away from the Poorhouse.

'And where are you now, you poor little soul? I pray to God that you're not suffering in any way!' A flash of anger lanced through him. 'And you, God? Why do you visit such dreadful sufferings on helpless, unprotected children? Why do you allow evil scum to flourish and prosper, and at the same time allow such agonies to fall on helpless children?'

He was roused from his bitter reveries by Elizabeth Henbath approaching and calling, 'Master Potts, I need to speak with you urgently.'

She came up to him, and seeing the instant concern in his face, smiled reassuringly. 'Not to worry, Master Potts, all is very well with little Georgina. But it is concerning her that I've come to see you.'

'What is it, Ma'am?' Tom instantly experienced the wild hope that this woman was going to volunteer to come and stay with Georgy at the Lock-up whenever he might be called out on duty.

'I'll be frank with you, Master Potts, and I speak on behalf of my sister as well as myself. We are of the opinion that the Lock-up is not a suitable dwelling place for little Georgina. During the year there are evil-doers of every degree; distressing and alarming sights and sounds, and at times even dead bodies within these walls, are there not?'

It was a confident assertion of fact, and without giving Tom any chance to answer she went on, 'This cannot be a suitable dwelling place for any young child. Least of all such an engaging and intelligent little girl as Georgina. With that in mind my sister and I have a proposition to put to you, Master Potts. Which is that you should apprentice Georgina to us for a period of seven years, during which she will be trained in all aspects of the crafts of millinery and mantua making.

'We do not require you to pay any premium to us for her apprenticeship, and her bed, board, education and upkeep will be our responsibility. You may rest assured, Master Potts, that she will not be put to any skivvying, for we already employ skivvies enough. However, my sister and myself will instruct her in the essential domestic arts so that should the happy day ever come that she wishes to wed a worthy husband, she will be well fitted to assume the duties of a married lady and to run her own household.

'In short, Master Potts, she will live with us as a full member of our family. She will be our de facto little sister. What do you say?'

Tom was quite taken aback by the generosity of this offer.

Knowing the sisters as he did, he was perfectly confident that
Georgina would indeed be treated by them as their little sister. He
mentally contrasted the bleak Lock-up with the Henbaths' comfortable home. The kindness and good humour of the sisters with his
mother's temperament. The hostile attitude of the general population towards the Constabulary and all those connected with it,
which would undoubtedly be visited on Georgy if she remained
living here with him. Yet still he could not instantly bring himself
to accept the loss of someone who brought such promise of filial
warmth, companionship and affection into his own unhappily bleak
home life. After a long pause he tentatively enquired, 'Would I
still be allowed to treat Georgy as if I were her uncle and she my
niece, and to share the expense, and experience of her upbringing
with you?'

Sensing his inner struggle Elizabeth Henbath smiled sympathetically. 'Of course you shall, Master Potts – that can be an
essential part of our contract if you so wish. Now come with me
to see Georgy, and to talk privately with her. If after that you
still harbour the slightest doubt that this new plan is not what
she truly wants, or not in her best interests, then we can revert
to our original scheme of merely instructing her for six days
each week.'

Tom's inner struggle continued as he walked to the shop with
Elizabeth Henbath, but in his mind he was already accepting that
it would be for the greater good for Georgy if she went to live
with the sisters.

'Look at me, Tom!' Georgy said excitedly and pirouetted before
him so that he could admire her new clothes, clean shining hair
and face. 'Look at my new clothes and ribbons!'

'You look wonderful, Georgy. Just like a noble lady,' he declared
admiringly.

'Come and see my room, Tom. Beth and Sarah say that I can
have it for my very own if I want it, and play with all these things.'

The room was fresh painted and spotlessly clean, with a fine
bed and an array of the sisters' childhood toys, dolls and books
around its walls.

Tom hid his pangs of sadness behind a smile. 'Do you know
something, Georgy, I believe that it would be really nice for you

to live here with Sarah and Elizabeth. They'll be your elder sisters if you want them to be. Would you like that?'

'Oh yes.' Her smile beamed, but then she asked seriously, 'But who will look after you, Tom, if I come to live here?'

'Oh, I shall do very well for myself, Georgy, and I shall come and see you very often. In fact you'll probably see more of me than you would if you stayed at the Lock-up, because as you already know I have to go away a lot to do my work. But when I come here to visit you no one will know where I am, will they? So I won't be called away. Now introduce me to all your toys and dolls.'

He spent the next hour with her and experienced a gamut of differing emotions: sadness and regret that she was not to be living with him; relief because of her patent happiness, but above all else a sense that this was what was best for her.

When he left she was playing contentedly with her dolls under the sisters' doting gazes, and he could not help but think with ironic amusement, 'I do believe they'll end up spoiling her rotten, and she'll become a right little madam!'

When he arrived back at the Lock-up his mother had gone out. Tom was relieved that he did not have to endure a diatribe. He went upstairs to the silence of his room and sat down on the stool by the window. He looked at his unmade bed and at the indent left in the pillow by little Georgy's head, and a wave of desolate loneliness swept over him.

FORTY-ONE

Noon. Thursday 25th October

Outside the windmill on Bridley Moor an excited crowd was being indignantly harangued by a half-drunk, muddy-booted peat-cutter.

'This aren't fair! It was me who found him, and by rights I should be able to charge them lot inside for entrance money for them to take a look at him. And charge you lot as well! It aren't fair, this aren't. I lost me morning's wages going all the way up into the town to tell his old dad where Joey Dowler was! It aren't fair! That lot inside aren't give me a penny piece for me trouble! And that bastard Bint is stopping me even stepping back inside, as well! It aren't fair!'

While Ritchie Bint guarded the doorway, inside the tower Tom Potts, Joseph Blackwell and Hugh Laylor were standing together before the dangling corpse of Joey Dowler.

'Well, you'd best get him down and taken to the Lock-up, Constable Potts. I trust you are available to carry out an immediate post-mortem examination, Doctor Laylor? Potts can assist you if it will save time.' Joseph Blackwell frowned sourly. 'And in due course no doubt my Lord Aston will insist on a midnight burial in the crossroads with a stake through the heart. He always feels most strongly drawn to repeat the barbarous practices of the Dark Ages.

'Now, if you'll accompany me, Doctor, I'll give you the written authorization for your task. Constable Potts, you will report to Doctor Laylor as soon as all preparations for the post-mortem are completed.'

When Blackwell and Laylor had gone Tom stood evaluating the scene. This was not the first time that he had seen a dead man hanging. As a youth he had gone with his father to witness the public hangings of criminals, and had also accompanied his father to two separate suicides by hanging.

Dowler's feet were only a few inches from the ground, with some bricks scattered beneath them. The rope ran upwards from his neck to pass over a protruding beam some ten feet from the floor and down to an iron ring in the wall.

'Did Dowler arrange those bricks to stand on, then kick them away and dangled?' Tom shook his head in puzzlement. 'I just can't understand why he should choose to strangle himself to death in that way when there are so many quicker, easier ways to die?'

He stepped up to the hanging man, staring hard at the pale face, blue lips and protruding tongue. The bulging eyes with greatly dilated pupils, the numerous small purple spots of petechial haemorrhaging on the conjunctivae, and the noose embedded almost horizontally in the fleshy neck. He lifted and closely examined the hands and fingernails, noting also the absence of

rigor mortis in the arms, shoulders and legs which indicated that
Dowler could have been dead for less than six hours or more than
forty-eight hours. However, the dryness of the visible excretion
of the bowels and bladder indicated it was the longer period since
death.

Frowning thoughtfully Tom summoned the visual memories of
the two hanging suicides he had seen as a youth. Their fingernails
were virtually torn off because they had scrabbled so desperately
to loosen the noose when they began to choke. But Dowler's
fingernails were all intact.

Tom stripped the jacket, waistcoat and shirt from the dead man
and carefully scrutinized the skin of the wrists and arms. There
were faint traces of what could be rope burns on the wrists, and
welts on the lower arms.

'Could these have been caused by Dowler having his arms
lashed behind him?'

Next Tom studied the knot of the noose on the back of the neck,
then went to study the end of the rope secured to the iron wall
ring. He recognized the noose knot to be a running bowline, and
the knot on the iron ring was a timber hitch. Both were traditional
nautical knots.

'Was Dowler ever a seafarer?'

Tom was suddenly struck by a realization. 'I'm toying with the
idea that Dowler could have been murdered! Surely if someone
was going to murder him, then they would have chosen another,
simpler method, such as poisoning, stabbing, shooting or simply
breaking his skull with a cudgel?

'The intact fingernails? I've both heard and read of cases where
the shock of a ligature tightening around the neck has resulted in
immediate unconsciousness. The nautical knots? Have I not utilized
running bowlines and timber hitches myself on occasion, and I'm
a landlubber.'

He shook his head dismissively. 'I need to stop letting my
imagination run riot. The sooner the post-mortem is out of the
way, the better.'

He went to the door and said to Ritchie Bint, 'We'll get the cart
and driver up here; and then we'll take the poor fellow down, wrap
him in the blanket and move him back to the Lock-up.'

He grimaced wryly. 'Do you know, Ritchie, I'm beginning to

wonder why the Good Lord is confronting me with so many suicides of late. Is He trying to tell me something, d'you think?'

'Is He trying to tell you that perhaps they are not suicides?' a voice whispered deep in his mind.

FORTY-TWO

Evening, Thursday 25th October

'Some talk of Alexander, And some of Hercules. Of Hector and Lysander, and such great names as these.'

The rousing song roared from the throats of the Apollo Glee Club and feet stamped in marching unison, shaking the floorboards of the Fox and Goose Select Parlour.

'But of all the world's great heroes, There's none that can compare, With a tow-row-row-row-row, To the British Grenadiers.'

Tom Potts and Hugh Laylor were returning across the Green from Joseph Blackwell's house after reporting to him following the post-mortem. Their findings on Dowler's corpse – the congestion of the brain, petechial haemorrhages in the trachea, larynx and epiglottis, fractured hyoid bone, ruptured thyroid cartilage and damaged sternomastoid muscles had persuaded them both that the cause of death was asphyxia by hanging or strangulation. Their successful collaboration on this second joint post-mortem had also kindled a closer amicable relationship.

'Will you not come in for a drink, Tom? It sounds as if it's a lively gathering,' Hugh Laylor invited. 'John and Richard will be there, and John Osborne is going to tell us about his plans for Halloween night. He's organizing the bonfire, and the Jack o' lantern procession.'

For a brief moment the thought of perhaps seeing Amy Danks was a strong temptation, but the dread of yet another public humiliation made Tom shake his head.

'No thank you, Hugh, I've no wish for another public bath at the hands of Maisie Lock. I prefer to take a private bath at the Lock-up pump instead.'

'Oh, nobody thinks any the less of you for what Maisie Lock did. In fact the majority opinion is that you behaved like a true gentleman, and kept your dignity. So come in with me and enjoy some jolly company. We can both do with a spree, after carving Dowler up. It'll take our minds off the prospect of our own inevitable mortality.'

The yearning to see Amy almost overcame Tom, but again he forced himself to refuse. 'No, I need to speak with Dowler's father, so I'll bid you a good night, Hugh, and I sincerely hope that you'll have an enjoyable time.'

They parted and as Tom walked away he found himself unconsciously marching in step with the beat of a further roaring chorus from the inn.

'So let us fill a bumper, And drink a health to those Who carry caps and pouches And wear the looped clothes . . .'

There was no light showing from the window of the Dowler hovel, so Tom knocked on the neighbour's door.

Hetty Drake's voice answered. 'Come in, whoever you am.'

'It's Tom Potts, Mrs Drake.' The cramped, sparsely furnished, single-candlelit room's ceiling was so low that Tom was forced to remove his top hat and stoop down.

'You'd best sit yourself down on that chair, my duck, or you'll get a crick in the back if you has to keep bending so low.' The woman chuckled in amusement.

Tom gingerly lowered himself on to a rickety chair. 'I wanted to speak to Master Dowler, Ma'am, but no light is showing and I feared he might be sleeping.'

'He is, and like a babby as well. The poor old bugger was so troubled by Joey being found like he was, I feared he'd drive himself half mad. So I give him a real good supping o' gin wi' a dash of laudanum in it to ease him to sleep.'

'That was very kind of you, Ma'am.' There was no irony in Tom's words. 'Tell me, did you know Joey Dowler well?'

'We've been neighbours all our lives. I've known him as boy and man. And truth to tell, I hadn't got much time for him as either. But this is a sad, strange way for him to end. Joey was the last bloke in this world that I'd ever have thought would have killed himself. He was always such a cry-babby when he suffered any pain.'

'Was he ever a seafarer?' Even as he voiced the question Tom felt surprised that he was asking it.

'Seafarer! Joey! Phooo!' She blew a disparaging raspberry. 'He'd not got the stomach for anything so hard as seafaring. All he ever did was odd-jobbing, and not too much of that neither. He was a lazy bugger, and a bit too fond of the drink for his own good.'

'Do you have any idea who gave him these odd jobs? What I mean is, was there anyone who regularly gave him work?'

'Well, it's hard to say really.' She furrowed her brows in the effort of remembrance. 'Over the years he was given tasks to do by lots of folks. These last couple or three years though, if I recollects rightly, he did say that he was doing quite a few for a bloke named Enoch Griffiths. He's got a farm out towards Ipsley way, I believe. In fact it was a woman who said she was Doll Griffiths who come looking for Joey the other day, saying that she'd got a little job for him. But o' course Joey wasn't here, was he? Could have been already dead by then, couldn't he?'

'Do you recall what day it was she came to see him?' Tom was being impelled by a vague atavistic hunting instinct.

'Tuesday morn, I think it was. Yes, Tuesday morn for definite. I told her to try the marsh beyond the windmill on Bridley Moor. She never come back here, so I don't know whether she found him or not.'

The atavistic instinct was strengthening rapidly now, and Tom decided he must follow it.

'Many thanks to you, Ma'am. I'll not trouble you further.' He rose to leave.

'What was it you wanted to tell Old Egbert? I can tell him for you, if you like,' Hetty Drake offered.

'Only that the post-mortem has been carried out, and we have to await the Lord Aston's decision as to the time and place of Joey's burial. In the meantime, Joey's body must remain at the Lock-up. But he is decently laid out in one of the cells, and Master Dowler may visit him whenever he cares to. If I'm not there when he does so, I shall leave instructions with my mother to allow him access.'

Hetty Drake smiled warmly. 'You're a kind man, Master Potts, and folks from Hill Street don't meet a great deal of kindness from their betters.'

'I'm most assuredly not one iota better than the people in Hill Street, Ma'am. In fact I hold to the firm belief that in this world we are all of us, whether rich or poor, equal in the sight of God.'

'Don't you dare let Old Egbert hear you say that, Master Potts,' she mock-scolded. 'He's a firm believer that God placed the rich man in the mansion, and the poor man at the gate.'

'I'll bear that in mind, Ma'am, when I meet Master Dowler. A very good night to you.'

Tom did not personally know the Griffiths family so he decided that before he went to speak with them he would try to find out more about their background. Now he headed for Silver Street, where Ritchie Bint lived. Located on the east side of the town's central plateau, it was one of the most notoriously rough and violent slums in the Parish, containing a large number of Needle Pointers as residents. A long crooked alley entered by an arch abutting the Red Lion Tavern, it was terraced with mean tumble-down tenements, which opened on to a square of older, larger, equally dilapidated buildings, two of which were registered as lodging houses.

Tom called into the Red Lion and found Bint sitting in the Tap Room playing dominoes with a group of other Needle Pointers, the table before them strewn with money. Tom's entrance was greeted with surly stares and derisive comments, but Ritchie Bint only grinned welcomingly.

'Pay no mind to these miserable sods, Tom. Am I being called out on duty? Bloody good job if I am, because these cheating buggers am fleecing me tonight.'

'I'm sorry to interrupt your game, Ritchie,' Tom apologized. 'But I wondered if I might have a word in private with you?'

'O' course you can, my mate.' Ritchie called to another man across the room. 'Shanko, come and keep this hand going for me, will you?'

Then he rose and led Tom out of the room and into the roadway.

'I need to know if you know anything about a man named Enoch Griffiths and his family,' Tom explained. 'They apparently have a farm tenancy out towards Ipsley, and a connection with Joey Dowler.'

'Oh yes, I knew Enoch Griffiths when his family was staying at Mother Readman's lodging house here in the Silver Street.

But his folks died when he was a young lad, and he was sent back into the Henley Parish Poorhouse with his sisters, because his dad and mam both had "right of settlement" there. I never seen him for years after that, but then he showed up here again about a few years past and he told me he'd got the tenancy of the Marlfield Farm down on the Icknield Street.

'Joey used to do odd jobs for him, and he told me that sometimes him and Enoch 'ud go travelling around doing a bit o' collecting and carrying, and buying and selling. Fair play to Enoch, he's done well for himself when you think that he started out as a raggedy-arsed poorhouse snot-nose.'

'What's Griffiths like as a man?' Tom was curious.

Bint shrugged casually. 'Well, I aren't seen that much of him as a man, but he seems alright enough. Joey reckoned he paid fair wages and didn't mind putting his hand in his pocket for the drink and grub when they was travelling.'

'Does Griffiths have his own wagon to do this collecting and carrying?'

Again the other man shrugged. 'I've no idea, you'll have to ask him that.'

'I will.' Tom nodded. A sense of keen anticipation was rapidly burgeoning in him, and the atavistic hunting instinct was now fully aroused. The impulsion to follow this fresh trail became overwhelming, and he told his companion, 'Thanks for the information, Ritchie. I'm sorry for taking you away from your game, and I'll leave you in peace to enjoy it.'

Bint looked disappointed. 'Do you not want me to come with you to see Griffiths?'

'There's no need, thank you all the same, Ritchie. I shall go and see him tomorrow, and I'll let you know if anything interesting transpires from my talk with him.'

'Well, if you do want me for anything tonight you know where to find me. I'll be here until Stop-Tap, and then at me house.'

They parted with a warm handshake and Tom went immediately to arrange for his use of Joseph Blackwell's horse at first light on the morrow.

FORTY-THREE

Evening, Thursday 25th October

By the fireside in the parlour of the pawnbroker's premises on the Unicorn Hill, Ishmael Benton sat nursing a bottle of gin, taking a sip of its contents from time to time. The news of the discovery of Joey Dowler's body was interesting him greatly, his cunning brain exploring if there could be any possibilities of gaining some advantage from the man's death. One theme occurred to him again and again.

'Why was Joey Dowler so agitated when I met him running away from Marlfield Farm?' Benton reflectively sucked on his decayed teeth. 'And did he top himself because he was so agitated? Has that bastard Griffiths had something to do with it? And if he has, how can I find it out and use it against him?'

In the shop at the front of the house Judas Benton was dealing with the customary Thursday rush of business from his more impoverished clientele. It was a long established practice for the majority of the Redditch workforce to be paid on Saturday afternoon. If the women were able to intercept their men and get the housekeeping money from them before they reached the taverns, then all would be well. The family would have money for rent, food, coal and candles, and to redeem whatever articles they had previously pawned. After the jollities and excesses of the weekend these same articles would almost inevitably be re-pawned on Monday, so that there was money enough to support the family's bodily needs until the following Saturday. For many, however, this fresh supply of money on a Monday would be exhausted by Wednesday or Thursday, and so necessitate a further visit to the pawnshop to raise a few more pence until payday.

Hetty Drake waited until the rush of business had slowed to a trickle before she entered the shop with a blanket-wrapped bundle.

Judas Benton grinned knowingly. 'I've got a good idea where this lot's come from, Hetty.'

'Well, Joey don't need no bedding where he is, does he, Judas?'
She grinned back at him. 'And until Old Egbert gets took on the
parish, I'm the one who's saddled wi' feeding and looking after
him.'

'You'm too soft for your own good, Hetty,' he scolded her
mildly. 'You've cared for the miserable old bugger for years, and
got little or no thanks for it. If it hadn't been for you the old
bugger would likely have turned over and died long since, for all
the good that bloody son of his was to him.'

'That's true enough,' she agreed. 'I had the Constable come to
see me earlier about Joey. He says the post-mortem's done and
dusted and that Old Egbert can go to see Joey in the Lock-up
whenever he wants.'

A wary gleam entered Judas Benton's eyes. 'Was he asking
anything about what might have caused Joey to top himself?'

'No.' She shook her head. 'He just asked about who Joey did
jobs for, and what day it was that Doll Griffiths come to see
Joey. I reckon he's going to call down Marlfield Farm and see her
about it.'

'Is he now?' Benton mused, and abruptly changed the subject.
'Let's have a look at what you got here, Hetty, and I'll see what
I can advance you on it.'

As soon as the transaction was done and Hetty Drake had left,
Judas Benton locked the shop, hurried to tell his brother what she
had said, and declared anxiously, 'Didn't I tell you that Potts is a
fly bugger, our Ishmael. I'm sure he's on to something! I should
never have got mixed up in this! I knew it 'ud all end bad! I knew
it!'

'Shut up, and let me hear meself think!' Ishmael Benton snarled.

Judas Benton stood fidgeting uneasily while the younger man
sat frowning in thought.

The shop doorbell jangled and women shouted.

'Where am you, Judas?'

'It's too early to be closed, you lazy bleeder.'

'Go and see to them, will you? Go on!' Ishmael ordered.

Judas Benton sighed resignedly and went back into the shop to
reopen for business.

Ishmael Benton was mulling things over and over again. 'How
much does Tom Potts know? How much does Doll Griffiths know?'

He thought deeply for many minutes, then suddenly rose and shouted to his brother. 'I'm going out, Judas. I'll be taking the dog cart, and be back in a couple of hours or so.'

FORTY-FOUR

Morning, Friday 26th October

'Has she sent you, Master? Has our Doll sent you?'

Tom reined in his horse as the young woman came running to meet him in the entrance lane of Marlfield Farm. He looked curiously at her; she was stockily built and dressed like a labouring man in breeches, short smock and hobnailed boots, with a man's wide-brimmed hat on her close-cropped head.

'Has who sent me, Ma'am?' he asked.

'Me sister! Our Doll!'

'Would that be Doll Griffiths?'

'O' course it is! I just told you, didn't I?' Her broad red face mirrored both irritation and distress. 'Her's gone, and we've been looking high and low for her. Our Deborah's out looking for her now. But Deborah told me to stay here in case our Doll come back while her was out looking for her.'

'And what's your name, Ma'am?'

'I'm Delilah. Me and our Deborah am twins, and Doll's our big sister, and Enoch's our big brother.' She was wailing in distress now. 'Our Doll's never gone missing afore. Summat must have happened to her! Summat bad!'

Tom could not help but feel sympathy, and he hastened to try and soothe her. 'I'm sure that nothing bad has happened to your sister. She's most likely gone on an errand, and is even now on her way back here.'

'How could her go on an errand, Master? Her was here when me and our Deborah went to bed last night, and when we got up this morning her wasn't here. How could her go on an errand in the middle o' the night?'

Tom could only shake his head. 'Well, I just don't know what errand it might be. But where is your brother Enoch?'

Now it was the woman who shook her head. 'I don't rightly know. He went away on Wednesday morn and our Doll said he was gone to do a bit o' business. He goes away lots o' times to do bits o' business.'

'And you've no idea when he might return?'

'No. He never tells me and Deborah when he goes and comes back. He only tells our Doll.'

Faced with her distress Tom, who had realized that she was somewhat mentally retarded, had to battle to overcome his own scruples against taking advantage of the simple-minded before he could ask her gently, 'Does your brother, Enoch, take his wagon with him when he goes away, Delilah?'

'Brother Enoch don't have a wagon no more. He used to have a wagon a few years since. But now if he wants a wagon he always sends Joey out with our horses to fetch one for him.'

Excitement started to pulse through Tom, and he had to force himself to keep his voice low and his tone casual. 'What sort of wagon does he like to use? The long roller-wheel ones?'

'Sometimes.'

'Was that the sort he had Joey fetch for him at the end of last month?'

'I don't know. What was last month?'

'It was September, Delilah, and it was very rainy at the very end of September, if you remember.'

She screwed up her beefy red face in the effort of remembrance, and Tom held his breath in anticipation of what he might discover in the next moment or two.

'Delilah!' Deborah Griffiths came at a run. 'Who's that you'm talking to?'

Tom dismounted and bowed politely. 'My name is Thomas Potts, Ma'am. I'm the Parish Constable.'

'Has you found her? Is our Doll dead?' Deborah's beefy face was bruised and swollen as if she had had a recent beating, and her expression was fearful. Tom instantly noted that her eyes were dulled like her sister's with mental retardation.

'No, I've not found Doll, and I'm sure that she is alive and well.' Tom hastened to soothe her fears. 'If something had happened to your sister, then the whole parish would know of it. I'm positive she's already on her way back from her errand.'

Deborah's manner veered abruptly to the aggressive. 'What's you been saying to me sister?' She turned on the other woman. 'What's this bloke been saying to you, our Delilah? You knows our Enoch don't want us talking to strangers! He'll give you a good hiding if I tells him, won't he!'

'You won't tell him, 'ull you?' Delilah whimpered in fright.

'I shall if you don't come along wi' me!' Deborah grabbed her sister's arm and pulled her at a shambling run back towards the farmhouse.

'Wait a moment, please.' Tom went after them.

'Just fuck off and leave us alone!' Deborah bawled with fear-invoked fury. 'Fuck off! Fuck off!'

Tom came to a halt, realizing that for now at least he would get nothing further from either of these women. For a while he stood undecided as to what he could do next. He was experiencing a rapidly strengthening suspicion that the apparent suicides of Alistair Carnegie, Adelaide Carnegie, Joey Dowler, and the disappearance of Doll Griffiths, could all be connected in some way, and that Enoch Griffiths was, or had knowledge of, the connecting link between them.

Some hundred yards due east from the farmhouse on the opposite side of the Icknield Street the land rose in an elongated hillock crowned with thick gorse. On that hillock the hidden watcher of the confrontation between Tom Potts and the Griffiths sisters closed his powerful spy glass with a sharp snap and mentally conceded, 'If your visit concerns what I think it does, then you're a sharp-witted fellow, Tom Potts. But I think I'm a few paces in front of you still.'

As Tom rode away from Marlfield Farm he decided that his next move must be to try and find out if Joey Dowler had borrowed or hired a roller-wheeled wagon during the month of September. He reasoned that if it was a regular occurrence for Dowler to take Griffiths' horses to collect a hired wagon then he was probably obtaining the wagons from the same supplier each time, and that supplier would not be far distant from Redditch. Tom remembered

Spicer's description of the children's wagon as being in a ramshackle condition.

'Who might loan or hire out a wagon in bad condition? Who would have wagons available for hire or loan?' He asked himself over and over again. 'I've been to every owner of roller-wheeled wagons in the Needle District and none of them had wagons hired or loaned out last month.'

Yet again he mentally went through the list of the wagon owners he had called upon. Then, abruptly, the memory of his conversation with Abel Morrall came into the forefront of his mind.

'He said that in September he'd sold a wagon which was in bad condition to a wainwright named Billy Nokes, who was going to break it up for spares. Could Billy Nokes have rented or loaned it to Joey Dowler? Well, that's easy enough to find out.'

Tom set out at a canter down the ancient Roman road towards the village of Alcester some seven miles southwards.

Before he had covered a mile he reined to a halt, mentally castigating himself. 'What in Hell's name is the matter with my brains? Let's put first things first! Didn't Ritchie mention that Griffiths was taken into the Henley Poorhouse because his parents had right of settlement in the parish? The refuge took in children from the poorhouses, so surely they'd have taken some from the local poorhouse? That could be the link between Enoch Griffiths and the Carnegies!'

He turned the horse and headed for Henley-in-Arden.

'Well this is an honour and a pleasure to be of service to you again, Sir.' The barber greeted Tom effusively. 'I trust I find you well in health and prospering in trade?'

'A trim of your hair, Sir. Of course, please be seated.'

'Did I know the Griffiths family, Sir? Oh yes. All we Henley people knew each other well in those days, Sir. Not like today when neighbours can hardly bother to pass the time of day with each other. It's all rush and bustle these days, isn't it, Sir?'

'Enoch? A very bright lad he was. Not like his sisters, they was all a bit backward, if you know what I mean, Sir. Their father took the family to live in Redditch when he found work there. But after him and his wife died the kids was all brought back to the Poorhouse in Henley here.

'It was the Carnegie family who took Enoch out of the Poorhouse and into their service. Very charitable of them, acting like true Christians so they were. I hardly set eyes on him for years after that. But later on I did hear that he'd left their service and was doing something in the carrier trade, and by all accounts he was rising in the world. But like I say, he was a very bright lad when he was a nipper, and if he was getting on in life, then good luck to him.'

'Farming now, is he, Sir! And got his sisters with him! Well I never! It just goes to show that bad beginnings don't always make bad endings, do they, Sir.'

'Thank you very much, Sir, this is most generous of you. I hope that I shall have the privilege and pleasure of being of service to you when you next visit Henley, Sir. A very good day to you, Sir.'

The excitement and lust of the hunt was pulsing through Tom as he mounted and headed for the ancient village of Alcester and Billy Nokes.

'Yes, Master Potts, I does sometimes rent wagons and carts out.'

'Round about the end of last month? Yes, I rented an old roller-wheel to a bloke from Redditch, name of Dowler. Joey Dowler.'

'No, they has to bring their own horseflesh. That's what made me wonder a bit about where a drunken waster like Dowler had got hold of a triple team. Bloody fine cattle they was as well, Cleveland Bays and a good sixteen hands high, all three of 'um.'

'Would I know the beasts again? Well one of 'um had a bald face. Seen plenty o' bald faces on the Clydesdales, but ne'er on a Cleveland afore.'

'What's a bald face? It's a white blaze that spreads to cover the muzzle and parts of the jaw and cheeks. Like I say, you don't normally see 'um on Clevelands.'

'When did he bring the wagon back here? Let me think now. It was on the Tuesday if I recollects rightly. Yes, that was it. The Tuesday of the second week in this month.'

'You're very welcome to any help I've been able to give you, Master Potts. Good day to you now, and if you ever wants to rent a cart or wagon then come and see me, and if I've got one available I'll give you a fair deal.'

Tom felt near to exultation as he rode away from the

wainwright's yard, promising himself, 'If Enoch Griffiths has a Cleveland Bay matching that description, then he's going to have to answer a great many questions.'

Because of the thickening dusk he decided to wait until the following morning before he returned to Marlfield Farm. He would take a spyglass with him and check on the grazing livestock at a distance before talking to the Griffiths family again.

FORTY-FIVE

Evening, Friday 26th October

'**H**er's gone! What d'you mean, her's gone? Gone where?' Enoch Griffiths' gin-laden breath gusted in a disbelieving snort against Deborah Griffiths' frightened face.

'We went to bed and when we woke up her'd gone, Brother Enoch,' she whimpered. 'And her never come back.'

'When did her go?'

'Last night.'

'Did her say anything afore her went?'

'No. We went to bed and when we woke up her'd gone. It warn't our fault, Brother Enoch. We hadn't done nothing to her. Honest we hadn't done nothing, had we, our Delilah?' She beseeched her sister to support her.

'Nothing, Brother Enoch. We hadn't done nothing.' Delilah Griffiths was as frightened as her twin.

For a few moments Enoch Griffiths stood breathing heavily, his yellow-brown teeth gnawing his lower lip, his fists spasmodically clenching and unclenching, while the two women crouched before him, shoulders hunched, bodies trembling.

He slumped down on a chair at the kitchen table and ordered, 'Get me some drink and vittles.'

They rushed to obey, stumbling into each other, fumbling and clattering utensils in their frantic haste.

Within brief seconds he had a pot of ale and a platter of bread, cheese and onions set before him, and he began to eat voraciously, taking slurping gulps of ale. The twins waited anxiously for his next command.

The process of satisfying his hunger and thirst served to calm his initial reaction to their news, and when he had eased his initial needs he instructed them quietly, 'Make up a pipe for me, Deborah, and you fetch me another pot of ale, Delilah.'

With heartfelt sighs of relief they hastened to bring him what he asked for.

He sat puffing out clouds of acrid smoke, carefully considering his next words.

'Now, my sisters.' He smiled at them and gestured to the other chair around the table. 'You sit down here wi' me. I'm not angry with you, and I'm not going to lift me fists to you, no matter what you tell me.' He beckoned coaxingly. 'Come now, sit yourselves down and be comfortable. Get yourselves a drink if you wants one, this ale is a bit o' good stuff, and I knows that you often takes a sly sip at it. Go on, Deborah, fetch a couple of jugs in and we'll all sup together in good companionship.'

She fetched the jugs of ale, and the two women giggling and fluttering grotesquely with relief and pleasure sat down and gazed at their brother with expressions of slavish worship.

'Here now, this jug is for you to share between you, and this jug is for me meself alone. Because I'm a big man with a big thirst.'

The twins chortled with delight.

'Take it turn and turn about to have a swallow now, my dears,' he told them jovially. 'You first, Deborah and then you next, Delilah.'

He waited while they drank and then said in a kindly voice, 'Now I want you to tell me all that you can remember about what's happened here since I went away.'

They both began to jabber excitedly, but he hushed them by putting his finger to his lips, and as they fell silent, he told Delilah, 'You tell me all that you can remember, Sister Delilah, and when you've finished our Deborah will tell me all that she can remember. Ready now – one, two, three, begin!'

FORTY-SIX

Morning, Saturday 27th October

On the hillock above Icknield Street the raindrops dripped from the branches of the clumped gorse bushes that Tom Potts lay beneath and low-lying mist blanketed the Marlfield Farm and its surrounding fields from his view. For more than an hour before dawn he had been hiding here, hoping for the clouds to rift and the rising sun to shine through and dispel the mist. The constant driving rain had saturated his clothing and billycock hat, chilled his flesh, and was now beginning to depress his spirits. For perhaps the tenth time he fumbled for his pocket watch and checked the hour. It was several minutes past eight o'clock, more than an hour since sunrise.

'I'm wasting my time here. There's naught else for it but to go directly to the house,' he decided.

He crawled on hands and knees from under the thick-laced branches and got to his feet, wincing at the stretching of his cramped muscles as he made his way down the steep slope. He had left his horse tied to another bush on the far side of the hillock concealed from the roadway but when he reached there frowned in dismay. The horse was gone.

'Where the hell are you?' He began to walk in ever widening circles, peering through the opaque swirls of mist, calling softly, 'Come now. Come now. Come now.'

'Come now! Come now! Come now!' Magnified by the mist, seemingly reverberating from all quarters, the sudden harsh shouting was interspersed with bursts of raucous, jeering laughter. 'Come now! Come now! Come now!'

Tom's initial reaction was nervous shock and he halted to turn round and round, desperately trying to locate the direction from which the shouts and laughter were coming.

A solid form loomed rapidly out of the mist, and Tom found himself face to face with Enoch Griffiths and the round black muzzle-hole of the long-barrelled gun he was aiming at Tom's head.

Tom involuntarily raised his hands to shield his face and stepped backwards. His heel snagged on a tussock of grass and he lost his balance and toppled backwards to thud down on to his arse.

Griffiths roared with laughter and lowered the weapon.

'There now, Constable Potts, that'll teach you not to trespass on my land, won't it?' he jeered. 'That's put the shits up you, aren't it?'

Heart racing, dragging in strangled gasps of air, Tom was unable to answer.

Griffiths used one hand to stroke the long barrel of the gun. 'This is a Baker rifle, this is, Constable Potts. I could take the eyes out of your yed at a hundred paces with this beauty.' He proffered the same hand down to Tom. 'Let me help you up, Constable Potts.'

After a momentary hesitation Tom took the offered hand and Griffiths displayed his immense muscular power as he yanked Tom back on to his feet. Then he pointed at the spyglass which Tom had dropped in his fright.

'There's no need for you to sneak around like a yellow-bellied cur dog to spy on me, Constable Potts. If you wants to know anything about me and my business, then all you needs to do is to come to my farm like a man and ask me whatever you wants to ask.'

Tom's face was burning with embarrassment and shame that he had reacted so cravenly to the other man's onset, and he was desperately struggling to at least make a show of composure. He swallowed hard, trying to ease the tension in his throat and mouth, and managed to blurt out, 'What have you done with my horse, Master Griffiths?'

Griffiths' strong yellow-brown teeth bared in a sneering grin, and Tom couldn't help but feel that he was facing a ferocious and deadly dangerous wild beast.

'Your horse, Constable Potts? How do I know that the stray I found on my land eating my grass the best part of an hour since is your horse? Have you got proof of ownership?' Griffiths was patently enjoying this baiting.

Tom was winning his inner battle to regain his self-control, and he sensed that, for the time being at least, his life was not in danger. He was able to speak more easily now, and to choose his words with care.

'No, Master Griffiths, I've no proof of ownership because in fact the mare is the property of Joseph Blackwell, Esq. I'm using it on his orders to carry out my duties.' He couldn't resist verbally striking back. 'I'm sure that he will greatly appreciate the care you've shown for his property. But whether he will accept your account of having found it astray, over my account of having left it securely tethered, remains to be proven.'

Griffiths scowled and Tom instantly regretted his own temerity, and could not help but add, 'But I'm sure that he will incline to favour your account rather than mine. Because after all, you're a man of property and I'm merely a lowly Parish Constable.'

Still scowling, Griffiths asked, 'What was it you were hoping to see through that bloody spyglass?'

Tom was abruptly consumed with anger at his own self-perceived cowardice, and was driven by his pride to respond bluntly. 'I was hoping to see a Cleveland Bay with a bald face. So to satisfy my curiosity on that score will you let me take a look at all your horses?'

To his utter surprise the other man's reaction was a chuckle of what appeared to be genuine amusement.

'Of course I'll let you look all my horses over, Constable Potts. They'm my pride and joy. You're hoping to see a bald-faced Cleveland, you say. Well I've got five Clevelands, and the finest of 'um is a bald face.'

He slung the Baker rifle over his shoulder and gestured invitingly. 'Let's go, Constable Potts. There's no time like the present to satisfy your wanting to see my horses, and me wanting to show 'um off to you.'

As they entered the farmyard the Griffiths twins came rushing out from the stable block and the caged dogs set up a furious barking.

'That's him, Brother Enoch! That's the bloke who was asking our Delilah all them questions! That's the one I fucked off!' Deborah Griffiths shouted excitedly.

'That's him, Brother Enoch! That's the bloke who was asking me all them questions!' Delilah Griffiths parroted her sibling.

'Am you going to shoot him, Brother Enoch?' Deborah asked eagerly. 'Am you?'

'Get back inside, the pair of you,' Enoch Griffiths roared. 'And get some vittles ready. Constable Potts is going to have some breakfast with me.'

Tom could only stare disbelievingly at the other man, who grinned at him and jovially invited, 'Now please accept my hospitality, Constable Potts. We'll have a look at my horses first, and then we can ate our breakfasts together just to show that there's no hard feeling on my part for your trespassing on my land and spying on me.'

The stables were large and clean, the walls freshly lime-washed, the stalled horses had reddish-brown coats, black manes, legs and tails, and were glossy with health and careful grooming.

'Here's my beauties, Tamper, Clamper, Stamper, Ramper and Lamper. Five of as fine Cleveland Bays as can be found in this kingdom,' Griffiths boasted proudly. 'There are none better for use as draft, riding or coach, and this 'un here is my particular favourite.' He walked to one stall which held a handsome stallion with a white blaze that spread across its muzzle, cheeks and jaw. 'Let me present Tamper to you, Constable Potts. He must be the bare face you was so interested in seeing. Aren't he a beauty?'

'He certainly is,' Tom was happy to acknowledge, and decided to take the offensive. 'And he's one of the team that you sent with Joey Dowler to collect the roller-wheel wagon from Billy Nokes' yard in Alcester at the end part of September, is he not?'

He found himself tensing involuntarily in nervous anticipation of Griffiths' reaction; and was hard put to hide his own surprised reaction when the other man told him readily, 'He's certainly one of the team I rented out to Joey Dowler in the last week of September, and Joey did say he was going to rent a wagon from Billy Nokes. Whether he did or no warn't any concern of mine. Joey paid me the hiring fee for my horses in advance, and I knew he'd take good care of them. I'd hired beasts out to him afore, you see, and he'd worked for me doing delivering and collecting when I was running my carrier business.'

'When did he return the team to you?' Tom queried.

'I was bloody upset when he did.' Griffiths scowled. 'Last thing at night it was when the bugger come knocking me up out o' me bed just when I'd got off to sleep. It was bloody Tuesday, second week in October. I remembers it well, because he was two fuckin' days late returning the horses. He'd promised me faithful that he'd have 'um back here on the Sunday afternoon previous. Then he had the cheek to ask me if I could wait for the extra money he owed for being so tardy in bringing 'um back. I charges double for any over-keep of the hiring, you see.'

Tom nodded. 'Well you're justified in doing so, Master Griffiths.'

Inwardly he was thinking ruefully that the other man's ready answers were totally opposite to the reaction he had been wanting to provoke. More in hope than expectation he enquired, 'Did Dowler ever pay you the extra charge?'

Once again the other man bared his big yellow-brown teeth in a snarling grin. 'Oh yes, he paid me alright, and on that very same night. The people I do business with knows better than to ever try and gammon me out of my rightful dues, Constable Potts.' He nodded as if to add emphasis to that statement. 'Oh yes, he paid me alright.'

'Do you know where he went with the wagon?' Tom pressed.

Griffiths shrugged his broad shoulders. 'Well he said something about doing a bit of collecting and delivering down Hereford or maybe Shropshire way. But I warn't really interested. So long as he paid me he could have gone to the fuckin' moon for all I cared.'

Frustration was gnawing at Tom. Despite the other man's apparent openness all his instincts were screaming at him that Griffiths was somehow involved in what had happened to the dead boy and the other children. Tom decided that the best thing he could do at this particular moment would be to go away and find a quiet spot where he could sit and think hard about how to progress this investigation.

'Well, thank you for your co-operation, Master Griffiths. I'll leave you in peace now.'

'Aren't you going to stop and have a bit o' breakfast with me? The girls will be sore disappointed if you goes without eating what they've took the trouble to cook for you.'

'Please convey to them my sincere apologies, Master Griffiths, but I have much work to do and cannot spare any more time here. If you could please return my horse to me I'll leave you in peace.'

'Ahhrrr yes, your horse.' Amused laughter rumbled in Griffiths' deep chest. 'I should think it's a fair way away from us by now, Constable Potts. Because the last sighting I had of it, it was going hell for leather down the road as if it had a red-hot coal up its arsehole. I tried to stop it, but it knocked me flying. I should ask the folks around Ipsley first if I was you. Somebody might have managed to stop it when it was passing through there.'

For a brief instant the mental image of his constable's staff crushing Griffiths' skull flashed through Tom's mind. 'Don't give the bastard the satisfaction of seeing you react in anger.' Tom summoned every atom of his willpower, and managed to force a smile. 'I shall take your advice on that score, Master Griffiths, and I thank you for it.'

A spasm of angry chagrin disfigured Griffiths' broad red face, and Tom drew considerable satisfaction at so sorely disconcerting his opponent. To twist the figurative knife in the wound he now began to whistle a lively air and sauntered out of the door hopefully portraying a state of utter insouciance. Then other ideas flashed through his mind, and he abruptly turned about and re-entered the stable.

Griffiths blinked in surprise. 'What brings you back?'

Tom smiled. 'I'm suddenly feeling the pangs of my empty belly, Master Griffiths; and if your kind invitation to have breakfast with you is still open, I'd be more than grateful to accept it.'

Griffiths hesitated as if uncertain, and then shrugged and nodded. 'Come on then. Like I already said, you're welcome to fill your belly at my table.'

As he followed Griffiths into the kitchen of the farmhouse the savoury smell of frying bacon, eggs and mushrooms wafted around Tom's head arousing a raging appetite.

The twins excitedly fussed around him, settling him into a chair at the table, bringing him a jug of ale, a platter heaped high with bacon, eggs, mushrooms, another platter with thick slices of fresh-baked bread and large knobs of salted butter.

An uneasy feeling of guilt struck through him, that he should be accepting this warm hospitality from these women when he had the ulterior motive of trying to prove the criminal guilt of the very brother whose food and drink he was now enjoying.

Tom forced his thoughts to centre on the dead boy and the little girl who had been spirited away from the Poorhouse. 'I'm doing this for them.'

Griffiths took a chair opposite Tom and began to eat and drink voraciously, completely ignoring his guest. The two girls stood side by side behind their brother's chair, their eyes avidly watching Tom's face, their mouths agape as if in wonder.

Tom was at first a little uncomfortable at being watched so intently, but that feeling soon passed as he concentrated on how to word the opening gambit which he hoped might cause Griffiths to give something away.

Tom finished the last remnants of his food, and Deborah instantly offered, 'Shall you have some more, Master?'

'No, I thank you, I'm full to bursting. That was a splendid breakfast, Miss Griffiths. You and your sister are very fine cooks.' Tom genuinely meant the compliment.

Both girls coloured with pleasure and simpered grotesquely.

Tom obeyed a sudden overwhelming compulsion to change his point of attack, and asked Deborah, 'Has your sister Doll returned, Miss Griffiths?'

The smile fled from her bruised face. She jerked her head round to stare fearfully at her brother.

Enoch Griffiths finished noisily chewing his mouthful of food and washed it down his gullet with a slurping gulp of ale. He belched resoundingly, and then told Tom, 'My sister Doll is up to her old tricks, Constable Potts. And if her warn't my kith and kin I'd be laying charges against her this very minute. Her's done this all too many times afore. She steals whatever money o' mine that she can lay her hands on, and then she buggers off on the piss.

'I was away on a bit o' business and she buggered off on the Thursday night, according to what the twins tell me. What they couldn't tell me, because they never knew, was that the bloody cow took twenty sovereigns from my strongbox. She'll not be back here until they've all been pissed up against the wall.' His teeth glistened in the familiar snarling grin. 'Or should I say, pissed straight down on to the cobbles, seeing as how she's a wench. I'd be very grateful if you'd keep an eye out for her when you're doing your rounds of the pubs, Constable Potts, and send me word if you sees her.'

'Would you not prefer me to take her to the Lock-up?' Tom probed.

The other man's snarling grin didn't waver. 'It would serve her right if you did, Constable Potts. But I don't want to make a public show of her, or get her into any trouble. It's a family matter, and that's where it stays, inside the family.'

'Your loyalty to your family is most laudable,' Tom commended, not entirely ironically because he could not help but question how his mother would react if he took so much as a handkerchief from her linen press. Then he reverted to his original plan. 'The Carnegie family, Master Griffiths? I don't doubt but that your loyalty towards them matched your loyalty towards your own family?'

For the first time Tom thought he detected a flickering of uncertainty in Griffiths' eyes. But after a momentary hesitation, Griffiths told him emphatically, 'I should hope it did! They were very good to me, and in return I served them well. I haven't seen any of them for years though. I went back to Henley when I'd made summat of meself and found that they were long gone, and nobody could tell me where they'd gone to.'

Now the snarling grin returned. 'That's another favour you could do for me. If you should ever hear anything about their whereabouts, perhaps you'd be good enough to send word to me. I should like nothing better than to see them again, and thank 'um for all their kindness to me.'

Griffiths slapped his hands down on the table in a gesture of finality, and rose to his feet. 'I'll have to see you out now, Constable Potts. I've got business to attend to.'

Tom rose also and Griffiths ushered him out into the farmyard.

'Good day, Master Griffiths.' Tom bowed politely. 'And thank you very much for the breakfast.'

'Good day, Constable Potts, and don't forget that your horse went southwards.' The confident, snarling grin was back on Griffiths' face once more.

'I won't,' Tom assured, and walked away.

As Enoch Griffiths watched the tall figure receding down the lane towards the Icknield Street, his snarling grin of triumph was superseded by a worried frown.

'You're a real fly bastard, aren't you, Potts? There's some mouths

I need to close before you get to open them, and I need to do it a bit sharpish as well.'

Tom's mood was also sombre. Although he was increasingly convinced that Enoch Griffiths was personally involved in the trafficking of the missing children, and an integral link in the apparent suicides of the Carnegies and Joey Dowler, he had not a shred of solid proof.

'What can I do now? What do I do next?' he asked himself repeatedly, until a small voice deep in his mind suggested: 'Perhaps it might be a good idea to go and find Joseph Blackwell's mare, before you're accused of horse-stealing.'

FORTY-SEVEN

Late afternoon, Saturday 27th October

The reason for this informal Saturday gathering round the long table in the vestry room of St Stephen's chapel was the pressing need to decide the disposal of the corpse of Joey Dowler.

Two magistrates were present. Both were clad alike in the black full-skirted coats, breeches and stockings of their religious calling; both favoured white, short-queued tie-wigs perched upon their heads. There the similarity ended, because the Reverend Percival Timmins was as extraordinarily pasty-faced, meagre-bodied, timidly spoken and presently sober, as the Lord Aston was extraordinarily purple-faced, grossly fat, aggressively spoken, and presently very drunk.

Now Aston was aggressively declaiming, 'I say that the Coroner's inquest verdict on Monday next must be suicide! And I say that after receiving that verdict we must uphold tradition, and bury Dowler under the Beoley crossroads at midnight, with a stake through his heart. All in favour indicate!'

Elegantly dressed, exquisitely groomed and pomaded, Hugh Laylor demurred. 'With the greatest of respect, My Lord, I fear that such a course of action would only serve to render this Parish an object of mockery.'

'How so, Doctor Laylor?' Aston glared.

'We are living in the modern age, My Lord.' There was the hint of a supercilious sneer in the curl of Laylor's shapely lips. 'Midnight burials at crossroads and stakes through hearts may well have suited their purposes in the Dark Ages, but this is the nineteenth century, not the ninth, and we are civilized Englishmen, not barbarous Jutes, Angles or Saxons.'

'I'll thank you, Sir, to remember that I have no need for any instruction in the history of my beloved country from you, or from anyone else throughout this Kingdom,' Aston growled. 'I'll remind you, Sir, that I hold Doctorates of Divinity and Philosophy, and have spent many years of my life in study and contemplation.'

Laylor's handsome features instantly mirrored utter consternation. 'My Lord, I hasten to apologize if my words could have been misconstrued to be any criticism of, or disagreement with your own views on this matter. I was in fact intending a sarcastic comment on the mores of the present age. In which the misguided souls, who are in such abundant numbers these modern days, sneer at the wisdom of our forefathers. I personally am in complete agreement with yourself, My Lord, that Dowler should be staked through the heart and buried under the crossroads.'

'Well speaking for myself, I don't give a bugger what's done with him. Just so long as it isn't going to cost the Parish any unnecessary expense,' grunted Samuel Smallwood, Needle Master and Select Vestryman.

'But surely digging a large deep hole in the centre of a busy crossroads is going to cause unnecessary delays and expense to travellers, and indeed to our own business deliveries and postings,' interposed the tall, distinguished-looking Charles Bartleet, Needle Master and Select Vestryman.

'Well, with all respect, My Lord and Gentlemen, I must confess to feeling uneasy at the thought of the stake so barbarously penetrating the flesh that is created in the image of Our Saviour,' Reverend Percival Timmins fluted nervously.

'Don't be such an old woman, Timmins. It was merely a man's prick penetrating a woman's cunt that created Dowler.' Aston reproved him coarsely, then turned to John Clayton. 'What's your opinion on this burial, Clayton?'

John Clayton was forced to make a very quick evaluation of

possible answers. He personally was opposed to the traditional practice of staking and burying under crossroads, regarding it as rank superstition which had no place in this modern age. However, down in Hampshire his widowed mother and spinster sisters relied upon him as their sole means of support, and although the stipend he received as Lord Aston's curate was small, it was all the assured income he had. If he lost his position then the situation for his dependants would became parlous in the extreme.

Clayton smothered his conscience and replied, 'I'm with you on this matter, My Lord.'

Joseph Blackwell, Esq. sat quietly observing his companions, and for the time being keeping his own counsel.

Outside the main chapel door Tom Potts stood sentinel, in company with Hetty Drake. Her kindly motherly features were drawn with anxiety.

'How much longer d'you think they'll be, Master Potts?' she kept asking at frequent intervals.

Each time Tom could only ruefully admit, 'I'm sorry, Mrs Drake, but I've no idea.'

'It'll be the death of his old dad if they stakes and crossroads Joey.' She shook her head worriedly. 'Joey being found hanging nigh on killed the poor old bugger wi' shock. I told him that it was all an accident. A bit of a game that went wrong. If Old Egbert finds out that Joey's been named as a self-murderer, it'll break his heart, so it will. Egbert's always been such a respectable man. Then there's Joey's bits and pieces, aren't there? They'll be all took by the Crown, won't they? God only knows they aren't much, but Egbert might get a few bob for 'um.'

The noise and bustle of the market ranged along the outside of the chapel yard wall was increasing in volume and density as the needle mills, factories and workshops released their workers and like a human flood they came in waves into the town centre.

'You've a busy night ahead of you, Master Potts.' Hetty Drake smiled sympathetically. 'It's odds on that Joey will have company in the Lock-up tonight, I don't doubt.'

'Let's just hope that that company will be alive and well, Mrs Drake,' Tom wished sincerely.

Two young women walked arm in arm past the chapel yard gate.

'There's Tom Potts,' Maisie Lock announced. 'And he's talking to a woman.'

Amy Danks pulled her friend to an abrupt halt. 'Let's go back and see who she is.'

They retraced their footsteps and both stared hard as they passed the entrance.

'That's Hetty Drake from down Hill Street,' Amy snapped angrily. 'She should be ashamed of herself setting her cap at Tom! She's old enough to be my mother!'

'No, she's not setting her cap at Tom. Hetty's not like that. She's a real decent sort,' Maisie Lock contradicted her friend. 'She told me that there was to be a meeting today to decide what's going to happen to Joey Dowler's body. Hetty's looked after his old dad for years, and she's real worried that they'm going to stick a stake through Joey's heart and bury him at midnight down Beoley crossroads. She says it'll be the death of his old dad if they does that.'

'Why should they do that to Joey? It's not right to serve a dead person so badly, and upset their family. It's not right to do it!' Amy thought that her point was eminently reasonable, and was shocked when her friend flared back angrily.

'Don't you know nothing, Amy Danks? When people kills themselves they commits the worst mortal sin possible, and they becomes the Devil's creatures, and their spirits roam the world doing harm to innocent people. So when they'm put in the grave the stake is driven through their hearts to fasten their spirits to that spot, so that they can't roam around doing evil. And they'm laid in the middle of a crossroads because the traffic over them crushes their spirits into little tiny bits that then wastes away to nothing. So they can never do any harm because there's nothing left of them.'

Amy instantly counter-attacked. 'That's bloody nonsense that is. People kills themselves because they're driven to do it. They should be buried properly and prayed for, not treated like some sort of evil spirit. I'm going to tell Tom Potts that he's not to let them do that to Joey Dowler.'

She ran into the chapel yard and up to the couple by the door. Tom was simultaneously shocked, delighted, and apprehensive.

'Is it true, Tom Potts, that they're going to drive a stake through

Joey Dowler's heart and treat him like an evil spirit?' She didn't wait for any reply. 'Well, if you stand by and let them do that, then I'll never speak to you again.'

'It's not Master Potts' fault that they're going to do that.' Hetty Drake sprang to his defence. 'He doesn't want that to happen to Joey any more than we do.'

'Then he must stop them,' Amy retorted.

'It's not been decided yet what they intend to do,' Tom said quietly. 'But I fear that my opinion won't have any influence on them either way.'

'That's you all over, isn't it, Tom?' Amy now sounded more sadly resigned than angry. 'You always put yourself down, and allow people to walk all over you. That's why I can't ever marry you, Tom. Because if you can't stick up for yourself, how can I ever be sure that you'll stick up for me and the children we should have.' Tears brimmed in her blue eyes.

He stood motionless, staring at her with dismay, not knowing what to do or say, when the stentorian bellowing of Lord Aston came from within.

'Potts, get in here this instant! This instant, I say!'

'Oh, Master Potts, please go in and find out what's to be done with Joey,' Hetty Drake pleaded.

'Potts? Potts? Where the devil are you, man?' Aston sounded furious.

'Please find out what's to happen, Master Potts. I can't bear not knowing a moment longer.' Hetty Drake's heartfelt plea swayed Tom and he entered the vestry room.

Aston glowered at him. 'What in Hell's name kept you, Potts? I've been shouting for you these last ten minutes. How dare you keep your betters waiting?'

Tom experienced a surge of bitter resentment that this arrogant, bullying, drunken sot should literally hold the power of life and death over other people purely by the accident of birth giving him the unearned advantage of wealth and possessions.

An angry rejoinder rose to Tom's tongue, but then instinctively he glanced towards Joseph Blackwell and saw the other man's thin lips mouth a silent negative. So he held his tongue and merely waited silently.

'You will make preparations to bury Dowler under the Beoley

crossroads this coming Monday midnight, Constable Potts,' Aston slurred. 'You will drive a stake through his heart when he is interred. Reverend Clayton will accompany you, and direct the proceedings.'

In his mind Tom could only see Amy's blue eyes brimming with tears, and hear again the sad hopelessness in her voice. *'You always put yourself down, and allow people to walk all over you . . .'*

He physically shook his head. All present stared wonderingly at him.

'Are you hearing what I'm telling you, Potts?' Aston stared quizzically at Tom's face.

Tom drew a long deep breath, and steeled himself. 'I am, My Lord. You are telling me to prepare to bury Dowler as a self-murderer.'

'And?' Aston questioned.

'I think it is the wrong thing to do, My Lord.'

There came a concerted gasp of astonishment from all around him.

'What?' Aston blinked owlishly in disbelief. 'Are you telling me that I'm doing the wrong thing?'

'I believe that you are mistaken in ordering this action, My Lord.' Now that the die was cast, Tom was doggedly determined not to give way.

'How dare you challenge my orders?' Aston bellowed.

Joseph Blackwell quickly rose from his seat and interposed himself between the antagonists.

'The constable is not challenging you, My Lord, he is merely advancing a personal opinion which he is perfectly entitled to hold.'

'Then let the lanky clown explain his opinion.'

Joseph Blackwell turned to the other men present and requested quietly. 'Gentlemen, would you be so gracious as to withdraw for a short time?'

Before Aston could make any comment, Blackwell frowned at him and said sharply, 'I really must insist on this, My Lord.'

With bad grace Aston scowled and slurred, 'Do as Master Blackwell asks, Gentlemen.'

'Not you, Constable Potts.' Blackwell detained Tom. 'I want

you to explain fully to Lord Aston your reasons for saying what you have to him.'

Tom's thoughts raced. It was the conversation with Hetty Drake and particularly the exchange with Amy Danks that had impelled him to speak out. He knew that to give this reason would only inflame Aston to derisively jeer, and guarantee his insistence on the crossroads burial and staking. He sought desperately for other reasons, and suddenly his mind found them.

'Very well, Sir. I shall explain my reasons in full . . . My Lord Aston, on the ninth day of this present month a seafarer named Matthew Spicer came to see me concerning some children who had been stolen from the Brimfield Poorhouse in Shropshire . . .' Tom spoke with a show of confidence he was far from feeling as he explained how he believed Dowler had been trafficking these children, one of whom was the dead boy found in the badger sett, and another the little girl who had been in effect stolen again from the Tardebigge Poorhouse. He finished by stating, 'I am positive that Dowler had accomplices, and these same accomplices killed him, My Lord.'

'Do you have any inkling who these accomplices might be, Constable Potts?' Joseph Blackwell asked.

'I have my suspects, Sir. But as yet no complete material proof that would satisfy a court of law.'

'How confident are you that you will in due course obtain such complete proof?' Blackwell was deliberately offering Tom further opportunity to press his case home.

'Totally confident, Sir, and this fact will be demonstrated in the very near future,' Tom lied with an air of utter certainty.

'Go and wait with the gentlemen outside, Constable Potts,' Blackwell ordered immediately so as not to allow Aston any chance of further questioning.

As soon as Tom had gone through the door, Blackwell declared exultantly, 'What a feather this will be in your cap, My Lord, to have been so instrumental in bringing a gang of such evil miscreants to justice! The whole of the county, nay the whole country, will be ringing with praise for your foresight. The Earl will be positively green with envy!'

He pulled his gold watch from its fob and glanced at it, then

exclaimed, 'Are you not engaged to dine with Lord Godericke at
Studley Castle tonight, My Lord?'

Aston blinked blearily with the effort of remembering. 'I do
believe I am.'

'Then permit me to call your manservant to escort you to your
carriage, My Lord.' Blackwell went to the outer door and shouted,
'Webster, your master wishes to leave now. You'd best bring the
coachman with you.'

Blackwell then moved to speak with the small group of waiting
men. 'Lord Aston will announce what type of burial Dowler's
corpse is to receive after due consideration of the Coroner's
inquest verdict, Gentlemen. So we may consider this meeting
ended, and I bid you all farewell. Except for yourself, Constable
Potts. I need to speak further with you after Lord Aston has left.
So wait here.'

Blackwell disappeared back into the vestry, and Tom went to
the chapel yard gate to tell Hetty Drake and Amy Danks.

'There's no final decision as yet about Joey Dowler's funeral.
But I'm very hopeful that he'll eventually receive a Christian
burial.'

'Oh, God bless you, Master Potts. I knew you'd speak up for
us. I'm going straight to tell Old Egbert he needn't worry about
it any more.' Hetty Drake beamed gratefully at him and hurried
away just as Tom was trying to disclaim any credit for the postponing of the crossroads burial.

Amy Danks remained, looking at Tom with an ambiguous
expression on her heart-shaped face.

He smiled tentatively at her. She frowned and stamped her foot
angrily. 'Why can't you do things to make me hate you, Tom
Potts?'

He gaped in shock. 'What sort of things?'

'Well, why didn't you tell Hetty Drake to bugger off and not
pester you about bloody Joey Dowler's funeral, for one thing? And
for another thing, why didn't you keep that scruffy little wench
to be a skivvy in the Lock-up for your rotten old bitch of a mother,
instead of finding her a nice home where she's already being
spoiled to death and taught to think herself to be Little Lady Muck
by those two soppy old maids? And why do you always have to
be so nice to me, no matter what I say or do that's hurtful to you?

Why can't you call me for the bad-tempered, spiteful cow I am
sometimes?'

Before he could answer, Lord Aston came staggering out from
the vestry supported on either side by his old servant, Webster,
and his coachman. Tom and Amy were forced to stand out from
their path to the carriage waiting outside the gate. Then Blackwell
appeared in the vestry doorway.

'Constable Potts, forgive me for interrupting your conversation,
but it is of the utmost urgency that I speak with you immediately.'

Amy's temper instantly flared again. 'Go to your boss, Tom
Potts. Deep down in your heart, being the Parish Constable is all
you really want to be, isn't it; and a wife and children would always
have to play second fiddle to that. So I'm done with you for good.'
She turned and ran, skirt and petticoat flying up around her knees.

'Constable Potts? I need to speak with you. Constable Potts?'
Blackwell's reedy shouted summons penetrated Tom's confused,
troubled thoughts, and it was with a feeling of almost relief that
he was forced to put Amy from the forefront of his mind and
answer to it.

'Now, Potts, give me the names of your suspects, and the reasons
for your suspicions of them. Which I don't doubt are well founded.'
Blackwell's thin lips quirked in a bleak momentary smile. 'For
apart from myself, I do believe that you're the shrewdest and most
cunning fellow in this entire county.'

'My main suspect is Enoch Griffiths. I think that he and Dowler
were acting in concert as child traffickers. Griffiths has strength
enough to have overcome and hung Dowler single-handedly.
Griffiths also had had close connection with the Carnegies, both
of whose deaths were classed as suicides, but could just as easily
have been murders.

'Griffiths' sister Doll has gone missing. He claims that this is
a frequent occurrence and that she is merely on a drunken spree
with money she stole from him. But my conversations with his
two younger sisters, both simpletons whom he obviously keeps in
terrified submission, lead me to the belief that Griffiths has disposed
of Doll also.'

'What about this fellow, Matthew Spicer, the seafarer?' Blackwell
queried.

Tom could only shake his head. 'I don't know where he is. He made many enquiries locally in an effort to find the wagon used by the traffickers, but I've not seen him since he first came to me.'

Blackwell closed his pale eyes and briefly mulled over what he had heard. Then his eyes opened.

'How are you going to prove Griffiths' guilt, Master Potts?'

Tom replied without hesitation. 'Frankly, Sir, at this present moment, I really don't know.'

FORTY-EIGHT

Late afternoon, Wednesday 31st October

S ince Monday people had been bringing scrap wood, dead branches of trees and shrubs and assorted combustible rubbish to the Green, and now in its centre the great mound of the bonfire was in its final stages of construction.

Tomorrow was All Saints' Day, the first day of November when the saints and martyrs of the Christian Church were to be hallowed, and tonight was the Christian All Hallows' Eve.

But on this night the flames of the great Halloween bonfire would not be leaping and roaring to hallow any Christian saints or martyrs, but would be celebrating a far more ancient tradition, the pagan Celtic festival of Samhain when the souls of the dead would revisit their old homes. These flames were to be lit to keep at bay the evil witches, ghosts, hobgoblins and demons of all kinds who would be roaming through the darkness of this night hunting for those human souls.

Tom Potts came walking back from the Pound meadow, halted on the Green to watch the bonfire builders, and contemplated what the night would bring for he and his fellow constables, Ritchie Bint and Charles Bromley. Even as he thought of the second name, he dismissed it from his reckoning.

'As always Charles will be at his usual post whenever there's a likelihood of fisticuffs. Hiding under his bedclothes behind barred shutters and doors. And who can blame him for that? Not I! Because I'd much prefer to be doing just that myself.'

'Master Potts, I was just on my way to the Lock-up to find
you.' Judas Benton came hurrying to join him.

'How can I be of service to you, Master Benton?' Tom asked,
noting as he did so that the man looked worried.

'It's our Ishmael, Master Potts. He's gone missing.'

'Gone missing?'

'That's what I said, Master Potts. I aren't seen hide nor hair of
him since last Thursday night. He said he was taking our dog cart
and he'd be back in a couple of hours at the most. And I aren't
seen neither him nor the dog cart since.'

'And this was last Thursday night, you say?' Even as Tom
sought confirmation the coincidence that Doll Griffiths had also
gone missing on that same night struck him.

'I do say!' Benton snapped irritably. 'How many more times
must I tell you?'

Tom had no real reason to think that the two disappearances
might be in some way connected, yet driven by a sudden strong
impulse he smiled and said, 'I shouldn't think that your brother
has come to any harm, Master Benton. He's most likely gone off
gallivanting with some woman or other. Perhaps with Doll
Griffiths?'

'Doll Griffiths!' Benton exclaimed.

For a fleeting instant Tom thought he detected alarm in the other
man's eyes and tone of voice. But then Benton went on hastily.
'Who's Doll Griffiths? Her aren't one o' my customers, that's for
sure. I knows everybody that I do business with, and this Doll
Griffiths, whoever she might be, aren't one o' my customers.'

Tom had to accept this assertion, and explain, 'It was just a
passing thought, Master Benton. But as to your brother's apparent
disappearance, I'm feared that there's little I can do. You could
have an appeal for any information concerning your brother's
present whereabouts broadcast by our Town Crier. Or advertise in
the Birmingham and Worcester newspapers, or even have posters
printed and distributed.'

'But that'll cost a bloody fortune!' Benton protested. 'I pays a
bloody extortionate amount o' bloody Parish rates and taxes, and
keeps you and your Ma in bloody free bed and board, and this is
what I gets in return. Bloody nothing! Well I'm going to complain
to the Vestry about you, my buck! You just wait and see if I don't.'

He stamped away muttering furiously to himself, and Tom could only smile ruefully.

'Constable Potts! Constable Potts!' A small slender figure came hurrying towards Tom from the busy group at the bonfire.

Tom sighed in resignation.

John Osborne was the master of the charitable Free School, which had recently been built and endowed by the Earl of Plymouth for those poorer boys of the Parish whose parents were prepared to release them for a few hours weekly from their multitude of menial jobs. He was also the self-important, self-appointed organizer and director of any public parish event for which he could lay claim to have the necessary esoteric knowledge and expertise.

Now with his magnified eyes blinking furiously behind the lenses of the pince-nez wobbling precariously on his long thin nose, he demanded pompously, 'Have you made all necessary preparations for the maintenance of the public order at tonight's festivities, Constable Potts?'

'Yes indeed, Master Osborne.' Tom took a sly delight in replying in the same pompous manner. 'I have issued instructions for the entire force of the Parish Constabulary to parade at eight o'clock this night before the main entrance of the Lockup. At which time I shall allot to them their various duties, and of course reiterate their obligation to keep the King's peace at all costs.'

'Very well, Constable Potts. I have the utmost confidence that you will do your duty to your best endeavour. Now I must leave you, because I still have a veritable mountain of tasks to complete. *Au Revoir*, Constable Potts.'

'*Au Revoir* to you, Master Osborne.'

They exchanged bows and Osborne hurried back to the bonfire. Tom chuckled wryly and went on his own way.

From their bedroom window in the Fox and Goose, Amy Danks and Maisie Lock watched him crossing the Green, and Amy sighed despondently.

'I'm sure he was having a joke and laughing with John Osborne.'

'Well if he was, why shouldn't he?' Maisie Lock snapped with a hint of asperity.

'Because he should be too sorrowful to be laughing and joking,'

Amy muttered resentfully. 'He should be feeling all out of sorts and depressed like I am.'

'You needs to make your mind up, you do.' Maisie frowned impatiently. 'Do you want him, or don't you?'

Amy's smooth brows creased as she considered her answer, then replied thoughtfully, 'Most of the time I do want to wed him. But I can't stand the way he lets his mother walk all over him, and I can't stand him being at the beck and call of everybody in the Parish.'

'He won't be at everybody's beck and call when he finishes being the constable; and his Mam aren't going to live forever, is she?' Maisie pointed out. 'And you could ask Jack Smith to wish a death spell on to her and hurry her into her coffin a bit quicker.'

Amy couldn't help but giggle. 'I wonder what he'd charge for that? God only knows his bloody scrying comes dear enough.'

Maisie giggled with her, and then suggested, 'Let's go and get the snails ready, and we'll do the pips after that.'

They hurried downstairs, took a flat dish each from the kitchen cupboard and went out to the rear of the building. In a damp corner of the garden they sought for their prey: snails.

'Don't use that one; black snails are unlucky,' Maisie reminded. 'Find a light-coloured one, they're the best for writing nice and clear.'

They found suitable snails, placed them on the dishes and went back to the bedroom. There the dishes were covered over and put under the beds.

Both girls were fervent believers that during the course of the night of Halloween the snails' movements would leave a trail of slime across the dishes which could be deciphered as the names or initials of their future husbands.

'I'm going to get up real early and see the name mine's writ for me,' Maisie declared. 'I hope it's somebody's name that I already fancies.'

'I know what mine's going to write,' Amy affirmed with sudden certainty. 'It'll be Tom again. Do you remember last Halloween when my snail left a big letter T on my dish, and it did the year before as well?'

'If I remembers rightly your snail only left a mess both times,' Maisie contradicted.

'It was only a mess to them who can't read properly,' Amy riposted.

'For me, with my good book learning, the letter T was as clear as could be both times.'

'Well ne'er mind that now; let's do the apple pips afore old Fatty shouts us back to work.' Maisie took her friend by the hand and led her downstairs to the back parlour where a fire burned in the grate.

'Where have you two been?' Fat Lily Fowkes was sitting at the fireside, curling her ringlets with a heated poker.

'Putting the Halloween snails ready. Are you going to do the apple pips with us?' Amy invited.

'I don't believe in all that rubbish. It's only for empty-yedded fools like you pair; and it's sinful witchcraft as well.' Lily snapped an irritable rebuff.

'Oh, you believes in it alright. But you daren't try it because you knows only too well that no bloke is ever going to want to wed you, you miserable cow!' Maisie snapped in return.

Amy took an apple from the cupboard and cored it, then carefully freed a single pip from the core and laid it on the table.

'Who's wants to go first?' she asked.

'You go first, then we'll see if it is Tom Potts you'm to wed – which I don't reckon it will be,' Maisie challenged.

'Alright then, I will.' Amy accepted the challenge with an outward show of confidence, but couldn't control the nervous inner tremors now that the moment of truth was facing her.

She drew a deep breath, screwed up her courage and, selecting a large pip, deftly positioned it on the top rung of the grate, reciting aloud as she did so:

> 'Your name, Tom Potts, must be,
> And hearken you must to me.
> If you love me, then bounce and fly,
> If you hate me, then lie and die.'

After a couple of seconds in the fiery heat the pip burst noisily and flew off the rung. Amy laughed in relief and crowed, 'There you see! There's the proof! Tom Potts is loving and faithful me, and to me only.'

'That's as maybe, but it still don't prove that he'll wed does it?' Driven by envy, Lily's denial was scathing. 'Tha prove that he loves you and he's faithful to you. But that's all it proves, aren't it? You still can't be sure that you'll wed him.'

'Oh yes she can!' Maisie affirmed confidently. 'Do the cheek proof, Amy.'

'Alright, I will.' Her confidence buoyed sky-high by the first result, Amy arranged four pips in a row on the table before her, and challenged Lily. 'Give me four known names of single chaps that are likely to be looking to get wed, and the last name you give must be Tom's.'

'Yes, and don't drag out the naming, Lily. Otherwise the spell won't work proper. You must think of all the names first, then when I give the word you must give tongue to them as quick as lightning,' Maisie ordered firmly.

Lily's fat red face screwed up with the effort of intense concentration.

Despite her newly acquired confidence, nervous tremors again troubled Amy, as she flexed her fingers and positioned herself.

Maisie excitedly cried out. 'One to be ready! Two to be steady! And three to go!'

Lily shrilled out four names. Amy's finger tips closed on pips, and stuck them against her cheeks. Hands flat on the table, holding her breath, Amy sat rigidly still with tension.

One pip fell, two more followed almost simultaneously, and Maisie screamed out delightedly.

'Tom's still stuck there, Amy.'

Amy gasped with relieved delight, as the fourth and final pip slowly peeled free from her glowing cheek and fell on to the table before her.

'There now!' Maisie crowed triumphantly. 'Put that in your bloody pipe and smoke it, Lily Fowkes. You've seen the proof with your own eyes now, haven't you?'

Scowling with chagrin the fat girl puffed to her feet and exited the room, slamming the door behind her.

'Right then, my girl.' Maisie clapped her friend on the shoulder. 'When are you going to tell Tom Potts that he can have your Banns called again?'

Amy's eyes danced with mischievous amusement. 'Oh, he hasn't suffered enough yet for letting me down like he did. I'll wait a while longer before I set that date.'

FORTY-NINE

Night, Wednesday 31st October

Throughout the streets, alleys and courts of Redditch, from the mean hovels of poverty and the fine houses of wealth, men, women and children had thronged on to the Green to surround the leaping, roaring flames of the great Halloween bonfire.

Jack o' lanterns, the hollowed-out pumpkins and turnips carved with demonic faces and lit from within by candles, were paraded before the onlookers by rival groups of youths, girls and children wearing grotesque masks and crudely fashioned costumes of witches and devils. Some innkeepers had set up drink stalls, which were doing a roaring trade. Peddlers and cheapjacks hoarsely touted their wares, while a few tramps were trying their luck at begging. Fiddlers, tin whistle-players and drummers formed an impromptu band and their music mingled with the hubbub of merrymaking. But even on this night of universal festivities the crowd had segmented into distinct entities. In one area were gathered the rougher elements from the slums; in another the respectable artisans, tradesmen, shopkeepers and clerks; in yet another the Needle Masters, manufacturers, property owners, prosperous farmers, professional and independently wealthy folk, many in open carriages and on horseback.

For several hours Tom Potts and Ritchie Bint had been patrolling together around the edges of the crowd, their constable's staffs carried discreetly low. Their colleague Charles Bromley had earlier that day remembered that he had a prior commitment to visit and help nurse his gravely ill sister in Birmingham, and to Tom's delight Gertrude Potts had selflessly volunteered to accompany her betrothed on his errand of mercy.

Midnight came, the bonfire was burning low having collapsed in upon itself several times, and the last of the crowd was dispersing. To Tom's relief although the drink had flowed freely there h

been no serious outbreaks of trouble except for a few heated argu-
ments and minor scuffles which the bystanders had quickly quelled
without need of any constabulary intervention.

As they neared the area where the self-appointed elite of the
parish had gathered, Tom thought he recognized the bulky figure
of Enoch Griffiths seated on a big powerful horse to the rear of
the remaining sparse groups.

'It's dropped again, Tom! That's about the finish I reckon.'
Ritchie Bint tugged Tom's arm and pointed at the bonfire which
had once again collapsed down upon itself and was now virtually
flattened, its glowing ashes sending only a spattering of sparks
into the air. 'We're about done here as well, aren't we?'

'Yes, I think we are, Ritchie, and I'll be glad to get to my bed,'
Tom agreed. He looked back to where the horseman had been, but
now there was no one there. 'Shall we head for home then?'

'We're going in opposite ways tonight, Tom.' The other man
grinned broadly. 'I've got to make an urgent call down Bridley
Moor where some slippery gentlemen should be waiting for me.'

Tom chuckled amusedly. 'Well take care the keepers don't catch
you with the Earl's eels. I don't want to lose my best deputy
constable to Worcester Jail.'

'Those buggers couldn't catch my old Granny.' Ritchie Bint
laughed as he walked away.

Rain began to fall as Tom headed towards the Lock-up and a
sense of loneliness came over him, accompanied inevitably with
his intense yearning for Amy and bitter regret over losing her.
Tonight while other men would be sleeping among their families
and loved ones, the only other human being within Tom's walls
would be Joey Dowler lying enshrouded in pitch-plastered canvas
in a locked cell.

Amy's parting words reverberated through Tom's mind. '*Deep
down in your heart, being the Parish Constable is all you really
want to be, isn't it; and a wife and children would always have
to play second fiddle to that. So I'm done with you for good.*'

Tears stung his eyes and he could only bow his head and mourn
his loss.

FIFTY

Early morning, Thursday 1st November

The frantic cacophony of the bells woke Tom from his uneasy slumber. He wearily pushed away his coverings and went through to his mother's room, opened the casement and poked his night-capped head out into the cold dull light of the drizzling near-dawn.

'Who's below there?'

The ragged-dressed, grizzly-bearded man stepped back and scowled belligerently up at Tom. 'It's Tommy Spragg, and I've been ringing this fucking bell for hours!'

Spragg was a very eccentric character employed by the Parish to do odd jobs such as street cleaning and general scavenging.

'What can I do for you, Master Spragg?' Tom asked.

'You can't do fuck-all for me, Tom Potts, but you must needs do a job for the Parish.'

'Jesus Christ!' Tom could not suppress a spurt of irritation, but managed to enquire politely, 'And what job might that be, Master Spragg?'

'You must needs get that dead bugger shifted off the bonfire! The Parish pays me to do a bit o' this and a bit o' that and a bit o' the other, but not to be a fuckin' undertaker!'

'Dead bugger! Bonfire!' It took Tom a couple of seconds to fully absorb this information. 'Who is it that's dead on the bonfire, Master Spragg?'

The man shrugged. 'I'm damned if I cares who it is. You needs must go and see for yourself.' He walked off, ignoring Tom's cries for him to wait.

Tom hastily dressed and ran to the Green. As he neared the ashes of the bonfire, which had been made sodden by the heavy overnight rain, he could see a figure lay prone, dressed in what looked to be a long robe, its face covered by a grotesque Halloween devil's mask.

He halted some yards away from the large circle of ashes and carefully studied the sprawled figure in its centre. It was indeed a human body dressed in a Halloween witch robe crudely fashioned from an old blanket daubed with various black and red satanic emblems.

Tom could see leading up to one side of the body a trail of deep indentations in the ash, and judged from their spacing and size that they had been made by a horse's hooves.

'So a horse carried the body, and it must have come here when the rain had fully quenched the heat because no beast would cross red-hot ashes.'

He crossed to the body, bent low to remove the mask, and gasped in recognition.

'Ishmael Benton!'

And almost simultaneously in Tom's mind the mental picture of Joey Dowler's dead face superimposed itself upon the grey face of this dead man: the blue lips, protruding tongue, bulging eyes with dilated pupils, petechial haemorrhaging on the conjunctivae, and the noose embedded virtually horizontally in the neck. The remaining short length of the noose rope had been cut off cleanly as if with a sharp knife.

'It's another death by hanging!'

'Who is it?' a voice called, and Tom started in surprise. He had been so intent on the corpse that he had not noticed the small group of early-to-work spectators which had gathered to watch him from some twenty yards distance.

He quickly wrapped the robe around Benton's head and upper body to hide his identity and the noose, then rose to his feet and told them, 'He's one of the beggars who were here last night. He must have collapsed and died when everybody else had gone home. Will you help me to carry him to the Lock-up, please?'

On the way to the Lock-up his volunteer corpse-bearers volleyed questions at Tom.

'What's he die of, d'you reckon? Was it the drink?'

'Did he have a heart attack?'

'How did he come to fall in the fire and not be all burnt up?'

'I'll know more when the doctor's had a look him,' Tom parried repeatedly.

With Benton placed in a cell, Tom ushered his helpers from the

Lock-up and then stripped the corpse. There was no rigor mortis present and no visible sign of wounds – only the dark patches of discoloration on the back and buttocks where the blood had collected and congealed after death.

'He's been dead for several days, and left laying on his back,' Tom decided. 'But where was he kept?'

He stood marshalling his thoughts, and grimly decided on an immediate course of action.

'I can't afford to shut me shop up at this hour o' the day; this is when the women brings in their bedclothes. I aren't got the bloody parish keeping me in clover, like you has. I has to earn me living the hard way,' Judas Benton complained resentfully.

'Master Benton, you said you wanted me to help you to find your brother.' Tom forced a smile. 'Let me assure you that this is just what I am doing. I'm helping you to find your brother. But you must come with me directly.'

The pawnbroker came out from behind his counter, and threatened, 'If you'm leading me on a wild goose chase, I'll be going straight way to the Vestry and claiming the loss of my earnings back from them. They'll soon put a rocket up your arse then, won't they just!'

'Indeed they will, Master Benton,' Tom agreed readily. 'And I shall be thoroughly deserving of that treatment, as well. Now we need to go firstly to the Lock-up where I've something to show you which hopefully will clear up this mystery.'

'You'd best hope it does, for your own sake, Master Potts. Or you'll be learning a lesson which you won't like at all.'

All through the walk up the Unicorn Hill, through the central crossroads, over the Green, Judas Benton kept up a tirade of whining complaints and threats of dire retribution should Tom fail to reunite him with his brother Ishmael.

Tom stayed stone-faced and silent, but inwardly was grateful that this abusively aggressive tirade was making it easier to smother his own troubling scruples over what he was about to do.

Tom unlocked the Lock-up door and went inside, asking Judas Benton, 'Could you wait here for a moment please, Master Benton?'

'Fuckin' Hell! How much more time and money am I going to have to lose?' Benton grumbled aggrievedly.

Tom went to the cell door and unlocked it, checked inside that all was as he had left it, and called, 'Come and have a look at this, Master Benton.'

Muttering angrily, Benton stamped up to Tom, who pointed into the cell and invited, 'Take a good look, Master Benton.'

Benton turned to look and his face blanched ashen-white. He emitted a shriek of horror and staggered backwards as if he had been physically struck.

Inside the cell, the naked dead man on the sleeping bench was propped up in a sitting position with his back against the outer wall, the noose rope dangling down his chest, his bulging eyes fixed in a sightless glare at the doorway.

Tom deliberately summoned the mental images of the faces of the dead boy and the small, terror-crazed girl, and these steeled him to act with merciless resolve.

He grabbed Judas Benton's shoulders with both hands and, shaking him hard, shouted threateningly into his face.

'Now's the time for you to tell me the truth, Benton! Unless you want to be sharing that cell with your brother! What devilry have you and Ishmael been up to with Enoch Griffiths and Joey Dowler? Tell me! Tell me this instant! Or I swear I'll see you hung like your brother was!'

FIFTY-ONE

Midday, Thursday 1st November

'So Judas Benton claims that he suspected his brother was somehow involved with Griffiths and Dowler to aid them in the unlawful trafficking of children, and he will testify to that effect.' Sitting behind his study desk, Joseph Blackwell rubbed his chin as he stared questioningly at Tom.

'Indeed he will, Sir, but only on condition that I keep him in protective custody in the Lock-up until Enoch Griffiths is arrested, and after that arrange for his further protection until Griffiths is hung,' Tom confirmed. 'So he's not the answer to the problems I'm facing in obtaining the concrete proof to ensure Griffiths is convicted.'

'And Ishmael Benton's death was by hanging?'

'Even without a post-mortem I'm confident that that's the cause of death, Sir,' Tom affirmed.

'Have you any thoughts as to who is responsible for this?'

'Yesterday afternoon, Judas Benton told me that during last Thursday night, Ishmael had gone out in the dog cart, saying he would be back within a couple of hours, but hadn't said anything about why or where he was going. Ishmael didn't return and hadn't sent any word as to his whereabouts since then.'

'And?' Blackwell's brow furrowed quizzically.

Tom chose his words with care. 'And, by coincidence, Enoch Griffiths' sister Doll also went missing during last Thursday night, and nothing has been seen or heard of her since then. I can't help but think that their disappearances are connected.'

'And?' Blackwell pressed.

Tom smiled with grim irony. 'The old saying has it that "all roads lead to Rome". Well, for me at this time, "all roads lead to Enoch Griffiths". I want to arrest him for the murders of Dowler and Ishmael Benton. Also I shall charge him with the murder of Doll Griffiths. I fully realize that this is a desperate measure, Sir, but as the old saying has it, "needs must when the Devil drives".'

A bleak answering smile curved Blackwell's thin pale lips. 'A desperate measure it is, to be sure, so bear in mind another old saying: "who sups with the Devil needs must use a long spoon". So take care in whatever you intend to do, for I've no wish to lose my Parish Constable. You may select any of my horses for your use. I bid you a good day, Thomas Potts.'

Blackwell bent his head, took up a quill pen, dipped its point into the inkwell and began to write with fine copperplate calligraphy into the large open ledger before him.

'Good day, Sir.' Heart beating with joyous relief that his temerity had been rewarded, Tom bowed and left the study. But even as he exited the house that joyous relief was superseded by a disquieting realization.

'I'll have to leave Ritchie Bint at the Lock-up to protect Judas Benton, so I needs must tackle Enoch Griffiths on my own. God help me!'

FIFTY-TWO

Evening, Thursday 1st November

There were only scattered clouds in the sky, but the thin sliver of the new moon cast little light on the rutted roadway and Tom, aware of his limitations as a horseman, kept his mount to a walk.

When he reached the entrance of the lane leading up to Marlfield Farm he dismounted and, leading the horse into the adjoining field, tethered it to a fence post. He took the brace of pistols out of his shoulder-slung satchel and checked their flints and charges. Then he replaced them and walked up the lane towards the farmhouse, keeping close against the thick hedgerows to aid concealment. As always whenever the threat of violent physical confrontation loomed Tom's nerves were jangling, his courage fluctuating, and he was battling hard against the almost overwhelming urge to turn and go back to Redditch.

When he reached the open gate of the deep shadowed farmyard he halted, expecting the dogs to start barking, but there was no sound from them, or any other sounds or signs of life from the stables and outbuildings. The only light showing came from the kitchen window and its outer door which stood ajar.

Tom frowned uneasily. 'Where are the dogs? Where is everyone? Is Griffiths hiding and watching me?' A shiver of fear coursed through him, and involuntarily his hand went into the satchel and gripped the butt of one of the pistols. 'Has Griffiths got a gun trained on me?'

The next instant self-disgust and anger surged through him. 'Stop being such a bloody coward, damn you!'

That surge of intense emotion spurred him on to sprint to the door of the kitchen, drawing the pistol from the satchel and slamming through the door, shouting, 'I'm Constable Potts, and I'm here in the King's Name!'

There was no one in the lamp-lit room. The range fire crackled cheerily, the table was laid out in readiness for a meal, with platters of bread, cheese and pickles, knives and spoons, jugs of ale and clean empty bowls waiting to be filled from the iron cooking pot of stew hung bubbling above the range fire.

The inner door swung open. Tom turned, pistol levelled, and the bulky figure and grinning, beefy-red face of Enoch Griffiths appeared in the doorway.

'I was upstairs, Master Potts, and saw you coming across the yard. You'm come in good time for your supper, I see. You must like my vittles well enough to come out all this way to taste 'um again.' He stepped fully into the room and gestured dismissively at Tom's levelled pistol. 'There's no need to be waving that bloody popgun around, Master Potts. There's no danger threatening you here. You'm in a friend's house now.'

Griffiths moved to the table and sat in the wooden-armed chair at its head. He waved towards the facing chair at the bottom of the long table.

'Sit you down there, Master Potts, and make yourself comfortable. Me sisters shouldn't be long in coming, and then we can start.' He chuckled throatily. 'I don't know about you, but I'm hungry enough to ate a bloody scabby babby, so I am.'

Tom kept the pistol trained on the other man. 'Where are your sisters, Master Griffiths?'

'The landlord at the Barley Mow down in Studley sent word that Doll was laying outside his door as pissed as a newt, so the twins has took the cart to fetch the thieving cow back here.' Griffiths laughed jeeringly at Tom's visible surprise. 'Did you think I'd done away with her or summat, Potts?'

Tom nodded. 'I did. Just as I think that you did away with Joey Dowler and Ishmael Benton.'

'What?' Griffiths scowled.

'You heard me, Griffiths.' Tom surprised himself by how steady his voice was, in stark contrast to his inner turmoil of nervous tension. 'I'm come here to arrest you for the murders of Joey Dowler and Ishmael Benton.'

'What?' The big man's ruddy face drained of colour. 'Am you telling me that Benton's dead?'

'You know well that he is, because you murdered him in the

same way that you murdered Dowler. You hung them both, didn't you,' Tom asserted confidently.

Griffiths shook his head violently and shouted, 'I've never killed nobody in me life! And the only thing I've ever hung was a bloody dog that had gone mad!'

Tom's utter distaste for this brutal, bullying man flared into anger and he spat out, 'The jury will decide the truth of that, Griffiths. Now hold your tongue, lie face down on the floor and clasp your hands behind your back! Move slowly and do exactly what I say, or I'll shoot you for being the mad dog you truly are. Move, damn you!'

Griffiths stared hard into Tom's eyes, and what he read in them persuaded him that it would be wisest to obey the command. He slowly levered himself from the chair, sank on to his knees and lay face downwards, grunting as he strained to join his hands behind his back.

Tom stepped to the side of the prone man, took chain manacles from his satchel and quickly secured Griffiths' wrists and ankles, then snapped, 'Get up.'

He gripped the back of Griffiths' coat collar and helped him to struggle to his feet.

'Now go out of the door, across the yard and down the lane,' Tom ordered, and warned, 'I'll be two steps behind you, and if you try anything on I'll put a ball through the back of your head without a moment's hesitation.'

'You'm making a big mistake, Potts,' Griffiths blustered desperately. 'I've never killed nobody in me life. I'm quick with me fists and boots, I admit. But I've never killed nobody!'

Tom rammed the muzzle of the pistol into the back of the other man's thick neck, and threatened, 'Shut your mouth, and move! Or I'll blow your head off right now!'

The ankle chain was long enough for Griffiths to shuffle small steps, still protesting. 'I'm an innocent man! I've never killed nobody!'

He lumbered awkwardly, chain rattling, out of the door and across the yard, and Tom followed closely behind, his pistol still cocked and levelled at the other man's head, his nerves stretched almost to breaking point.

They were halfway across the yard when from the lane beyond

the gate came the thudding of horses' hooves, the trundling of iron-shod wheels, and the bouncing beam of a cart lamp.

'Me sisters are back,' Griffiths shouted thankfully. 'Our Doll 'ull tell you now that I've not killed nobody.'

From the deep shadows of the stables wall came two small flashes of light coupled with simultaneous sharp cracking reports of shots, and a heavy impact thudded against Tom's shoulder-hung satchel sending him staggering sideways. Even as he staggered he instinctively switched the aim of his pistol and fired back at the site of the flashes.

High-pitched shouts sounded from the lane, and again impelled by sheer instinct Tom ran towards the gate shouting, 'Don't come any closer, girls! Stay back! Stay back!'

The oncoming horse and cart clattered to a halt. Tom crouched low and fumbled in the satchel for his other pistol, felt the tear in the leather, and the dent in the pistol butt impacted by the lead pistol ball which, half-flattened, had dropped to the bottom of the satchel pouch.

He squinted his eyes to peer through the darkness. The black outstretched heap that was Griffiths lay motionless.

'Griffiths, are you hit?' Tom called softly, but received no answer, and his heart missed a beat when suddenly the beam of light from the cart lamp shone fully on him, and Deborah Griffiths' plaintive voice sounded from the gateway.

'Master Potts, our Doll is woke up, and her's shit herself. We needs to get her in the house and clean her up.'

Tom's eyes involuntarily shut tight as he awaited the crack of the report and the impact of another pistol ball tearing into his flesh.

'What was you shooting at, Master Potts?' Deborah Griffiths questioned curiously. 'Was it a rat? Only we don't get many rats in our yard. Our dogs am very good ratters, you know.'

'Get into cover, woman, and douse that bloody lamp!' Tom shouted, and tried to scramble out of the beam of lamplight. 'Someone's trying to kill us!'

But she stayed where she was, tracking him with the lamp's beam, calling plaintively, 'What d'you mean, Master Potts? Is it me brother? Has he lost his temper again? He does that a lot, you know. But he never kills us, he only knocks us about.'

'God help me!' Tom pleaded desperately and was about to ri

and hurl himself at her to get the lamp doused when his name was called.

'Tom Potts, can you hear me?' The voice was strained and faltering. 'I mean no harm to you, Tom Potts. Look, I'm throwing my pistols from me. I mean no harm to you. Look!'

Tom turned his head, stared hard, detected movement low down against the stables wall, heard the sound of metal clattering across the cobbles.

'I've thrown my pistols away, Tom Potts. Please, come to me, I fear I'm done for, and I must tell you things. There's no more killing will be done now.' The weak voice was cut off by choking coughs.

Against all his natural urge for survival, Tom found himself instinctively believing that the voice was truthful, and rising erect on legs that felt weak and shaky, struggling to firm his voice, he called back, 'Wait a moment, and I'll come to you.'

He went first to Deborah Griffiths. 'Give me the lamp please, Miss Griffiths. I need to see how your brother fares.'

The black outstretched heap stirred into life, and Enoch Griffiths bellowed furiously.

'Oh, I'm alright, but it's no thanks to you, you great lanky streak o' piss! Now get these fucking manacles off me!'

'Just stay where you are,' Tom shouted as he ran past Griffiths towards the stables and found the assailant sitting with his back to the wall. He drew a sharp breath of surprise when the lamp's beams shone upon the ashen face of Matthew Spicer.

'Where are you hurt, Master Spicer? What can I do to help you?'

A fit of coughing shook Spicer's head and a thin line of dark blood snaked from the corner of his mouth. 'You've gunshot me, Tom Potts. There's nothing you can do to help me now.'

'Let me take a look.' Tom crouched to open the other man's coat but Spicer pushed his hands away.

'I've seen enough bloodshed and death to know when a wound is mortal, Tom Potts, and I know that I'm dying fast, and in all truth it will be a blessed relief for me. What I want you to do is listen to what I have to tell you. Will you do that for me? Will you listen without interruption, because I've not time nor strength enough left in me to enter into debate over what I say to you.'

Tom nodded. 'I will listen, Master Spicer. Please, speak on.'

The wounded man coughed again and more blood snaked from his lips, but he still was able to speak with some degree of clarity.

'To begin with, Tom Potts, I'm not the uncle of little Jack Telton, I'm his father . . .'

Tom's breath hissed in shock, but he said nothing, and remained crouching and listening intently as, shaken by repeated fits of coughing, voice becoming ever weaker and more laboured, the other man related his story.

Then in a final fit of blood-spattering, choking and coughing, Matthew Spicer slumped sideways and died.

Tom gently laid Spicer's body on its back, crossed the arms upon the chest, used his fingers to close the glazed, sightless eyes. He rose to his feet and sighed in self-disgust as burgeoning guilt assailed him.

'Please God forgive me for killing this man. It all happened so quickly and my reaction was purely instinctive.'

'Get these bloody manacles off me.' Enoch Griffiths had stealthily come near and had overheard most of what Spicer had told Tom. 'I heard him confess to killing Dowler and Benton. So get these off me and beg my pardon, why don't you?'

Tom shook his head. 'You're staying under arrest. I'm still going to charge you with the kidnap and illegal trafficking of children; and with being an accessory in the murder of Jack Telton.'

Griffiths slowly shook his head from side to side, and Tom could hardly credit his senses as he heard the rumble of laughter coming from Griffiths' mouth.

Unable to stop himself, he demanded, 'Will you still find it so amusing when you're standing in the dock, Griffiths?'

Griffiths stared straight into his eyes, and sneered. 'You and I both know very well that I'll not be standing in any bloody dock. Because you and I both know very well that you've no proof that I've ever done such things, and anybody like him laying there who could claim they had proof is now dead. You've just shot your own star witness, and all he had was what he claimed the men he murdered had told him.

'Now I could be a star witness against you, couldn't I? I could tell the magistrates that I watched you shoot down that bloke laying there after he'd chucked his pistols away and was trying to surrender to you.'

Tom's angry retort spilled from his lips before he could bite back the words. 'And what's to stop me shooting you now, Griffiths, and telling people that it was Spicer's ball that hit you?'

Griffiths jerked his head in the direction of the gate, where the dark shapes of his three sisters were huddled together.

'I don't reckon that you'd kill them three to keep them from telling that they saw you kill me, Constable Potts.' He proffered his manacled wrists towards Tom. 'So, why don't you just take these off? You've most likely just saved my life and I'm very grateful to you for that. So I'm prepared to let bygones be bygones, and not lay any complaints against you for wrongful arrest.'

For a period an inner battle raged within Tom, then from the depths of his mind it seemed another entity whispered, 'Box clever and bide your time, Tom Potts. Bide your time.'

Without uttering a word Tom unlocked the manacles and stowed them in his satchel.

Griffiths' brown-yellow teeth bared in a grin of triumph. 'Now you'm showing a bit o' sense at last, Constable Potts.'

Tom stayed silent.

Griffiths jerked his head towards the dead man. 'He needs to be shifted afore the vermin starts making a meal of him.'

Now from the depths of Tom's mind came Joseph Blackwell's voice: *'Who sups with the Devil needs must use a long spoon.'*

Tom mentally nodded in affirmation, and aloud requested politely, 'Please may I have the use of your horse and cart to carry him to the Lock-up, Master Griffiths?'

'You may indeed, Constable Potts, and the use o' me sisters to get him there as well.' Brown-yellow teeth bared again in a triumphant grin, Griffiths turned and bawled at the huddled women.

'Deborah, Delilah, get our Doll indoors and then fetch the cart here to me. Look sharp now!'

FIFTY-THREE

Early Morning, Friday 2nd November

Tom's mood was sombre as he rode at walking pace, the horse and cart driven by Deborah Griffiths following a few yards behind him. The town's streets were deserted, the only signs of life the occasional gleam of candle or lamplight from a window in a silent building.

At the Lock-up Tom dismounted and tugged on the iron bell pull. Before the clanging echoes had ceased, bars and bolts rattled, the door swung inwards and Ritchie Bint welcomed him.

'Am I glad to see you, Tom! I was beginning to fear that you'd got yourself into trouble.'

'In a manner of speaking, I did,' Tom confirmed dryly.

The cart creaked to a halt, and Ritchie Bint frowned curiously. 'What's this then?'

'It's a dead man,' Tom explained. 'Come, help me get him inside. I'll tell you all about it then.'

It was a few hours later when the town was stirring into life that Tom stood before Joseph Blackwell's study desk and again related the events of the previous night and the dying words of Matthew Spicer.

Matthew Spicer had said that he was a merchant ship captain who had mainly spent his shore time in America since he was a boy. During one of his voyages to England he had seduced, then deserted a young woman when she fell pregnant. But this mean act had preyed on his conscience for years, eventually driving him to return to England to find her and try to make amends. He discovered that she had given birth to his son, Jack. She had later had a brief, childless marriage with a man named Telton, then had been been widowed and died leaving Jack to the care of the Brimfield Poorhouse.

Spicer had arrived at the Poorhouse just after Jack had been sent away, and immediately set out to search for the boy. Eventually he had succeeded in tracking down Joey Dowler. He had forced Dowler to tell the full story of Jack's death, and had freely admitted to Tom, that Spicer's own torment of guilt had been the main impulsion for the vengeance he then determined to wreak on the gang of child traffickers. Deciding on Enoch Griffiths as being their leader, Spicer planned to prolong his torment of Griffiths by firstly killing his close associates, then Griffiths' sisters, and lastly Griffiths himself. He deliberately chose to hang Dowler and Ishmael Benton to unnerve Griffiths.

As his recital of Spicer's account came to a finish Tom drew a long breath and admitted ruefully, 'I've been drawing wrong conclusions from the very beginning of my investigation. I can only blame my own conceited stupidity. It seems that although Enoch Griffiths is most certainly a brutal bully and a vile trafficker of children, he is innocent of the murders I suspected him of committing.'

'And what of the other children that were in the wagon with the boy Telton?' Blackwell asked now.

'Ishmael Benton told Spicer that they had been sold on auction to paedophiles and would now be impossible to trace.'

'Could Spicer have had any connection with either of the Carnegies, do you think?'

Tom shook his head. 'I don't believe so. But the little crazed girl, who Spicer named as Sukey Crawford, and was stolen from our own Poorhouse by the woman claiming to be Adelaide Carnegie, was one of the children on the wagon with Dowler and Griffiths. Griffiths was in service with the Carnegies for several years. He readily talks of it himself, but claims not to have seen them since leaving their service. But the thought still nags at me that Griffiths is somehow involved with their deaths.'

Tom paused, frowning in frustration. 'I keep racking my brains, yet can find no satisfactory answers to my own questions.'

Blackwell smiled bleakly. 'Be that as it may, Thomas Potts, yet in the eyes of the world you will have undoubtedly scored a triumph by solving the murders of Dowler and Benton, and despatching their killer to the next world. Thus saving the expense of a costly trial – and, might I add, giving me the pleasure of yet another opportunity to crow over those among my own worldly Lords and Masters, who sometimes misguidedly question my championing of your talents.'

'But I didn't solve their murders,' Tom pointed out.

'The world does not need to know that fact. Now let us arrange what must be done. Doctor Laylor can do the post-mortem on the man Spicer tomorrow, and you can assist if he needs you to do so.'

'With respect, Sir, I can't say that I would be happy to assist at the post-mortem of a man who's death I've caused,' Tom objected.

'With equal respect, Thomas Potts, let me point out that doctors all too often are called upon to do the post-mortems of patients whose deaths they have themselves caused with their damnable treatments and potions.' Blackwell wheezed with amusement at his own sally. 'I fail to see any difference in this particular case, and I'm confident you will cope admirably with the task.

'I will hold the inquest on Monday morning at the Fox and Goose, and the verdict will be justifiable homicide in defence of the lives of yourself and Enoch Griffiths. Make sure that Griffiths is there to testify on your behalf. Are there any other matters you need to tell me of at this time?'

'Only that Judas Benton is demanding that he be allowed to remain under our protection. He's claiming that Griffiths will murder him at the first opportunity.'

'And it'll be good riddance to bad rubbish if Griffiths should do so. Send Benton packing, and release his brother's body to him. You may also notify Dowler's relatives that they must remove him from the Lock-up. Give Parson Clayton notice of this.

I reserve for myself the pleasure of informing Lord Aston that there will now be no necessity for stakes through hearts and cross-roads burials. I bid you a good day, Thomas Potts.'

FIFTY-FOUR

It was a favourite saying in the Needle District that if a man farted at the Headless Cross Tollgate, it would be the subject of gossip at the Bordesley Tollgate before the smell had dissipated. The news of the shooting at Marlfield Farm did not spread quite so quickly, but well before midday it was the subject of talk throughout the entire district. As always in the telling and retelling of a story the actual facts became somewhat distorted and by the time it reached the Fox and Goose the three pistol shots fired had become repeated fusillades of musketry, and depending on who was relating the story the toll of casualties varied between three and thirteen.

Amy had been visiting her mother that morning and did not hear the news until she returned to the Fox and Goose just after midday. As she entered the Select Parlour, Lily Fowkes hastened to tell her the story.

Amy's face blanched with dread as she asked, 'Is Tom one of the dead?'

'No, but one bloke told me that he's badly wounded.' Lily Fowkes couldn't resist adding a spiteful barb. 'It's a good job that you finished with him, aren't it? Because from all accounts he'll be crippled for life, and you'd have been saddled with a useless cripple and a lifetime of poverty and hardships if you'd wed him when you was supposed to. You've had a lucky escape, my wench.'

'You'm talking rubbish as usual, you spiteful cow!' Maisie Lock interjected angrily. 'Nobody's told me that Tom Potts is wounded!'

'Simmy Docker told me that he'd seen Tom Potts being carried into the Lock-up by Ritchie Bint and another bloke, and that he looked like he was breathing his last.' Lily Fowkes flared angrily back. 'Tom Potts could well be dead by now, and most likely is.'

Heart thumping, breath half-strangled with distress, Amy could bear no more. She ran headlong from the building and across the Green to the Lock-up, where she frantically tugged on the bell pull. After what seemed to her agonized mind to be endless time, but was merely seconds, the door opened and Ritchie Bint appeared.

'You'll pull that handle off the wall if you keeps swinging on it like that, my wench.' He grinned.

'Is Tom dead?' She could hardly bear to formulate the question.

'Tom, dead?' he exclaimed. 'Who's told you that load o' bollocks?'

'He's still alive then?'

'O' course he is.'

'Is he very badly hurt?' she pleaded.

'Only in his bloody pocket.' Bint chuckled. 'He might have to buy another satchel; the one he's got has an 'ole in it now.'

She felt light-headed with relief. 'Where is he? I want to see him.'

'You've only just missed him, my wench. He only left a little bit afore you came here creating such a bloody ruckus.'

'Where's he gone?'

'He's gone to see a wench he's fond of.' Bint winked broadly. 'He's a devil for the wenches is our Tom.'

'He's gone to see a wench he's fond of?' Amy repeated his words, hardly able to accept what she had heard. 'A wench he's fond of?'

'Oh yes.' Bint grinned. 'Powerful fond of her, he is.'

A white heat of jealous fury flooded Amy's mind and she blurted, 'Well you can tell him that I'm done with him forever. And tell him from me that he can go to pay court to any wench that he wants to, and I shan't care. Because I'm never going to even spare him a look ever again.'

Before Bint could say anything, she was gone, running headlong across the Green.

'Look at my new Sunday bonnet and gown, Tom. Auntie Sarah made the bonnet for me, and Auntie Beth made the gown. But I sewed on the ribbons all by myself.'

Georgy pirouetted proudly as she displayed her new clothes and Tom smiled fondly at her. 'They are truly beautiful, Georgy, and you'll be the Belle of Tardebigge Parish when you go out wearing them.'

'Were you very fritted when all those bad men shot their guns at you, Tom?'

'There was only one man, and I don't believe he was really bad, and it all happened so quickly that I really didn't have the time to be very fritted. But afterwards, when I thought about it, yes, I was very fritted.'

'Auntie Beth and Auntie Sarah say that you're the bravest man in the whole parish, and that I'm very lucky that you're my new uncle. I think I am, as well.'

'And I think that I'm very lucky to have you for my new niece, Georgy.'

'You stay there while I go and fetch my kitten. Auntie Beth and Auntie Sarah got it for me yesterday. It's a girl so I'm going to name her Polly. Auntie Beth and Auntie Sarah and me are going to have a christening service for her, and afterwards a party with lots of cakes and ginger pop. You can come to the service and the party as well if you like.'

'Thank you, I'd very much like to come. When is it going to happen?'

'After we've been to chapel on Sunday. Parson Clayton is going to come back here with us and do the christening service and then stay for the party. I'm really looking forward to it, Tom. I've never been to a party before.'

As Tom looked at her piquant, happily smiling face he was suddenly overcome with poignant regret that he had not been able to save that other pitiful small girl and find her a loving home.

'I'm going to keep on searching and won't stop until I discover what has become of the poor child,' he vowed silently. Then the voice in the depths of his mind questioned, 'But now, where can you even begin the search?'

And he was forced to admit that at this moment he had not the faintest idea.

FIFTY-FIVE

Morning, Monday 5th November

At ten o'clock in the morning the Select Parlour of the Fox and Goose was to become a Coroner's court. Except for the tables retained for the use of the Coroner and his clerk, and sufficient chairs for the most important spectators, all other furnishings had been removed to create standing room for the lower ranking spectators. Directly in front of the Coroner's table the corpse of Matthew Spicer, shrouded but for his features, lay in an open coffin with a peeled onion in his mouth and a nosegay of herbs on his chest to overlay any encroaching stench of an unduly rapid decay of flesh.

Because of the sensational nature of the case under enquiry a large crowd had gathered outside the inn to seek admittance, many of the rougher elements among them still noisily half-drunk from their weekend debauches.

Tom Potts and Ritchie Bint were standing guard at the inn's entrance. Tom had been able to accept that he had acted by instinct when he'd returned Matthew Spicer's fire, and he was able also to accept that it was Spicer's own actions that had brought about his death. But knowing what had driven Spicer to commit those actions, Tom could not help but feel that both Dowler and Benton had deserved to die, and that Enoch Griffiths was equally deserving of death.

The fact that throughout the weekend he had received plaudits from a wide variety of people for solving the murders of Benton and Dowler, and saving the life of Griffiths, both embarrassed and dismayed him.

'I've done neither one nor the other,' he told Ritchie Bint repeatedly. 'And when I tell anyone that fact, they then insist that I'm behaving like a true Englishman by being so modest.'

Ritchie Bint only laughed and told him, 'Take full advantage of it while you can, Tom, and when they want to buy you a drink, then get as drunk as a bloody Lord on their money. I should if I was in your place, I tell you no lie.'

Also for Tom the days and nights since he had returned to the Lock-up from visiting little Georgy had been overshadowed by Ritchie Bint's account of his encounter with Amy Danks. He had called three times at the inn to try and explain about the child, but each time she had refused to speak to him, and this morning she had completely ignored him in the fleeting instances he had seen her.

Under strict orders from Lord Aston himself, only men were to be admitted into the inquest and Tom and Ritchie Bint had to give priority of entrance to the rich and powerful of the Parish: the Needle Masters, the professional men, the independent gentry, the successful factors and traders. Long before the hour of ten o'clock so many of these had come that there was no room left for any of the lower orders in the packed Select Parlour, where the air was thick with tobacco smoke and loud with noisy talk and laughter.

Landlord Thomas Fowkes and his entire staff were struggling to cater to the thirsty throats clamouring for brandy, whisky, gin, wine, ale and cider. Ever eager for more profit he had obtained the permission of Lord Aston to allow the lower orders into the Tap Room and the Snug, and to open the outer windows and inner doors so that the proceedings could be relayed to both rooms and to the drinkers in the street outside.

Enoch Griffiths was ensconced in the rear private parlour waiting to be summoned to give his evidence, while Doctor Hugh Laylor, who with Tom's assistance had carried out the post-mortem, was seated in the Select Parlour among his peers.

At five minutes to ten o'clock Joseph Blackwell Esq, Reverend the Lord Aston, Reverend Percival Timmins and Curate John Clayton came from the chapel in a procession of pairs. Strutting at their head was the schoolmaster, John Osborne, specially appointed for this auspicious day as Usher to the Coroner's Court.

Wielding a short crown-topped baton, pigeon chest puffed with self-importance, eyes watering with excitement behind the wobbling pince-nez on his long nose, Osborne was shouting repeatedly, 'Clear the way! Clear the way for His Majesty's Coroner, and for the Reverend my Lord Aston! Clear the way! Clear the way!'

A drunken wag reeled out from the crowd by the door and pranced about in front of the procession, shouting, 'Clear the way for all the Lord bloody Mucks. Clear the way for all the Lord bloody Mucks.' Until a sharp crack across the side of his head from Ritchie Bint's staff sent him reeling back into the cheering, jeering crowd.

Lord Aston nodded approvingly and told Joseph Blackwell, 'It was a wise decision of mine to appoint that man as a constable, was it not, Master Blackwell?'

'Indeed it was, My Lord. A most wise decision.' Blackwell smiled ambiguously.

Aston frowned. 'What's his name again? At this moment it escapes me.'

'Bint, My Lord. Richard Bint. He's a Needle Pointer by trade, and a noted pugilist.'

'Yes alright, thank you very much, Blackwell,' Aston snapped pettishly. 'There's no necessity to relate all the details. I know them all very well.'

'Indeed you do, my Lord,' Blackwell agreed smoothly. 'It's well known that you are a master of detail.'

The group entered the Select Parlour. Joseph Blackwell took

the seat at the table behind the coffin. John Clayton in his capacity as Coroner's clerk sat at the side table which was furnished with ledger, inkwell, a shaker of blotting powder and a selection of quill pens. Aston and Timmins were seated in the most prestigious of the spectator positions at the very front of the audience.

At a signal from Blackwell, John Osborne called the room to order, Ritchie Bint bellowed to the crowd outside to be silent, while Tom cautioned the Snug and Tap Room. The hubbub quietened until only the occasional belch, suck of tobacco pipe, snort of snuff, cough, or hasty slurp of drink broke the silence.

Then Lily Fowkes called from the Snug. 'Have I to stop serving altogether then, Pa? Only there's another regular just come in. What shall I do for him?'

Various obscene suggestions were shouted and greeted with roars of laughter and cheers, and it took another several minutes for order to be restored. But once it was the proceedings moved forward with smooth rapidity. Doctor Hugh Laylor gave his evidence as to the actual cause of death. Tom gave his evidence. Then Griffiths testified that without Thomas Potts' intervention it was certain that the entire Griffiths family would have been murdered by this homicidal maniac, Spicer.

The Coroner's verdict was that Matthew Spicer's death was a proven case of 'justifiable homicide' and that no charges would be brought against Thomas Potts, to whom the Court also gave its commendation.

The verdict was greeted with general applause, and Tom was immediately besieged by men eager to shake his hand and buy him drinks. But he was able to make a quick escape by insisting that he must immediately transport Matthew Spicer's corpse back to the Lock-up.

He and Ritchie Bint with a couple of helpers loaded the coffin on to a handcart and trundled it back to the Lock-up. When it was safely locked into a cell Tom told Bint, 'I've some good news for you, Ritchie. Joseph Blackwell has agreed that any time you must lose from your actual work to carry out parish constables duties, such as this morning for example, will from now on be recompensed from the Vestry Chest. Of course it will not be as much as you would earn at the Pointing, but it will offset some of the losses of wages you incur.'

Bint chuckled and winked slyly. 'Just between you, me, and the gatepost, Tom, I'm finding that being a deputy parish constable is paying me very well as it is. But o' course I'm more than happy to accept the offerings from the Vestry, and I thank you very kindly for pressing Blackwell to do this. You'm proving a good friend to me, Tom Potts, and come the time o' need, you'll not be regretting that friendship.'

Tom felt truly moved by the other man's words, and had to swallow hard to dispel the lump that had risen in his throat.

'Now what's the drill for tonight?' Bint questioned. 'I reckon we'll both be needed on duty. Guy Fawkes night always gets a lot livelier than Halloween, don't it?'

'It does indeed,' Tom acknowledged wryly. 'God pity the poor animals that'll have fireworks tied to their tails before this night's over and done with. Perhaps we'd both better get some rest while we can, and I'll meet you by the bonfire at seven o'clock.'

FIFTY-SIX

As soon as the mills and factories and workshops had stopped working the noisy gangs of excited children swarmed through the town with their home-made 'Guys', fashioned from straw and rags with rotting turnips or cabbages or lumps of dried mud for heads.

> 'Spare a penny for our Guy!
> Spare a penny for our Guy!
> If you've not got a penny,
> A ha'penny will do.
> If you've not got a ha'penny,
> A farthing will do.
> If you've not got a farthing,
> Then may God bless you!'

Unfortunately for the children, because it was a Monday, most adult pockets were almost empty of money, and their shrill-voiced supplications garnered very few coins.

By seven o'clock a large crowd of men, women and children on foot, on horseback, in carriages and in carts had gathered around the great mound of the unlit new bonfire built on the ashes of the Halloween bonfire. There was a different atmosphere in the crowd tonight. Halloween was an ancient custom, its origins lost in the mists of antiquity, but Guy Fawkes night was a celebration of national identity. A proclamation of England's religious freedom from the dominance of any doctrine of faith other than its own national creed.

The crowd watched and waited as John Osborne, the self-appointed director of the Guy Fawkes night celebrations, marshalled the members of the torchlight procession. Glorying in his role he strutted along the ranks of men and youths, shouting instructions.

'Wear your coats and waistcoats inside out, because sometimes the pitch drips from the torches and it's the very devil to clean it off your clothes afterwards! March in threes, keep to the pace and don't break ranks, and most importantly, do not play silly buggers with your torches. It's only the bonfire and the Papist traitor "Guido Fawkes" to be put to the torch tonight, not the town or its inhabitants!

'Try to keep in time with the drums, and sing out loud and clear. But only sing out the proper words. I expressly forbid any utterances of foul language or obscene rhymes, or any insults or abuse offered towards your masters or your betters. Is that understood?'

Only a few scattered 'Ayes' came in reply, and Osborne scowled and reiterated his demand.

This time he was answered by a single disgruntled voice bawling, 'For fuck's sake, Schoolie, will you give over and let us get to marching. It could come on to rain cats and dogs while you'm standing there bloody well scrawkin' your yed off.'

Thunderous applause from both spectators and marchers greeted this sally, and Osborne was forced to accept defeat. Scowling in outraged indignation, he shouted, 'Be it on your own heads then, and if it becomes a shambles then remember that you've only your-selves to blame. Drummers, take post! Marchers, light your torches!'

From one to another and another to another in rapid succession the torches glowed and spluttered into life with leaping red-yellow flames and swirling plumes of grey-black smoke.

The marchers held their torches high. Three drummers, toting a big bass drum and two smaller kettle drums, took position at the head of the long triple lines. John Osborne took position two paces in front of the drummers. He waved his torch from side to side above his head then pointed it forwards and shouted, 'By the left! Quick march!'

The bass drum thudded, the kettle drums rattled and the lines stepped off, then with one tuneful voice leading, the entire procession took up the rhythmic chant, repeating it over and over again.

> 'Remember remember the fifth of November,
> Gunpowder, treason and plot.
> We'll have no foreign Popery here,
> In Protestant England, we hold so dear.
> God save the King!'

This culminating exhortation being thunderously roared out with all the power of straining lungs and throats.

As the torchbearers circuited around the main streets of the town centre many of the spectators went with them, adding their voices to the chant until it seemed that the whole sky was resounding with its echoes.

Tom and Ritchie Bint stayed and patrolled around the unlit bonfire to guard against any mischievous pranksters who might try to light it prematurely – a frequent enough occurrence on bonfire nights.

'God save the King!'

The concerted roar carried clearly across the rooftops to the ears of those who had remained on the Green.

'Bloody King! He's a fat useless bugger that I'd never wish God to save,' Ritchie Bint hissed scathingly. 'Nor any other of the ruling bastards who grind us into the dirt and live like Lord and Lady Muck on our sweat and blood.'

'Don't let Lord Aston hear you say that, Ritchie.' Tom smiled. 'Or he'll have an apoplectic fit.'

'And that'll be a good riddance to bad rubbish as well.' Ritchie Bint hawked and spat to give emphasis to that opinion, then asked Tom curiously, 'Are you a loyal subject of King George, Tom?'

Tom pondered for some moments before answering thoughtfully.

'Loyal to him as an individual, no! In fact I fully concur with your opinion of him and of our ruling class.

'Yet on the other hand, I'm proud to be an Englishman, and I live in hopes that some day we shall manage to create in this country a truly fair and just society in which all of us, whether high or low born, will be treated as being equal under the law.'

'Amen to that!' Bint grinned. 'But I wouldn't bet on you being able to hold your breath until it comes about.'

'Remember remember the fifth of November, Gunpowder, treason and plot . . .'

The drumbeats and chanting sounded from the crossroads and the long line of torches filed back on to the Green and formed a close circle around the bonfire mound.

'We'll have no foreign Popery here, in Protestant England, we hold so dear. God save the King! God save the King!'

With a final resounding cheer the flaming torches were hurled on to the bonfire and within brief seconds flames snaked across the tarred, oiled wood and rubbish and took hold. The great mound hissed and crackled and roared like a living entity and the sheets of flame soared skywards, their glaring light bathing the rapt, excited faces of men, women and children, lighting the facades of buildings, flashing from panes of glass, while the smoke-laden breezes carried the myriad glowing sparks far and wide over the roofs of the town.

'Burn Guy Fawkes! Burn Guy Fawkes! Burn Guy Fawkes!'

The cry was raised and spread throughout the crowd, and now the strongest and most daring boys began to brave the flesh-scorching heat and dash forward to try and hurl their Guys into the flames. Each successful attempt was wildly applauded, and the hurler lifted on to the shoulders of his friends and paraded through the cheering spectators like a champion gladiator, the pain of his scorched skin temporarily eclipsed in the ecstasy of his triumph.

When the last Guys had met their fiery fates, and the first sagging and crumpling of the bonfire mound began, the vendors of sweet-meats, pies and drinks came to cry their wares. A wide space was cleared on the greensward. Fiddlers, penny-whistle players and drummers struck up the old tunes of England: 'Blow Away the Morning Dew', 'Nothing At All', 'Matty Groves', 'Early One

Morning', 'The Wild Rover', 'There is a Tavern in the Town', 'There was a Lover and His Lass'.

Gentlefolk and working folk, rich and poor, men and women, youths and girls, old people and children chose their partners for the traditional country dances and became as one in the unison of rhythm, sound and movement.

Tom Potts and Ritchie Bint continued their patrol, but now they were watching out for opportunistic predators of all types. Tom found himself paying particular attention to the children, and each time he saw one who was apparently alone, or appeared to be in any distress, he was quick to go to them and check that they were alright.

Enoch Griffiths swaggered up drunkenly and accosted Tom. 'You'm a proper joker, you am, Constable Potts. I was having a chat wi' Judas Benton earlier tonight and he told me how you tried to force him to tell a load o' lies about me and his brother Ishmael selling kids to chavy-shaggers. I can't credit that you should think me capable of such wicked doings.'

Griffiths' foul breath filled Tom's nostrils, and such intense repulsion for the man's sweaty, wet-lipped, drink-slackened face coursed through him that he was amazed at the calmness of his own voice and measured words as he heard himself replying.

'Yes, indeed I do credit you with such, Master Griffiths, and there is one small service you could do for me this very moment. You could give me the names and addresses of those paedophiles that you've been selling helpless children to these last few years.'

Griffiths' leer did not falter. 'Now why would you want to get in touch wi' chavy-shaggers, I ask meself? Is it because good-looking women like Amy Danks buggers you off, so you'm desperate to shag anything, even little kids? Goodnight to you, Constable Potts.'

As he swaggered away there was murderous anger in Tom's brain, and an overwhelming impulse to crush Griffiths' skull with his staff. As if he could read minds, Ritchie Bint grabbed Tom's arm and growled, 'No you don't, Tom. This isn't the time nor the place.'

Even as he spoke the music stopped, the dancing ceased, and as the finale of the night's celebration a few rockets soared into

the air and exploded in cascades of brilliant flashes to be greeted
with cheers and applause.

The murderous anger slowly ebbed from Tom's brain, and he
told Bint, 'You may let my arm go, Ritchie. I'll not do anything
stupid.'

'Good! And don't pay any heed to what that cunt said about
Amy. Now I've got an errand to do, but I'll not be gone more than
a couple o' minutes or so.'

Tom continued to patrol through the now dispersing crowd, his
thoughts centred sadly on Amy.

'I just have to accept the fact that inevitably Amy will some
day fall in love with and wed another man. I can only hope and
pray that he'll be a decent, kindly soul who'll love and cherish
her as much as I do.'

In the Fox and Goose the staff were calling time and when Ritchie
Bint went into the Select Parlour, Maisie Lock told him, 'You're
too late for serving, Ritchie Bint; the taps are closed.'

'I'm not come for drink. I need to have a private word with
Amy.'

'What about?' Amy Danks questioned.

'I said it was a private word I wanted wi' you,' he reiterated.

'Oh, alright. But make it quick,' she snapped impatiently and
led him into the passageway.

'Now just listen and don't interrupt,' he ordered. 'That young
woman that Tom went to see last Friday is named Georgy Hanover
and she's eight years old. She's the little wench that's living wi' the
Henbath sisters. Now Tom's one o' the finest men I've ever known,
and he worships the ground you walks on. If you've got any sense
at all in your noddle, you'll wed him just as quick as you can,
because you'll never find a nicer, truer-hearted, more decent a bloke
in the whole o' Christendom. And that's a fact, that is!'

He turned on his heels and left her.

'Georgy Hanover. Eight years old. The little wench that's living
with the Henbath sisters.' Amy whispered the words over and over
again.

It was past midnight when Enoch Griffiths came back to Marlfield
Farm, reeling drunk and in a vicious mood. As he dismounted in

the farmyard he lost his balance and tumbled on to the ground. He raised himself on to his hands and knees and bellowed furiously, 'Get out here, you fuckin' cows! Get out here! I'll learn you, you lazy stinking bitches. Get out here!'

His three sisters were in the lamp-lit kitchen, each bearing on their faces and bodies the swollen cuts and bruises of the savage beating he had inflicted on them earlier that day. Deborah and Delilah clung together like children, whimpering in helpless terror.

Doll Griffiths stroked their bloodied heads, crooning soothingly to them. 'Don't be feared, girls. Don't be feared. He'll not hurt you ever again!'

She lifted the axe from the side of the cooking range and went out into the yard shouting at the top of her voice, 'I'm coming, Brother Enoch! You be easy now. I'm coming!'

FIFTY-SEVEN

Mid-Morning, Tuesday 6th November

When John Clayton came to the Lock-up he looked disgruntled, and the instant that Tom and he were seated in Tom's bedroom he blurted, 'May God forgive me for it, Tom, but there are times when I despair of the human race!'

'Why so?' Tom asked.

'I've just called on Egbert Dowler and Judas Benton to discuss the funerals of their respective relatives, and you'll not believe what I'm going to tell you.'

'Oh, I most likely will believe you, John. After all you're a man of God.' Tom smiled.

'Well, both the corpses are in Judas Benton's shop, and he and Egbert Dowler are charging tuppence to view them, and they're doing a roaring trade. Half the town seems to be queuing up outside the shop.'

Tom was not disturbed to hear this; it was fairly common among the poorer sections of society – where the living had to share their very limited home space with the dead up until the day of the burial – to display a family member's corpse and charge a penny fee to anyone who wanted to view it.

'Well, both men committed evil crimes and their causes of death were most unusual, John, so of course a great many people are curious to see them. Whenever I've a body here in the Lock-up I commonly get people asking me to let them see it.'

'Yes, I fully recognize that death holds a great fascination for people, and I don't condemn the poor who try to earn a few pence in this way,' Clayton readily accepted. 'But when I asked Benton and Dowler to set a date for the funerals, they told me they couldn't do so because they had no way of knowing how many people would be coming to view the corpses during the next few weeks. When I pointed out that in a matter of days the corpses would be very unpleasantly noisome, Benton said a bit o' stink had never bothered him in the slightest. Then I said to him that close proximity to two dead men for an extended period might well be bad for his health. He very coolly answered that he'd never heard of a dead man getting out of the coffin and harming a living man.'

Tom couldn't help but quip, 'We must live in hopes that in this particular case there will be an exception to that rule, John.'

The clergyman's tough features creased in a wry smile. 'I'll second that, Tom, and just have to trust that our Lord will forgive me for my lack of charity. Now the reason I'm here is to let you know that the Vestry will be meeting this afternoon to discuss what's to be done with Spicer. From his own account he'd no blood relations in this country and had spent most of his life at sea or in America, so there's little chance of tracing any "right of settlement" he may have had in this country. Personally I see nothing else for it but to bury him in the paupers' patch in the Monks' Cemetery.'

A rush of guilt assailed Tom, and he shook his head. 'No, that won't do, John. I'll pay for his burial plot, funeral and a headstone.'

'I fail to see why you should do that, when it was only by the grace of God he failed to kill you,' Clayton protested.

'It was Griffiths he was trying to kill, not me,' Tom asserted firmly. 'And I'll give him a decent burial. In all truth I'm doing this mainly for my own sake, in the hope that it will perhaps assuage a little of the guilt I feel for killing him.'

'You've no reason to feel any guilt whatsoever,' Clayton stated positively. 'You were doing your rightful duty. In fact in one way his death was a mercy for him. His conscience over what had happened to his son would have undoubtedly been a grievous torment to him for the rest of his years.'

The clanging of the bells interrupted their talk.

'I'll just go down and see who that is.' Tom rose.

'I've got to be going anyway.' Clayton rose also. 'Old Widow Hinge is near to her time and I promised I'd call in and pray with her. Do you want me to tell the Vestry that you intend to pay Spicer's burial costs?'

'Indeed I do,' Tom confirmed.

They went downstairs to the front door, and when Tom opened it his breath caught in shock to find it was Amy waiting outside.

'I can only say hello and bid you a good day, Amy, and good day to you also, Tom. I sincerely hope it will prove to be such for both of you.' Clayton smiled warmly and left them staring at each other with nervous uncertainty.

It was Amy who broke the strained silence, her manner tentative. 'Ritchie Bint told me about the little girl you've befriended. I've brought these for her.' She held out a small bundle wrapped in clean cloth. 'They're ginger snaps. I hope she likes ginger snaps; all children do like them, don't they?'

'Oh, Amy!' Tom could barely answer, his heart was beating so rapidly. 'Oh, Amy!'

'Well, does she like them or not?' Amy's own anxiety made her demand with a touch of asperity in her tone. 'Why won't you tell me?'

Tom disregarded the sharp edge of her voice; he saw only the tremulous emotion in her eyes. He reached out and enfolded her hand and the bundle of ginger snaps in his own hands, and said gently, 'Oh yes, Amy. Georgy loves ginger snaps, and she will tell you that herself if you'll come with me to present these to her. Please come with me to see her. She's a sweet child, and she's had a very hard life. She'll love meeting you, and I'm sure that when you speak with her you'll love meeting her also.'

Tears brimmed in Amy's eyes, and Tom could feel the stinging of tears in his own eyes. He drew her close and took her in his arms, whispering hoarsely, 'I love you, Amy, with all my heart and soul. Your happiness is more important to me than anything else in this world. I will do anything you ask of me.'

He felt her body tremble, and then with shocked dismay heard her giggling. The next moment she told him breathlessly between her giggles, 'First you can stop crushing the ginger snaps between us, or else they'll be only crumbs when we give them to Georgy. And then you can go and tell Parson Clayton that he's to call our Banns again. And then you can set about finding a comfortable place for your mother to live in. I shall do all her housework, cooking and cleaning for her, so she'll have no cause to grumble, will she, miserable old bat that she is. But before all that you can take me inside the Lock-up where nobody can spy on us kissing. Because I've got my reputation as a good-living woman to safeguard.'

FIFTY-EIGHT

Morning, Sunday 11th November

> 'My beloved spake, and said unto me,
> Rise up, my love, my fair one, and come away.
> For, lo, the winter is past, the rain is over and gone;
> The flowers appear on the earth;
> The time of the singing of the birds is come,
> And the voice of the turtle is heard in our land.
> Here endeth the Lesson.'

John Clayton closed the vast bible and stared up at the North Gallery. His eyes sought and found Amy and Tom sitting together and his tough features were softened by the happiness of his smile as he announced, 'I publish the Banns of Marriage between Master Thomas Potts, Constable of this Parish, and Miss Amy Danks, Spinster of this Parish. If any of you know cause, or just impediment, why these two persons should not be joined together in holy matrimony, ye are to declare it. This is the first time of asking.'

Seated directly behind Amy, fat Lily Fowkes whispered spite-fully, 'It makes a change for Tom Potts to be here for his Banns, don't it?'

Maisie Lock angrily rounded upon her, but before she could utter a word Amy turned her head and smilingly interposed. 'Shush, Maisie! Poor Lily's beside herself with jealousy. She's to be pitied, not blamed.'

John Clayton waited for a few seconds but no objection was voiced. Then he said to the congregation, 'Let us now join together in Hymn Two Hundred and Eight. "Praise ye the Lord, ye servants of the Lord".'

The congregation rustled and rose. The opening drone of the organ sounded, then died away as the outer door crashed open and a stentorian shout brought all heads turning towards the man hurrying to the pulpit.

'I beg you to excuse my interruption, Reverend Clayton, but it is of the utmost urgency that I speak with Constable Potts.' Hugh Laylor's features were flushed with excitement.

'Of course, Doctor Laylor.' Clayton pointed at the gallery. 'He's up there.'

'I must speak with you immediately, Tom! Will you come with me?' Laylor beckoned animatedly.

Tom looked at Amy in concern, but she only smiled and pressed his hand with her fingers.

'You go, sweetheart. Just take care to be back at the Fox in time for my party, and don't you dare be late for it, or you'll make me a laughing stock again.'

It was Amy's betrothal celebration, which was to be held in the Select Parlour where even at this moment the early guests were gathering.

'I'll not be late, sweetheart,' Tom promised.

Necks craned and curious stares followed the exit of the two men.

'We'll go to my house, for there are two gentlemen there that you must meet with, Charles Hewitt and Henry Atkins.' Laylor's speech was as hurried and excited as his pace and manner. 'Hewitt is a proprietor of madhouses, whom I've had professional dealings with on many occasions. The last time I met him he told me that he had acquired a brilliant young protégé named Henry Atkins whom he was convinced would find the cure for all types of insanity. And by God, it appears Atkins is near to doing just that!'

As he entered the drawing room of Hugh Laylor's house, Tom halted and could only stand rigid-bodied, gazing in utter amazement at the small girl sitting with composure on the lap of the young, slender-bodied man, all her attention centred on the doll she was cuddling.

Noting Tom's reaction the older man, Charles Hewitt, beamed with delighted gratification. 'I do believe that you recognize this child, Constable Potts. Might you be able to name her, I wonder?'

Tom was forced to breathe deeply and marshal his thoughts before venturing, 'I think her name could be Sukey Crawford.'

Hewitt clapped his hands in delight.

It was at this point that Laylor made the introductions. Mutual bows and acknowledgements were exchanged, after which Charles Hewitt related why he and his friend had come to Redditch.

'We are here because we have heard of your successful investigation into the dreadful murders of Ishmael Benton and Joey Dowler, and the talk of child-trafficking. It was Benton who brought the child to us because she appeared to be hopelessly crazed with insanity, and was suffering dreadful torments because of that condition. He told us that she had been bound as a Parish Apprentice to a man named Enoch Griffiths, and that Griffiths was a most cruel and brutal master to his apprentices. We paid Benton double that premium to persuade Griffiths to release the poor child and give her over to our guardianship. We wanted to cure her by treating her with my esteemed colleague's method, the scientific application of the "Etheric Fluid".'

Hewitt shook his head regretfully. 'Sadly, her mind was so grievously damaged that it has not been possible to restore it to complete health and memory.' His manner brightened. 'But what has been achieved, as you are witnessing, is that her torments have been banished from her mind, and she lives in peaceful contentment. Perfectly happy so long as she is with Henry or myself or our manservant, Mackay. Also, of course, we employ a most godly and kind-hearted woman to cater for – as I can now name her – to cater for Sukey's intimate feminine needs and bodily functions.'

Tom spent a further hour talking with the two men and closely observing little Sukey Crawford. As he questioned and listened, his thoughts were very mixed. Initially his reaction was utterly cynical. 'Two rats leaving a sinking ship!' But as time passed that reaction began to seem unduly harsh. He could see that the child was well cared for, and apparently contented. Remembering the last time he had seen her he was forced to acknowledge that there had been a remarkable transformation in her general well-being. He repeatedly asked himself: 'If I took her from these men on the grounds that she was an unlawfully trafficked child, would it improve her life in any measure?'

The harsh answer to that question was 'No'. She would revert to being a Parish orphan, and it was highly unlikely that anyone – including himself, he accepted shamefacedly – would be prepared to take in and care for such a mentally afflicted child for the rest of their days.

Eventually he steeled himself to ask Hewitt, 'What will eventually become of her if she remains with you? Because she is an expensive burden to carry, is she not?'

'Let me be brutally frank, Constable Potts,' Hewitt answered hesitantly. 'Her continued visible contentment and well-being are our future financial fortune. She is the living proof that Henry and myself are the finest practitioners in this country for the entire or partial curing of insanity. For that reason she will be protected and cherished by us for hopefully her entire life.'

'Are you both prepared to turn King's Evidence and testify that Enoch Griffiths was unlawfully trafficking children?' Tom asked next.

'We are.' The answer came without hesitation.

'Very well, Gentlemen. Then I shall do my utmost to ensure that Sukey remains in your care.'

'What will you do now, Tom?' Laylor asked.

'I'm going to Marlfield Farm to take Enoch Griffiths into custody.' Tom's face was grim, and successive waves of apprehension and excitement were coursing through him. 'Until I actually have him securely locked away, I would advise you gentlemen to take all precautions to keep Sukey and yourselves safe.'

*   *   *

An hour after Tom had left Laylor's house he was in the Lock-up charging his pistols and readying the chain manacles when Amy came to him.

'Everybody's at the party, Tom. We're all waiting for you. What are you doing with those guns anyway? Really, Tom, this is too bad of you to keep us all waiting like this.'

'I'm truly sorry, sweetheart. I was coming this very minute to tell you.'

'Tell me what?' She frowned ominously.

'That I've got to go and arrest a man. I've been running around like a mad thing arranging for horses and finding Ritchie Bint. That's why I couldn't come and tell you before now.'

'But why do you have to go and arrest him now? Why can't you wait until after my party?' she challenged forcefully. 'Why can't you let Ritchie Bint do the arrest by himself? He's a lot tougher and stronger than you anyway. He'll manage it very easily by himself. Don't you dare let me down again. I'll never forgive you for it if you do!'

For long moments the temptation to defer the arrest, to defer the dangerous, perhaps deadly confrontation with a desperate Enoch Griffiths, and instead go to the party with Amy threatened to overwhelm Tom.

At last he sighed heavily and slowly shook his head. 'I'm truly sorry, my love, but this man must be arrested without delay. I'm the appointed Constable of Tardebigge Parish, and I can't send another man to do what it is my own paramount duty to perform. I must lead the way in making this arrest.'

He bowed his head and despondently waited for the figurative axe to fall, for Amy to spurn him for the last and final time.

Instead he felt her fingers touch his cheek, and heard her saying softly, 'I suppose I just have to live with the fact that you wouldn't be my Tom Potts if you sent another man in your place. Come to the party as soon as you can, and don't you dare get hurt.' She kissed his cheek and then was gone in flurry of skirt and petticoats.

It took more than a few moments for Tom to stem the tears that were threatening to fall from his eyes, and when he finally left the Lock-up he was buoyed up with elation.

FIFTY-NINE

The two men reined in their horses as they reached the entrance of the lane that led into Marlfield Farm. The scene before them was an idyll of pastoral peace: horses, cattle and sheep grazing in the fields, birds chirruping among the branches of the neat-trimmed hedgerows, a long plume of smoke rising from the chimney of the farmhouse.

Tom took the brace of pistols from his shoulder-hung satchel, checked their priming and flints and handed one of them to Ritchie Bint.

'How d'you want to play this one, Tom? I'll be the vanguard, shall I?' Ritchie Bint's eyes were glowing with excitement, and Tom, all too conscious of his own present apprehension, both admired and envied his friend's fearlessness.

Tom shook his head. 'No, Ritchie, you'll not be the vanguard. Instead of launching a frontal assault, I think we'd best try and box clever today. Griffiths is a cunning man, and he'll have got plenty of firepower close to hand. I want you to go on foot, keep in cover and circle around to the rear of the house. When I judge that you're in position there, I'll ride up the lane and when I reach the farmyard I'll shout for Griffiths to come out and speak with me. My shouting will be your signal to close in, because I'm confident that Griffiths and his sisters will all be focussing their attentions on me, and not be aware that you're behind them.' Tom smiled wryly. 'From that point onwards, we'll just have to play it by ear.'

Bint grinned and dismounted, tethered his horse to the hedgerow out of sight of the farm buildings and, utilizing available cover, quickly disappeared.

As Tom waited he deliberately summoned memories of his father whom he had so loved and hero-worshipped, vowing in his mind, 'I'll not shame your memory, Father. I'll not act the coward, no matter what lies ahead. I'll see it through to the end, I swear to you!'

He judged that sufficient time had passed and, summoning all his fortitude, kneed his horse into a trot. As soon as he passed through the farmyard gateway he shouted with all the force of his lungs.

'Enoch Griffiths, come out and face me! Come out! Come out!'

His hand went into the satchel and closed on the butt of the pistol within.

'Enoch Griffiths, I want to speak with you. Come out!'

His breath hissed sharply as the kitchen door opened and first one, then two, then three figures emerged and came to stand in a row a couple of yards in front of him.

'What's all this ruckus for then, Master Potts?' Doll Griffiths, wearing a shabby black gown and bonnet, demanded indignantly, while flanking her, Deborah and Delilah, be-smocked and breeched, simpered and giggled bashfully.

'I want to speak with your brother. Where is he?' Tom's gaze flicked rapidly around the potential places where Enoch Griffiths might be hiding in ambush.

'He aren't here.' Doll Griffiths' bruised features were impassive. 'He's gone from here for good, so he has. Went days ago, so he did.'

'Where's he gone?'

'I'm buggered if I know.' Doll's lips twisted in a snarl, displaying her solitary long jagged tusk.

'Most likely gone to Hell, I should reckon. But he aren't here, and he's never coming back here. That's certain sure, that is.' From inside her bodice she pulled a folded piece of paper and stepped up to Tom, proffering it to him. 'Read this. It's what he left when he went.'

Tom scanned and read aloud the crudely penned, badly spelled, unpunctuated note.

'Doll I'm gone and I'm never coming back you can have the farm and the stock I'm done with it forever you'll never see me again Enoch Griffiths.'

'You can look all over here for him if you wants, Master Potts. But he's gone and he's took all his clothes and stuff with him. The bastard took all the money we'd got here as well. Fuck him!' Doll spat out viciously.

Her attitude and words held the ring of truth, and Tom found that he believed her. Nevertheless he still wanted to make a search of the farm. He shouted, 'Ritchie, it's all clear here!'

Ritchie Bint appeared in the kitchen doorway, grinning broadly. 'I've already had a quick gander through the house, Tom. There's neither hide nor hair of the bastard, and none of his clothes from the look of it.'

The two men spent the next two hours painstakingly searching through the length and breadth of the land and the buildings, but found nothing. They ended their search at the large pigsty, where several exceptionally fat pigs grunted and rooted amongst the heaps of stinking food waste, thick layered straw and their own urine and faeces.

Doll Griffiths came to join them. 'They'm fine beasts, aren't they? My pride and joy, so they am. I feeds 'um on the fat o' the land, so I does. I even gives 'um fresh meat as a treat sometimes. They thinks it's their birthday then, so they does. You should see the speed they gets the meat down into their bellies.'

She burst into fits of hysterically raucous laughter, holding her sides, tears of merriment streaming down her cheeks, as she cried out gleefully.

'That rotten bastard brother o' mine couldn't a-bear my pigs. He hated 'um, so he did. That's the best of it! He hated my pigs, and used to kick the shit out of them just to spite me. But it's me and my pigs that am having the last laugh, not my rotten bastard brother! My pigs thought it was their birthday again last Tuesday when I give 'um a feast o' fresh meat. You should have seen 'um chobbling that fresh meat down!' She walked away, her shoulders shaking with laughter.

Both struck at the same instant with the same sudden conviction, Tom and Ritchie Bint's eyes simultaneously locked and held in a startled, almost incredulous stare.

'Are you thinking what I'm thinking?' Tom asked.

Ritchie Bint nodded. 'I reckon I am.'

Then he grinned and told Tom, 'And I'll tell you summat: I aren't going to be buying any pork, ham or bacon from the butcher that buys these pigs.'

Tom grinned back. 'Me neither, my friend. I'd feel like a cannibal. Come on, let's get back to Redditch. There's a party we have to go to.'